*Flavia ran through the moonless night
to her own secret place in the garden.
Here she could weep at the injustice,
the cruelty of the Duke. He was sending
her year-old baby away from her—to
Germany and . . . discipline!*

Suddenly she became aware of the scent of tobacco, the red glowing tip of a cigar. A man sat smoking in the shadows.

"Forgive me," she said, aware she had been weeping a long time. "I thought this place deserted."

"Don't apologize. Each heart has its hell."

His voice. His voice! *Don't imagine things, Flavia. Don't break your heart more than it is already breaking.*

"Do you desire escort?" he asked.

"No thank you, sir. I know my way. I'm the Duchess of Tewksbury."

"Your voice," he said, his shoes scraping stone as he rose. "It reminds me of . . . You!"

"You . . ." she breathed. *Run! Run back to Tewksbury!* But her feet would not obey her mind, and she found herself flying into his arms.

"Don't tell me," he ordered. "Don't tell me why you ran away that night. I fear to hear it. I've searched for you for almost two years. God, how I've searched!"

Flavia lifted her wet face in joyful surprise.

"And I have searched every face . . . but now, now what can we do?"

Beyond the Dawn

Jo Ann Wendt

WARNER BOOKS

A Warner Communications Company

Again, to Phil . . .
and to my wonderful sons, Paul and Ross

I would like to acknowledge two men and a woman who are woven, invisibly, into the fabric of this book. The first is Gottlieb Mittelberger, who, in the year 1750, set sail from Amsterdam to Philadelphia on the mission of delivering an organ to the German Lutheran Church in New Providence, Pennsylvania. Mittelberger recorded his journey, his compassionate eye taking in everything. He leaves us a rare legacy—a brief but poignant account of the harsh life endured by the indentured servants who poured into the American colonies, willing to trade four to seven years of servitude for ship passage to the New World.

The second man deserving acknowledgment is my literary agent, Arthur Schwartz, whose enthusiasm for the manuscript, whose critical expertise and keen sense of plotting made me strive to do my best.

Finally, I want to acknowledge the woman who took my dream and made of it a reality, the woman who took my manuscript and made of it a book. She is my editor, Fredda Isaacson.

Jo Ann Wendt
San Jose, California
September, 1982

Beyond the Dawn

Chapter 1

London, January 1752

THERE WAS NO MOON. A mist rose from the black waters of the Thames, sending up the dank odor of river slime. The mist mingled with inrolling winter fog. Fog and mist curled over the waterfront like a shroud, hiding the coach-and-four that waited on the quay.

Alert to waterfront dangers and armed with cudgels, three footmen guarded the coach. The footmen sniffed the fog, listening. From a jumble of dilapidated taverns near the quay came the loud roistering of sailors well into their cups.

Footsteps sounded. The guards tensed. Two heavily painted prostitutes with identical orange hair and dirty red petticoats drifted out of the fog and floated toward the coach.

"A moment of joy, dearies? Ten minutes of heaven?" they called to the footmen.

The burliest of the footmen stepped forward, tapping his cudgel to the palm of his hand.

"Begone," he growled.

The women retreated into the fog with thin, complaining whines.

Inside the coach a girl waited, head bowed, hands clasped as if in prayer. But if the truth were known, she was not praying. She clasped her hands to keep them from shaking. Her fingers twitched nervously, wanting to find the gold ruby ring and twist it. But the hands were ringless.

Despite the warmth of the dark wool cloak that covered her slender body from head to toe, she trembled. At the slightest noise—a raucous echo from the taverns or the muted jingling of horse harness—her head jerked up. Her eyes lit with panic.

And *such* eyes, thought elderly Simon Beauchamp as he watched his niece in the dim flaring light of the coach lantern. Eyes like wild doves. No, Simon corrected himself, her eyes were like lotus blossoms, such as grew in far distant lands. What a rare color! A brilliant turquoise when her mood was sunny, unworried—a jade green when she was frightened, as now.

As he sadly watched her, her incredible eyes lifted to his, imploring.

"I—I—*am* doing the right thing, Uncle Simon?"

It was less a question than a prayer. He leaned forward, patting a small hand so stiff and cold that it jolted his very soul.

"You are doing the only thing possible," he assured her quickly.

Sadness tugged at his old heart. She was his favorite, the eldest of his brother's six daughters. It had given him no pleasure to marry her off at fifteen to the fifty-year-old duke. And tonight gave him no pleasure; it revolted him.

When the panic did not subside in her eyes, he repeated what they'd spoken of privately many times before.

"Your madman of a husband is too vain to admit he cannot father a child. He is obsessed with siring an heir for his dukedom. His first two duchesses died without giving him an heir." He paused, going on as gently as he was able. "Must I remind you how he behaved to them when they proved barren? He sent the first to his estate in Germany, where she lived friendless and neglected. In her unhappy state, she fell prey to illness and died. A similar fate befell his second duchess."

"I don't want to be sent away!"

He sighed unhappily.

"You have been his duchess four years and there has been no child . . ."

He watched her eyes widen into pools of green terror.

"I would fear *death* less than I fear *tonight*," she whispered, scarlet patches suddenly blooming on the high, delicately formed cheekbones.

Simon felt a surge of pity. Instantly he chastised himself for it. Sentiment must have no part in this. His niece must do what she must do: lives and fortunes depended upon it.

Leather cushions squeaked beneath him as he shifted his bulk forward, taking her young hands into his large, time-scarred ones.

"Think of your father," he exhorted softly. "You love him, but you must realize your father is a fool about finances. Money flows through his fingers like water. He is deeply in debt to the duke. He depends upon the duke to underwrite his every frivolous whim. He counts on the duke to grant your sisters handsome dowries when they come of age."

"Don't, Uncle Simon," she begged.

But he pressed on. He knew she hated to hear ill of her father, but as family mentor he could not afford pity.

"What would happen if the duke sent you away? Think. Would you see your father cast into debtors' prison? What then would become of your mother and sisters?"

He was satisfied when the small hand he held gave a violent shudder. She had always been the responsible one, the dutiful one, devoted to her family.

Suddenly she tossed her head in frantic appeal, clutching his hand with both of hers.

"Uncle Simon, advise me. Tell me what to do. I shall do anything. I swear it!"

Simon Beauchamp eased his tired, pain-riddled body into the cushions, comforted by her passionate outburst but saddened. She was the daughter he'd never had. He loved her.

He sighed, a sigh that terminated in a wheeze of poor health. It was a cruel world that required one's daughters be used as pawns. She was waiting for him to speak, her eyes imploring him for a wisdom he wished he possessed. She was so small and frightened sitting there in the smoky lantern light. He cleared his throat. The words he was again forced to say stuck in his craw like grit.

"Deceive your husband. Bear a child, Flavia."

She said nothing. The only sound was her panicky, uneven breathing. When the rhythm of her breathing changed, when it deepened in resignation, he knew she'd come to terms with it at last. When her voice broke the silence, it was the voice of a lady. Dignified. Calm. Only an occasional quaver betrayed her.

"This . . . this man you have selected, Uncle Simon. He . . . resembles the duke?"

Simon smiled at the girl's intelligence.

"Dark eyes, dark hair. Taller and more robust. But any child born would be accepted as the duke's."

She closed her eyes, paling.

"This . . . man . . . is young and healthy?"

He leaned forward, squeezing her stiff cold hand.

"I have ascertained it, Flavia. By discreet inquiry."

Her incredible eyes seemed to fill her face, and she searched his face as though searching out Holy Writ.

"You are positive I shall never see the man again, after tonight?"

Simon smiled sadly.

"He is a colonial, Flavia. A shipmaster. His ship is the *Caroline*. He sails for Virginia colony tomorrow on the tide."

Watching her, Simon feared she would hold her breath forever. He could see the pulse thudding in the fragile hollow at the base of her throat. She grew deathly pale.

"He will *not* know who I am?" she begged.

Simon shook his head, hating to say what must be said. He cleared his throat.

"He thinks you a—a whore, Flavia."

"Oh!"

She lapsed into shocked silence.

Simon let the minutes pass. He didn't press. But when the ten o'clock watch was called by the quay watchman, Simon knew he must prod.

"Little Flavia," he said softly, "it is time."

Bone-chilling winter fog swallowed her up not five steps from the coach. Its cold wet fingers probed into the hood of her cloak, curling round her neck. She shivered, clutching her cloak closed. The fog billowed so thick over the ground that she felt she would trip on it. Her footsteps sounded distant, far away, as though they did not belong to her. She walked quickly, lest courage fail. Her short, panicky breaths drew in the fog odors of rotted wharf timbers and damp chimney smoke.

As the glowing windows of the tavern grew to life size, her steps faltered, then stopped. Fear hammered through her. As though to provide a staccato for her fear, the screams of alley cats pierced the fog. Something shot past her, hissing. She whirled in fear, trying to see the coach. One moment she could see it, the next she could not. The rolling fog was playing hide-and-seek with it. She started to run for the coach, then jerked herself back.

You must do it, she told herself fiercely. *For your own sake. And for Papa.*

Boots clattered over cobblestone, running frantically.

"Did ye get his purse, matey?"

"Ay," a disembodied voice answered somewhere in the fog. "But I lost m' pigsticker, I did. Stuck in his ruddy rib, it did."

Flavia flew toward the tavern in panic and jerked open the door. Odors rushed at her: beer, male sweat, filth, frying fish. Laughter and drunken cursing rumbled from the public room to the left. The dark staircase was straight ahead, as Uncle Simon had said. She bolted for it, but a hand shot out, seizing her cloak. Flavia yelped in fright. The hand belonged to a brassy, orange-haired woman who popped out of the shadows and gave Flavia a vicious shake.

"Say, now, you! Cast off. This tavern is *our* terr'tory."

Flavia instinctively jerked her cloak free of the clutching hand and lunged away from the smell of overpowering perfume.

Another woman drifted out, identical to the first.

"Aw, leave 'er be, luv. Can't yer see she's a *lady?*"

Terrified, Flavia backed away, then whirled and bolted up the staircase, escaping the women. Their crude cackling laughter and screaming perfume pursued her to the top. When she looked down, a drunkenly weaving man had joined the women. He put one booted foot on the first step and leered up at her.

"Care for a bit of company, me pretty?"

Flavia panicked. She flew along the corridor to the end of it, then fell panting against a greasy wall. Overhead, a befouled oil lamp sputtered. Grotesque shadows performed a macabre dance in the lamplight. A rancid smell hung in the hall.

I can't do it, Uncle Simon! I can't! I'd rather die!

Just then, a booted step sounded in the stairwell. Then another. Freezing in fear, she hugged the wall, pressing into the shadows.

Chapter 2

"TEN O'CLOCK AND SHE'S A FOGGY NIGHT . . . ten o'clock and the fog's rollin' in . . ."

The watchman's call, muted by fog and the closed wood shutters of the window in the hired room above the tavern, evoked a string of soft curses from the bed where Garth McNeil lay whiling away the time by balancing a half-empty brandy bottle on his broad, sun-browned chest.

"Damnation, where *is* the little tart!"

With a quick movement he sat up and caught the bottle in a practiced hand as it tumbled. Ramming cork into bottle, he threw it aside. The bottle bumped over crude floor planks.

He was due back at the *Caroline* within the hour. If he were an honest man, he reflected wryly, he'd admit he needed a whore about as desperately as he needed a cannon blast through the head. The Baroness Annette Vachon had taken care of that during his short London stay. He grinned, rubbing a jaw that cried for shaving. Savoring the deliciousness of the memory, he chuckled. If *that* was how a baroness behaved in bed, he could hardly wait to graduate to a viscountess.

McNeil lunged up from the bed. His boots hit the floor with a bang. He grabbed a ruffled shirt of cream silk. He was into it in two impatient shrugs, ramming shirttails into expensive, well-tailored breeches. He grabbed his coat.

He'd not wait for the whore. He didn't need her. In fact, he made it a practice to avoid whores. He wanted no part of the "French disease."

The heels of his boots pounded across the room to the door. He wrenched up the door latch. Then, as though controlled by invisible wires, his hand was stayed on the latch, unmoving.

The old man had tantalized him with the offer to procure a bewitching girl. First, there was the puzzle of the man himself. A stately well-to-do old gentleman procuring flesh? Ridiculous. Second, there'd been the portrait. The painted miniature, which the old gentleman had carefully drawn from his cloak pocket, was a portrait of a creature so delicate, so stunning that Garth had laughed in the man's face. A whore, indeed!

Now he stood still, remembering...God, what eyes. Bright blue, flecked with green. The eyes glowed from a heart-shaped face framed by a mass of coppery hair. He remembered the delicate hairline, the widow's peak giving the face an aura of unbelievable sweetness.

For a long time, he stood scarcely breathing. He let his hand fall from the door latch. Recrossing the room with slow uncertain steps, he retrieved the brandy bottle from where it had rolled, uncorked it and drank.

He wondered if the girl could be a highborn lady from one of London's secret clubs, clubs in which jaded ladies sold themselves for thrills or for money. But such women usually were "sold" by foppish young men who minced about in lace suits and diamond ear studs.

He laughed. "You're a fool, McNeil," he told himself. "The old fox has a game. He means to pass off some well-used slattern as the wonderful creature in the miniature. Her face will be a battlefield of pox pits. The pits will have been puttied over with wax and powdered until she looks like the bottom of a flour sack!"

He snorted in amused self-derision as he lifted the bottle once again. Brandy burned a trail of fire down his gullet. He thrust cork into bottle and slung the bottle away. But this time it broke. The acrid scent of expensive French spirits curled into the air, mingling with the rancid smells of the cheap oil lamp and the unswept room.

That did it. He'd not wait.

He was at the door in two impatient strides. He wrenched it open. Suddenly, out of the corner of his eye, he saw furtive movement in the hall shadows. Instinct served him well. His hand shot to the knife sheathed at his waist. A hundred ports from London to the Indies had taught him what to do. He froze. He'd not move a muscle until his eyes began to focus in the dimness. Gradually, the shadowy apparition became a live figure. He caught his breath.

It was she.

He would know her anywhere, even though the eyes were not turquoise as in the miniature, but green. Green as a rare brocade from the silk islands. She was swathed in a dark hooded cloak. Soft tendrils of coppery, fog-dampened hair escaped from her hood and framed a startled, heart-shaped face.

He could do nothing but stare. She was exquisite. Under the glare of his fierce concentration, the girl's chin began to tremble. Small and perfect white teeth tugged at a full lower lip.

Stupidly, he continued to stare, his throat tightening in an emotion he could not put a name to. He caught the faint scent of heather, the fresh young smell of her mist-damp skin. The scent of her made him tremble.

I want her, he thought foolishly. I *want* her.

He floundered to find the voice that seemed lost. When he found it, it was not the confident voice that commanded the *Caroline*. It was husky. Boyishly vulnerable.

"Come in."

She wavered in indecision, and again he caught his breath. Would she bolt? Flee and be lost to him forever? His heart thudded at the thought.

"Don't go. You've the right room."

Flavia felt faint. Had she ever been so terrified? Not since she was fifteen and found herself standing in a cheerless but magnificent bed-chamber. She'd clutched her wedding bouquet as she now clutched the edges of her cloak. She'd stood frozen, as now. The door had opened... the duke had strode in, cold-eyed and haughty... and then...

She shuddered away the memory. Her stunned gaze flew to the tall stranger's face. How would he treat her? Like the duke? She shivered again.

"The hall is cold, miss. The room is warmer."

Flavia swallowed as he came toward her with the loose, casual stride she'd noticed in colonials who called upon the duke. She flinched as he reached for the cold hand that clutched the cloak.

"Damnation, you're freezing."

She was swept into the room before she could thaw and run. Her heart jumped like a rabbit as he dropped the crossbar on the door with a loud clunk. He went to the fireplace and fed a tired fire. Afraid to look at him, afraid to think beyond the moment, Flavia turned and desperately surveyed her surroundings. She'd never been in such a hovel. Rough planks served as floor and wall. Both were pock-marked with knife gouges as though tenants used them as targets. Dust balls as large as kittens skittered with every stirring of her skirts. A table, two chairs and a bed furnished the room. Hastily her eyes fled from the bed. Each nervous breath she drew smelled of hard spirits, and fish that were frying in grease somewhere in the noisy bowels of the tavern. She could hear a fight breaking out. Furniture crashed belowstairs. Voices shouted.

"Come to the fire."

His calm voice made her jump. Swallowing hard, she gingerly obeyed. But when she did not come close enough, he took her firmly by the shoulders, stood her in front of the crackling fire and slowly rotated her as though she were a piece of cheese being toasted on a stick. She was shaking so badly that several minutes passed before she realized his hands were surprisingly light and gentle. His gentleness gave her courage to steal a quick look at his face.

Dark hair was brushed casually back from a lean weathered brow. His skin was the rough tanned skin of men who are at home on the sea. Command shouted in the line of nose and jaw, but a loose easy mouth hinted at an even temperament.

Almost, her galloping heart slowed a bit. But then, suddenly and without warning, he stopped toasting her and pulled her hard against him, crushing her to his chest. She cried out in panic, feeling his heartbeat invade her.

"Don't, sir! Please! What—what do you want!"

He stared down at her, a startled look crossing his face. Then amusement began to crinkle at the corners of his eyes.

"What may I have? What are my choices? Perhaps you've brought a bill of fare for me to select from."

Flavia blinked in fear. If he was making a joke, then she didn't understand. She tried to twist free.

"Please, sir!"

"Yes, quite right. Let's not waste time. Begin."

His hands fell away and he seemed to expect her to do something. She backed away, her eyes flying to the door.

"Well?" he said, chuckling. "Do you expect me to take my pleasure through cloak and gown?"

McNeil was confused at the blank, nervous look she gave him. Why was the whore nervous? Surely she could see he wasn't a perverted customer. He smiled, amused at the thought. Then the smile died as amusement flickered into suspicion. A normal whore would be stripped to her chemise by now, eager to complete the transaction and move on to other customers. A normal whore would already be kissing him in feigned passion as her mind totaled the number of coins she might earn before light once more crept over the Thames.

He studied her with narrowing eyes.

"What is your game? You and the old man?"

She jumped.

"Sir?"

"Your *game*. You're a shill, aren't you. Your master has learned that I carry the profits from the *Caroline*'s cargo."

She shook her head with such fear that she confirmed his suspicion. He drew a harsh, painful breath. Of course the old fox would employ an innocent-appearing creature such as she. She was the perfect shill. Her sweetness could set any man off guard.

His mouth tasted suddenly sour. He hardened himself against the rush of sentimental disap-

pointment that came like a flood. He was thirty
years old and by now life should have made him
a cynic, he thought. Hadn't experience taught
him that the prettiest apple was the one most
likely to be rotten to the core?

"Order the brandy from the innkeeper," he
commanded, taking a step toward the trembling
girl. "You've been instructed to get me drunk
and steal my purse, have you not!"

"Sir—please—I don't understand—"

Her playacting infuriated him.

"Then understand *this*. My crew waits below.
They are armed. One word from me and they'll
scour the waterfront for that thieving old fox. I'll
drag the both of you to the nearest magistrate."

Flavia choked on terror. She backed away
from furious eyes, the warily hunched shoulders. Backed away until a wall came up against
her. Uncle Simon! A magistrate? The duke finding out? Terror chilled her to the bone, swallowing
up the earlier fear of going to bed with this
stranger—swallowed it up as a large fish swal-
lows a smaller one.

"Please, sir? Not the magistrate—I'll do
anything."

He laughed unkindly.

"I wager you *will*."

Furious at being deceived by such sweetness,
McNeil strode to the quaking girl. Three jet
black buttons clasped her cloak at the throat.
With an angry wrench, he yanked them open.
The cloak slid down the silk of her modest
gown, falling to the floor with a swish. Roughly,

he grabbed her. Sour disappointment roused him to cat-and-mouse cruelty.

"Shall I let you leave?" he said, with no intention of doing so. She quaked in violent hope. Bright blue color swirled into the green of her eyes.

"Oh, yes, sir. Please, sir."

Then, as suddenly as the hope had risen in her eyes, it receded, dying. She dropped her head.

"No, sir. I—I—can't, sir."

Dumbfounded, he forgot he was toying with her. He stared down at her, unable to comprehend. She wanted to go. But she couldn't. Why? Slowly, comprehension dawned.

Of course she couldn't leave. Not without earning some coins. Her master would flog her. He swallowed, trying to fight the pity that rose. This delicate creature coming under the whip? It sickened him.

He stomped on the tender feelings with steel boots, growling, "If you're staying, do not waste my time. Begin! Kiss me."

To his irritation, her dark velvety eyelashes began to shine with wetness. She squeezed her eyes shut. She drew an agonized breath. He could feel her heart quake. Obedient to his surly command, she worked shaking hands up his chest. She curled ice cold fingers around his hot neck. Eyes still squeezed shut, she tilted her face up to his. She pursed her lips like a child.

McNeil was stunned. My God, had the whore

never been kissed? He wanted to laugh. But somehow he could not. The sweet earnestness of the gesture disarmed him. Vengeful lust wavered and began to fade. A quieter feeling came.

Softly he kissed the pursed, trembling lips.

"You kiss like a child," he whispered.

Her eyes flew open, flying into his. For a jolting moment something electrifying passed between them. Call it discovery. Call it the sweet stab of something neither of them had felt before. Her trembling lips ventured a shy half-smile.

"I'm sorry, sir," she whispered.

"Don't be. It shall be my pleasure to teach you."

His mouth came down and Flavia's heart fluttered in stirring excitement. She was afraid of this man and yet at the same time she felt an odd, insane trust. He kissed her and then she understood his gentle criticism. No one had ever kissed her like this! Certainly not the duke, who called kissing a filthy habit. Certainly not her parents or Uncle Simon.

Her pulse raced in fear and anticipation for what must follow as he drew his head back and whispered, "Your mouth is sweet as honey. I've never tasted sweeter..."

A gentle desire pounded through McNeil. He felt a fierce surge of protectiveness for the trembling girl. God, she was a delicate thing. So slender she could be lost in a man's arms.

He picked her up and carried her to the bed. She stiffened in seeming fear until he kissed away her resistance. When she wilted against his warm body like a flower wilting in the sun, he slowly peeled away her clothing. It was like peeling away the petals of a rose.

He took her. It was a slow, joyous taking and he was gratified when her small body flushed suddenly with heat and she gasped under him.

"Oh!" she said timidly, her eyes widening in surprise.

McNeil was amazed. Amazed and exhilarated. Had the little whore never... ? Incredible.

It was a wildly happy moment for him. It was like the first time he'd taken the wheel of the *Caroline* and felt her respond to his slightest touch. He smiled down at the blushing girl in his arms.

"'Oh!'" he teased softly.

He gazed upon her flushed loveliness. Shyly, she met his eyes and smiled. For an endless moment they gazed at each other. Not as whore and hirer, but as man and woman.

Then her dark lashes fluttered. She looked away in some nameless emotion. But when he bent to kiss her again, he did not have to tease her mouth open as he'd done at first. With a shy generosity that both charmed and puzzled him, she lifted her velvet mouth.

"Two o'clock and a thick fog... two o'clock and all's well..."

Deep in the shadows of the bed, Flavia Rochambeau, duchess of Tewksbury, fearfully held her breath as she listened to the fading, fog-muffled cry of the watchman. Belowstairs, the brawling revelry had faded, too. A man still sang drunkenly. A whining woman—the tavern-keeper's wife?—loudly complained of the night's damages.

The hour was late. The deed, done.

More than done, she reflected, flushing in sudden shame as her mind raced over the past hours. She drew a quick, dizzying breath, then fought to expel it slowly, silently.

She mustn't wake him!

Gentle as he'd been, she still feared him. His overwhelming maleness, tempered with a playful air, had shaken her to the core. He'd set her brain spinning.

No, she mustn't wake him. After the second time he'd taken her, he'd drowsily amused himself by teasing her:

Did she like ships? Good, for she'd soon be on one. He was taking her to Virginia to be his mistress.

Did she have skills to fend off lunatics? Yes? Good, for she'd soon meet his younger brother, who behaved like a lunatic over pretty women.

Did she like the color red? Good, he would buy her a dozen red dresses on the morrow.

Sleepily kissing her bare shoulder, he demanded to know her name. Fortunately, Flavia was spared replying. Sleep carried him off in a sigh of satisfaction.

Now he lay heavy beside her, his brown lean arm flung over her. She breathed quietly. But the warm scent of him set her heart fluttering.

So this was what *it* was meant to be.

So this was the man-woman thing.

How could she have known? The passionate lovemaking of this handsome, playful stranger in no way resembled what passed for the duke's marital act. True, the duke was old and his stern German heritage outweighed the Englishman in him. But, more, he was devoid of passion. Even at fifteen, she'd sensed that.

His twice-weekly visits to her bedchamber were prompted by desire for an heir, not desire of a woman. He dispatched his duty with hurried distaste. He never fondled her, never kissed. If any passion throbbed within the duke, that passion was directed to his magnificent collection of jade carvings. Already, hundreds of priceless Oriental pieces filled Tewksbury Hall's receiving rooms.

Tewksbury Hall... Flavia breathed softly, musing. God willing, nine months from tonight the corridors of Tewksbury would echo with the birth cry of a future duke or duchess. If a son, the baby immediately would take the duke's lesser title, his German title, marquis of Bladensburg. And she would be safe! Safety for everyone—herself, Papa and Mother, her sisters. Perhaps the duke would honor her long-standing request. Elated over his heir, perhaps he'd grant Uncle Simon a stipend and allow Uncle Simon to retire from his clerical post at the Board of Trade.

Her breath caught with hope, but then she sighed. No. The duke would not. The duke sat on the Board of Trade. He was adamant about keeping Uncle Simon in his post. Flavia found the duke's attitude a grievous mystery. The duke was rich; Uncle Simon, old and ill.

The stranger stirred on his pillow. Flavia held her breath. He mumbled, groped for her shoulder, patted it and then sank into deep sleep. Flavia watched him. Shame kindled in her cheeks as she gazed at him. Shame for her sin, shame for the feelings he'd awakened in her, shame that the rest of her life would be ruled by deceit.

Deceit.

If this night didn't bring a child, she would be forced to . . . She wrenched her face away, her pillow rustling. *Dear God, no! No one else! Not after the wonder of tonight!* Heart hammering, she lay there praying for a child and alternately begging God *not* to give her one. She trembled at the thought of the duke's shrewd eyes inspecting his heir. Suppose he grew suspicious? Panic surged. She must get back to Uncle Simon, back to the coach, to Uncle's house, where she was presumed to be spending the night.

The sea captain's arm was dead weight upon her. His breathing was deep, calm. She must go. Uncle would be pacing the alley, eaten up with worry. The hour was terribly late.

Flavia cast her eyes about the room, getting her bearings. The room was poorly lit. The oil lamp scattered grotesque shadows that changed form with each flicker of flame. She made out her cloak, lying in a dark heap on the floor. Petticoats and bodice topped a broken chair.

Her chemise and stockings rested beneath his breeches on the floor beside the bed.

Holding her breath, she carefully lifted his leaden arm and inched out from under his hot embrace. Icy sheets met her legs, an icy floor her bare feet.

Escaping the bed, she dressed in haste. When a silk petticoat rustled going over her head, she caught her breath. She froze, her eyes leaping to the bed. But he slept on. Snatching up her cloak, she stole to the door. Her heart hammered as she eased up the heavy crossbar. Luck was with her. The battered old door with its decoration of knife scars opened without comment.

Hovering on the threshold, she permitted herself a glance at the figure on the bed. His hair was shockingly dark against the pillow. It had not seemed so when she was close. She had a sudden urge to cross the room and study the color of his hair, drinking it in, engraving the detail in her memory, where she could keep it and cherish it forever. But this she knew to be foolishness. Foolishness born of the stress of this unnatural night. Still, she hovered, gazing wistfully at him.

I shall never see him again. Never.

She knew she should feel profound relief. But somehow the finality of it settled into her heart like a stone. She could feel tears gathering. She blinked them away.

"I don't even know your name," she whispered softly. "Only that you are captain of the *Caroline . . .*"

In the sputtering lamplight, he moved restlessly in his sleep. Flavia caught her breath. Sweeping her eyes over him one last time, she turned and slipped into a hallway that reeked of fish and ale. Soundlessly, she pulled the door shut.

Fighting tears, she flew down the ill-lit passageway, and stumbling blindly down creaking uneven stairs, ran out into the fog and into her godfather's comforting arms.

Chapter 3

September 1753

Almost two years later

TEWKSBURY HALL WAS ABLAZE WITH
LIGHT. Set against the starless London night and
the black flowing river, the seventy-room ducal
mansion glittered like a fairyland.

Within, countless candles of the finest bees-
wax flamed in ornate silver and brass sconces.
The melting wax sent up a delicate, expensive
fragrance. In the east and west wing ballrooms,
crystal chandeliers were springing to life. Footmen
in black and gold livery tiptoed to each chandelier, lifting long brass candlelighters to candles
nestled in crystal. The candle wicks caught fire
one by one, and prisms of light shot out from
chandeliers and went spinning over a polished
rich walnut dancing floor. The immense empty
chambers reverberated with the discordant sounds
of violins tuning up.

Out of doors, the dark rolling grounds of Tewksbury twinkled with diamondlike light. Brass lanterns burned everywhere: lanterns dotted the vast gardens; lanterns marched down formal French terraces to the river; lanterns converged on red-carpeted landings where wealthy guests would arrive in private river barges; lanterns lit a newly constructed gazebo at the water's edge where more violinists sent gay tunes out upon the night waters.

The duke of Tewksbury had spared no expense to ensure that the first birthday of Robert Charles Neville Rochambeau would be the crowning event of London's social season.

Flavia's silver kid slippers clicked nervously down the marble corridor of the east wing. Obedient to the duke's wishes, she'd spent the day under the exhausting ministrations of dressmaker, hairdresser, perfumer, jeweler—every sort of sycophant. Their incessant chatter, their bickering, had driven all rational thought from her mind. But perhaps that was to the good, she reasoned wearily. Tonight she must not think too much. She mustn't brood. For this eve of her son's natal day awakened all the old fears. It awakened all the old yearnings too, she was forced to admit.

It had been almost two years. Where was "he"? Was he alive and well? What might he be doing at this very moment?

The yearning that had been her legacy since the night on the quay, welled up. Fed by the festive occasion, the yearning throbbed with fresh intensity.

Oh, why couldn't she forget the man!

With a vividness that made her ashamed, she remembered his gentle touch, his masculine smell. When she closed her eyes at night to sleep, he was there; and though she might weep in helpless frustration, she couldn't help remembering his thrilling kisses.

Lost in memory, she shivered. The brisk click of her heels slowed. Her steps flagged. To remember such things was to open herself to jeopardy. To yearn for him was dangerous. What of her position? What of her parents? And Robert?

She drew a scared, determined breath. Above all, she must protect the baby. No hint of scandal must touch him. She was well aware that at his birth London wags had amused themselves by joking about the duke's late-found virility. People had dredged up tittle-tattle about the duke's previous duchesses.

Terrified that gossips might cast their malicious eyes upon *her*, she'd withdrawn like a turtle into its shell. Gradually, her warm, trusting nature had chilled to ice. In less than two years, the open-hearted girl had become the cool, unapproachable duchess of Tewksbury.

If the metamorphosis had displeased her puzzled family and her friends, it had pleased the duke, Flavia mused unhappily. The duke disliked females who wore their feelings on their sleeves. The new, aloof Flavia was more to his taste. She realized he'd paid her the ultimate compliment when, during their dreary dinners in the immense dining hall, he'd begun to assault her with dry little histories of his jade collection.

Secure in the knowledge that an heir slept in the nursery, he'd dispensed with visits to her bedchamber. In this Flavia had felt relief, for his cold, efficient performing of marital duty left her sobbing into her pillow for that which was lost to her ... for that which must *always* be lost to her if she intended to protect her son and herself.

Wearily, she sighed in resignation. If life was to be loveless, then so be it. There were other satisfactions. There was satisfaction in lavishing love upon her adorable son. There was satisfaction in seeing Papa prosperous and happy, in shepherding her younger sisters into good matches.

But, for herself? The question hung in the air.

She frowned in determination. Straightening the shoulders that felt so burdened, she said aloud, "I *shall* survive."

"M'lady?"

A young footman with scared, inquiring eyes bobbed out from his post in the corridor beside an enormous Flemish tapestry. Flavia stiffened, controlling the impulse to shriek in startled surprise. She'd not seen the lad, as his livery blended into a tapestry scene depicting the crusaders' march to the Holy Land.

He ducked his head in a nervous bow. "M'lady?"

Flavia shook her head and granted him a chilly smile. It was a smile that served her well these days, keeping all persons—highborn or low—at arm's length. The carefully cultivated smile isolated her, kept her safe from kitchen gossip and the more vicious snipes of the well-born. Head high, she swept past the boy without replying.

Her light step echoed down the corridor, carrying her to the balcony of mirrors that overlooked the white marble entrance hall below. A marble staircase curved downward from each side of the balcony. As she lifted her skirts slightly to descend, cloth-of-silver peeped from beneath her gown, swirling at her ankles. Clicking down the snow white staircase, she anxiously studied her repeating image in the mirrored panels that followed her down. Her anxiety lessened with each candle-lit image.

She looked every inch the duchess. The duke would be pleased. Her girlish mass of red hair had been tamed to a sleek sophistication. Washed three times by a clucking covey of hairdressers, her hair had been brushed dry, then drawn to the crown of her head and coaxed into a tumble of Greek curls that emulated the Greek statues of Tewksbury Gardens. A tendril of burnished hair curled at each ear, softening the blaze of diamonds that trembled there.

Her gown was French, as the duke had commanded. An acclaimed dressmaker had been summoned from Paris. The result—dazzling. Even the difficult-to-please duke deemed it worthy of the occasion.

The gown was a sweep of ivory satin. The neckline was low and trimmed with flowerlike ivory satin petals. Each petal was encrusted with seed pearls and brilliants. Cloth-of-silver underskirts rippled at the hem of her gown as

she moved, lending a silvery grace. She wore
diamonds on her fingers, diamonds on her wrists
and the famous Tewksbury diamond pendant
upon her white bosom.

With a last anxious glance in the glass, Flavia
stepped from the staircase, releasing her skirts.
The heavy satin woofed softly as it settled round
her. She hurried on, her step echoing in the
entrance hall, her step clicking over a floor of
snowy marble that had as its center the ducal
crest worked in black and gold marble. From
their posts near the tall, ornately carved double
doors, footmen bowed as she passed. A glance
out the Venetian glass windows assured her all
was in readiness outside, too. The duke would
find nothing to criticize. Torches flamed along
Tewksbury's quarter-mile carriage drive. Footmen
waited in the flaring light to help guests alight
from conveyances that would range from Uncle
Simon's modest landau to coaches crested and
trimmed in gold leaf.

Flavia shivered. She wished the coaches, the
river barges would never arrive. She dreaded
tonight. She dreaded the natal day congratulations that would bubble so effusively from smiling mouths while malicious eyes narrowed and
darted between her young figure and that of the
aging duke. She shuddered. Then, sensing the
eyes of servants upon her, she swept regally on.

The duke waited in the Hall of Portraits in
the west wing. As was his custom in unoccupied
moments, he was studying the heroic-size paint-
ings of titled Englishmen and equally titled

Germans. His own likeness, Germanic and severe, hung in the place of honor.

As Flavia entered, her heart drummed with the trepidation she always felt in the duke's presence. Hearing the rustle of her gown, he turned abruptly. She dropped into a graceful curtsy. When she rose, he was fitting spectacles upon the bridge of his long Roman nose. Clasping his hands behind his stiff black brocade coat, he studied her without expression. As he did so, Flavia's cheeks warmed in humiliation. She was the duke's property. She was his to inspect. Still, she thought in a flush of anger, it is degrading. She fought the impulse to fidget under his gaze; the duke disliked females with fluttery hands.

At last he removed the spectacles, folded the wire temples with maddening slowness, and replaced the spectacles in an inner breast pocket.

"I approve," he said in his chill, thready voice.

Flavia let out her breath in relief.

"Thank you, sir," she said softly.

"Not at all."

He continued to inspect her, his cold eyes traveling from her crown of Greek curls to her silver slippers.

"I believe I shall have you painted as you are tonight. The new portrait shall replace the current one hanging in the Hall of Duchesses. That likeness lacks—" He tossed a ruffled wrist in an aristocratic gesture. "—lacks dignity," he finished.

Flavia flushed. She knew the duke disliked

that portrait. In it, she was all hair and eyes.
And her face was not the oval perfection of her
predecessors.

She swallowed. "My only desire is to please
you, sir."

It was true, fervently true, she admitted to
herself. The duke displeased was a man to be
feared.

"Of course." He accepted the homage as his
due. He granted her a rare, careful smile. "You
do please me, my dear."

Flavia's eyes widened in surprise. The duke
seldom praised. Hardly knowing how to respond,
she lowered her eyes to the Oriental carpet that
lay like an island in the huge polished hall. She
curtsied once again.

"Thank you, sir."

He gave a pleased nod at her response and
moved toward her on thin legs that were almost
comic in white silk stockings and enormous
ribboned knee clocks. With stiff formality he
offered his arm.

"Come, my dear. We shall greet our guests
on this the first natal celebration of my son."

His thready voice rang with pride, and
obediently Flavia took his arm and moved with
him to the corridor of bowing footmen.

"You've viewed my new jade piece, Flavia?"

Carefully, she considered her answer. His
Grace was easily irritated at an ill-chosen word
about his jades.

"The vase is magnificent, sir. It's not nephrite
jade but jadeite, isn't it? If I'm not mistaken, sir,
a vein of dark green imperial jade runs through

the lip of the vase. Only a master craftsman carves imperial jade."

His eyebrows lifted in pleased surprise.

"Very good, my dear. You're learning." He drew a proud, deep breath. "The piece," he said, "is a treasure!"

Flavia knew that to be true as she moved down the corridor on his arm. She dared not ask where he'd got the "treasure." The duke didn't seem to acquire his Oriental pieces at auction, as other people did. The pieces simply appeared in Tewksbury Hall. No money seemed to be paid.

Alert to London shipping news ever since the night on the quay, she'd gradually become aware that the duke's jade collection increased whenever certain colonial ships were in port: *Bountiful Lady* and *Virtue*. Those ships had once been investigated on charges of smuggling. The charges had been dismissed as false by the Board of Trade. The duke sat on the board; Uncle Simon served as chief clerk to the board. Flavia shivered. The duke's wealth seemed to increase every year.

When they reached the black, white and gold entry hall, the duke suddenly glanced down at her.

"I have been contemplating the Tewksbury lineage, Flavia. Continuity of line is best ensured by multiple heirs, do you not agree?"

Flavia's fingers contracted violently on his stiff brocade sleeve. Her heart stopped. Unable to speak because of dread for what surely must come next, she could only nod.

He took the nod for acquiescence.

"I shall resume calling upon you," he said meaningfully. "If I *may,* my dear?" His tone was polite but patronizing—the tone of a man who cannot imagine any reply to him in the negative.

Flavia felt ill. Very, very ill. Forcing back tears that sprang up, she swallowed with difficulty.

"My—my only wish is to be your dutiful wife, sir."

He granted her an approving nod.

"And so you are." He patted her tightly curled hand, then drew it to his lips and kissed it.

"Tonight, my dear? After the ball?"

Her eyes flew to his in stunned disbelief. Dear heaven, not tonight! Not *this* night of all nights. Not *this* night when her mind was so full of "him."

The duke was waiting. It was foolhardy to make the duke wait. She forced out the only acceptable answer.

"Tonight, sir," she whispered, trying to smile.

He began to say more, but his discourse was arrested by the excited shouts of coach footmen, the loud squeaking crunch of carriage wheels on the crushed stone drive. Becoming the perfect host, the duke left her side.

Flavia was left alone in her agony, standing stiff and solitary in the center of the entry hall. The imposing black and gold crest under her feet seemed to swallow her up.

As footmen tugged open the carved doors, and laughing guests spilled over the threshold, she felt something die within her. What it was, she couldn't name. But its death left an emptiness in her soul.

The Baroness Annette Vachon lay curled against him like a contented cat. Garth could almost hear her purr. He smiled to himself as her fingernails traced his shoulder, then trailed to his chest. The nails played idly there for a time—twisting tufts of hair—then trailed lower.

He held his breath in anticipation.

With a sultry laugh, she shifted up on her elbow. Her raven tresses spilled to his chest like fine silk. She was in one of her playful and generous moods. The forty-four-year-old baroness dipped her head...

He felt the pleasure build slowly, in golden, ever-widening rings. His ears filled with the roar of his own desire. His blood raced. Slowly she took him to the brink. Then, as he teetered on the brink of release, she suddenly rolled away, giggling. Kittenish, she skittered to the edge of the bed, grabbing at a wrapper of Chinese red silk.

"Damnation, Annette! Teasing bitch!"

With a growl, he lunged for her, catching her arm. He wrenched her to the center of the bed, and her giggles rippled as he flung her to her back and held her down. Still giggling, she gasped for air and struggled, her dark hair a silken fan on the pillows.

"Not again, McNeil," she scolded, laughing. "My maids must dress me for the ball. Let go."

He did not.

"Will you never learn, Annette? A tease must expect to pay the piper."

"But the duke of Tewksbury's ball—" She broke off, giggling.

"I don't know Tewksbury. I don't give a fig for his ball."

He pressed his mouth hard against hers, and slowly the laughter died in her throat. She ceased her struggling. Her body tensed, and he watched the dark flashing eyes mellow to a familiar glow. With an excited shiver, she reached for him.

The coach jolted along, rocking, pitching. Even with Annette's footmen running ahead lofting torches, the driver failed to avoid many of the chuckholes.

Inside the coach, sitting next to Annette, Garth McNeil propped his feet upon the seat opposite and eased down into the sumptuous leather to endure the short journey to Tewksbury Hall. Yawning, he let his eyes slide shut. He was tired. Annette Vachon's bed was not famous for the sleep it provided.

He began to snooze. His nap was interrupted by a smart tap on his shoe. He ignored the imperial summons and snoozed on. She tapped again with her ivory fan. This time, insistently.

McNeil opened one eye to a slit.

"Not again, surely?" he said dryly.

The baroness tossed her beautifully coiffed head in feigned disgust. "Really, McNeil. I don't know why I put up with you."

He gave her a lazy grin. "*I* know why."

She whacked at him with her fan, then speared his propped feet with an annoyed look.

"Remove your feet from my cushions. You should respect my possessions."

McNeil did not remove his feet.

"As I respect their owner?"

For answer, she threw her fan in pique and turned away. McNeil chuckled. Why did he enjoy provoking her so? Wasn't it enough that he exasperated her by calling her Baroness, when the proper mode of address was Lady Annette? Ah well, he thought, perhaps I enjoy playing the role of the colonial-born clod.

Annette retreated into injured, haughty silence. But experience had taught McNeil that the silence would not last long. His mistress was not one to endure much in silence. He was right. Only a minute passed before she swung her head to him.

"You *do* love me, McNeil."

"Have I ever said so?"

She shot him a look of pure fury, and he was surprised at the hint of tears in the hard, dark eyes. He'd gone too far. He sighed. There was no need to hurt her. She made his London stopovers pleasurable. Annette was a generous lover and, in her own greedy and having way, a sweet one. He found the difference in their ages—her forty-four to his thirty-two—to be a positive factor, not a negative one.

He resolved to make amends. He retrieved the fan for her, and slipped his arm around her

waist. When, with a happy, forgiving sigh she
settled against him, he kissed the beauty patch
she wore on her cheek.

"You *do* love me," she reiterated.

McNeil felt a surge of annoyance at the old,
wearying theme. He'd heard it for the past
three years.

"I love to *bed* you," he corrected.

She lifted her head, her lips forming a pout.

"So! You still fancy yourself in love with that
dock whore who warmed your bed one drunken
night and then vanished." She tossed her head
in contempt. "You *still* search for her," she
accused.

McNeil stiffened. He pulled his arm from her
waist.

"If I do, it does not concern you, Annette."

She swung toward him in irritation.

"In love with a doxy! Pah. Do you know the
life span of a dock whore, McNeil? The slut is
long dead of disease. Forget her."

He winced. Hadn't that been his agony these
past two years? Hadn't that worry consumed
him during his voyages? He'd searched. Judas,
how he'd searched! He'd hired a dozen men to
comb London. He'd offered rewards to tavernkeepers and prostitutes.

"She's dead," the baroness said.

The furious eyes he turned upon her would
have stilled the tongue of even the bravest man,
but Annette ignored his fury. Tactlessly, she
pressed her case from another direction.

"Only God knows how much money you've
wasted in your search."

He looked at her sharply, his eyes narrowing as a suspicious thought formed. The carriage jolted into a pothole. The lantern swung in its leather harness.

"Only *God* knows?" he asked acidly.

Her scared eyes told him he'd caught her. So she *had* been nosing into his activities. She fluttered her lashes, suddenly playing the coquette.

"If I make it my business to delve into your life, it is only because I love you, McNeil."

He sat on his temper, sat hard. Damn her bold, interfering ways! Judas. A vile new thought began to form, choking him. Had Annette thwarted his search in some way? She had money enough to do it.

He gave her a long, hard look. She misread his look and slid coyly to his lap, her silk petticoats rustling. She teased his angry, unyielding mouth with butterfly kisses.

He burned with anger. He had the sudden urge to demean her, humiliate her. Roughly, he took her into his arms and wrenched at the gown lacings that ran along her spine, wrenching them loose. She jerked upright in surprise.

"McNeil? What are you doing?"

He smiled with distaste.

"The only thing for which you have any talent, Baroness."

She tried to lunge away, and for once she did not giggle. She drew quick, panicky breaths.

"But in my coach? I never!"

He laughed unkindly.

"Then it's time you did, Baroness."

She cried out in fresh protest and twisted away. But he held her with one hand and angrily snuffed out the coach lantern that rocked gently at the window.

"McNeil! No!—we're nearing Tewksbury Hall—think how I shall look!" But by the time her words were out, she lay under him in a crush of silk.

To Flavia's immense joy, Simon Beauchamp was among the first guests to arrive. She knew it cost her uncle great effort to attend. His health had deteriorated in the past two years, and he preferred a quiet evening at his own fireside.

She hurried forward. In younger, more carefree days she would've run laughing into her uncle's arms. Those days could be no more. Uncle Simon seemed to understand, but his eyes were the sadder for it. With old-fashioned decorum, he bowed low over the jeweled hand she offered.

"How very good of you to come, Uncle Simon."

"Only the grave could prevent me from honoring your son's natal day, Flavia."

He smiled, but it was a solemn, questioning smile. In it she read unspoken concern for her well-being.

"All is well," she said quickly. "Truly, Uncle Simon."

The quaver in her voice threatened to betray her, and she slid her eyes from his. To hide the emotions that churned, she smiled with a brightness she didn't feel. Taking his infirm arm, she plunged into diverting chatter as she led him across the entryway.

"Come, Uncle Simon. Salute the duke, and then I shall take you in. Father is already at the gaming tables. Mother is in the west ballroom, keeping a hawk's eye on Harriet and Phoebe. At thirteen and fourteen, the girls are already such minxes, Uncle. You'll laugh! They browbeat Mother into letting them wear grown-up gowns. But Mother insisted they tuck a lace fichu into their necklines. I'm positive Harriet and Phoebe intend to let their laces slip the moment Mother turns her back."

Her uncle was silent. Gamely she chattered on.

"I can't wait for you to see Florentina. She's so beautiful tonight! She's sixteen now, you know. When that handsome young baronet from Edinburgh sees her tonight, he is sure to speak to Father. Oh, and Valentina! There has never been such a lovely seventeen-year-old. Wait until you see her. I bought her a gown of ruby-colored silk. With her black hair and bright blue eyes, she's—"

She fell silent as the stern set of her uncle's jaw told her he'd not been deceived by her playacting. His frown deepened as she led him slowly toward the cluster of guests where the duke held court, proudly and arrogantly receiving congratulations on his son's first birthday.

Simon Beauchamp scowled.

"So everyone is happy but you, Flavia."

Her eyes fled from his. She wanted to deny

his statement, but could not. She couldn't lie to
Uncle Simon. Their hearts were too close. Together, they guarded the secret upon which her
safety and the prosperity of her family depended.
She patted his arm helplessly.

"I have my son. I have my sisters. I have
Mother and Papa and you. I—I have many
blessings, Uncle Simon."

He fumbled for her jeweled hand, covering it
with his swollen, rheumatic one.

"Perhaps, my child. But were it within my
power to grant it, I would wish you blessed with
one thing more."

She raised her eyes, questioning.

"Love," he said simply.

The baroness was predictable. First she raged,
pelting him with fan, reticule and calamanco
dancing pump. Then she hurled curses that
would've made a sailor blush.

Amused, McNeil eased into the cushions to
ride out her temper. Soon, her railing was punctuated with a few stray giggles. At last she
threw up her hands and burst into low throaty
laughter.

"McNeil, I don't know why I put up with
you!"

He cocked his head.

"Shall I refresh your very short memory,
Baroness?"

She giggled, low and sultry.

"And shall I put your prowess to the test,
Captain?"

"Touché."

It was his turn to chuckle. He was satisfied she had no part in thwarting his search. Annette's character was too straightforward for that. He struggled to relight the gently rocking lantern and turned, studying her with grudging admiration. In the long run, he thought, good humor carried a woman further than good looks. Annette was past forty. Yet she would outlast her peers in desirability.

Breaking into a happy smile at the look in his eyes, she slipped to his lap. She gave him a light, forgiving kiss. Fumbling, he helped her repair her dishabille. The baroness sighed in contentment, her flighty thoughts springing ahead to the ball at Tewksbury. McNeil chuckled as she entertained him with outrageous gossip concerning the duke. Like a malicious but delightful kitten tossing a mouse about, she pounced on the duke's long-delayed fatherhood, on the failure of his first wives to produce an heir.

"There is talk," she confided happily, "that his first wives are not dead but alive, and sold into an African seraglio!" When he made no response, she demanded, "What do you think of *that*, McNeil?"

He eyed her solemnly.

"An excellent solution for unmanageable wives. I shall recommend it to your husband, the baron, when next we meet."

She slapped at him with her comb, but would not be put off track. She leaped back to her gossip, unsheathing kitten claws upon the current duchess.

"I should like to believe Flavia cuckolded old

spindle shanks," she went on, wetting one finger with her tongue and repairing a disarrayed curl. "But, alas, she lives like a nun. No one can be found to say a word against her." She sighed in disappointment.

McNeil said dryly, "How uncooperative of the duchess."

Annette gave him a quick sharp look, then giggled.

"McNeil, there is nothing so dull as a faithful wife."

"Is that the opinion of your husband, Baroness?"

He found himself on the receiving end of a flung comb.

It was Garth McNeil's first party at a ducal estate and he was amused to note that in tone it didn't differ from a public ball in Williamsburg, which one might attend for the price of a three-shilling ticket.

As in Williamsburg, each element sought its level. Avid horsemen gathered in groups, talking horses while their wives fussed at them to dance. Gamblers sought the gaming rooms while *their* vexed wives took pains not to appear vexed. The politically minded flowed to the smoking rooms. The young unmarried people danced every dance in the brightly lit ballrooms. The elderly claimed comfortable settees on the fringes of the dancing, their cheeks growing pink with wine and misty-eyed reminiscence.

"Come, McNeil," Annette said, firmly taking his arm. "We must find old spindleshanks and present you."

He moved with her through the glittering, expensively dressed assembly.

"And how will you present me?" he asked in amused curiosity. "As your dear and long-lost cousin?"

Discreetly, she stabbed him in the rib with her fan as her rustling skirts guided him on. "Stop it. I shall introduce you as shipmaster of the *Caroline*, prime shipper of Vachon chinaware, business associate and close friend of my husband."

His mouth twisted in a wry smile as they drifted through the music and gaiety, heading for the east ballroom.

"Ah, yes. My close friend, the baron." He paused. "But tell me, Baroness, what does my close friend the baron look like? Tall or short? Thin? Fat as a cow?"

She shot him a black look.

"McNeil, do behave."

"Say please."

Temper flared in her eyes. Then she giggled. "*Please.*"

He bowed.

"I shall be the personification of gravity, Lady Annette."

McNeil was annoyed at the surge of instant dislike he felt for the duke of Tewksbury. He did not usually find himself condemning a man at a glance. America-born, he always granted benefit of a doubt. Still, he felt his hackles rise as he and the duke exchanged the expected amenities in the ballroom. He loathed everything about the man: the peacock strut, the arrogance, the glint of hardness flickering in the cold eyes.

His hostility growing by the moment, McNeil clenched his jaw and spoke as little as possible. Annette chattered on brightly, oblivious to the polite contempt in the duke's smile.

"The baron regrets he cannot attend tonight, sir," she bubbled on in high spirits. "Business detains him on the Continent. Where is Her Grace? Shall we have the honor of seeing your son, the marquis?"

The duke warmed slightly in pride.

"I have ordered the nurses to awaken him and bring him down." He paused.

"However, Her Grace has seen fit to contradict me." Displeasure moved across his features, hardening his mouth. "Her Grace has gone to fetch him herself. She insists he be wakened gently. She coddles him," he said with distaste.

Annette burst into good-natured laughter.

"But he is only a baby, sir!"

He gave her a chilling look.

"He is the marquis of Bladensburg and the future duke of Tewksbury. He cannot begin to learn his duties too early."

McNeil's stomach turned. With a bow that barely qualified as polite, he excused himself. He needed air. There was a taint to the duke that sickened him.

Ignoring the flirtatious glances and fluttering fans that ushered him through the crowd, he made his way out and headed for the gaming rooms.

* * *

Flavia chewed her lip as she hurried along the corridor, her son heavy and wiggling happily in her arms. She was worried. She knew she'd displeased the duke. And in front of guests. She hadn't meant to speak up. But her heart had rebelled at the thought of the German nurses roughly rousing Robert from his sleep. The nurses toadied to the duke. They would've wrenched Robert awake with the greatest speed: rough hands, loud voices, bright candlelight. At least she'd spared Robert that. She'd wakened him softly, with coos and kisses.

Aware of the two stern nurses trailing behind, exchanging frowns of disapproval, she faltered as she approached the ballroom. Her heart was heavy with dread. Would the duke have forgiven her peccadillo? Or would he hold it against her, meting out some future punishment? She remembered a past springtime when she'd unknowingly infuriated him by romping with a kitchen puppy through a garden plot of bright yellow daffodils. The duke did not speak of the incident. However, the next day all dogs were banished from Tewksbury.

Kissing the baby's cheek, she drew a deep breath for courage and stepped into the ballroom. She forced a serene smile to her trembling lips as the sea of guests parted for her with appropriate admiring cries for the baby. Approaching the duke with a poise she didn't feel, Flavia searched His Grace's face for some signal of mood. His lips smiled, but his eyes were flint.

She looked away in panic. *Dear heaven, he's furious with me! What will he do?*

Immediately, silk-gowned and jeweled women flocked forward, cooing, clucking, petting the baby, uttering little cries of compliment that were meant for the duke's ears.

"But he is *precious,* sir," the Baroness Vachon bubbled to the duke after warmly greeting Flavia. "See how he clings to his little mother. Aren't they sweet together?"

Flavia's hope for clemency sank. Annette Vachon meant well, but she couldn't have said anything more damaging. In fear, Flavia glanced at the duke. He continued to smile, but the flinty eyes were coated with frost.

"Maternal attachment interferes with the process of education," he said testily.

The baroness laughed, and Flavia's hope sank further.

"Nonsense, sir! Babies need their mothers."

The duke stiffened.

"It has never been so for the dukes of Tewksbury. We are reared without maternal coddling. It prepares us for our station in life."

He smiled at Annette and then at Flavia, but Flavia trembled at the thought of what might lurk behind the smile.

"I shall return Robert to the nursery," she offered quickly.

The duke checked her with a frown. "Allow the nurses to do it, my dear." He signaled to the nurses who'd trailed after her. As a stout humorless nurse reached for Robert, he shrieked,

clinging to Flavia's neck. She feared to comfort
him with soft patting. Under the duke's forbid-
ding eye, she could not. Helpless, she let the
stout woman wrench him from her arms. Robert
wailed. The wails cut a path through the
sympathizing guests and faded into the corridor.
Flavia stole a look at the duke. Clearly he was
displeased with his son's performance.

"You see, sir?" Annette Vachon pressed tactlessly. "A baby needs his mother."

"He needs discipline," the duke snapped.
"And he shall have it. Tomorrow he goes. To my
estate in Germany. To Bladensburg. There he
shall be reared by nurses and tutors who do *not*
coddle."

It was a stab. Without thinking, Flavia cried
out, "No! Not yet! I know that Tewksbury heirs
must spend their boyhood at Bladensburg, but
Robert is still a baby, sir. He's—"

Controlled anger glittered in the duke's eyes,
cutting her off.

"You disagree with my decision, my dear?" he
asked pleasantly.

Guests murmured, drifting away. Flavia stared
about her blankly, seeking support that was
nonexistent. Even Annette Vachon had turned
from the subject and was flirting with a French
count. The orchestra swung into a rousing German march, and she forced her numb gaze to
the duke.

"Please, sir? Don't send the baby away—don't."

His face was implacable. The music grew
louder, its rhythmic cadence square and thumping.

Coldly, the duke said, "It is time for us to lead the grand march, my dear. Will you grant me the honor of taking my arm?"

Dazed, Flavia complied. Like a puppet responding to its puppeteer, she moved with the duke to the head of the ballroom where the march would begin. Stunned and heartsick, she hid behind the duchess of Tewksbury's cool, serene smile.

The party was endless. Finally, Flavia found an opportunity and fled into the darkness of the garden. Her heart was bursting. She desperately needed to weep. Needed to release the heart-deep sobs that had been choking her during the past hours of obligatory dancing.

While tears were a luxury any Tewksbury kitchen maid could afford, the duchess of Tewksbury could ill afford them. Even in the supposed privacy of her apartment, there was always a servant about, eager to ingratiate herself with the head steward by reporting on her mistress. Tears, laughter, a cross word or even a happy shout—all were reported and eventually reached the duke's ear, and the duke would lecture her on the theme of dignified self-control.

Blinded by tears, she fled down the path, her slippers crunching the mollusk-shell path. The garden was empty. A chill damp breeze had begun to blow off the Thames, chasing in even the most ardent lovers.

There was no moon, but Flavia needed none. She knew every inch of the garden. It was her only refuge at Tewksbury. She knew everything about it, even knew where wild rabbits hid from

the gardener's swinging cudgel. Slipping from
the white shell path, she left the formal part of
the garden and found the dirt path that cut
through a thicket of small trees and wound
along the riverbank. She ran. When she reached
her private place by the river where trees shielded
her from view of greenhouse and tool sheds, she
sank into the inky darkness and sobbed. Her
cries were wild and raw, her few sobbed words
incoherent. She wept as she'd never wept before.

When her emotions were spent, she knelt
there, numb and exhausted, beyond caring that
the damp grass was spoiling her gown. She
bowed her head. Bowed it to the inevitable.

Robert will go...the duke will have his way...

She was empty. Only gradually did she become aware that life still went on all around her.
She could hear distant violins. The river lapped
soothingly at the shore. A hint of the sea came
to her in the damp-smelling river breeze. She
breathed deeply and caught the startling aroma
of tobacco.

Turning quickly, she saw the red glowing tip
of a cigar. A man sat smoking, deep in the
shadows. She prickled, then squelched the fear
as an unworthy one. If the man meant her
harm, he'd have done her harm by now. She'd
been weeping a long time.

"Forgive me," she said timidly. "I thought
this place deserted."

The cigar glowed to brightness, then faded.
Smoke lingered in the air for an instant, then
wafted off in the wind. Flavia found the smell
oddly comforting. At last the man spoke.

"Don't apologize. Each heart has its hell."

The words were terse but not unkind. The accent Yankee. So he is America-born, Flavia thought sadly. There were many at the ball. Flavia had met several and danced with two. It was all the rage for highborn ladies to dally with handsome colonials, bringing them to parties in lieu of an absent husband. Gossips said Annette Vachon brought a colonial tonight, but Flavia hadn't seen him.

The colonial didn't intrude by speaking again. She was grateful. A less sensitive man would've attempted to offer comfort. Her gown rustled as she rose to leave.

"Do you desire escort?"

His voice. His voice! *Don't imagine things, Flavia. Don't break your heart more than it is already breaking.*

"No, thank you, sir. I know Tewksbury as well as I know the back of my hand. I'm the—" Her voice fell away, and she found herself wondering at her impulse to confide in this stranger. "I am Flavia Rochambeau...the duchess of Tewksbury," she finished without heart.

She would've had to be deaf to miss the harsh intake of breath that came from the darkness.

"Then I understand," he snapped, and she sensed he truly did. She was aware that the duke's cruel decision about Robert had been pounced upon by gossips. The tale had gone flying. No doubt it had been served up with the iced lobster in supper rooms, dealt out along with cards at gaming tables, and passed from

fluttering fan to fluttering fan in the two ballrooms. No one could fail to know.

"Thank you," she whispered sincerely.

For response, he moodily slung his cigar at
the Thames. She watched it go. It was a tiny
comet, trailing angry fire, then vanishing into a
black watery void.

She knew she must weave her way back to
the violin music. She mustn't linger and further
anger the duke. Yet she was loath to leave. The
quiet colonial exuded a strength, a comfort.
God knows, she thought, I am badly in need of
such.

"Your voice," he said, his shoes scraping stone
as he rose. "It reminds me of—no. No."

Her heart was suddenly a pendulum, swinging between hope and dread.

"Sir? Your voice, too... it... "

Just as he moved toward her, the moon forced
its way through the dark, rain-laden clouds. The
moon peeled back the clouds, layer by layer,
and then sprang out, huge and white. Light
flooded the riverbank.

"You!" he cried out.

"You..." she breathed.

He took three wild steps toward her, then
froze as though he feared a closer look.

"Is it you?" he demanded. "Is it?"

Flavia swayed, her mind reeling. Safety lay in
denial. Safety for herself and Robert. *Run! Run
back to Tewksbury!* But her feet would not
obey her mind. Instead they obeyed her heart,
and she found herself flying into his arms.

"Yes! Oh, yes," she gasped as he crushed her to his banging heart. At his touch, his smell, she began to weep with stunned happiness. Holding her as though he would never let her go, his lips went to her hair and pressed against its silken strands.

"God," he whispered, his voice shaking with reverence, "God..." He held her tight and she wept against his warm, thumping chest. "To find you here, to find you the duchess of Tewksbury... I don't understand. That night on the quay. Why?"

Shaking with emotion, she looked up at him, helpless to explain, helpless to excuse herself. But his eyes met hers with bewildered gentleness.

"Don't tell me," he ordered. "I fear to hear it. I fear I can't bear it." He cradled her in his arms, rocking her, brushing his lips in her hair.

"You stole my heart that night. I've searched for you for almost two years. God, how I've searched!"

Flavia lifted her wet face in joyful surprise.

"I searched, too," she admitted with a sob. "Every face that came to Tewksbury, every face in the theaters on Drury Lane and at the parties the duke took me to. Oh, I don't even know your name."

He took her face in his hands, and she drank in his dark eyes.

"Garth," he said softly. "Garth McNeil."

"Garth," she repeated in a hushed whisper. She shivered, sensing a boundary had been crossed. She now knew his name, and his name would forever define the boundaries of her life.

She shivered again, only half sensing what that might mean.

"Flavia," he said softly, tasting her name. "Flavia... Flavia..."

Scattered heavy drops of rain pelted suddenly from the closing sky. The moon darkened.

"Where can we go, Flavia? To talk? To be alone?"

She shivered in fear. She mustn't! She *must* go back to the ball. If the duke...

"The greenhouse," she whispered. "But only for a moment. We mustn't be discovered."

The greenhouse smelled warm, moist and earthy. Blossoming gardenia and fruit-laden lemon trees filled the air with fragrance. As soon as the door closed behind them, they were in each other's arms. They kissed in anguished passion, and their few words were utterances of love, pledges of commitment, confessions of need. They touched each other, their eager hands trembling at the sweet wonder of stroking the beloved brow, the cherished face.

"Now that I've found you, I won't let you go. Sail with me. Leave the duke. Forget your life here. I love you, Flavia!"

She uttered a little cry, pressing her face to the thudding pulse that throbbed in his strong, warm neck.

"Please, Garth, don't. It's madness! Don't torture me by saying such things. If I went with you, the duke would find out. He'd have you killed! Oh, I love you too much to put you in danger."

"Nonsense," he began, then stiffened as a

noise came from the adjoining section of greenhouse. A clay pot crashed to the ground. Flavia jumped in fear.

"A cat," Garth suggested, his hands tightening on her shoulders. "But you must go. You'll be missed, and," he added reluctantly, "the Baroness Vachon will miss me."

He swept her to the door and wrenched the door open.

"Come to me tomorrow. On the *Caroline*."

Flavia trembled.

"No," she said, and then, as his hand touched her face, "yes, oh, yes!"

She moved to go, but he caught her hand.

"That night on the quay. Have you . . . done such things often?" His voice was tight, tortured.

She shook her head.

"Never before. Never since."

His sigh was one of deep relief.

"Then why *that* night, Flavia?"

She glanced into the darkness. Rain was beginning to spit down. The ballroom music was muted now, as though windows had been shut. What could she say? She couldn't tell him he had a son. He was the sort of man who would move heaven and earth to claim what was his. He would confront the duke, and what would the duke do to the baby? And to her? She shuddered away the answer and floundered for a gentle lie to tell him, a sweet lie, the sweetest lie she could think of.

"I—I—was starved for love."

She reached out, touching his face.

"And Garth . . . that night, I—I found it."

* * *

With a last look at his puzzled brooding face, she flew into the night and back to the mansion. Shaking with emotion, she found a maid to help rub the grass stains from her gown and repair the wisps of hair that had loosened during Garth's kisses.

She struggled to slow her banging heart, to regain her poise. With great difficulty, she strove to pull on a mask of cool serenity. She was hostess. She *must* resume her duties.

Torn in half by the equally powerful tugs of ecstasy and dread, she went out to dance with her guests. As she danced, conversing politely, her heart shouted, *He loves me! I love him! Oh, God, what should I do?*

Uncle Simon was the only guest who sensed her agitation. He drew her aside, linking her arm under his as he strolled from the noisy ballroom toward the cloakroom.

When they were free of the throng of guests, Uncle Simon said, "You've done an unwise thing tonight, Flavia."

Her knees went to water. *Garth. The garden.*

He went on, "You have publicly questioned the duke's right to raise his son as he wishes. That was dangerous. His Grace is extremely angry with you, Flavia."

She gulped air in relief.

"But my baby—I—I shall apologize to His Grace."

"See that you do, child. I fear the duke's temper. A streak of madness . . ." Uncle Simon's voice trailed off into a wheezing cough.

At the cloakroom he sent one footman for his landau, another for the cloak. Tiredly, he shrugged into the cloak, turned and kissed Flavia on the cheek. He'd taken no wine, and his breath smelled of illness. As Flavia helped him to the door, the duke's German steward strode in, bowed to Flavia and thrust a package at Uncle Simon.

"Mr. Beauchamp. His Grace would be pleased if you would take these papers to the Board of Trade immediately and file them. In the *usual* manner."

Flavia's breath caught in outrage.

"It's the middle of the night! My uncle isn't fit to—"

"Your Grace!" Uncle Simon checked her, then slowly reached for her hand, bowed over it and kissed it. "Your Grace, I shan't detain you. You have your duties; I have mine."

She breathed in tight, jerky spasms as she watched Uncle Simon go. When his landau had clattered off, she remembered the steward. The man was a sycophant. He would rush to tell the duke about her outburst unless she somehow apologized. She turned to do so. But except for footmen, the entry hall was empty. The steward had flown.

When the ball ended and she could at last escape to her apartment and undress, she fell into bed, emotionally exhausted. She drifted toward sleep even as she fought against it.

That the duke did not come in, that he'd omitted the marital visit he'd requested, scarcely made a ripple in her mind.

*   *   *

She awoke to bright sunshine and a tap on the door. One of the duke's newly hired German maids came in bearing her usual morning cup of chocolate. Bleary-eyed, Flavia reached for the cup. It flashed robin's egg blue in the sunshine, its gold rim glinting, contents steaming chocolaty and rich. She brought the cup to her lips.

Ten minutes after she'd drunk it, she knew the chocolate had been drugged. A hundred hammers pounded her skull. Her heart was a clock gone mad—now racing, now refusing to tick. She tried to lunge out of bed, but the bedpost danced away and she fell into a chasm. From the bottom of the chasm she could see the pink and gold walls of her bedchamber begin to tumble. Faster and faster they spun, until a door in one wall opened and the duke's German steward tumbled toward her. Flavia blinked. The steward splintered and now there were six of him tumbling closer, ever closer.

"Help me," she whispered.

But even as she begged, she knew it was too late. Everything was slipping away. She felt someone pick her up and drop her onto the bed. Then the bed dropped away and was falling. She fell with it. Into oblivion.

Chapter 4

GARTH MCNEIL WAS BLIND DRUNK. He'd been drunk for a month. Drunk ever since the duchess of Tewksbury had taken sick and died.

Lying in a nest of stinking bedding, he groaned. He cursed the consciousness that stirred in him as sunlight filtered through the unboarded space in the broken window. He rolled from its stabbing light. He fumbled in the sour sheets for his bottle. He found it. With shaking hands, he guided it to dry, crusted lips.

Empty!

He launched a torrent of invectives at the offending bottle. He cursed it thoroughly, as though it were the embodiment of the pox that had taken Flavia. Drunkenly, he snaked his way to the edge of the bedstead and drummed the bottle against the floorboards, signaling the innkeeper below.

He needed rum. Much more rum. Conscious-

ness was not to be borne. Pain...too much
pain...memories that slashed like scimitars.

His risky visit to Tewksbury Hall, where he'd
waited for news in the crowded receiving chamber, along with other solicitous callers, the chilling
verdict of smallpox, the violent banging of his
heart when he arrived to find servants draping
doors and mirrors with black bunting, his stunned
disbelief and then the crashing despair, his inevitable acceptance of her death when Flavia's
own nurse nervously recounted to him Flavia's
last moments.

"It was my sad duty, sir, to accompany Her
Grace to the gates of her Reward. I myself
closed Her Grace's lifeless eyes and placed the
pennyweights upon them...I myself closed
her..."

God Almighty! No more of it!

With a bellow of inner torment, McNeil
clutched the bottle and savaged the floor with
it. The bottle shattered. Splinters of glass shot
into his hand. He didn't feel it. He scarcely
noticed the blood. He slumped to the bed.
Numb. Exhausted. Around the bed, the water-
stained walls revolved like a Dutch windmill.
His leaden eyes closed.

The door creaked open. McNeil did not trouble himself to flicker an eyelid.

"Uncork it," he snarled. "Be quick."

There was a light step, the brisk rustle of a
gown. A bottle was slapped into his demanding
hand with more force than was necessary. McNeil
grasped his salvation. Greedily, he sucked in
the amber fire. The acrid, memory-expunging

smell of rum filled his lungs. Then, mixed with
the rum aroma, came the scent of perfume.
McNeil stiffened. It was not the familiar stench
of the innkeeper's wife, who divided her time
between serving up and tending her flock of
randy-smelling goats.

McNeil wrenched his eyes open. Red silk and
a tumble of glossy black hair jarred into focus.
He shut his eyes in disgust.

"Get out of here."

Unperturbed, the baroness sat upon the bed,
setting the bed to rocking, and McNeil knew—
knew beyond doubt—that for the first time in
his life he was going to be seasick. Totally,
ingloriously seasick.

He lunged for the edge of the bed, racing the
rising gorge. He began to retch. With her neat
little kid slipper, the baroness toed a slop jar in
the general direction of his misery. As he emp-
tied himself, she watched without a murmur of
pity. When he was done, she got up, fished a
towel from the room's debris, wet it in the
cracked, slow-leaking pitcher on the washstand
and dropped it into his waiting hand.

"Devil take you, Annette," he muttered by
way of thanks.

She laughed her soft throaty laugh.

"You're welcome, McNeil."

She sat down heavily upon the bed. Again the
bed rocked like a cradle. McNeil swore, gritting
his teeth against the threatening gorge. He
retrieved the bottle, which was two-thirds spilled,
its rum soaking into the straw mattress. He
drank. The rum burned its way down, a snake of

acid. He choked, swallowed, choked, until the painkiller had done its work.

The baroness watched without comment. Garth glowered at her. Then, sickened at the cloying taste of rum, he flung the bottle at the wall. It hit with a crash. For a moment, a sunburst of amber appeared on the gray plaster. Then its rays dripped downward into ordinary stain.

The baroness was unflappable. She continued to study him with her dark, good-humored eyes.

"Go away!" he roared.

She shook her head.

"You stink, McNeil," she offered cheerfully, wrinkling her nose in distaste. "Tell me, McNeil, do you intend to stay drunk forever? Or only until the *Caroline* is impounded and you are arrested for thievery?"

McNeil opened one eye. What the hell was the bed-craving bitch blathering about? The *Caroline* in jeopardy? Stiffly, he raised up on one elbow. A seedy alarm coursed through him. The *Caroline* was his responsibility. The crew depended upon him.

Finding she had captured his attention, the baroness did not mince words. In her forthright way, she stated the case bluntly.

"The duke of Tewksbury has obtained papers for your arrest. On the night of the ball, you stole two of his priceless jade carvings. Even now, the magistrate and his men are thrashing about the waterfront, searching for you."

McNeil was stunned. He sat up, instantly sober.

"That's nonsense."

"I know. But the carvings *were* found aboard the *Caroline*. In *your* cabin. In the desk containing your private captain's log."

McNeil couldn't take it in. He staggered to his feet. Dizzy as a landlubber on high seas, he braced himself against the bedpost.

"I don't believe it."

For response, Annette went to the door, flung it wide and beckoned into the hallway. A young man with scared eyes and a wig that didn't fit edged into the room sideways, as though ready to bolt.

"Who the devil?" McNeil growled.

The young man ducked his head, swallowed, opened his mouth to speak. Annette cut him off.

"Footman to the duke of Tewksbury. It was he who planted the jades in your cabin. A clever choice of emissary by the duke, was it not? If the boy succeeds, fine. If he is caught and tells his story, who will believe it? The duke merely accuses the lad of stealing and stowing away to the colonies. The lad is thrown into Newgate to rot."

McNeil's head spun.

The young man fell to his knees. "Please, sir, I be fearful scared. I've runned from my post. Footmen what does favors for His Grace's steward, them footmen has a way of disappearin'. Please, sir, take me to the New World?"

Garth scowled, scarcely hearing the boy's plea. He tried to think, tried to make his pickled brain work. For some reason the duke wanted all eyes on the *Caroline*. Why? His meeting with sweet Flavia could not have been the reason. Their few moments in the garden had been chaste and short . . . a lifetime too short.

As he stood thinking, Annette dismissed the boy, sending him to the *Caroline*. He shook his head to clear it.

"McNeil, wake up!" Annette scolded. "There's not a moment to waste. The duke is sparing no effort to have the *Caroline* impounded. Thus far, he's not been successful."

She swept through the room, muttering after his boots. When she found the boots, she threw them at him.

"Get dressed. I have ordered the baron's steward to do everything possible to delay impoundment. But it won't last forever. Your first mate, Mr. Jenkins, has obtained clearance from the harbor master. The *Caroline* sails on tonight's tide, before Tewksbury can do further mischief—"

She broke off, breathless. Garth drove a foot into a boot, listing a little as he lost his balance. Damn! He was captain of a ship first, a man second. The *Caroline* was his responsibility. He would see her safely to Virginia. He owed that much to his stockholders. After that, he could drown himself in rum, drink himself into the very oblivion that held Flavia.

As he wrenched open the door, the baroness flung herself against it. Twisting under his arm, she placed her hands upon his chest in warning.

"McNeil, you *shan't* leave on your own two feet. It would mean instant capture."

Stupidly, thinking slowly because of the alcohol, he stared down at her urgent face. Her eyes were startled starlings.

"Then how?"

She petted his grizzled cheek, touching it gingerly as one touches an animal that both charms and frightens.

"You shall be carried aboard in a wardrobe trunk belonging to the Baroness Annette Vachon."

"What!"

"The Baroness Vachon sails to America to inspect her husband's land holdings. She travels with a dozen large trunks. *No one*—magistrate or harbor master—would have the audacity to search those trunks."

He stared at her. For the first time in many weeks, a thin smile strained over his lips. He was baffled. Amazed. To think this cheerful titled wench had courage enough, brains enough, to arrange such a deception.

She sensed his thoughts and bridled.

"Jackanapes! There is more to me than tail and tit. As you would know, if you took the trouble to find out."

She pushed past him in a huff, and McNeil found himself swaying like a stripling in a hurricane. To steady himself, he reached for her arm. Coordination failed him. He ended up with a handful of silk skirt. He was surprised when she did him the kindness of not pulling away.

"Annette," he said softly. "You place yourself in danger for my sake. Why?"

She colored slightly. For a moment, her brassy confidence wavered. She shrugged the moment away and eyed him boldly.

"Because you amuse me, McNeil," she said crisply. "Were you thrown into Newgate, darling, I should be deprived of my amusement, should I not?"

Her retort hung in the air. Brittle as ice in January, and as much a lie. McNeil did not know what to say. But even in his alcoholic fog, he knew he would despise himself if he deceived this gallant woman.

"I don't love you," he said bluntly.

In a snappish gesture, she jerked her skirt from his hand. "'Love'!" she said scornfully. "Every woman knows she must choose between love and amusement. I find amusement the wiser investment." She granted him a dazzling smile. "It is far less costly, is it not?"

He grinned. A weary, soul-wracked grin. So, she understood. Knew the limits of their relationship and would not complain when more was not forthcoming. He found building in him the urge to fondle her chin, as one fondles a dear relative. He did so, and earned her ire for it.

"Damnation, McNeil!" she said, slapping away his hand. "I may be old enough to be your mother, but may I roast in hell if I let you treat me like it. Now, come. Pay attention. Let us tend to the details of your departure."

A quarter of an hour later, the baroness threw a gray cloak over her silks and swished to the door.

"Oh," she called back in her artless way, "I near forgot to tell you. The queerest happenstance, McNeil. That dull little duchess of

Tewksbury? She's died of the smallpox. Had you heard?"

McNeil sucked wind. His head roared. Something violent smashed about in his ribcage. *She's dead, McNeil. Accept it. The kindest thing you can do for Flavia is to pretend you never knew her.*

He took a deep breath.

"No," he said with deadly calm. "I hadn't heard."

Chapter 5

"TRY 'NUTHER SIP, DEARIE. There, that's a luv."

Flavia's throat was as parched as a desert. She desperately craved the water that someone seemed to be holding to her cracked lips. But she couldn't swallow. The water trickled down her chin.

"Don't be wastin' it, luv. Little's enough yer ration."

The cup was offered again. Flavia struggled to swallow. She was disoriented. Her head was spinning. Every bone and muscle in her body ached. Her eyelids were leaden. Try as she might, she couldn't force her eyes open.

There was the roaring sound that never ceased, and she felt bruised, as though her bed were flinging her from bedpost to bedpost.

Where am I? Oh, my throat! Why does it burn like fire? And my bed—why does it buck and pitch so? If I could have something hot to drink—send the maid—

"Please," she croaked in an unused voice, "I want my tea."

A cackle of laughter hit her full in the face along with a gust of breath well laced with garlic.

"Her wants tea!" the garlic voice crowed. Flavia flinched as the laughter cackled forth again. This time, there was an answering echo of snickers and jibes.

Flavia tried to open her eyes. They were gummy, stuck. As though she'd slept weeks.

"D'ye make me yer servant, luv? Step 'n' fetch yer tea, do I?" Laughter and garlic breath hit Flavia. She flinched. "Even be I of a mind t'do it, luv, I cain't. 'Tis Wednesday. Tuesday and Satiddy be hot food day. No, luv, you'll make do w' tack and water. Like the rest of us."

While the words were rough as chopped kindling, they were delivered without rancor. Even in her delirium, Flavia had sensed the woman's goodwill. Her racing heart slowed to a gallop. She rubbed her eyes open.

Slowly, things came into focus. She was in a darkish place, a cubbyhole. There was barely space to sit up. Similar cubbyholes honeycombed the strange room. Hammocks hung everywhere. The only light was sunlight from a square grating in the low ceiling. The pitching room vibrated with noise. Babies cried. Men argued and swore. Someone was reading aloud in German. Female voices whined in complaint. But worse than the noise and the terrifying feeling of being packed in like herrings was the smell. The odor of vomit, unwashed bodies and un-emptied slop jars assailed her quivering nostrils. She fought the impulse to gag. Instead, she shuddered.

"Where am I?" she begged the woman who hunkered near on the bunk. "Where—what—"

She tried to sit up. The woman firmly pushed her back against the thin, rancid-smelling mat covering the slats of the bunk.

"Yer still tiddly, luv. Rest a mite."

Flavia's head spun woosily from the effort to get up. She fought fainting.

"Please—where am I?"

Instantly, she was enveloped in garlic breath and laughter.

"Why, yer 'board the *Schilaack*. Bound for the New World. 'N lucky to be, dearie. The cap'n, he balked at signin' you on. He don't hold w' rum drinking. Specially in females."

Flavia blinked, trying to comprehend.

Slowly, the speaker came into focus. She was a thin young woman, stringy-haired and cheerfully unkempt. Her lean face exuded a peasant strength. Her cheap serge bodice was grease spotted and open to the waist. An infant sucked at one flaccid breast, a whimpering girl of about five clung to her skirts, jealously watching the baby feed, and making furtive snatches at the breast. The woman permitted the behavior for a bit, then lost patience and smacked the child.

"*Whu—whu—whaaaaa*," wailed the fair-haired little girl, and the woman comforted her by giving her a moment's suck.

Flavia's head whirled. She couldn't take it in. Aboard a ship? It wasn't possible. She pulled herself up and sat holding her careening head.

"Please. There's some mistake. Take me to the person in charge. I—I'm the duchess of Tewksbury—"

The young woman burst into a delighted cackle.

"And I'm the Virgin Queen, luv."

Flavia panicked. She had to make her listen. Had to make someone listen.

"Please! I *am* the duchess. If you'll find the duke for me—"

She was cut off by riotous laughter from a motley assortment of the curious who'd begun to gather at the bunk. The young woman laughed so heartily that her breast jumped from the child's mouth. The child screamed in anger, and the deprived baby shrieked with her. Into this mindless, madhouse cacophany boomed a deep, steadying voice.

"Here now, Mab Collins. What's amiss, wife?"

The largest, homeliest man Flavia had ever seen blocked out the room as he squatted beside the bunk. Flavia shrank from him, but the little girl dove straight into his enormous arms. Even the baby flailed its tiny hands, cooing happily.

Still laughing, Mab Collins wiped her streaming eyes and said, "Obadiah Collins, meet the duchess of—of—" She burst into new laughter.

Flavia was as offended as she was bewildered.

"Tewksbury," she said tightly. "I am duchess of Tewksbury."

Mab Collins tittered behind a corner of her

apron, but Obadiah Collins did not laugh. He swung kind glowing eyes at Flavia, then shook his head at his wife.

"'Tisn't the Lord's way, Mab Collins, to tease a poor sick lass," he chided gently. His ingenuous gaze traveled back to Flavia. With a quiet shyness that was incongruous to his size and appearance, he said, "Sister, true happiness be found in the Methody way. Forsake strong drink. Turn to the Lord, Sister. There's naught He'll not forgive ye, if ye'll but repent."

Flavia was stunned. It was like waking up in another world. Her mind went spinning, clutching at memories, clutching at anything that might serve as anchor. She could remember nothing past the night of the ball. Oh! Garth McNeil! There'd been his kisses. Rapture so exquisite she'd never dreamed such happiness could exist between man and woman. Then, slipping through the night and into Tewksbury . . . sleep . . . morning . . . the cup of chocolate . . . the world spinning out from under her . . .

"Please!" she begged the big man. "I *must* see the person in charge. There's been a mistake."

Mab Collins tittered.

"On the Sabbath, luv. After prayers. That be the *only* day the cap'n tends to the whinin' 'n' caterwaulin' of bondslaves."

"'Bondslave'!"

Flavia froze, her mind rejecting the incredible thought that was beginning to build.

Obadiah Collins frowned lovingly at his wife.

"'Tis a poor way to state it, Mab Collins. Indentured servants we are, and proud to be.

'Tis nothing dishonorable, exchangin' a few years' honest work for ship passage to a land of milk and honey."

Flavia stared at the couple blankly. Her heart thudded in her throat. She fought acceptance of the incredible thought. Surely the duke had not—surely no man could be so cruel—

Mab Collins patted her husband.

"Obadiah's indenture will be short, as he's a cabinetmaker. Cabinetmakers, they's rare as hens' teeth in the New World. The cap'n will sell Obie for four years, plus one for the babes' passage." She shrugged the baby to her breast. "I be set to serve six year as kitchen drudge." She threw her husband a proud look. "'Course Obie will buy out my indenture soon's he be a freeman and layin' by cash."

She cocked her head curiously at Flavia.

"How long's yer indenture, dearie?"

Flavia sank back upon the smelly mat, her eyes filling with tears that smarted like fire as they trickled down the chapped, neglected skin of her face. So she and Garth had been discovered in the garden . . . the duke had been told. Nothing else could have inspired so cruel a vengeance.

"Yer indenture," Mab prodded impatiently. "How many year?"

Flavia closed her eyes, closed them as though to shut out all memory of things that could never be again. Garth McNeil . . . her son . . . her family . . .

"I don't know," she whispered desperately. "I don't know!"

*   *   *

"Seven years!"

Flavia's anguished outcry was swallowed up in the sounds of winter wind whistling through the rigging, winter swells hammering the ship's wooden hull. The *Schilaack* pitched, plunging into a particularly wicked trough between waves.

Flavia went pitching forward. Her chapped red hands flew out. She caught herself against the captain's writing table, which was pegged to the deck. She hung on while the *Schilaack* righted itself, bucking skyward with a long sucking roar.

For the offense of touching his table, she earned the Dutchman's scowl. But she was beyond caring. Three weeks in the hellhole that served as the indentureds' quarters had deadened her sensitivity. The weeks had been an eternity of seasickness, black despair, and of waiting her turn to speak to this stern, unfeeling tyrant.

And now to be told seven years!

It can't be, she thought, paralyzed with shock.

It can't.

Seven!

Why, I shall be old before I'm free again!

And my baby—a grown boy!

Aghast at the terrible perfection of the duke's punishment, Flavia could only stare blankly at the hardened Dutchman who was holding court on deck, dispatching of petitioners with an alacrity that bespoke his contempt of the indentured.

Irritably, the captain jabbed a finger at Flavia and went on in broken English.

"Thy name iss not—iss not—"

He jabbed a finger at her.

"Rochambeau," she shouted above the wind. "Flavia Rochambeau."

The captain's disbelieving laugh was half snort, half bellow. Flavia's stomach knotted in helpless anger. Her eyes dropped to the deck she'd been forced to scrub only yesterday.

While she clung stubbornly to her name, she no longer claimed to be a duchess. Almost a month in the bond hold had taught her that. Her fellow passengers had leaped upon her title as a pack of dogs leap after a rabbit.

They tormented her. They taunted, jeered. The children had made up singing games, with her the butt of their joke. And she'd gathered the unwanted attention of men who tried to touch her breasts whenever she forced her way through the crowded hold to the vile slop bucket that served as the only privy, behind a curtain of tattered sail.

But the women, excepting Mab Collins, were cruelest of all. Their jibes were tipped in the poison of jealousy. They jeered at her dainty ways, mocked her speech. They roared with laughter when she shrieked upon finding lice crawling in her own hair. During deck scrubbing, one of them always contrived to spill a bucket of cold seawater on her, soaking her to the skin.

The meanness had gone unchecked until Obadiah Collins put an end to it. Exploding in righteous indignation, that gentle giant made it known he would tolerate no further baiting of Flavia. Each night she thanked God for Obadiah's presence. No person, male or female, was foolish enough to risk the big man's wrath.

"Thy name iss—"

Flavia jerked herself to alertness. The captain thumbed through his log, his irritation increasing with each page he was forced to search. At last he stabbed a long yellow fingernail at an entry.

"Hah! Jane Brown!" he read victoriously. "Come *Schilaack* September the thirteen." He glared up at her, his bearded mouth twisting in contempt. "Come *Schilaack* drunk."

Flavia's mouth flew open in protest. Then she shut it tiredly. What was the use? The Collinses had told her she was "Jane Brown" from the first. They even remembered her solicitous "cousin" who'd brought her aboard. And she'd wakened in rude clothes reeking of rum.

A dry hysterical sob forced its way up through her despair.

"I *am* Flavia Rochambeau!" she cried out.

But the captain wasn't listening. He'd already dismissed her and was dealing with two brothers who argued hotly about the possessions of a third brother. The man had died of consumption just an hour before in a bunk near the one in which Flavia and the entire Collins family were crammed.

She turned away, sickened for herself and sickened at the avarice exploding behind her. While the brothers railed, the captain thundered, cursing the untimely death. He could not collect passage if a bondman died before the ship passed the halfway point in the journey. Had the young man lingered, the captain could have tacked the indenture on to that of the young man's widow.

Sick, despairing, wishing *hers* was the body being passed out of the humanity-packed, fetid hold, she pushed her way through the throng. Her ears were deaf to the insults that trailed after her.

"Ay there, Duchess. Crawl over to me hammock t'night 'n' I'll give ye somethin' from the duke!"

"Blimey, Duchess! Where's yer diamond and rooooby tiara? Lost it in the privy bucket, has ye?"

"Coo! Ain't so proud now 'at she's dirty as the rest o' we!"

There was a crevice, a little "hidey" place as the children called it, between the starboard rail and a dozen water barrels that were strapped between cabin wall and rail. Only a child or a slender adult could slip in. Flavia made for the haven and squeezed into it. Alone, she clutched the rail and rested her burning face on her hands.

She felt defeated. Empty. The ship rolled under her. Whitecaps smashed at the hull, sending spits of foam flying. The spits sizzled on her hands for an instant, then melted away. She was too tired to think. Too tired to live.

Am I dead to everyone who loved me? Does only my husband know I'm alive? Oh, why haven't I the courage to end it! The sea beckons...

But she had neither the courage to die nor

the energy to live. And prayer had deserted her weeks ago. There were only two thoughts, burning like candles, that kept her spirit from being totally extinguished.

Garth.

Robert.

In the past week she finally had come to terms with the fact that she would never see them again. But as long as she lived, she could send them her love with every breath she drew. Perhaps her fervent love thoughts could find their way across time and distance, blessing her beloved two.

She knew she must never seek them out. The duke must never suspect what Garth had been to her. He must never suspect Robert. For if he did, she knew he would kill them both.

She swallowed hard. Her heart ached. God, how it ached. Leaning back upon the gurgling water barrel, she raised her face heavenward and sought solace in the winter sky. Clouds galloped overhead like gray mares, free and unfettered. Cold rain spat down. She drew one last long breath of sweet air before turning toward the foul hold.

"Let someone give my son the love I cannot give," she whispered passionately. "Let someone give Garth—"

No, no. It was all too much.

Numb and beaten, Jane Brown turned and descended into the squalid darkness.

Garth McNeil shucked boots and stockings and scrambled up the fore-rigging in the moonlight.

There'd been an odd humming sound from the after shrouds. A frayed rope? He had to find out. He was a careful sailor and tolerated no sloppy sailing or worn, weakening equipment.

Hanging on in the wind with the *Caroline* bounding under him, he found nothing amiss in the after shrouds or futtock shrouds. He climbed up into the fore-topmast rigging, checking the foot ropes and the lower fore-topsail braces. All was well. He continued to climb up into the bright moonlight, up to the fore-topgallant mast. There he hung on in the wind and looked out at the sea. The sea was painted with moonlight, and the night was as light and bright as day.

At sea a month now, McNeil had fallen to taking the night watch from eleven bells to three. It was a lonely watch and counterproductive to his efforts to forget Flavia. Still he persisted in the watch, perversely torturing himself in the quiet hours by thinking of her. At the end of the watch, he would go to Annette's cabin. These days he went there with intense urgency. It wasn't the urgency for simple animal release. It was the urgency to forget.

But on Annette's side, McNeil knew she interpreted his passion as increasing affection. She reveled in it. Annette was blooming like a girl in first love. McNeil knew he should set her straight in the matter, but he made no effort to do so. He wasn't thinking of Annette. His head was full of Flavia.

The *Caroline* leaped into a deep trough between waves, throwing him against the rigging.

He shook his head to clear it, then called up to the man aloft and exchanged a few words.

He scrambled down the rigging, jumped to the deck and pulled on stockings and boots. He began his usual night prowl of the sleeping ship, listening for any change in the hum of the rigging, alert to any discordant creaking of wood spars or ship's hull. He took a lantern and went down into the cargo hold, checking for any sign of shifting among the lashed-down crates. All was as it should be.

His prowl completed, he returned to the moonlit deck, checked the Jacob's ladders at bow and stern, then had a few words with Harrington at the wheel. The ritual finished, he treated himself to a smoke.

He'd not smoked half the cigar before his unwilling mind ran back to Flavia. He ached. Normally cynical about women and what they had to offer, McNeil was at a loss to explain his feelings for Flavia and why he grieved so sorely. The cynic in him said that real love—if there was such a thing as *real* love—came gradually, if ever; "instant" love was merely lust masquerading in fine clothes. But the man within denied it. What he'd felt for Flavia had been love. That love had been born full-grown the moment he'd opened that tavern door on the quay and looked into those vulnerable eyes. He knew it now.

He was confused by all of it. Why had sweet Flavia played the harlot that first night on the quay? Why?

Seeking answers, he'd questioned the duke's young footman during the voyage, and by now the lad must think him mad. When the lad said things about Flavia that were unbearable, Garth tongue-lashed him into scared silence. Eager to toady to the ship's master, the boy spouted gossip willy-nilly. Garth found it hard to sort truth from lie.

Only one thing stood out in a certain light. The duke had chosen Flavia as wife because Flavia's mother had been a prodigious child-bearer. The duke expected Flavia to produce as her mother had done. He demanded heirs. An odd, unformed thought stirred in him like a hazy dream, then faded as a brass bell sounded.

Three chiming strokes rang out in the wind and echoed out over the moonlit sea. There was the tramp of feet, the usual cries of instruction as the watch changed. He surrendered his watch to Jenkins, exchanged a few words and turned to go. But he didn't go. He stood in the stern of the ship, watching the foamy churning wake. An odd thing about churning wake. Stare at it long enough and it conjures up pictures. A girl's white skin, a dewy cheek damp from running through fog...

A light step sounded behind him on the deck. He turned. Annette's blue silk wrapper shimmered in the moonlight as wind ruffled it. Her dark hair was unbound and feathering in the wind. She smiled.

"Come to bed, Garth."

He slung his dead cigar into the sea and strode toward her. She came into his arms, and he was jolted by the warmth of her body. He'd not known he was so cold.

He sought her mouth. He kissed her with fierce, bruising urgency.

Chapter 6

"JANE?"

Flavia woke instantly, the way she'd always done at Tewksbury when Robert was fretful with teething and the mother in her would not permit deep sleep. She shifted up on one elbow, careful not to wake the Collins babes, who snuggled warmly against her, one at each side. She rubbed her tired eyes.

"Yes, Mab? What's wrong? He's not worse?"

In the dim light of the hold's single sputtering lantern, she sensed rather than saw the young woman's shoulders slump forward in despair.

"Jane, he be raving. He be all the time tryin' to git up."

"I'll help."

Flavia eased her weary body from the bunk. She covered the sleeping children, pulling the dirty wool blanket up to their thin chins. She shook out her creased and wrinkled serge skirts. Like everyone else, she slept clothed. At least now she had her own bunk. Bunks had become available as the arduous voyage took its toll among the indentured.

Scurvy and ague plagued the ship. It hit the big strong men hardest. And growing children, of course. One raw potato and half an onion a week did not suffice in containing the sickness, and the captain had done nothing to ease their plight. Greedy, eager to pass the halfway point and realize full profit from bondslave contracts, the Dutchman drove his ship hard. He set his course due west across open wintry seas rather than follow the longer course that trailed the African coast and the Caribbean, where the *Schilaack* might put in for fresh water, oranges, lemons, green vegetables. The result of the Dutchman's avarice was drinking water gone brackish in the barrel, sea biscuit crawling with worm, salt pork gone putrid and lives lost.

Flavia was outraged at the man's inhumanity. A dozen times a day she vowed to see him punished, and a dozen times a day came face to face with the reality of her own impotence. She was no longer duchess of Tewksbury. She was a bondslave. She hadn't the power to order punishment of a gnat.

Groping through the bunks of the snoring, Flavia made her way to the Collins bunk. That everyone should sleep unperturbed while Obadiah Collins fought for his life did not surprise her. Each family had its share of misery, and in the past weeks she herself had helped sew many an infant or small child into a pillowcase before the stricken parents consigned the small bundle to the dark cruel sea. And the latest outbreak was raging now—dysentery.

Obadiah lay burning with fever. Tossing and heaving about the bunk in his delirium, the big man kept casting off the cool wet cloths Mab placed on his brow and chest.

"Mother, be we halfway?" he demanded, not waiting for an answer but raving on, repeating the question over and over.

In the flickering light, Flavia met Mab's terror-filled but determined eyes. Flavia and Mab had made a pact. Obadiah was not to know the halfway point had been passed two days before.

Mab took a deep breath of the foul sickly air.

"Course we ain't halfway, y'big dummox! Now bey' silent and git well, hear?"

Mab's roughness was sham. Flavia knew Mab was straining to behave normally so as not to raise Obadiah's anxiety. For a few minutes it worked. The big man's hands ceased their delirious fidgeting. His breathing seemed to ease. But Flavia was alarmed. With such fever, he should be oozing sweat. Obadiah, however, lay hot and dry as a desert baked in noon sun. Each breath he drew was echoed by a watery whistlelike sound.

To hide her mounting fear, Flavia plunged into helping Mab.

"Mother?"

Obadiah knocked away the cup Flavia was holding to his parched lips. He reared up, searching for Mab's face and not finding it, although his wife hovered only inches above his head.

"Mother? Be we halfway?"

Mab choked off a cry. Shaking, she jammed the knuckles of her fist into her mouth and bit them until they bled.

Flavia struggled with the man, urging him to lie down. He seemed unaware of her. Blindly, Obadiah continued to seek his wife.

"Y'been a good wife, Mother. I'll not have y' saddled w' servin' my indenture. If I'm to go, I'll go now—before—before—" Burning with fever, he lost his train of thought. He sank back on the hot pillow. "Before—before—the spring violets does poke up theys bonny heads b'hind the barn—"

Mab was weeping openly now. Great huge tears rolled down her thin cheeks, carving clean channels in the permanent grime of her face. She swiped at the tears, then grabbed her husband's hand. She flashed a fierce look at Flavia.

"You be talkin' pig shit, Obadiah Collins! Now you git well or y'll git the back o' my tongue, the likes you never heard afore, nor want to!"

At her familiar scolding, a fleeting half-smile played over the big man's face. He seemed to drift into peaceful sleep. But only seconds later, he resumed his restless tossing.

"Be we halfway?" he demanded, and then, "Mother. Read t' me!"

Mab shivered violently. With visible effort, she pulled herself together.

"Y'know I can't read, y' big stupid ox." Her voice softened. "Jane be here. Jane kin read."

She nodded at Flavia, and Flavia drew Obadiah's Bible from beneath his pillow where he always kept it. She knelt beside the bunk, close to the big man's head. The dim light of the captain's begrudged "sick" lantern flickered upon his flushed skin.

Softly she whispered, "Obadiah? What will you have me read?"

For a long time he made no answer. Then, just as Mab and Flavia nodded to each other, acknowledging his sleep, Obadiah's mouth twitched.

"Isaiah," he whispered weakly, "the twenty-fifth chapter."

Flavia thumbed through the worn Bible, seeking her place. She began to read, softly and without haste. As she read, the big man's breathing grew more and more labored. When the ominous wheeze began to accompany each whistling breath, Mab seized her husband's hand and thrust it to her heart, holding it there as though to will him the strength of her own sound young body.

Flavia choked. She stopped reading, but Mab gave her a fierce nod. Swallowing the anguish she felt for these two good people, Flavia blinked back tears and found her place in the text.

"He will swallow up death in victory," she read quietly, "and the LORD GOD will wipe away tears from off all faces; and the rebuke of his people shall he take away from off all the earth; for the LORD hath spoken it."

"I'm glad he didn't live t' see this day."

Mab's voice was dull and lifeless, like her empty eyes. She sat defeated on the far end of the bunk, her shoulders hunched, her arms listlessly holding her stomach.

Flavia could find no word of comfort to offer. So she said nothing. She went on with her sewing. She was embroidering a small cross on the pillowcase. If time permitted before the brief service on the stern deck, she would embroider birds and flowers too. She stitched steadily, oblivious by now to the continuous hubbub in the indentured hold. Women whined, men harangued one another or gambled for buttons at cards, children played games, the sick moaned. Flavia heard none of it.

The death of the baby had been inevitable, she reflected. When Obadiah died, Mab had gone into shock. Her milk dried up. Flavia had scoured the hold for a willing wet nurse and, for a time, she found one. But the Collins infant was a difficult charge. No nursing mother was strong enough or willing enough to put up with its demands. For a time, Flavia sustained the baby on boiled barley water and molasses that she begged from a crew member. But the baby developed fever.

"Mab?" she said gently. "Would you like to look at her one last time? Before I sew the pillow shut?"

The young mother's shoulders convulsed.

"No!"

However, Mab instantly negated her answer by swinging around to stare at the tiny body lying clean and tidy at the bottom of the bunk. A slow smile came to her lips and lingered.

"Purty, weren't she, Jane?" She looked from

the infant to Flavia and back to the infant. "'N' smart she were, too. Like her Pa."

"Oh, yes," Flavia agreed quickly.

It was a merciful lie. In truth, Flavia had suspected the baby was not quite right. Its muscles had been flaccid. Its splayed, flattened nose resembled the idiots who were beaten into begging outside the theaters on Drury Lane. Flavia had tossed them shillings whenever the duke had taken her to the theater.

Mab's baby had cried day and night. In no way had the infant reminded her of Robert with his bright-eyed intelligence, his eagerness to reach out for the world and capture it. Yet she'd fought for the baby's life. When it died she felt a deep grief. Her hands grew still in her lap.

"Shall you want to sew the pillow shut, Mab?"

Mab swallowed.

"No!"

But instantly she snatched the threaded needle from Flavia's hand and set to work. When she was done she picked up the small bundle and held it tightly to her bosom, rocking back and forth on the bunk to a dirge that only she herself heard.

At last the Methodist preacher summoned them. Together—hatless, shawlless—they climbed up into the cutting winds of winter.

If life had been hard with Obadiah alive and offering protection, it became harder now. Stripped of the good man's shelter, Flavia felt thrown to the wolves.

Again Flavia found herself the target of taunts,

the recipient of lustful suggestions. The decent
folk did not torment her, but the riffraff did. She
managed to stay clear of the male Newgate
convicts with whom the Dutchman had filled up
his shipload of bondslaves. But the women were
impossible to escape. The more slatternly the
woman, the more Flavia's beauty and daintiness
seemed to rankle. The crones took umbrage at
everything she did. They jeered at her attempts
to wash and cleanse herself. They hooted whenever she scrubbed lice from her thick coppery
hair in a bucket of icy seawater. They delighted
in tripping her on the stairway whenever she
hauled bedding up into the sunshine. They
made fun of her when winter swells gave her
seasickness and she lay in her bunk, green with
misery.

Her few belongings were quickly stolen. Flavia
learned never to leave her bunk without taking
shawl and cloak. Mab had made her a gift of
Obadiah's Bible. This she kept safe, deep in a
pocket of her serge apron. For safety and for
warmth on the frigid ship, she and Mab shared
a bunk. Mab's five-year-old Sarah Bess slept
tucked between.

The voyage was an endless hell, each day a
greater torture than the day preceding. For the
first time in her life Flavia knew hunger. Often
she found herself praying for the release of
death, but in the next breath she'd fervently
cancel that prayer. The world might be a desolate place, but it was still the world Garth
McNeil inhabited. And Robert. While her beloved ones lived, she too would cling to life with

all the tenacity she could muster. She would never give up. In this she recognized a surprising new strength and will. No longer was she the meek girl who'd gone dutifully to Tewksbury Hall, a bride of barter. She was changing.

As the hellish voyage went on, measles broke out below deck and grief-maddened mothers lost more children to the sea. Conditions above deck deteriorated, too. When the captain was not about, the hangdog crew exhibited a new surliness. The English crewmen fought with the Dutch. Both grumbled at the captain's choice of route and cursed the ship's food, though they fared ten times better than the indentured. At least crewmen got ale to drink and a belly-warming ration of rum each night to help ease the cold and pain. Fearing the captain and his awesome power to punish with the cat-o'-nine, the crew restricted their complaints to muttering in their beards.

The long voyage stirred in the crew a randy fever. The sailors hungered for a woman. When bond servants took air and exercise upon deck, the crew's salacious eyes raped even the ugliest crone. Alarmed, bondmen kept a watchful eye on their womenfolk. Flavia no longer went on deck except in the company of a kind Dorsetshire farmer and his family.

Despite precautions, the worst did occur.

Grieving for Obadiah and the lost baby, Mab had tossed and turned in her bunk one night, unable to find sleep. So she'd taken her cloak, crept up out of the dark pitching hold and lurched along the safety rope to the indentureds' deck. There, she leaned over the rail, shivering in the biting wind, searching the cold glittering stars for solace. In her grief, she'd not been aware of the big tar until he grabbed her from behind.

She screamed, but the scream died in the winter wail of the rigging. The tar clapped a paw over her mouth and dragged her off her feet, pulling her into a candle-lit cubbyhole where three others waited, their eyes twitching, their tongues darting along weather-split lips. Mab knew. She went into a frenzy. She fought, but they were upon her at once, gagging her mouth with her own stocking. They took her, passing her from one to another until the last gleam of lust faded from the wolfish eyes. Then they beat her. Calling her Newgate trash, they warned that the captain would not give a moment's ear to a slut's accusations. They thrust her, brutalized and dazed, out onto the deck.

Flavia woke just as Mab fell against the bunk. In the dim light, Mab's face was gray. Blood flecked the corners of her mouth. She was shaking. She worked her lips, but no words came out.

Flavia knew instantly.

"Mab!" she cried, then choked off her outcry at Mab's shaking, mute hysteria. Throwing back the filthy blankets, she flung out her arms. Mab fell into them.

"Oh, no, no," she crooned, clutching Mab's icy shaking body. Not knowing what to do, what to say, she could only rock her in her arms.

Mab began to sob against her breast. But the

sobs were thin, keening squeals, like the cry of some small tortured animal. Terrified, at a loss to know how to help, Flavia held her tight, rocking her back and forth until at last the hysteria was spent and Mab collapsed, exhausted in her arms.

It was a full hour before Mab could speak of it. Then, she poured out her rape in a gusher of long angry whispers and longer, deadly silences. She told her story over and over, her thin body turning to ice as she recounted each violence. Flavia held her, listening in horror, rage increasing with every word she heard.

At last, Flavia was able to persuade Mab to lie down. Shaking with fury, Flavia covered her with all of their blankets, cloaks, and even shawls. She tucked the soundly sleeping Sarah Bess close to Mab's back. She fetched water. Mab sipped it, then gagged it up into the apron Flavia yanked from her own waist.

"Rest, Mab. I'm going to the captain. The sailors must be caught and punished."

Mab reared up, eyes large with fright. She caught Flavia's hand, and Flavia was jolted by the iciness of it.

"No!" she whispered. "'Twill do no good. The cap'n won't care a flea. Y'see, 'tis true—I be—I—"

She lost heart. Sinking back upon the dirty mattress, Mab turned her face to the bulkhead.

"'Tis true, Jane, what the men say. I be Newgate trash. Obadiah, he found me in jail when he come t'preach. He bought me out and wed me proper."

Flavia's heart rushed out to her. Helpless to help, she squeezed Mab's cold hand. Mab turned her head and looked at her. In the dim light of the sick-lantern, Mab's eyes begged for understanding.

"It ain't like I never was took afore. I was. Ever since I come ten years old. My mother's man, he...things as that, they goes on reg'lar where I was birthed. It's jist that since Obadiah— since Obie—"

Flavia swallowed hard, her rage choking her. Did no one care that humanity was so brutish? Did not even *God* care?

Her throat tightened. "Hush, dear. Sleep. Try to sleep, Mab."

Again, Flavia tucked the coverings round Mab, gently stroking Mab's bruised cheek as she waited for the bounding ship to do its cradle work.

Mab's eyes flickered open one last time.

"You'll stay close, Jane?"

"I'll stay close."

Flavia knelt on the bunk, keeping watch as Mab descended into jerky, fitful sleep. She knelt there, listening to the night sounds in the stinking hold—night sounds that would have shocked Flavia Rochambeau, duchess of Tewksbury, but that were commonplace to Jane Brown: A baby whined in fever. A child begged for water. A woman sobbed, and two men snarled in argument over a vanished pewter shoe buckle. In a distant part of the room, there came the labored groan of a woman delivering. The midwife's whine tangled in the patternless whine of the feverish tot. "Push harder, luv. Ye'll not be rid of your trouble until ye push harder."

Daylight seemed an eternity in coming. Finally, gray light began to filter through the sailcloth that had been nailed over the ceiling grate to keep out the winter wind. Mab woke. She lay there, hard-eyed, unblinking, staring at nothing. The hardness in. her face frightened Flavia.

"Mab? Are you all right?"

Nothing.

"Mab?" Flavia waited. "Please, Mab. Speak to me."

It was several more minutes before Mab shifted up on one elbow, patted Sarah Bess's dingy yellow curls, then turned flinty eyes on Flavia.

"Jane, I want you t'learn me t'read and cipher," she began, her voice shaking with vengeance. "You got lady ways, Jane. I want to learn 'em, too. I want t'learn everything. I want t'make my *own* way in the world. I don't never want another man near me. And not near Sarah Bess, neither. I spit on 'em. I spit on *all the men in the world.*"

"Land! Land ho! Blessed Providence has brought us through—the journey is ended—land—"

At the bondman's shout, Flavia sprang up from her bunk where she'd been mending a stocking. She flew toward the ladder as the hold exploded in happy hysteria. Stinking bodies surged forward, clamoring and clawing to be first on deck. Flavia found herself thrust aside by two

women. She pushed back, clawing her way to
the deck, too.

Heedless of the captain's rule restricting the
number of bondslaves on deck, the indentured
boiled out of the hold. Even the desperately ill
spent their last iota of energy to drag themselves topside.

Flavia pushed her way across the packed deck
to Mab, screaming, "We did it! We survived!"
But Mab was silent. She stared westward at the
hazy indistinct landmass, her face wet with tears.

"There it is, Jane," she said. "My Obadiah's
dream."

Flavia wept, too. All around her, men and
women were falling to their knees, weeping and
giving thanks to God that the voyage was done,
the hell finished. Those who wept hardest were
the grieved souls who'd buried family at sea.
The Methodist preacher stepped forward and
led the assembly in prayer. Only the cocky and
hardened of heart did not bow a head or bend a
knee.

On Christmas Day, 1753, the *Schilaack* dropped
anchor off the Carolinas. Forced from her course
by savage winter storms, the ship was far south
of her destination, and the captain was vexed.
He vented this vexation on the indentured. He
reduced their already slim rations. To appease
his crew, he lay in port for several days. The
crew was permitted ashore in shifts; the indentured were not. They must stay aboard until
sold or dead.

So Flavia and Mab could only lean on the
ship's rail and stare with yearning at the town

where smoke curled up from cozy fireplaces within English-style houses, where townsmen trod with casual indifference upon precious, solid ground. After months of sea, the sight of a mere tree was thrilling. The sight of a lady riding to market in a horse-chaise seemed as thrilling as any Drury Lane theater performance.

"Oh, Mab, it's *good* to smell land again."

Flavia bubbled in enthusiasm, momentarily forgetting that when she again stepped upon land, she would be stepping into seven years' servitude.

Gossip spread that the Dutchman would not sell indenture contracts here in the South where profits might be lower than in the North. Plantation agents rowed out to the *Schilaack* daily to persuade the captain to part with able-bodied laborers. Plantation blacks, they complained, were useless in winter. Accustomed to the ovenlike heat of Africa, new slaves tended to sicken in hard weather and it was difficult even to beat them into resuming their duties.

On the third day, word galloped through the ship that the captain would sell contracts of any sick bondslaves who wanted to leave. And parents who intended to sell their children to pay for passage might do so here, also. The Newgate convicts were to be sold off, too, and Mab tartly observed to Flavia that in this action the Dutchman was only covering his own "arse." Any Newgater with an ounce of gumption would shinny over the side as soon as the *Schilaack* anchored in a decent-size port.

Thirty convicts were sold and five sickly men

who managed to appear healthy when the plantation agents interviewed them. Six families parted with several of their children. As she watched the children being lifted down into the waiting dinghies, Flavia's heart twisted at the weeping farewells and the shouted, hollow promises:

"Be a good lad to yer master, Jimmy-James! We'll come git ye, soon's we's on our feet and in the money!"

"Sally Nell, stop that caterwauling! You be eight year old, gal. Lud! Ye want yer new mistress to think you a snively babe?"

"You be a stout, good worker for your master, Edmund! You hear, boy? Show 'em how ruddy good a ten-year-old lad can toil."

The children's misery tore at Flavia. She suspected that parents who parted with their children at the first easy opportunity had no intention of redeeming them. She suspected the parents would harden their hearts, turn their backs upon the past and forge into their own selfish futures in the New-England. She could only hope the children were going to Christian families where they'd be treated as the law prescribed. For their indenture was to be a long one. Regardless of their age now, bound children must serve until twenty-one.

Alert to profit, the Dutchman increased his profits by buying fresh produce on land—cabbages, stored autumn apples, potatoes, onions, pumpkins—and reselling it to the indentured at an elevated price. Starved for fresh food, bondsmen willingly spent their last shillings for it.

Flavia longed to buy, but could not. She

hadn't a penny, let alone a whole shilling. And she had nothing to trade. Mab was in the same straits, having spent her last coins for a blanket to shroud Obadiah. Flavia trembled with desire for a fresh apple. When someone purchased and bit into an apple, she had to turn away from the sight to keep from doing violence. She squeezed her eyes shut. Her mouth watered. She could almost feel the taut moment when apple skin broke under teeth. She could taste the spurt of juice, the cool mealy pulp of the fruit. Gladly would she have traded all the banquets she'd eaten at Tewksbury Hall for one small green apple.

"Catch, Jane!"

Flavia's eyes flew open as something hard and heavy landed in her lap. She stared at it in disbelief, then seized it, brought it to her mouth and sank her teeth in. Mab and Sarah Bess climbed into the bunk, devouring *their* apples, skin, seeds, core and all. For several minutes, Flavia felt herself in heaven. Daintily licking the last of the juice from her fingers, she turned to Mab with a breathless laugh.

"How? However did you manage it?"

Mab winked.

"Kiped it."

Flavia gasped. Her first impulse was to scold. But in that, she recognized her own lack of honesty. She'd coveted that apple. She'd wolfed it. And while she wolfed it, she hadn't worried a whit if murder had been done to obtain it. She shook her head ruefully. *I'm not different from the others. I, too, will do almost anything to survive*. She shivered, then sincerely thanked Mab.

"How did you—ah—*kipe* it?"

Mab's grin was all ginger and spice.

"Come on. I'll learn ye. You kin help."

Flavia choked.

"Mab, I couldn't!"

Mab nodded encouragingly.

"But I'll learn ye. It be right easy, Jane."

Flavia laughed in dismay. How could she explain? Mab didn't see her protest as a matter of morals but as a matter of craft.

She tried to explain gently, but Mab wasn't listening. She'd already lifted Sarah Bess to the floor and was brushing the little girl's skirts straight.

"Y' remember what I learned ye, Sarah Bess?"

The child stuck her thumb deep into her mouth. She sucked twice, then nodded solemnly, her fair dirty curls bobbling on her shoulders.

"Then say it, luv," Mab urged.

Sarah Bess's thumb came out with a wet pop. She looked up at her mother.

"Daddy, Daddy, Daddy," she chanted.

"Then what, luv?"

Sarah Bess thought earnestly. She explored the roof of her tiny mouth with the wet thumb.

"Umm, umm. I—I—hangs onta the man's leg at the apple bag. I don't let 'em shake me off."

Mab patted her daughter's head.

"Good girl," she said and turned her attention to Flavia. "Jane, you kin be decoy. Them shit-face tars, they does pop theys eyes when *you* walk on deck, luv. When I makes the high sign, like this"— Mab scratched the tip of her nose with one finger—"Y' feints a rum gipper. Y' pulls y' skirt up, jist so." Mab demonstrated. "Y' rubs y' gipper, up 'n' down, up 'n' down."

Flavia blinked in disbelief.

"Mab, I can't!"

Mab paid no attention. Her quick fingers flew to Flavia's bodice. A tug here, a yank there, and the cleavage of Flavia's breasts glowed white and delicate against the harsh serge of her soiled gown.

"There," said Mab with satisfaction. "Give 'em that t' lay theys shit-eyes on, and I kin kipe a *dozen* apples."

Flavia stared at her in astonishment. For several long moments Flavia hesitated, dangling from the silken thread of indecision. Cling to her principles and starve, sicken? Perhaps die and never see Garth or the baby again?

She swallowed. She gave Mab a decisive nod, and the trio trooped up into the winter sunshine. As Flavia's foot hit the deck, she wavered, squeamish. *Suppose we get caught? We'll be whipped! Oh, the humiliation—*

"Come on!" Mab ordered.

Numb with fear, Flavia set her mind to obey. It wouldn't do to endanger Mab by failing her part. But she felt her face go scarlet. The rush of blood to her head only seemed to enhance her prettiness. On the crowded deck where produce was being hawked, several men turned sharply to gawk at her. Their eyes traveled to her small revealed bosom. And when she bent, raising her skirt at Mab's signal, hardly an eye went anywhere but to her shapely stockinged calf.

"Daddy, Daddy, Daddy!" wailed Sarah Bess.

Flavia gulped and raised her skirt all the way to her knee.

In the ensuing days they ate well. Mab's repertoire of ruses was large. Potatoes, onions and even cabbages followed hard on the heels of the apples. Flavia was appalled at how little shame she felt wolfing the life saving food. The small amount of shame that she *did* retain she banished by sharing with others too sick or too penniless to buy.

As for Mab, she felt no shame. Obadiah's holiness had worn off. She was hardened by her rape. Once again she became the London drab who must either live by her wits or cease to live at all.

In a matter-of-fact fashion, she taught Flavia her street craft, offering it as fair exchange for the tutoring she received from Flavia. Aghast at Mab's casual attitude toward crime and yet unwilling to hurt her feelings, Flavia listened with fascination. Mab instructed her on everything from how to steal a loudly cackling hen (Thrust it into a thick sack; the hen will think it's night and will go to sleep) to how to pick a pocket (Choose a *fat* man; he will get winded chasing you and soon abandon pursuit).

In turn, Mab devoured all Flavia taught. Flavia found her quick, intelligent. Mab rarely made the same mistake twice. She could read now, write and do sums. For practice, she ciphered on the rolling floor with a piece of chalk she stole. Earnestly she studied Flavia's mannerisms and speech. She aped her walk, her carriage. She grilled Flavia about society parties. She stole a piece of parchment, folded it into a fan and spent hours practicing ladylike fan flutters.

Eager to learn lady ways, Mab still dug her heels in and balked at basics.

"Bathe? All over? In the altogether? Jane, it ain't decent! I'll jist dab at m' face with a cloth, every week or so."

Flavia sighed. It was a recurrent argument and one she had no hope of winning.

"Ladies *bathe*, Mab."

"But why? What fer? It ain't healthy."

"*Isn't* healthy."

Mab blinked.

"That's what I said, Jane."

Flavia threw up her hands. She tried again.

"A lady takes care not to smell bad, Mab. A lady *never* has lice in her hair."

Mab drew her knees up. She hunched in the bunk, hugging her long legs. She rested chin on knees. She drifted in stubborn thought.

"A few cooties never hurt nobody."

"*Anybody.*"

"Yes," she agreed, brightening. "M' Uncle Ezra, he took a bath once. Come down with the ague and turned up his toes not a week later."

Flavia tried a new tack.

"Mab, if you washed your hair and bathed and perfumed yourself, I'm sure you would be quite lovely."

The young woman sat up, startled. A slow, incredulous smile lighted her face.

"Naw!" she said, then quickly, "y' think so, Jane?"

Flavia smiled.

"I *know* so."

The *Schilaack* sailed north. She raised Cape Fear, skirted the outer banks of Raleigh Bay, navigated the sound and dropped anchor at New Holland.

Starved for diversion after the monotony of sea travel, Flavia hung at the rail with Mab, watching commerce unfold in the small port. Ton after ton of iron goods and farm tools were hauled down the plank. Countless tons of pig iron and hogsheads of tobacco were trundled up into the ship.

Again, agents clamored to buy skilled bond-slaves. Any cooper, shoemaker, farmer, cabinet-maker, blacksmith or school teacher found himself courted. Often, a bondman negotiated his own indenture, selecting among several would-be masters. It was not so for the young, the old, the sick or the female. Flavia shivered inwardly, afraid to guess what her own fate might be. She'd seen enough to hope for service on a large plantation. There, a servant would not be overworked. Poorer masters who owned only a farm or a small business were a different matter. They exhibited a pinched, niggardly attitude as they shopped for flesh aboard the *Schilaack*.

Flavia sensed they'd demand more than their money's worth, working their few hard-pressed servants from dawn until the extinguishing of night candles. Seven years in *their* employ and she would emerge a worn woman.

With the ranks of the indentured reduced, the *Schilaack* made for the strait of Cape Henry and Cape Charles. On the first day of February she dropped anchor at the port of Norfolk.

Here commerce began in earnest. Shipping agents bargained for the cargo of Dutch lace, English wools, satins. Delft tiles, china, pewter and silver were sold into the keeping of agents. Hogsheads of tobacco were rolled aboard, ton after ton of them until Flavia feared the very ship must sink.

The remaining skilled bondmen were snapped up and plantation agents lost interest in the ship. Flavia was dismayed. Now she would fall into the hands of an independent. She could only hope her master would be humane. When she voiced this hope to Mab, Mab hooted.

"Pish!" she said, having reluctantly abandoned pithier expressions under Flavia's tutelage. "*Good* master? They's no such thing! If y' master wants to bed you, Jane, he'll bed you. 'Twon't bite his conscience no more'n a flea biting a dog. Come Sabbath, he'll march hisself to meeting, all pridey and proper, like he never had him a lusty notion in his life."

Flavia was stunned speechless. In her most severe imaginings of servitude in America, her mind had not gone to *that*.

Quickly, more to assure herself than Mab, she

blurted, "It's against English law to abuse a bond servant."

Mab gave a hard laugh.

"That it is, luv. And when y' master comes pussyfootin' round y' bed, *you* be sure and tell him so."

Mab's inference was sobering. Flavia knew it couldn't be true. Still she found herself warily judging the flesh shoppers. If an eye flickered with the slightest hint of lust or cruelty, Flavia resorted to the ruse Mab taught her. She'd whip out a kerchief that she and Mab had stained with red paint borrowed from a cabinetmaker's stain box. She'd cough violently into the kerchief. The would-be master's eyes would bulge with horror. He'd hustle away at once. He had no intention of purchasing the dread lung disease, no matter how prettily it was packaged.

At Norfolk Flavia saw her first American woman. She was a Mistress Sewell and she came aboard on the arm of her husband who was shopping for a stout Dutch drudge, one skilled in tending dairy cows. Flavia ached with longing as she drank in the woman's smart ensemble. She wore thick plush green velvet. Jacket and skirts were topped by a cape trimmed with ermine tails. Her hands were gloved in soft black kid and diamond earbobs flashed in the winter sunlight. A handsome hat and muff of fox fur rippled in the chill breeze.

Flavia sighed. She'd forgotten how wonderful it felt to wear beautiful clothes, to wear warm clothes. Unconsciously, she shrank inside the rough serge cloak.

"Mr. Sewell!" the woman trilled brightly as she trailed along on her husband's arm. "Mr. Sewell, I've a mind to buy a new serving girl."

"You've Tansy and Queen," he countered agreeably. "And Noah, my dear."

She made a face.

"Africans, Mr. Sewell!" She pouted, flirting up at her husband through a thick fringe of lashes. "How can Sewell Hall become known for its genteel entertaining if bush slaves oversee the serving? You'll recall what happened last July, Mr. Sewell. When the kitchens grew too hot." She paused for effect. "Tansy simply shucked petticoats, bodice and stays. She carried the roast meats to the dining table in her *shift*."

"And Noah trooped in wearing only his shirttails." He chuckled. "I thought it funny."

Mrs. Sewell drew herself up.

"I, Mr. Sewell, did *not*. I daresay Lord and Lady Carlisle still grow faint when they remember."

"I daresay they've forgot," he said pleasantly.

She shifted her tactics.

"If I bought an English girl who could read, write and cipher, I could use her as my secretary. She would supervise serving too, of course. She could assist me with my accounts. She could pen invitations to our dancing assemblies, and I could dictate my correspondence." She paused. In a burst of fresh inspiration she added, "In her spare time she could assist the tutor, spelling the little ones."

He laughed merrily.

"You would work her to death in six months, my dear."

Her eyes narrowed. As Flavia watched, fascinated, Mrs. Sewell arranged her lovely features in the manner of an innocent who's been wrongly accused.

"I do believe, Mr. Sewell, you have no appreciation of how hard I toil for Sewell Hall. Merely assigning the slaves' tasks employs the shank of my day. Some evenings, Mr. Sewell, I am faint with weariness. Though far be it from me to let one word of complaint escape my lips. I am your dutiful wife, Mr. Sewell. Your happiness is my sole concern."

He sighed.

"Very well, my dear. Buy your girl."

She swung around with glee, the lovely long fur of hat and muff shivering like wheat in a field.

"This one, Mr. Sewell."

Flavia jerked, finding herself at the end of a pointing gloved finger.

"Do you suppose she reads, Mr. Sewell? Has she lice? Oh, dear, do you suppose she had a promiscuous life and carries the French disease?"

Flavia flushed. She looked down at her feet. It was humiliating to be examined by a woman so clearly her inferior. The duchess in Flavia flared. She lifted her head high.

"I can read," she snapped, deliberately ignoring the other queries and omitting the obligatory "ma'am."

"Write and cipher?"

Flavia bit back her anger.

"Yes."

The woman swung her head to her husband. She gave him a flirtatious, helpless glance.

"Bondslaves will tell you *anything*, of course, Mr. Sewell. They are every bit as bad as Africans," she said, contradicting the argument she'd used just moments earlier. "Test her, Mr. Sewell."

The man reddened.

"If you want her, my dear, *you* test her."

There was a flurry on deck, as the woman sent a half-dozen tars scrambling for slate and chalk. When the materials were brought, she thrust them at Flavia.

Flavia seethed. How dare this common, ill-bred American treat her so! Shaking with fury, she squeezed the chalk. She paused. A quotation from Obadiah's Bible flew into her mind. Swiftly she penned:

Proverbs 9:13: *A foolish woman is clamorous; she is simple, and knoweth nothing.*

For a moment there was silence. Then Mr. Sewell burst into hearty laughter. His eyes twinkled.

"By God, wife, she'll do. She'll do."

Mrs. Sewell pursed her lips, waiting for her husband's laughter to abate. She was not intelligent enough to know she'd been insulted, but the expression on her face was one of confused displeasure.

"I think, Mr. Sewell, she will *not* do."

Without another glance, she gave Flavia her back. She turned to Mab, and instantly Flavia

regretted venting her pride. Sewell Hall might
have been an easy post. The master seemed a
good and kind man, the mistress too vain and
lazy to generate overly much work.

"Now *this* one, Mr. Sewell," the woman began, putting a finger in Mab's face.

To Flavia's amusement, Mab immediately drew
out her red-stained kerchief and coughed violently
into it.

The weather changed. Winter deepened. Arctic
winds swept down for one last onslaught before
the advent of spring. The Chesapeake Bay
threatened to freeze, and the captain grew eager to set out for London. He redoubled his
efforts to rid himself of the remaining bondslaves.

Sarah Bess was sold at Norfolk. Mab fought to
keep her, but the Dutchman had his way. He
refused Mab the option of extending her own
indenture to cover the child's passage. He pointed out that Mab already had her own contract to
serve plus Obadiah's four years. With additional
time to serve for the little girl, Mab would
become unmarketable and he would lose his
profit. He pointed out that he'd already been
generous. He'd not charged her for the dead
infant although the baby died past the halfway
mark.

As before, Flavia raged inwardly at the man's
lack of compassion. She shook with frustration
at her own inability to help. Were she Flavia
Rochambeau, duchess of Tewksbury, she could
make Mab's life come right again in a trice. But

she was Jane Brown. For all she knew, Jane Brown's lot could become harder than Mab's.

Forced into complaisance, she could only stand at the rail, her arm around a stiff and sullen Mab as the dinghy carrying Sarah Bess pulled away from the *Schilaack*. In the dinghy, Sarah Bess howled in hysteria, both her small thumbs pressed to the roof of her mouth. As Flavia held Mab, her own wounds opened. Pain knifed into her. Robert. Her bright-eyed darling baby. Wrenched from her embrace at the ball. She could feel the sudden emptiness of her arms as the nurse grabbed him. Robert's terrified screams seemed to mingle with the fading screams of Sarah Bess.

When the dinghy disappeared amidst harbor traffic and the child's fair head could be seen no longer, Flavia squeezed Mab's stiff unresponsive shoulders.

"You'll see her again someday," she tried. But even to her own ears, the words were hollow, devoid of conviction.

Mab said nothing. She stared out over the choppy gray water. Her lips twitched, as though in the bleak interior of her soul she wrestled with some new resolution. At last she turned. The burning defiance in her eyes scared Flavia.

"Mab? Promise you'll do nothing foolish?"

Mab uttered a cheerless bitter laugh.

"'Foolish'? Nay, Jane. For the first time in m' life I aim t' do something smart."

Flavia raised her eyes to Mab's, questioning.

"I aim t' run away."

Chapter 7

"How tiresome to have to wear black to the royal governor's birthday ball. Black ill becomes me. I wonder if I mayn't get away with wearing the scarlet silk gown. Just this once?"

Getting no response, the baroness shifted up on one elbow and shook her silken mane. Dark tresses tumbled over a pleasantly plump white shoulder, a full bosom. She drew up the cambric sheeting of the four-poster bed and tucked it into her cleavage.

"McNeil. You're not listening."

Lying back in Annette's bed in the lavish, French decorated house she'd rented on North England Street in Williamsburg, Garth McNeil grunted sleepily.

"True. I'm not listening."

The baroness curled thumb and forefinger. She snapped him smartly on the taut nipple of his bronzed muscular chest. He jumped. His eyes flew open.

"Bitch!"

She giggled her low, sultry giggle, then bent to him, tonguing small purring kisses into the abused spot. McNeil relaxed. Eyes closing, he dreamily let himself enjoy the cool sweep of Annette's perfumed hair on his chest, the warm throbbing promise of her breasts. God, he was tired! He was in between sailings. It was already May. Since his February arrival in Virginia, he'd made three sailings to Barbados. Next week would see him off to England with a full load of tobacco.

Work was the palliative. Work was the key to forgetting. Exhausted, he sometimes fell into his bunk at night without a single thought of Flavia. So he pushed the *Caroline* at a furious pace. The crew thought him mad. Harrington and Jenkins grumbled, but his brother and partner and his stockholders were ecstatic. McNeil was making them rich, and making himself rich too, as by-product of the work frenzy.

While he sailed, Annette stayed in Williamsburg. Charmed by what she called "the provinces," Annette had rented the most elaborate mansion available in the capital. She entered the social scene with the zest of a child discovering an old-fashioned but delectable sweetmeat. As a titled lady, she had the run of the Governor's Palace. If a baroness ranked low in London peerage, in the colonies she glittered like a queen.

"Bother! Must I wear mourning to the ball?" Annette reiterated. "Is it too soon to wear red? What do you think, McNeil?"

He chuckled. Annette's new sense of propriety amused him. Being "queen" had its shortcomings, evidently.

"Go in the altogether if you wish."

She pretended shock, then giggled and gave him a playful slap. She pulled herself up to a sitting position in the middle of the canopied four-poster. She collected the sheet and draped herself.

"It's not as if the baron and I married for love, McNeil. The marriage was an arrangement. A convenience. He wanted my wealth. I wanted his title. As for bed—" She shrugged prettily, giving McNeil a wry smile. "He... he... preferred boys."

There was something in her voice—a catch, a faint quaver—that stirred loyalty in McNeil.

"The baron," he snapped, "was crazy."

Instantly he regretted his gallantry. Annette's face lit with love. Judas! Now he'd be forced to set her straight, to make it clear once again. Why couldn't she accept things as they stood? They were lovers. Nothing more.

Sighing happily, she slipped into the crook of his arm and lay beside him. Her fingertips traced feathery circles on his chest, his hard belly.

"Still, I *do* hate being a widow," she simpered

in a little girl voice he'd never heard her use before.

McNeil stiffened. So she thought to trap him, did she?

"Then marry, damn it!"

She gasped. She wrenched herself from his arms, flung herself off the bed, and angrily yanked on a green silk robe. She rammed her feet into silk slippers.

"You—you colonial barbarian!" she sputtered, flinging back her dark tresses with the backs of both hands. Her eyes shot dark fire. "Am I to suppose you will *never* marry me?"

He sat up. He matched her angry glare.

"You would be wise to suppose nothing else."

She flinched before his coldness.

"You—you—"

"Attila the Hun?" he teased imprudently.

Annette let out a howl of frustration. She whipped off her hard-heeled slippers. McNeil ducked and feinted as the slippers came winging at him.

Missing her quarry, Annette shrieked in frustration. She whirled around, and with a comment that left him in no doubt about the origin of his birth, she flounced from the room.

The door banged shut with a tremendous crash. Alabaster vials of perfume danced on the marble-topped dressing table. On a green damask cushion in the recessed windowseat, Annette's napping cat sprang up, arching with a hiss. The loud bang reverberated through the mansion, and McNeil lazily watched a few specks of dust filter down from the disturbed green silk draperies, the tiny dust motes twirling in the afternoon sunshine.

He relaxed, satisfied. This was the Annette he preferred. Not whining and begging to become his wife, but passionate and hot-tempered as a mistress should be. The baroness was never so good in bed as after a tantrum.

At that thought, lust began to stir again in his groin. He turned his head on the pillow, watching the door with more than slight eagerness. Annette was predictable. He did not have to wait long.

The door swung in with a furious push, then crashed shut. Again, the cat hissed, glass rattled, dust motes went spinning. Annette put her back to the door, leaned upon it and tightly crossed her arms over her bosom. Fire blazed in her eyes.

"*Why*, McNeil?" she demanded loudly. "*Why* won't you marry me?"

He grinned. Ignoring her question, he drew back the rumpled sheet. He patted the bed. At his unspoken but clear invitation, she jerked her head aside with a curse and would not look at him. But the color heightened in her throat, and McNeil did not miss the taut sudden lift of her breasts that always signaled her own rising desire.

Angered, she pretended to stare out the window. Pretended interest in the green vista of formal garden rolling into pasture where fluffy white Merino sheep wandered, tugging at sweet spring grass.

He waited until the time was right to speak.

"Annette," he coaxed, "come here."

She seemed to wage some inner battle for a minute or two. At last she turned and came toward him. The silk of her exotic robe rustled sensuously as she slowly made her way across the room.

She stood before him, seemingly undecided as whether to laugh or to cry. Her hands fluttered at her sides.

"Damn you, McNeil," she whispered helplessly.

With a rueful laugh, she came into his waiting arms. McNeil's throat thickened with urgent desire. He roughly unrobed her. He kissed her with fierce, savage hunger, and for the next few minutes he took not one thought for his sweet Flavia. For a few minutes his devastating loss was as far from his mind as Williamsburg from the moon.

When he lay back, sated, all senses at rest, the baroness lazily rolled toward him.

"*Why*, McNeil?" she demanded with sleepy good nature. "*Why* won't you marry me? I make you happy in the bedchamber. We are friends as well as lovers. I'm rich. I'm not unattractive. I would be a charming hostess for your house on York Street."

As though to endorse her mistress's proposal, Annette's white long-haired cat leaped to the bed, nuzzling McNeil's hand, begging for a head scratch. He shoved the cat off the bed and dropped his hand on Annette's back.

He placated her with a lazy pat on the fanny. "Go to sleep."

But she would not be placated.

"Is it because I'm older than you?" She waited

for an answer. When it didn't come, she tried again. "Is it because I can't give you children?"

The question irritated him.

"Go to sleep, damn it."

McNeil rolled away, punched his pillow and settled into his nap. Marriage? Children? God knows, such subjects had been foreign to his mind until Flavia. The huge-eyed girl had stirred alien feelings in him. An adventuring, seafaring man all of his life, he'd never yearned for hearth or home. Until Flavia.

The baroness sensed she'd struck pay dirt.

"It *is* the issue of children."

He emitted a growl of protest.

"Let me sleep," he ordered, "or you'll find yourself treated *exactly* like a wife. I'll beat you."

She giggled, then lay back with a long sigh.

"What vain creatures men are. They set such store in having an heir." She giggled her low throaty giggle. "Like old spindleshanks, the duke of Tewksbury, McNeil? Lord knows what he did to get *his* heir! It's rumored that he poisoned his first two duchesses because they proved barren. Though some say he sold them into an African seraglio and only pretended they died of illness."

McNeil had gone tight as a coiled spring at first mention of Tewksbury.

"Be silent, Annette," he warned.

Ignorant of his relationship with Flavia, she blithely rattled on.

"Of course, he finally got his long-awaited heir from poor dead Flavia. But I wonder . . . suppose Flavia cuckolded him? Suppose she saw

the handwriting on the wall . . . married several
years and no sign of children. Suppose she
assumed it was the duke's fault? Suppose she
assumed the duke was unable to father a child?
Suppose she decided to lie with a servant to get
with child? Suppose—"

McNeil lunged out of bed. His heart raced
like a ship before the west wind. Blood hammered thickly in his jugular, thundered in his
temples. His vision went black. He couldn't
see. Yet, for the first time, he saw clearly. Judas,
how stupid he'd been! How blind! She'd come
to him that night on the quay, frightened to
death but determined to see the liaison through.
His heart stopped as the enormity of what he
now knew hit him like a lightning bolt.

I have a son! he exulted. *My Flavia is dead,
but our son—our son lives!*

Galvanized into action, he seized his clothes
and threw them on. He had to get out. Had to
think, plan . . .

Forgetting the baroness existed, he wrenched
the door open, strode down the hallway and
vaulted down the stairs, two at a time. Annette's
alarmed voice echoed after him, fading under
his strident, booming footfalls.

"McNeil? What . . . where are you going?
McNeil? You won't forget you're escorting me to
the governor's birthday ball tonight? McNeil?"

Chapter 8

May 1754

Chestertown, Maryland

"JANE! JANE BROWN! Get down here, you worthless chit. Earn your keep, girl. 'Tis Market Day. You've the hens to do, peas and lettuce to pick. Your master's not yet seen hide nor hair of his breakfast. Must I sing my lungs out? Jane!"

Flavia groaned. The straw-filled mat snapped crisply under her as she stirred. Surely she'd been asleep no longer than five minutes. She was bone-weary. Every muscle hurt. Even in her dreams she'd gone on stooping and bending, stooping and bending as she and Neddy planted the huge garden in beans.

She forced her eyes open. Blinking, she tried to get her bearings in the windowless loft. A dull gray glow illuminated chinks where chimney mortar pulled away from siding.

Dawn? Already?

Flavia's heart jumped in dread. She flung herself up, her shoulders twitching in sharp recall. She'd no desire to feel Mistress Byng's switch once again.

Swiftly, she threw on the ill-fitting muslin clothes that marked her a bond servant. She grabbed a mobcap. There wasn't time to wash or even pull a comb through her thick coppery curls. Such niceties would only earn her a thrashing at best. Mistress Byng would accuse her of primping.

She hoped fervently that Neddy was awake and about his duties in the barn. The boy was simpleminded. Given a specific duty, Neddy would plunge in at once. But let a bird fly by or a dog bark, and Neddy was as easily distracted as a three-year-old. His poor, undeveloped brain could not find its way back to the assigned duty. As a result, Neddy got more than his share of beatings.

Her heart ached for the boy. Bound to Josiah Byng at the age of six, Neddy was now fifteen. He must serve until twenty-one. Even at twenty-one, Flavia doubted the Byngs would take pains to explain freedman status to the boy. Doubtless they would use fear and food to keep the lad bound to them for life.

Not daring to take time to straighten her cot, Flavia rushed down the creaking loft ladder and into the large lime-whitened kitchen that was the center of the Reverend Josiah Byng's modest house.

The fire was already blazing in the hearth, a

sure sign that Flavia's day would be an unpleasant one. As she hurried to the larder cupboard to start the corn cakes, Mistress Byng hauled herself up from lighting the fire. Her lips puckered.

"I shall speak to the magistrate, Jane. Your slugabed ways cost me dear. The magistrate shall be persuaded to indemnify me for your laziness. He shall extend your indenture by a year."

Flavia swallowed back rising anger. It was Mistress Byng's usual threat. In the first months, Flavia's knees had gone watery with fear whenever she heard it. And she heard it often, being all thumbs at servant work and unable to please. But now she knew her rights. An indenture could be extended only if a bond servant ran away or stole.

"The time can't be more than half-past four o'clock," she returned coolly. She lifted a heavy piece of crockery from the cupboard and measured cornmeal into it.

"'Tis Market Day and well you know it, girl. Market Day requires an early rise."

Flavia sighed tiredly.

"I prepared everything last night. The cheeses are wrapped. The tins of butter stand in cold water in the springhouse. The egg basket is packed."

"Packed well?"

"Yes, ma'am."

"Last Market Day it was *not* packed well. You let Neddy carry the basket, and three eggs got broke before they could be sold."

Flavia's head throbbed. She was tired. The woman's shrill voice gave her a headache.

Incautiously, she blurted, "*You* packed the eggs last time, ma'am. *You* told Neddy to carry the basket."

Mistress Byng's small hard eyes lit with challenge.

"Oho, missy! Saucy, ain't we? Shall the magistrate hear of it? Have a yen to ride Chestertown's public whipping post, do you?"

Flavia reddened in anger. Her headache banged, increasing. Its throbbing pain made her throw caution to the wind.

"I know the law," she said softly. "Insolence must be proved before the judge will condemn a bond servant to the post."

Mistress Byng's sallow complexion darkened, and instantly Flavia regretted her boldness. Oh, why had she risen to the baiting? Now the heartless woman would revenge herself where it tortured Flavia most. She would vent her anger on Neddy.

Before Flavia could offer an ingratiating apology, the kitchen door banged open. Neddy came tramping in, his bare feet caked with barn soil. He was a gangling boy, all wrists, elbows and feet. Sudden growth had rendered his breeches short.

As he entered, his eyes flew to Flavia in unabashed adoration. His slack mouth achieved a clumsy smile. Clumping across the clean pine planking, he toted a bucket of fresh cow milk.

"Uh, uh, Jane—uh, uh—Neddy 'member. Uh, uh, uh—Neddy—uh, uh—milk Daisy."

Flavia threw him an encouraging smile.

"Good boy, Neddy."

She rushed to rescue the bucket lest the boy spill, earning himself a scolding or worse. Mouth slack, Neddy stood basking in the warmth of her praise. Like an eager puppy, his eyes begged for a pat on the head. She gave it and Neddy glowed. Excited, he gestured toward the door.

"Uh, uh—Neddy—uh, uh—go milk Daisy, uh, uh."

Flavia shook her head.

"No, dear. You just milked Daisy, remember? You may milk her tonight. After supper."

Neddy's eyes brightened with a new thought.

"Supper—uh, uh—Neddy eat—uh, uh."

Concerned to get the child out of the house when the mistress was in one of her foul moods, Flavia whispered, "Hush, Neddy. Good boy. Run and take Daisy to pasture. Do it for Jane?"

But her ploy didn't work. Loath to leave her, Neddy dawdled, and Mistress Byng was across the kitchen in a trice. Lips pursed, she peered into Neddy's bucket.

"Why, there's dirt in the milk!"

She swung round at the boy. "You drooling fool. Jane," she commanded, "fetch the switch."

Neddy's glee died. Confusion filled his eyes, then fear. He began to blubber. He was almost the size of a man, but he plucked at Flavia's skirts, trying to hide.

"It's only a speck," Flavia said. "I'll strain it, ma'am. The milk will come good as new."

But Mistress Byng didn't want solutions. She wanted revenge. Striding to the stone wall that housed the fireplace, she seized a willow switch from where it hung among iron skillets. She swooped back upon the howling terrified boy.

Aghast, Flavia threw her arms around the child. "Please! Don't beat him, ma'am. He doesn't understand."

But the switch reared upward, knocking into a bunch of dried herbs that hung from the beam along with smoked hams and bacon. A shower of aromatic bits floated down, increasing the woman's vexation.

"'Understand'?" She smote the boy on his bare, defenseless legs. "There's only one way to train a fool. Understanding must be beaten into him."

Neddy screamed as the switch reared up again. Flavia shut her eyes. Before the blow could land, a door opened and the Reverend Josiah Byng emerged from his study. The clergyman's face was red with irritation. Tearing off his reading spectacles, he gave the proceedings an ill-tempered glance.

"Neddy again! How many times shall he interrupt my morning prayers? Wife, give me the rod. I shall take him to the woodshed and chastise him proper."

"No! Oh, no, sir—" Flavia cried out, but Josiah Byng silenced her with a baleful look.

"God bless you, Mr. Byng," Mrs. Byng simpered. "It quite puts my arm out of joint, disciplining the lad."

To Flavia's despair, Neddy was wrenched from her arms and was dragged, howling, across the kitchen and out the door.

"Spare the rod," Josiah Byng intoned loudly as the beating commenced, "and spoil the child."

With tears for Neddy welling up, Flavia blindly turned to her chores. Through the boy's screams, she could hear the whistle of wood and the splat when it found its target. Her hands shook as she rushed to slice the bacon, layered it in a long-handled black skillet and settled it upon a trivet in the fire. Flicking tears from her eyes, she cracked eggs into the cornmeal, added leaven, wheat flour and milk, and stirred furiously. As Neddy's howls of pain and terror came, tears spilled down her cheeks and into the batter.

Mistress Byng was satisfied.

Forgetful of the morning beating, Neddy trudged along at her side in the May spring sunshine, his eyes wide with childish delight. It was Market Day, and he was happy. For a few hours he was free of the Byngs, and he was in the company of his beloved "Jane." When he tramped through a mud puddle, joyously splashing and setting his sack of trussed hens to cackling in terror, Flavia didn't scold him for it. Let him have his fun, she thought.

Her spirits always lifted on Market Day, too. Though she must sell Mrs. Byng's wares and account for every penny, the day afforded a measure of freedom. There were friends to talk with, news to glean. She'd made friends among Chestertown's indentured. One or two were well-bred like herself. It wasn't an uncommon practice among English gentry to discipline an incorrigible son or daughter by sending him or her to the colonies under indenture.

Above all, Market Day always brought news of Chesapeake Bay shippers. Sometimes she heard tidbits about McNeil & McNeil. Already she'd learned that Garth and his brother owned two ships, that Garth had houses in Williamsburg and in Hampton, Virginia. News. Her pulse raced in anticipation. Shifting the heavy egg basket to her other arm, she quickened her step and hurried Neddy along with his load of cheeses and chickens.

The wagon road twisting down into Chestertown teemed with market-goers and smelled of the baaing, bleating, mooing livestock that was being driven to market. Chestertown's dogs loped along the road, assaulting everything that moved with wild, hoarse barks, and farm boys hallooed at one another above the chaos or shouted jibes as they prodded a cow or sheep toward Chestertown.

Steering Neddy along, Flavia absorbed all the sights and sounds. An itinerant fiddler shuffled along, practicing his notes as he went. With the deftness of a dancer, he avoided fresh piles of steaming manure without missing a note.

Two girls with long sticks drove a flock of geese. The geese waddled along, rearing up and hissing whenever a barking dog ventured too close. One of the town's ne'er-do-wells came cantering down the center of the dirt road on his big bay, scattering livestock and people alike.

"Neddy!" Flavia grabbed the boy's sleeve, pulling him out of the way. The rider on the bay was Jimmy Barlow. Thundering through the flock of frantically honking geese, he laughed uproariously as the goosegirls flew to round up their scattered charges. Jimmy Barlow turned in his saddle, laughing even harder at the stick the saucy goose-herder jabbed meaningfully in his direction.

"The back o' me skirt to ye, Jimmy Barlow!" she shrieked. "The back o' me skirt!"

Flavia hurried Neddy on. The boy had a tendency to stop and gawk at everything. If she missed getting a prime selling spot under the huge oak tree by the jail, Mistress Byng would be in a sour temper for a week. If the wares weren't mostly sold by noon when the Reverend and Mrs. Byng rode stylishly into town to watch the public punishments, Flavia would earn their wrath.

And they'd not be late *this* Market Day, she reflected bitterly. The punishments were much too titillating for the Byngs to miss. There was to be a hanging, two runaway indentured youths were to be whipped, and Mary Wooster, a gentle fifteen-year-old bond servant, was to be punished at the whipping post for the crime of bastardy.

Flavia shuddered.

She urged Neddy along. Hurrying, she made her way down Water Street, wistfully admiring the three-story red brick mansions that sat proudly overlooking a waterfront dotted with sailing ships. She hurried toward Market Square. She got the last spot under the oak tree and spread the small tarpaulin, arranging Mrs. Byng's wares as invitingly as possible. Taking the trussed hens from Neddy's sack, she smoothed their jostled feathers as best she could without getting her fingers viciously pecked.

Both business and gossip commenced briskly in the gay, festive atmosphere of Market Day. Flavia sold eggs to the owner of the new White Swan Inn and a chicken to a well-dressed woman who dispatched it by Negro slave to her house on Water Street. She sold a cheese to a man who irritated her by pinching her cheek and whispering that she was to have a shilling if she'd meet him at the Rose and Crown. She turned her back on him.

"Jane! Jane! Have you heard? The Hamilton-St. James players are in Annapolis! And straight from Drury Lane."

Flavia whirled round with a smile. It was Elizabeth Simm, another indentured girl. Long before she'd met Elizabeth, she'd heard her story from wicked tongues that delighted in telling it. Betsy Simm was the wild youngest daughter of a Yorkshire earl. Given to bedding down with handsome stableboys, Betsy had been packed off to America in punishment. Unrepentant and undaunted, Betsy continued to scandalize Chestertown just as she'd done Yorkshire.

"Jane, Mrs. Eustacia Hamilton-St. James is touring in *Flora; or a Hob in the Well*. And think of it! She's to perform several nights in Chestertown before the company journeys to Williamsburg."

Betsy's dark eyes danced.

"Oh, I should *like* to be an actress, Jane. Do

say you'll come into town when Mrs. Hamilton-St. James performs. Come with me."

Flavia laughed. "I haven't a penny, let alone three shillings for a ticket, Betsy."

The girl made a face. "That's the trouble with you, Jane. You think to catch flies with vinegar. I, my dear, catch flies with sugar." She popped her hands on her shapely hips, pushing out her breasts and raising one arched eyebrow. "A bit of sugar sprinkled on one's master's nose can have its rewards, Jane."

Flavia was taken aback. "Hush, Betsy," she sputtered. "Someone will hear."

Betsy snorted, running one hand through thick black hair that was bereft of a proper servant's mobcap.

"Lud, what do I care? I haven't a reputation worth guarding." She turned, laughing and surveying the growing crowd to find promising-looking young men. She whirled back to Flavia.

"Sugar!" she advised with a wink, adding, "I've seen how the pompous Josiah Byng looks at you, Jane, when you are unaware. Mark my words: clergymen are the worst. They love to sin, so's to give the Almighty the pleasure of forgiving them."

"Betsy!" Flavia hissed in dismay. But the girl's wild spirit had already leaped far afield from the subject.

"Oh! There's Jimmy Barlow!" Betsy cried out, half dancing, half skipping into the crowd, pursuing her quarry.

Flavia felt shaky. The thought of Mr. Byng

daring to kiss her, daring to touch her, was an appalling one. It made her sick. She was furious with Betsy, more furious than Betsy's casual teasing warranted. Was it because Betsy confirmed the suspicion that Flavia already had about Mr. Byng? What would happen to her? What did this hopeless future hold?

When the gentle young indentured schoolmaster approached her, hoping for conversation, her thoughts were still on Mr. Byng, and she cut the young man short. He left with his spirits dragging, and instantly Flavia regretted her rudeness. Dennis Finny was a good man. He was also her source of news. He'd leaped upon her supposed keen interest in ships, and he always brought Chesapeake Bay news to share with her on Market Day. Twice he'd mentioned the Caribbean sailings of the *Caroline*.

The day grew noisy and warm. Liquid refreshment flowed at the White Swan, and outside that public house the rough class was already engaged in "Indian wrestling" and betting on the matches. Drawn by today's hanging and the crowd such a spectacle would gather, a soul driver had come to town. The soul driver herded a pack of bondslaves to auction. The people looked to be Germans, and no doubt the man had bought them at a lot price from some ship in Baltimore.

Flavia felt a rush of sympathy for the forlorn new arrivals. Pinch-faced and gaunt from the voyage, the bondslaves stared about them, bewildered. Flavia knew what it was like to be bought by a soul driver, to be driven like sheep from town to town until sold. While Mab Collins had been sold immediately to a woman who kept an inn in Williamsburg, Flavia had struck buyers as being too delicate for hard work. She'd not been sold until Chestertown, some one hundred twenty miles north of Williamsburg.

She'd gone to the Byngs and had thought herself lucky at first. Wasn't Mr. Byng a clergyman? But as it turned out, Mr. Byng was *not* the ranking clergyman in Chestertown. While he aspired to the church of St. Paul's in the parish, he was forced to make do with a simple chapel of ease. This grated on both the Byngs, and they lived in daily hope that the elderly rector of St. Paul's would pass on to his reward, clearing the way for Mr. Byng.

Noon came. The Byngs arrived. As usual, Flavia found herself enduring humiliation.

"Hawk your wares, girl!" Mrs. Byng advised loudly. "You've lungs, Jane. Use them. Cheeses will not speak up and sell themselves, you ignorant chit."

Flavia bit back a tart reply and angrily kept her silence.

"Mind you, I shall require a strict accounting of the money. Get rid of any notion you may have, Jane, of foxing me out of my due."

"I am *not* a thief. You've no right to say I am!"

"Saucy chit! Speak back to me, will you? Well, I shall *see* about that when you return home, girl."

Flavia sighed in relief when Mrs. Byng lost interest in baiting her and sauntered off to find Mr. Byng and to lunch at the White Swan.

Neddy rambled back and Flavia fed him leftover corn cake for the noon meal. He begged for cheese. She said no, fearing the risk. But then, still smarting from Mrs. Byng's insults, she took a cheese and boldly sliced off a large wedge. Let the switch fall where it may. Neddy was a growing boy. He would have his nourishment.

As she sat nibbling corn cake with Neddy in the dappled shade of the oak tree, Betsy Simm danced up again. Betsy's cheeks wore the telltale flush of too much ale.

"Jane, there's a man in the White Swan asking after you. A German. He's been eyeing you all morning. A lover, Jane?"

Flavia's heart stopped. Her fingers turned to ice as blood drained away. She dropped her tidbit of corn cake, and a sparrow swooped down from a branch and snatched it.

"Wh—where?"

"He's right over—" Betsy swung round, pointing. "Lud, he's gone." She twitched her hips in vexation, then giggled. "Good riddance, I say. The German was young, but he'd a mean look to him. Lud knows what he'd ask in bed, Jane." Whirling around, Betsy blew her a giggly kiss and skipped off through the crowd toward the White Swan.

A chill passed through Flavia. Beginning to shake, she crossed her arms on her chest and hugged herself. Her heart banged. She scarcely heard Neddy's plea for more food.

A German . . . was he an agent sent by the duke? Or simply a passing traveler who spots a

pretty girl and asks about her? She breathed
deeply, trying to calm herself. German settlers
abounded in the colonies. She couldn't fear each
one. Yet the incident left her shaken. If the man
was sent by the duke, then she *was* being spied
upon. Her heart flew in fear to the baby and to
Garth. She must watch her step. She must
never put Garth or Robert in jeopardy.

Market Day had suddenly taken on another
dimension, another tone. Trying to shuck off the
anxiety, she gave Neddy her attention and threw
herself into lighthearted conversation with every customer who stopped to buy. But the sense
of threat made her smiles tremble.

*Be Jane Brown and you live; attempt to be
Flavia Rochambeau and you die.*

Public punishments began at two o'clock. The
crowd gathered noisily outside the jail. Schoolboys hooted in excitement and jostled one another. The riffraff was already drunk, and the
rosy cheeks of the female gentry said they too
had taken a rum toddy to calm themselves for
the exciting sight of a man swinging by his
neck from the gallows.

Flavia's heart pounded in dread. She wished
she could take Neddy and go. But the Byngs
would have her skin. Mr. Byng maintained that
a soul received cleansing when it witnessed
"justice."

A youth of seventeen was first. Fortified with
rum supplied by friends, the youth swaggered
to the whipping post with an insolent grin. He

doffed a red-and-white-striped sailor's cap and bowed mockingly toward the jailer. The riffraff in the crowd hooted in glee and applauded.

The jailer, who also held the paid position of public whipper, stepped forward. He was a brutish, dirty-looking man with a big belly and greasy unclipped hair. He stripped the young man of his shirt. He grabbed the youth's right wrist and roped it to an iron ring in the crossbar of the post. He dealt similarly with the left wrist.

Across the street at the White Swan, the court secretary emerged from dining, using a silver pick to clean his dinner from his teeth. The pick glinted in the sun. The man walked casually to the jail, mounted the steps and took his place. From his breast coat pocket he drew out papers and began to read.

> *"Let it hereby be known that one Peregrine Jones hath been found guilty of offending the goodly citizens of Maryland by deserting his master and running away from his indenture, being caught in the port of Annapolis preparing to flee to the West Indies."*

The crowd murmured and the man read on, loudly.

> *"Let it hereby be known that one Peregrine Jones is sentenced to serve one additional week for each day he hath stolen from his master. Let him receive twenty lashes, goodly applied, to his bare back."*

The secretary looked up, hid a burp of indigestion in his fist and said, "Proceed."

Flavia swallowed in dread as the lad planted his bare feet on either side of the post. He gripped the iron rings. With a tipsy shout to his friends, he bowed his head.

The lash snaked out, cracking.

"One!" shouted the crowd.

The boy flinched, but threw up his head laughing. Egged on by the crowd, the boy laughed through five cracks of the lash. Then his laughter hollowed off and died. He drew a rasping breath. He gritted his teeth.

Blood was rising now, bright red, glistening. The lash came down again and again to the crowd's gleeful count. At last it was over, and only then did Flavia realize she'd been holding her breath. She gasped dizzily.

The boy was untied. He staggered off on the arms of two boisterous ne'er-do-wells.

The second youth was not so brave. Flavia wept at his screams. Neddy, confused by the cracking of the whip and upset by Flavia's tears, opened his slack mouth and howled. For this he earned a cuffing from a spectator. Quickly, Flavia pulled Neddy out of the crowd and settled him on the ground under the oak. She gave him the empty basket and the dipper to play with.

Mary Wooster was dragged forth next. Only fifteen, the girl was frozen with fright and had to be pushed and prodded to the post.

The jailer stripped her bodice to the waist. The crowd snickered and Mary's fair, freckled complexion went scarlet, then white as death. In her distress, mother's milk dripped from her full, young breasts. Like the youths, she was tied to the rings, and Flavia's throat went dry with horror.

"Let it hereby be known that one Mary Wooster, bond servant to the honorable A. Bartholomew, hath been found guilty of offending both the Lord God Almighty and the goodly citizens of Maryland by willfully committing the crime of bastardy. Said fornicator shall indemnify her master for days lost in childbed. Said fornicator shall also be fined sixty pounds of tobacco or twenty lashes, goodly applied, to the bare back."

Flavia winced. Oh, why didn't the man responsible come forward? Why didn't he redeem Mary? No servant girl could have such riches. As Flavia held her breath, Mary Wooster lifted her head for a moment, as though she too hoped the merciful might happen.

The judge read on:

"Let it also be known that one Mary Wooster hath offended her God and the good citizens of Maryland by her obstinate and unholy refusal to name the man, that he too might be cleansed by just punishment. For her refusal, let her be fined an additional ten lashes, goodly applied, to the bare back."

"No," Flavia whispered.

The girl's eyes widened in terror. She was still searching the faces of the crowd in dazed disbelief when the first lash cut into her delicate white skin.

"One!" the crowd shouted.

At the blow, Mary Wooster reeled into the post, her feet going out from under her. She gave an agonized cry. She found her feet just as the crowd roared "Two!"

She went reeling under the blow. As the third and fourth struck her, she shrieked, "Help me, sir! Please help me!"

The whip snaked out a fifth and sixth time. The girl screamed in hysteria and yanked her wrists raw where ropes bound her. By the tenth, her eyes rolled in her head. By the fifteenth, she'd fainted away. She hung senseless from the ropes, the joints of shoulders distended like some plucked and dressed fowl hanging in a butcher's window.

Sick with tension and revulsion, Flavia leaned against the rough trunk of the oak. She held her stomach. Squeezing her eyes shut, she tried to blot out the sound of whip on flesh, the cries of the crowd.

When it was done, the jailer loosed the ropes and the girl melted to the ground. A bucket of water was dashed upon her, and then the crowd lost interest. The hanging was next. With an excited surge, the spectators flowed past the whipping post, poured into Water Street and headed out of town to the public field where the gallows waited.

Revolted, sick at heart, Flavia struggled to compose herself. On wobbly legs she made her

way to the post, sank to her knees and began
tending the girl. With Neddy's help she moved
the girl into the cool shade of the trees and gave
her water. Slowly, Mary Wooster came to her
senses, opened her eyes and took in her surroundings. Gulping the water Flavia held to her
lips, she whispered, "It hurts, Jane. Lud, how it
hurts."

The girl hugged the ground, afraid to move.

"Mary? I'm going to clean your wounds with
water, then butter. The butter will heal. But
there's salt in it. It will sting."

The girl nodded. Her eyes were dark bruises.

Flavia worked gently. Still the girl writhed
under her gentlest ministration, biting back moans
of pain.

"There, Mary. It's done. It's over with."

The girl said nothing. Tears collected in the
dark eyes. She didn't move.

"'Tisn't done, Jane," she whispered. "'Twill
be done me again in a year."

Flavia stared at her, not understanding.

"I'm with child."

Flavia caught her breath. Stroking the child's
sweat-dampened hair from her forehead, she
whispered, "Oh, Mary! You must report the
man. He must be punished. Tell your master.
You're an Englishwoman. Under English law
your master is obligated to protect you—"

She was silenced by Mary's bitter laugh.

"Tell my *master?*" she said in a voice venom-
ous with sarcasm. She laughed harshly. "Ay,
Jane, I shall certainly tell my *master!*"

Flavia sank back on her haunches, appalled at

the girl's inference. That a child should be treated so! And by her own master! The injustice of it made her seethe. She was helpless to help.

Choking back anger, she whispered, "Come, Mary. Neddy and I shall help you home."

That night, in her bed, she wept bitter tears. Tears for Mary and for herself. What would the future bring? What would become of her?

Chapter 9

TIME DRAGGED ITSELF FORWARD, advancing with the discouraging hesitation of a failing clock. Flavia felt its lethargy deep in her soul and saw it reflected in the weather.

May in Maryland was hot. June, hotter. In July breezes from Chesapeake Bay ceased, and Maryland became an oven. By August, she gladly would've died for just one breath of cool English air.

While plantation owners and bondslave masters retreated to shady verandas and sipped cooling drinks, slaves and servants found their work doubled.

In addition to Flavia's regular chores, there were corn rows to hoe and vegetables to pick and preserve. Untaught in such things, Flavia was slow, clumsy and a vexation to her mistress. The work was endless. Water had to be drawn and hauled, bucket by bucket, to the parched garden. The chickens, made ill-tempered by the heat, had to be caught and dipped into sulfur water to cure summer nit. Cooking had to be done in a kitchen so hot that it rivaled the cookfire.

All of this Mistress Byng oversaw from her chair on the veranda, and she was satisfied with nothing that met her eye. "Jane" was lazy; Neddy, stupid and bungling. Even in the evening Flavia was expected to account for her time. As she rested on the porch, she had the previous fall's hickory nuts to crack and pick out.

Occasionally a chore was a pleasant one. Fond of terrapin steak, the Reverend Byng often sent Neddy to the creek to spear terrapin with a lance. But the boy couldn't go alone. Alone, he'd forget his mission and simply play in the water. So Flavia was ordered to help Neddy. Quick to realize Mistress Byng would deprive her of any chore she took pleasure in, Flavia pretended indifference to the outings.

But she gleaned a bit of happiness from the peaceful afternoons of wading in the creek. The mud bottom was cool to her feet, the water clean. Green leafy branches arched over the creek, and sunlight filtered through thick leaves, dappling the water as she waded.

While Neddy was powerful enough to thrust the lance through the fifty-pound tough-shelled terrapins and hoist them out of the sucking mud, he wasn't keen enough to find their hiding places in the mud bottom. Flavia did this for him and helped him clean what he caught. Everything must be salvaged. Even the shell.

Mrs. Byng sold the terrapin shells to a comb and button maker.

When the terrapin work was done, Neddy would play in the water until he tired. Then he'd nap on the creek bank, and Flavia would steal upstream to bathe and wash her hair. She reveled in the private moment. Sitting on the bank in her wet shift, she'd brush her hair dry to the slow, peaceful gurgle of the stream. She would treat herself to daydreams. She would think of everyone she'd ever loved, saving her two best-beloveds for last. Was Mother well? Papa and the girls? Uncle Simon? At first she'd feared the duke would harm them. She no longer feared that. She guessed the duke had made it appear that she'd died. He would only attract suspicion if he abused his "dead" wife's family.

She would think of Robert and Garth. She would think how she must preserve their safety by never attempting to see them again, and her tears would gather.

Besides terrapin hunting there was one other chore Flavia didn't despise although it put her in close proximity to Mistress Byng. That was reading. Mrs. Byng couldn't read long without eye pain. Flavia had to read aloud to her.

The chore was a welcome one. Exhausted from hoeing alongside Neddy in the hot, airless garden, she cherished an hour on the veranda when she might do nothing more strenuous than read. And if she hadn't hated Mrs. Byng so intensely, she might even have found humor in the woman's choice of reading material.

If Mr. Byng were home, Mrs. Byng called for readings from the Bible or from Jonathan Edward's *A Faithful Narrative of the Surprising Work of God*. If Mr. Byng were gone, Mrs. Byng pounced on penny tracts describing women's ravishment by frontier Indians, or gazettes, which Dennis Finny, the indentured schoolmaster, brought over from the Tate plantation.

The gazettes were old by the time they got to the Byngs, but the gazettes were Flavia's only contact with the world beyond Chestertown. They contained news of the colonies and of London.

Sometimes there was news that made her heart jump. News of the *Caroline!* Slowly she would read aloud the *Caroline*'s sailing dates, her ports of call, her tonnage of barrel staves picked up in Annapolis for shipment to molasses-producing plantations in the Caribbean. On *Caroline* news days, Flavia floated through her chores in a daze, too happy to notice her bondage. But there were other gazette days that threw her headlong into despair as she read aloud to Mrs. Byng.

"Speak up, Jane. Louder. Your pudding-mouth will be the ruination of my ears."

Flavia swallowed. It was a sultry August afternoon and she was sitting on the veranda steps, a new but well-thumbed *Virginia Gazette* in her lap. She tried to see the words of the article she'd just begun to read, but her churning emotions sent black dots whirling over the paper. Her hands shook as she smoothed the page and read on.

"Escorted by Cap—Captain Garth McNeil to the Governor's Royal Birthday Ball on the twelfth of this Instant, was the Baroness Annette Vachon. The bereaved widow—widow—"

Her voice broke and she ceased reading. Widow? Annette a widow and living in Williamsburg. Free to set her cap for Garth? She was stunned.

"Really, Jane! Read on. Have you a mouth full of mush today? Then chew it up or spit it out, girl."

In misery, Flavia found her place and read on. The article said nothing more about Garth but described Annette's fashionable black gown, her black ostrich headdress. The remainder of the piece focused on the ball itself. Festivities lasted three days. The sweetmeat table held seventeen different desserts. Grouse, cracked crab and oysters highlighted the feasting. The governor presented a silver salver as door prize on each of the three days, and, finally, it was the opinion of the writer that the portraits of King William and Queen Mary, which hung in the main ballroom, were badly in need of cleaning.

Finished reading, Flavia let her hands fall disconsolately to her lap. The gazette slid to the ground, and Flavia stared at it, not seeing it, not hearing Mrs. Byng's chatter.

Would Garth marry Annette Vachon?

Despair welled up, despair at the thought of Garth marrying Annette or marrying anyone. She dropped her head to her hands. She felt weary. Defeated. Even old. When Mistress Byng sent her to the kitchen to start supper, she went obediently, went on numb, wooden legs.

Once, the arrival of Dennis Finny with a new gazette had brightened her day because the paper might hold news of Garth. But now the arrival of a gazette cast a shadow. She would stiffen and tense at the first sight of the gentle Quaker schoolmaster bounding across the fields from the Tate plantation.

Would *this* gazette be the one announcing Garth and Annette's marriage? If so, how could she bear to read it?

She grew curt with Dennis Finny. Although she knew he brought the papers to please *her* and not the Byngs, she ceased to thank him for the courtesy. She accepted his offering with an indifferent nod.

Dismayed, the gentle young man tried his best.

"Mistress Brown?" he said as she gave him her back and made to enter a house. "Will thee sit upon the porch step and converse a moment?"

"No," she snapped. Then, softening at the dashed look on his face, she added, "I'm extremely busy, Mr. Finny. My duties will not wait."

"Of course. I understand."

But the hurt in his quiet gray eyes told her he did *not* understand. He gave her a puzzled, apologetic smile. He bowed. Clapping his hat upon a head of pale, thinning hair, he walked out of the dooryard with touching dignity. At the gate in the low stone fence he paused. Hesitantly, he came back.

"It may be, Mistress Brown, that I have unknowingly offended thee in some way?"

"You've not offended me," she said, fearfully scanning the gazette he'd given her for news of Garth. There was none. She felt giddy with relief. Relief brought a smile to her lips, and at her smile, Dennis Finny brightened.

"I'm glad I have not offended thee, Mistress Brown. I would sooner die than offend thee."

Flavia's eyes widened in surprise.

He blushed. Reddening like a beet, he ducked his head in an awkward bow, clapped hat to head and scurried off.

She didn't know whether to laugh or cry. Laugh at the thought of a Quaker schoolmaster courting the duchess of Tewksbury, or cry at the sudden, paralyzing realization that her future was unlikely to hold anything *better* than Dennis Finny.

Leaning against the porch rail, she blinked back hot tears. But more gathered. Tears of resignation.

A shrill cry came from within the house.

"Was that Dennis Finny again?" Mrs. Byng called. "I shall speak to the magistrate, Jane. Mr. Finny is *not* to waste your time. Lollygagging about in the shank of the day, indeed! I shall report him to his master, to Mr. Tate."

Flavia wiped away her tears with a corner of muslin apron.

"He brought a gazette," she called unwillingly.

"Ah? Did he, indeed?"

Mrs. Byng's voice sweetened.

"A fine lad, Dennis Finny! D'ye suppose he

intends to hunt grouse this coming autumn? I
shouldn't be averse to receiving a brace of fine,
fat grouse. Tell him, Jane," she ordered. Her
voice warbled up to its usual high pitch. "Still,
he is *not* to waste your time. You may tell Mr.
Finny for me, missy, that if he intends to wear
out the floorboards of *my* veranda, he is expected
to turn his hand to a task. If he's of a mind to sit
on *my* steps, he can well put his idle hands to
cracking nuts or shucking dried corn."

When Flavia made no reply, Mrs. Byng raised
her voice.

"Jane! Stubborn, uppity chit! Did you hear
me?"

Flavia descended the veranda steps and strode
toward the garden without answering.

Next to penny tracts and the gazettes' social
news, Mrs. Byng doted on gazette subscriptions
offering bounties on runaway bond servants. In
this Mrs. Byng took perverse pleasure. She
knew it cut Flavia to the quick to read aloud
about her fellow slaves' suffering.

*"Runaway on the twenty-first of this Instant,
after a whipping, from This Subscriber in Kent
County, an Irish Servant Man, Valentine Flaherty.
He is about nineteen, a great lusty Fellow, somewhat pock-broken, wore his own hair but may
cut it off, has a sour pinched looking Countenance. Having on when he went away snuff-
colored Breeches, Ditto shirt, a homemade brown
cloth coat and a green silk Handkerchief. Whoever takes up said Servant and Secures him in
any Jail so that his Master can have him again,*

*shall have Forty Shillings and Reasonable charges
paid by,*

> *Edward Fitz-William, Esq.
> Wig Maker, Kent County"*

Poor young man, thought Flavia with a sigh as she finished reading and put the paper down.

"Read it again, Jane," Mrs. Byng directed, leaning forward in her veranda chair to swish a rag at a cluster of flies that gathered on her empty rum toddy cup.

"And attend to what you're reading, missy. On Market Day you must keep your eyes peeled for runaways. I shouldn't take it amiss to get myself forty shillings for no work but looking."

Flavia's stomach lurched in disgust, but she complied with the order and read the boy's description once more. When she finished, Mrs. Byng granted her a rare, peevish smile.

"I don't wonder but what I might not give *you* a shilling or two of the reward, Jane, if you'll but keep your eyes peeled and fly to the jailer if you spy the runaway."

Flavia's eyes flashed with anger. Quickly she looked down at the gazette to hide her hot feelings. Fly to the jailer, indeed! Rather she would fly to the young man and warn him to run.

"Jane! Are you *listening?*"

She jumped as Mrs. Byng's fan rapped her shoulder.

"I'm *hearing* you, ma'am," she said sarcastically.

Mrs. Byng's weak eye twitched. Sensing she

may have been insulted, but unable to put her finger on the insult, she smoothed her own ruffled feathers by attacking.

"Where is your mobcap, chit? Put it on at once. Attire yourself decent."

Flavia looked up in genuine surprise.

"The day is so hot. I'm cooler without the cap."

Mrs. Byng gave her a baleful look.

"Your hair is an affront to Nature, Jane. Only a wanton or a slut has hair the color of yours."

Flavia's cheeks heated in anger.

"It is the hair God was pleased to give me!"

"Yes! And He gave it to you that decent folk could easily spot a wanton and be warned. In like manner, He gave red hair to Jezebel and to Eve. The Reverend Mr. Byng says it is so."

It was infuriating, but Flavia bit back the words she wanted to hurl. There was no argument to be offered for "Mr. Byng says it is so." She studied her hands in her lap, refusing Mrs. Byng the satisfaction of knowing she'd upset her. But Mrs. Byng found her composure incensing.

"Oh, yes, girl. Mr. Byng discerns a wanton spirit in you. He warned me of it. Mr. Byng intends to keep a close watch on you, missy."

Flavia flushed in anger. A close watch? During the past weeks Mr. Byng's eyes had followed her every movement. At times she felt stripped naked. And she was uncomfortably aware that the last time she'd bathed in the creek someone had spied from the bushes. She'd heard furtive slaps, as though someone battled insects. That night Mr. Byng came to supper with his face mottled with red chigger bites.

"You are wasting my time, Jane," Mrs. Byng said. "Read on in the gazette. Read the rest of the bondslave subscriptions. And mind the detail. On Market Day you are to keep your eyes peeled."

Flavia sighed and picked up the gazette. She began to read with deliberate slowness. Detestable as the subscriptions were, they gave respite from garden work.

"Runaway from the Mistress of Spencer House, a genteel Williamsburg lodging place, an English Servant Woman called Mab Col—"

Her voice stuck in her throat. For several seconds she couldn't breathe. Fear pounded in her breast.

Mrs. Byng turned sly eyes upon her.

"Do you know the bondwoman, Jane?" she asked with feigned pleasantness.

Flavia blinked. She drew a steadying breath.

"No," she said firmly. "No."

Willing herself to be calm, she rushed on with the reading. She mustn't arouse Mrs. Byng's suspicions. For what if Mab traveled north, counting on Flavia to hide her? In the eight months since they'd parted, they'd exchanged letters only once. Postal fees were too dear to permit more. But Mab's one letter had hinted at escape.

Burying her face in the gazette, Flavia read on aloud. She knew she must read every word as it stood because Mr. Byng often read the same material aloud in the evening. Where profit was concerned, Mistress Byng stayed alert. If Mrs. Byng suspected deception, she would watch Flavia carefully and Flavia would find herself powerless to help Mab.

In a deliberately bored manner she read:

> "—an English Servant Woman called Mab Collins. Said Servant is about twenty-three years of Age, a tall, pridey woman having insolent eyes and hair of no special coloring. She hath a tart mouth and Thieving ways. When she went away, clothed herself in her mistress's black Allopeen Cloak with Silver buttons. It is supposed she will endeavor to pass for one Mary Percy, having Stolen her Indenture with a Discharge thereon."

Flavia paused for breath. Sending up a quick fervent prayer of Godspeed for Mab, she rushed to the finish:

> "Whoever takes up Mab Collins and Secures her so that her Mistress may have her again, shall receive, besides what the Law allows, Four Pistoles if taken in Virginia, Six if taken in Maryland and Eight if taken in New-York, paid by,
>
> > Mrs. Eliza Spencer
> > Spencer House for Genteel
> > Gentlemen
> > and their Ladies,
> > Williamsburg"

When Flavia fell silent, Mrs. Byng stood up in thoughtful concentration.

"*Six* pistoles, Jane. A pistole holds its value far better than shillings." She frowned. "Keep your eyes peeled, Jane. You hear?"

Flavia looked away, hiding the fearful excitement that danced in her eyes.

"Oh, I shall, ma'am," she promised. "You may count on it."

Chapter 10

GARTH MCNEIL's footfalls echoed with hollow resonance as he hurried up the spiraling uneven stone steps of the castle keep. The keep was the last remaining tower of what once had been Castle Bladensburg. Here each feudal Germanic lord of Bladensburg had sought to "keep" his lady and his children safe in times of siege. Encircled by its own small moat, the keep had once been the center of a proud castle. Now it looked down upon tumbled ruins, and its moat was a shallow ditch overgrown with scruffy trees, choked with wild honeysuckle vine.

McNeil vaulted up the steps, ignoring the gloomy stone alcoves where once frightened ladies had clutched their children as they peered out narrow archers' slits to watch the terrible battle unfold.

McNeil reached the top of the keep and went out into the sunshine, leaving gloom behind. A square scalloped wall circled the top of the

171

keep, and from here a marching army could be seen at ten miles' distance. But an ancient medieval army was not what McNeil was interested in. He was here to absorb the lay of the land, the layout of Bladensburg.

He prowled the wall. Below lay sprawling ruins where wild flowers grew upon stone outcroppings. Peacocks roosted upon ruins, and their peculiar shrieks echoed off the stones and out over the river that ran past Bladensburg. A hundred yards north of the keep there began a formal garden, terraces that marched up to an imposing three-story villa. McNeil looked at it with distaste. The duke of Tewksbury's German bastion.

He went to the north side and studied the densely forested countryside. The Rhine River snaked through the land, rushing north, rushing toward the lowlands of Holland, rushing toward Amsterdam. In Amsterdam, the *Caroline* waited.

He paced the windy tower, studying river and rolling countryside, planning...

"It's a lovely view, isn't it, Captain McNeil?"

McNeil started. Jerking around he found Eunice Wetherby smiling up at him. Miss Wetherby was a plain young woman with a pert, birdlike face and hennish, fussy ways. Her young but spinsterish bosom rose and fell breathlessly as though she'd found the climb to the top of the keep taxing. As he looked at her, she smiled eagerly. Then, perhaps fearing her smile had betrayed too much, she reined it in to controlled, ladylike dimensions.

McNeil smiled back.

"The view is *very* lovely," he said, pointedly looking at her and not the view.

She reddened at the possibilities underlying his words, ducked her head and turned away slightly, pretending to study a fishing boat that was passing. Her manner corroborated what McNeil suspected: Eunice Wetherby fancied herself in love with him.

He scowled in irritation. It didn't fit his plans to have Lord Wetherby's cousin following him about like a devoted puppy. She could be a danger. Unknowingly, she could scuttle his mission, sabotage his careful plans. And those plans had been long in the making.

His scowl deepened as he forced Lord Wetherby and Eunice from his mind and concentrated upon his mission. The past months had been intense. The coming months would be more so.

It had begun in May, three days after the governor's royal birthday ball in Williamsburg. Abandoning a ragingly furious Annette with no more adequate explanation than "Keep my bed warm, Baroness," he'd sailed out of Norfolk. He'd caught the prevailing westerly winds and loosed the *Caroline* to run before them. Like a mistress flying to her lover, the *Caroline* flew toward England.

Matching the loosed madness of the *Caroline,* McNeil's own thoughts and passions rioted. Wildly, he vowed to confront the duke and demand his son. This foolishness he likely would've committed had the *Caroline* magically leaped between Norfolk and England in a day.

And it would have meant the death of his son he realized after he'd finally cooled down.

For the duke of Tewksbury had struck him as a ruthless man. If the duke should learn that Tewksbury blood didn't flow in Robert's veins, the duke would not hesitate to—God! McNeil was stupified at the thought of what he might have brought upon his son by rash action. No, he must *never* confront the duke. He must *never* endanger Robert's life.

From an extreme of foolhardiness he'd swung to meekness. For a time, he meekly planned only to try to catch a glimpse of his son. Simply a hasty glance through a nursery window. Then, so be it. But he yearned to lay eyes on the boy, yearned to look and absorb the boy into his heart, keep him there in the center of himself where he kept memories of Flavia.

He was almost inured to the unhappy idea of contenting himself with just seeing the boy when he'd awakened one night in a cold sweat, in bondage to a new and infinitely chilling thought: he'd learned of the existence of his son by piecing bits together. A chance remark by Annette had been the catalyst, the spark that exploded those bits and caused them to reassemble in his mind in new, meaningful shapes. Suppose the duke had a similar experience. Suppose His Grace put the bits and pieces together. What would the duke do? Would he hesitate to have Robert murdered?

The horror of the thought choked him day and night. With desperate urgency, he knew

what he must do. To save the boy, he must steal
him.

Cool-headed at last and as much the master
of himself as he was master of the *Caroline*, he'd
made his plans. Three weeks out of Norfolk, the
wind-favored ship penetrated English waters. A
few days more and the *Caroline* dropped anchor
at Plymouth.

From Plymouth, Garth sent Tom Jenkins, his
trusted first mate, to London to make discreet
inquiries: was the colonial Captain McNeil still
wanted by authorities on charges of stealing a
jade piece from Tewksbury Hall?

Jenkins brought back the answer. No. Not
only no, but all charges had been dismissed as
an unfortunate administrative error. The error
had been laid to a steward of the duke, and the
erring steward had been discharged.

"The bastard!" Garth had snarled to Jenkins.
"His Grace wants all swept under the rug and
forgotten. Why?"

Jenkins had smiled his solemn, intelligent
smile.

"I pursued that question, sir. And very handy
was the fifty pounds you sent with me. I greased
a few palms, loosened a few tongues' w'rum."

"Well?"

"I got nothing certain, Captain. A tad here, a
tad there. But tads add up, don't they?"

"And?"

"And it looks like His Grace planted the jade
on the *Caroline* for an interesting reason. He
wanted all eyes on the *Caroline* while a certain

other ship sailed out of London, with no port authorities botherin' her. His Grace chose the *Caroline* because you was the only shipmaster at the ball that night. When that certain ship sailed out safe, His Grace dropped the charges, sayin' that the jade found on the *Caroline* was *not* his."

McNeil had ruminated long on the information.

"What ship was His Grace protecting? And why? Smuggling?"

Jenkins had shrugged.

"No tellin', sir. There was a dozen ships in and out at that time—the *Cluny,* the *Aberdeen,* the *Bountiful Lady,* a Dutch ship called the *Schilaack...*" Jenkins had gone on naming them. Then he'd tossed in a tidbit of gossip: not six weeks after the death of his wife, His Grace had wed his late wife's sister Valentina.

As the days went on, Jenkins's theory of why Tewksbury dropped charges had satisfied Garth less and less. It was too simple. He'd chewed at the mystery. Gradually, his puzzlement had chilled to new apprehension. Suppose, as sweet Flavia lay in her death agony, she'd let slip the truth about her son. Supposing the duke *knew* and was biding his time to strike against the boy?

McNeil had gone numb with fear. The child was helpless. A potential pawn in a vicious and deadly game.

Learning that Robert was kept at Bladensburg, the duke's Rhine River estate in Germany, McNeil had sailed for Amsterdam with a shipload of

English trade goods. Though his heart was in his mouth for fear of what might be happening at Bladensburg, he conducted his Amsterdam business at a leisurely pace, accepting all social invitations that came his way. At each dinner or ball he probed the guests, sifting out those who might suit his purpose.

The Wetherby party had suited him best. The party consisted of six young persons and two elderly chaperoning aunts. Lord Wetherby was an English earl from Sussex. He was also a penniless spendthrift who sailed through life leaving a wake of unpaid tailors and irate shop-keepers. Eunice Wetherby, his cousin, was unmarried and about twenty-three years old. Her marital chances had suffered, no doubt, because of her guardian's embarrassing financial state. Three male cousins and Eunice Wetherby's female companion completed the party. Lord Wetherby was in Amsterdam, preparing to take a holiday junket up the Rhine. Lord Wetherby carried letters of entry, inviting his party to stay at German estates on the Rhine, including Bladensburg, the estate of the duke of Tewksbury.

Flirting with Eunice Wetherby at a ball, McNeil had easily insinuated himself into the circle of Wetherby females. Access to Lord Wetherby's circle was equally easy. The young spendthrift enjoyed nothing so much as keeping company with an openhanded rich colonial. When McNeil offered use of a Rhine River barge he'd hired, Lord Wetherby had jumped at the invitation. McNeil had found himself in the inner circle.

"You're frowning, Captain McNeil."

Garth jerked as Eunice Wetherby's anxious voice broke into his intense thoughts.

"I should not have come up to the top of the keep, Captain McNeil. I fear I'm disturbing your meditation. I fear you're angry with me."

He'd not been aware of the ferocity of his concentration until Eunice's voice ended it. Collecting himself, he cast a last glance out over the rolling forest, then turned, forcing a smile.

"Angry with *you*, dear Miss Wetherby? Impossible."

She flushed. She looked away, then peeked back at him. A sudden half-shy, half-bold expression crossed her face. She gazed up at him. To ignore the invitation in her eyes would've been ungallant. So he bent and lightly kissed the dry, trembling lips. She drew back in propriety. But not immediately. Blushing deeply, she forbore commenting on the daring intimacy. Instead, she gulped air and chattered on as though it had not happened.

"Captain McNeil, my aunts sent me to find you. The tour begins shortly. The chief steward will lead us through Bladensburg and explain all its treasures. We mustn't miss the tour."

She drew a shallow, uncertain breath and echoed her own words. "We mustn't miss the tour?"

Her eyes begged him to disagree, but he would not. Involvement with Eunice Wetherby must be proper and superficial. He would leave her virginity intact. Let someone else reap it.

There would be unhappiness enough for the young spinster when he would suddenly receive news of his "aged, ailing grandmother," and would leave at once.

"I—I—suppose we could miss the tour," she whispered fearfully.

He gave her a hearty smile.

"Miss it? Not for the world, Miss Wetherby. I know how fervently you've looked forward to examining His Grace's Oriental collection. My arm, Miss Wetherby?"

The corners of her mouth twitched in vexation, but the expression was gone in an instant. Granting him a bright smile, she accepted his proffered arm.

He escorted Eunice down the ancient stone stairwell that spiraled gloomily down the castle keep. Her voice echoed off the stone walls as she chattered happily.

There was a slightly proprietary weight to the small hand on his arm, and the bounce in her step as they crossed the castle yard, scattering peacocks, was unnervingly victorious. He led her along, up the terraces, through the garden and into the villa where the Wetherby party was assembling in a sunny, greenery-filled breakfast room.

As he and Eunice stepped into the fragrance of fresh coffee and warm yeast buns, all heads swung their way. Eating stopped. Conversation died, then instantly resurrected itself and burst on with masquerading gaiety. But eyes met knowingly. Lord Wetherby winked at a cousin,

and behind fluttering fans the fat, chaperoning
aunts nodded to each other excitedly. Garth
drew a deep breath.

*Wonderful, McNeil, wonderful. You're as good
as trussed, tied and delivered to the butcher's
block.*

"There are one hundred and fifty-six mullioned
glass windows in Bladensburg Hall. Each window reaches the height of twelve feet and spans
three feet. The glass is imported from Venice.
You will notice, my lord, my ladies, gentlemen,
that each pane of glass is beveled. The mullioned
fittings are brass. The brass is acid-bathed so as
not to distress the eye when sunlight enters the
window."

"The draperies, Parkinson?" It was the fatter
of the two aunts who spoke.

"Flemish, my lady," replied the English steward whose job it was to extend the absent duke's
hospitality. "If you will kindly examine the warp
and woof of the weave, my lady, you will note
that each tenth thread is gold dipped. It is the
gold that brings an especial luster to this fine
Flemish silk."

Lord Wetherby yawned.

Lord Wetherby and his cousins lasted through
the draperies, an El Greco, a life-size tree of
jade, and a tall curio case containing golden
multiarmed tantric buddhas. Murmuring apologies, the men drifted off to sample the duke's
riding stock. As the men left, McNeil was suddenly aware of Eunice's hand tightening on his
arm. It was only a slight pressure, but he was

surprised at the imperiousness it conveyed. He was both amused and irritated. So he was the property of a plain-faced, twenty-three-year-old spinster, was he?

The gesture was annoying enough to make him wheel round and join the men. But he didn't. While the tour was merely recreation for the ladies, it was a crucial event for him. If he were to make a success of stealing Robert, he must familiarize himself with every inch of Bladensburg. He must be aware of the location of every window, every door, every corridor. He must know where any odd creaking board lurked and how to avoid it in stealth of night. He must count the servants, become familiar with the routine of each. Were footmen posted at night? Or did all servants, except the night steward, retire and sleep soundly in belief that nothing wayward ever occurred in the country?

He must find out. He must leave nothing to chance.

"As you enter the west receiving room, my ladies, sir—"

The party flowed on, moving toward the nursery wing. On the pretext of studying a tapestry, McNeil extricated himself from Eunice and dawdled in the rear. From the moment he'd stepped from the barge to the grounds of Bladensburg two days earlier, he'd been tense and alert, waiting—no, damn it, *yearning*—for a glimpse of the boy. Today's tour provided the first opportunity to go near the nursery. As the others drifted on, he lingered in the corridor, his throat dry, his senses heightened.

Suddenly, behind the great double doors of the schoolroom, a young child's laughter bubbled up. The happy laughter was followed by the sound of a switch coming down hard upon soft flesh. There was a terrible pause. Then, heart-wrenching sobs that played upon McNeil's nerves like a saw upon tin. He froze, horrified.

A pedantic dry voice rose shrilly above the crying.

"I warned you, my lord. You are *not* to play, young sir. Your father, the duke of Tewksbury, has entrusted me with teaching you your letters. Now then, pay attention, my lord. His Grace, your father, was a fine reader at the age of three. His Grace could read Latin and Greek at the age of five. You *must* emulate His Grace, my lord."

But the sobs still came, and along with them, babyish catches of breath. McNeil's anger knew no bounds. His hands shook. Lest he wrench open the doors and smash the face that belonged to the dry, pedantic voice, he strode rapidly away and caught up with Eunice.

The incident banished any doubt he harbored about the morality of his mission. Robert must be taken away.

On the third day of their stay he chanced upon Flavia's portrait. Deferring to Lord Wetherby's aunts' request, the chief steward had ordered the dust covers taken off all of the ancestral portraits in the main ballroom. Flavia's was among them.

A dozen times a day McNeil found himself standing in the empty, echoing ballroom, staring hopelessly at her. It was a moving portrait and it awakened all the old grief. Girlish and innocent, she'd been painted perhaps in the opening weeks of her marriage. Her huge young eyes shone with hope and with a trusting belief in the goodness of life. There was a shy eagerness to please in the set of her mouth, and her loose, casually arranged hair made her seem a country girl on holiday.

Physical pain, the same incapacitating pain he'd suffered in those first weeks after her death, stabbed at him again.

The heels of his boots stirred dust devils as he hurried across the castle yard to join the Wetherby party down at the boat dock. A pleasure cruise on the barge was the agenda, and pleasurable or not, McNeil had to attend. Eunice Wetherby expected it. And it was in his best interests to meet Eunice Wetherby's expectations.

He was about to descend the brick steps that wound down to the river when a flurry of noise and activity caught his attention. Across the yard, near the stables, three grooms huddled round a saddled white pony. The pony shifted from hock to hock as the grooms attempted to settle a wildly struggling small rider on its back. The would-be rider squalled in terror, pitching away from the pony.

"No! No!" a tiny, sobbing voice shrieked.

McNeil halted in midstride, his heart wheeling, blood pounding in his throat. Could it— *was* it—

He knew it was. Without thought, he charged

across the yard, grabbed the first groom, flung him into the dirt and went for the second.

"Put the child down," he roared. "Idiots! Can't you see he's frightened?"

The groom he'd flung was kneeling in the dirt; shaking his head like a stunned dog. The other two grooms stared, flabbergasted at the interference. Even the child in the oldest groom's arms stopped crying and stared at McNeil. The boy's cheeks were a wet testimony to his misery. His little chest heaved with silent sobs.

It struck McNeil like a thunderbolt. A two-year-old was not a boy, but still a baby. Tenderness welled up like a choke. He swallowed. Then swallowed again.

"Put him down," he ordered softly.

Intensely, he drank the baby in as the befuddled groom hastened to obey. He was Flavia's. No one who'd known her could doubt it. The sweetness was there. And the face that verged close to being heart-shaped. But the eyes were McNeil eyes. And the dark hair. A cowlick swirled at the crown of the baby's head, exactly where McNeil's own cowlick made mischief, defying the comb.

Gazing at his son, he could hardly breathe. He stared. *Oh, Flavia* . . . but the chief groom had recovered himself and was smarting with anger. Unable to discern whether McNeil was an important personage or just an interfering guest, he made do with shooting him a sullen look.

"'Tis my task to teach the marquis to sit a

horse. If my lordship don't ride good by the time he be three, it's my *post* I'll be losing."

Tearing his gaze from the baby, McNeil raked the groom with furious eyes.

"Proceed to teach him as you are doing, and you shall lose *more* than your post, I promise you!"

The groom muttered a bit to save face, then fumbled for his cap, pulled it off and held it against his chest in an unconscious gesture of obedience.

McNeil squatted and smiled at the baby. Robert stared back, sucking his thumb.

"You're afraid of the horse, Robert?"

The tiny chest began to heave again. The thumb was sucked in, up to the last pink knuckle.

"Would you like to ride on my shoulder? You can sit here." McNeil patted himself. "We'll pretend I'm a horse."

Robert stared warily. For several moments he made no response, but McNeil could see the child's every thought reflected in his eyes. In this, the child was pure Flavia. All of Flavia's feelings had lived naked in those large lotus blossom eyes. He watched as the tot struggled with the proposal. The dark eyes flashed first with fear. Fear slowly disintegrated into doubt, doubt into the natural inclination to play. At last he nodded, and McNeil shakily held out his arms.

His tiny son flung himself into them. At the sweet innocent smell of babyish flesh, McNeil's heart thundered. He fought the urge to hug him close, to kiss the tear-streaked cheek. He wanted to whisper "You shan't cry any more, Robert. Papa will see to it." But he couldn't. He swallowed hard.

"Up?" he asked thickly.

"Up!" Robert echoed.

Carefully he settled the child upon his shoulders. Two firm small legs straddled his neck. Holding him with both hands, McNeil stood slowly and began walking about the castle yard. At first, his hair was gripped tight in fear. Gradually, fear faded. A bubble of noise that was almost a giggle popped out. Then another and another, until the child chortled joyously. Letting go of McNeil's hair, Robert flailed chubby hands, whipping his horse.

"Go!" he chortled. "Horse go!"

McNeil went. For several minutes they trotted round the castle yard. Then, casually, McNeil strolled toward the white pony. By degrees, he introduced the boy.

"See the horse's eye," he encouraged.

Robert jiggled excitedly.

"Eye! See eye!"

"See the horse's mane."

"Horse! Horse mane!"

They played for a quarter-hour while the chief groom and the undergrooms watched sullenly. When McNeil judged the boy'd had enough, he lowered him from his shoulders and reluctantly returned him to the groom.

"See that you teach him to ride in slow, easy steps. As I have demonstrated."

The groom's sulky expression came just short

of disrespect. Well aware of the folly of insulting
a Bladensburg guest, he checked his temper.

"'Tisn't His Grace's way," he muttered.

McNeil turned and stared the man down.

"It is *my* way," he said in a voice that left no
room for negotiation. "You would do well to
adopt it. In fact," he added with a cold little
laugh, "I insist!"

He was satisfied at the scared, cowed expression that passed over the groom's face. Then,
lest he totally humiliate the man and stick his
son with the consequences of the man's temper,
he quickly strode off without a backward look.

Behind him, a small vulnerable voice rose,
calling after him.

"Up?" the voice pleaded. "Up?"

Forcing himself to ignore the endearing summons, he straightened his shoulders and hurried down to the boat dock. Everyone was
assembled, sitting in the canopied barge, sip-
ping wine, waiting. Eunice Wetherby had saved
him a seat beside her.

A hunter's moon, huge and heavy, crouched
upon a forested hilltop and flooded the Rhine
with invading white light as McNeil launched
the skiff, unfurled its single sail and watched the
sleeping port of Köln shrink behind him. The
night was hushed and quiet. Everyone slept,
except for an occasional dog baying at the moon.

McNeil grasped the tiller and bent to the
night's tense work. He'd taken every precau-
tion. The Wetherby party was now staying in
Köln, on the estate of Lord Wetherby's German

cousin. McNeil's room overlooked balcony and garden. At this moment, a candle burned at the writing desk and a man—McNeil at a glance—hunched over a book at the desk. The man was Jenkins, his first mate on the *Caroline*.

The sail upriver from Köln to Bladensburg ate up two precious hours, McNeil judged, gauging time by the rising moon. He was careful to cling to the shadowy shore with its overhang of trees, and eluded customs houses by lowering the mast and slipping under the chains that stretched from river island to shore.

When the castle keep reared its head in the bright moonlight, he drew a deep breath of relief. So far, so good. He beached the skiff in a stony cove south of the boat dock. Shucking boots and stockings, he leaped into the cold water and dragged the boat ashore. Barefoot, he ran through trailing willows, then scrambled up the rocky slope that led to the ancient castle yard. In the bright moonlight, the tumbled ruins cast deep, velvety shadows. Sprinting from shadow to shadow, he worked his way through the yard and up into the terraced gardens.

Bladensburg slept. River rats running freely in garden and castle yard were a sure sign of it. The only unbolted door would be at the night steward's post. McNeil had studied the man's habits during the Wetherby party's two-week stay. At precisely midnight, two o'clock and four, the steward marched out with a lantern to patrol the grounds. The steward's route was the same each night: the gardens, then the stables, then the castle yard as far as the keep, then

down the stone steps to the boat dock, back up
the boat stairs, again through the garden and
into Bladensburg Hall for a pint of beer. The
duration of the patrol was thirty minutes. Sixty
minutes if a housemaid awaited the steward at
the boat dock.

Breathing raggedly, McNeil settled into the
shadows to wait. Time passed. The moon continued to rise. At last, the night steward's door
creaked open. Lantern light bobbed into the
night and swung through the garden. When the
lantern bobbed down to the second terrace,
McNeil shot for the door, eased it open—lifting
to ease the hinge—and let himself in.

He listened. All was silent except for the
pounding of his heart. A lantern burned on the
steward's untidy table, and a cat slept curled on
a chair. The smell of beer was heavy.

Drawing on wool stockings that he'd secreted
in the breast of his dark shirt, he moved swiftly
down the long polished corridor that cut Bladensburg in two. At the wide center staircase,
he crouched in the shadows, listening. Nothing.
Skipping the second and the ninth creaking
steps, he moved up the staircase and into the
upper corridor, then the nursery wing.

Out of nowhere, a cat suddenly meowed. He
froze, cold sweat breaking on his forehead. The
cat came padding to him out of the darkness.
She arched against his ankles, mewing, begging
for a scratch. He scratched the cat's ears to
quiet it, then pushed it away.

Noiselessly, he hurried down the corridor to
Robert's sleeping-room and put his ear to the

door. This would be the crucial part. He was aware that a nursemaid slept on a cot in an adjoining room, keeping her door ajar in the event the child awoke and cried out for her. Taking a deep breath, McNeil put his hand to the metal door latch. As his fingers touched it, the latch suddenly began to turn in his hand. He lunged away, leaping into shadow and sucking his body tight to the wall.

The door opened without sound. A fair, braided head peered out cautiously. A soft whisper broke the silence.

"Vilhelm? Is you? Vilhelm?"

McNeil gripped the wall. He didn't breathe.

She wandered out into the corridor, glanced first in McNeil's direction and then the opposite. Giving a breathy little giggle, she ran down the corridor, her white flannel nightdress flapping. A shadow appeared suddenly at the end of the corridor. There was a flurry of whispers. A furtive giggle. The couple disappeared.

McNeil released his breath slowly. Darting back to the door, he listened again and then let himself in. The room was bright with the light of the huge hunter's moon. A door on the far wall stood ajar, and from it came the deep snores of still another sleeper. It was the second nursemaid. Quietly, he stole across the room and closed out the stout German snores and huzzahs.

He drew back the sleeping-curtains at the boy's bed and sat to waken Robert gently. He touched his cheek.

"Robert?"

With the alacrity of the innocent, the child woke. Having never experienced fear in the safety of his bed, he exhibited none now. He merely blinked in curiosity. As his dark eyes studied McNeil in the moonlight, a lopsided smile grew on his lips.

"Up?" he croaked in a sleepy voice.

"Shssh. Shsssh, Robert. We'll play 'horse' later. Will you come with me?"

For answer, the child sprang up and flung himself into Garth's arms.

"There, there," he whispered, choking at the sweetness of his son's response. He patted him awkwardly. "We'll play a game, Robert. In the game you must be very, very quiet. Quiet as a mouse. Can you do that?"

"Yes!"

"Shsssh!"

"Shsssh," the wide-eyed child mimicked, trying to please.

Garth grinned despite the tense sweat that was beginning to bead on his forehead again. Digging into his pocket for the sweetmeats he'd brought for just such a contingency, he popped one into Robert's mouth. The boy's eyes lit with delight. He chewed solemnly and silently, licking the sweet drool that seeped from the corners of his mouth.

"There, old man," Garth whispered, tucking an extra sweet into the chubby, eager fist. "That should keep you quiet as a mouse."

Harrington was waiting on the wharf in Köln. Already the sky was a leaden gray, and a thin pink line was forming on the eastern horizon just as the skiff bumped gently against the pilings.

"You've the landau?" McNeil snapped tensely, handing up the sleeping bundle.

"Ay, Cap'n. The horses are strong and fresh."

"Head directly for Amsterdam. Change horses as often as needed. Travel day and night, if need be. Settle the boy aboard the *Caroline*, and Harrington—"

"Cap'n?"

McNeil stared at the small bundle and fought the urge to go to Amsterdam himself. No. It would be stupid and foolhardy. When servants at the Köln estate of Lord Wetherby's cousin came with morning chocolate, McNeil must be in his bed, as though he'd passed the night in sound sleep.

"Treat the boy as though he were your own flesh and blood," he said at last to Harrington. "Dress him in clothes suitable for play. Give him plenty of food and plenty of sunshine. Let him get dirty if he chooses. I want him to look like—like an Amsterdam street urchin."

Harrington's ruddy face wrinkled in perplexity. He stared at the child sleeping peacefully in his arms.

"Who be the lad, Cap'n?"

McNeil laughed softly.

"What a forgetful old bastard you are, Harrington. The boy is a beggar orphan. You found him yourself in the alleys of Amsterdam. You rescued him, saving him from certain starvation."

Bewildered, Harrington blinked.

"I did, Cap'n?"

"You did. And I congratulate you, you charitable old sea dog."

Garth smiled wearily, and at last Harrington's canny, trusting grin came into play.

"That I did, Cap'n. I well recall it."

McNeil grinned, then tiredly looked up at the lightening sky.

"Off with you, then," he said.

"Right, Cap'n." Wheeling round, Harrington loped down the wharf to the waiting landau where two sleek chestnut horses pricked up their ears at his approach.

Harrington stopped and swung around.

"Cap'n? What do I call 'im?" he called back in a loud whisper. "What be the little lad's name?"

McNeil rubbed his jaw wearily, the tension of the night draining away.

"How should *I* know?" he hissed. "*You* found him. That makes *you* his godfather. *You* name him."

"Me?"

Harrington broke into a slow grin.

"Why, Cap'n—*Trent* be his name. After me own pa."

"Trent, it is. Now, go. Hurry. God be with you."

He waited until the landau clattered off, rattling softly over the cobbled streets of Köln. The echo of the landau faded, melding into the soft bump-bump of the skiff nudging the pilings. When he could hear it no more, he shoved off. Daybreak's wind was fresh and cool, sweet as a prayer. As he maneuvered the skiff into its home cove, he cast one last anxious glance at the town of Köln and its empty cobbled streets.

"And God be with *you*, Trent," he breathed. "God be with us both."

"It is a great tragedy," declared the fatter of the two aunts as she sat at the table, spooning the last bit of a meringued plum jelly into her mouth.

"A great, *great* tragedy," echoed the second aunt in predictable fashion as she gazed round the banquet table, blinking at each person in turn.

The fatter aunt stayed her spoon against the crystal dish. "It quite takes the pleasure out of a holiday upon the Rhine. Do you not agree, Captain McNeil?"

McNeil opened his mouth to utter some bland, noncommital response, but evidently no response was wanted, for the aunt merely gave him a vague smile and chattered on in all directions.

"Steward? See to the wine, please. Lord Wetherby's goblet is quite neglected. As is Lord Sutherland's. And I fear our dear Captain McNeil may expire of thirst if something is not done immediately."

She paused for breath. "La, I am ever so fearful that the pathetic little body will come floating up to the surface of the river one day, just as we are attempting to enjoy an outing on the barge. La! I daresay my heart should fail me at such a sight."

"I should faint," Eunice put in quietly, gazing up at McNeil with a shiver of helplessness.

McNeil roused himself to smile fondly at her. He had to, he reminded himself sourly. Eunice Wetherby was now his "intended," his betrothed.

He frowned at the wineglass as it was being filled, then picked it up and drank. Events had made the betrothal imperative. The duke's head steward at Bladensburg was no fool. With swift, Germanic thoroughness he'd launched an immediate investigation into the marquis's disappearance. He'd scrutinized the guest list. Suddenly it had seemed imperative to have a sound reason for being attached to the Wetherby party. What better reason than being betrothed to Eunice Wetherby? It would squelch any suspicion the duke might have. And Robert would be safe . . . safe . . .

Eunice was smiling at him possessively. He lifted his glass and sipped again. The betrothal papers had been signed. He'd negotiated the dowry with Lord Wetherby at the young man's insistence. Lord Wetherby suggested two thousand pounds. McNeil could do nothing but agree. However, Lord Wetherby hadn't ten pounds, let alone two thousand. Could he borrow the sum from McNeil? To hold in trust until the marriage took place?

For the sake of his son, McNeil had checked his temper and had written a draft on his London bank for two thousand pounds. He doubted he would ever see that money again. But, for the boy? And for the memory of Flavia?

"Oh, I should faint, also, if the body came floating up. Indeed I should," murmured Eunice's mousy, mild-mannered companion. The young woman spoke seldom, and McNeil thought her about as remarkable as wallpaper. Her rare outburst finished, the unremarkable Abigail Turner faded back into her meringued plum jelly and fell silent.

"Stuff!" said Lord Wetherby, who was bored by the two-week-old topic. "Anyone for a hand of whist?"

Cautiously, McNeil stirred the waters.

"Perhaps the marquis of Bladensburg did *not* drown. Perhaps he was abducted and is being held for ransom."

"Whist?" Lord Wetherby tried again, hopefully.

But it was too late. McNeil's interjection stirred up a new buzz of excitement among the ladies. Feminine voices burst out like a spring shower.

"There has been no ransom demand."

"The child's nightdress was found, wet and washed up on the riverbank."

"The child's footprints were found in the wet mud."

"The duke believes him drowned. It is said the duke is in an insane fury. He will close up Bladensburg."

"The child is definitely drowned, Captain McNeil," the fatter of the two aunts summed up. "All facts point to it. The child woke because of the bright hunter's moon. He wandered through the house and found his way out while the night steward patrolled. With a child's natural fascination for water, he wandered down to the river and—" She paused, shuddering. "And disappeared into it." She shuddered again, as did all the women.

"Whist?" tried Lord Wetherby.

"La, Captain McNeil, I blame the tragedy on the moon, the bright hunter's moon."

Eunice's gown rustled a bit as she twisted in her chair to gaze up at Garth.

"I fear no one slept well under that moon," Eunice said, smiling up at him. "Even *you* were up and about, Captain McNeil."

It was a harsh jolt. His blood began to pump, surging in thick violent thumps. The smile on his face froze to wood. While he waited in dread for Eunice to speak on, he seemed to live out a lifetime. His senses drank in every detail in the room; the dark paneled walls, the faded Flemish tapestry of The Last Supper, candlelight catching the silver epergne filled with green grapes, a dot of plum jelly on Lord Wetherby's collar ruff...

Eunice blushed shyly. "Auntie and I couldn't sleep. So we strolled the garden. We saw your window, Captain McNeil. You were sitting at your writing table, reading by candlelight."

Relief brought buckets of sweat. He could feel his own juices ooze under the brocade waistcoat, the ruffled Holland shirt. Thank God for Jenkins!

"Ship's paperwork," he murmured to Eunice, then turned attention from himself with a quiet "Bladensburg has suffered a great tragedy."

"A great *great* tragedy," the fatter aunt chimed in.

"The *greatest* tragedy." Second aunt.

"I should faint if the little body—" Eunice reiterated.

"Indeed, I should faint, also." Eunice's shadow.

"If not whist, then, backgammon?"

Chapter 11

THE SAME HUNTER'S MOON that witnessed the disappearance of the young marquis of Bladensburg witnessed another, humbler event that night in August of 1754.

Dennis Finny proposed.

Had Flavia been listening, had she been giving the earnest young Quaker her full attention as they sat on the Byng steps under the enormous rising moon, she'd have stopped him before he reached the point of declaration. She'd have spared Dennis the humiliation of rejection.

But she hadn't been listening. Mesmerized by the glorious moon and the fragrance of wild honeysuckle that rambled in the ditch beyond the stone fence, she'd been deep in her own thoughts. Dennis Finny's voice drifted to her as a soothing, background lull. His voice blended softly with Neddy's happy laughter as the boy knelt in the dirt not far from the veranda steps, playing with a new red top the schoolmaster had carved for him.

Immersed in the tranquillity of the beautiful night, she was remembering Robert. And Garth. She ached to see her beloved two. Ached to hold each of them in her arms.

So it was with a jolt that Dennis Finny's words came through to her.

"What I am striving to ask, Mistress Brown— what I am awkwardly attempting to say—is—is— forgive me, but I have lost my heart to thee, Mistress Brown. If thee could forsee any possibility of happiness in union with a lowly schoolmaster, I should find myself the most blessed of the Lord's creatures."

"What?"

Flavia turned to him, puzzled.

"Mr. Finny, you are not suggesting—"

She stopped with an incredulous laugh that she quickly bit off, seeing the agony rise in his eyes. A crimson streak burned slowly up his throat. For a moment his face quivered naked and defenseless under her startled gaze. Then he swallowed and went on bravely.

"Please, Jane, I mean to have my say. Laugh if thee must," he said softly, "but I will have my say."

"Mr. Finny, I cannot—" She got up.

"Please, Jane," he said with firm dignity, "hear me out."

His eyes shone so naked and vulnerable that she would've had to be made of stone to refuse his request. Falling silent, she accommodated him and sat, praying she would find kind, nonwounding words to turn him down.

Distracted by her movements, Neddy looked up and held the top toward her. "Make go!" the boy demanded, then swung his head to Dennis. "Fix! Dennis fix!"

With gentle forbearance the young schoolmaster reached for the top, carefully wound the thin leather cord round its rim and returned the top to Neddy, patting the boy's head. It was a tolerant, merciful gesture and it touched Flavia's heart. Most men were surly with Neddy, uneasy that such a big strong body should be indwelt by an infantile mind. The more robust Neddy grew, the more townsmen seemed to resent and fear him.

Neddy scrambled down onto the hard-packed dirt to play with his top, and Dennis Finny turned to her, his eyes shining with an adoration that frightened her.

"Mr. Finny, I feel it only fair to warn you that I can never—"

"Jane," he said softly. "I'll have my say. Please listen."

Her shawl had slipped from her shoulder onto the step and lay there, gray and plain in a puddle of bright moonlight. Unaware that he did so, Dennis Finny reached for the fringed edge of it and reverently fingered it as he spoke.

"As thee must know, Mistress Brown, my master has been just and fair throughout the whole of my indenture. While I tutor his children in Mr. Tate's schoolhouse, I am allowed to add town children to my class, at the fee of five shillings monthly. This profit is my own, and I've not spent a penny of it. All is invested in tobacco. Returns on that investment have been gratifying."

Flavia nodded. The young Quaker's integrity and business sense were highly regarded by both bondslave and citizen.

"God willing, my indenture is satisfied in January, and Mr. Tate will fulfill his part of the contract. Five acres of bottomland will be ceded to myself."

He glanced up in a quick, shy bid for her approval, and she smiled uncertainly, neither wanting to encourage such confidentiality nor discourage it.

"So I hear, Mr. Finny," she offered noncommitally. "With your profits you will build a schoolhouse on the bottomland and take in paying students."

"That *was* my intention."

He shot her a quick look, then averted his eyes. Nervously he twisted the fringe of her shawl.

"I propose to give *thee* my savings, Jane. To redeem thy indenture."

At first she was certain she'd misheard. Then, as the enormity of the gesture sank in, she gasped.

"Dennis, no. I cannot accept your money. I cannot marry you—no—not ever."

He silenced her outburst with a nod both

humble and strangely dignified. Doggedly, he pursued his thesis.

"Thee does not love me. This I understand and have understood from the first. Whether thee will marry me or whether thee will not, I *will* see thee freed from the Byngs. A few pounds is a small price to pay for thy happiness, Jane."

His voice shook passionately, and she could only stare at him in shocked disbelief. Had ever anyone made a more selfless gesture? His offer made her tremble with selfish longing. Free? Oh, how she longed to be free of the Byngs! But at the expense of a fine young man for whom she could feel nothing stronger than fondness, respect?

No. Impossible.

Abruptly she stood, and the shawl came with her, its fringed edge tugging from his fingers. Startled, he stared at the fringe, then slowly, regretfully opened his hand and released it.

"I've insulted thee," he whispered. "Forgive me."

She moved to retreat into the house, then stopped and turned to him. On impulse, she kissed his hot cheek.

"You've not insulted me, Mr. Finny. On the contrary, you've honored me. You are a fine man, Dennis Finny. I'm honored to be your friend."

He winced at the word "friend," and she grasped for kinder words to use, words that wouldn't wound this gentle large-hearted Quaker.

Softly she said, "I feel true affection for you, Dennis. But it's not wifely affection, and therefore I cannot marry you. It would be unfair of me. I could never give you the love you deserve."

He looked up, his eyes dying. One last fiery coal of hope blazed up, lighting those eyes for a moment.

"Marry me, Jane! I shall ask nothing of thee," he vowed passionately. "All I ask is to sit at fireside at day's end and partake of thy sweet companionship. Nothing more would I force upon thee. I swear it!"

She stared at him, her heart thudding wildly. To be free of her indenture? Free? Oh, think of it! But at what price? To give herself to a man she didn't love and, ultimately, to cheat both of them of happiness. No. Dennis deserved better. His selfless offer bore testimony to that.

He was holding his breath, waiting for her answer, oblivious to Neddy, who knelt in the dirt pounding the red top against the ground, crying, "Fix! Dennis, fix!"

"Jane?" he whispered, his voice shaking.

She looked into his eyes, then gazed away and shook her head.

"No."

A small word, only a whisper. Still, it closed the issue as effectively as if it were the massive olivewood doors swinging shut at Tewksbury Hall.

He groaned. It was a soul-burdened groan that ended in a heavy sigh. He seemed to grapple inside of himself, searching for a smile.

At last he found one, drew it out and fitted it sadly upon his face.

"I'll teach Neddy to use the top," he said softly. "Then I'll be going."

If she'd assumed that was the end of Dennis Finny, then she'd reckoned without knowing the strength of the quiet young Quaker. For he was back at the Byngs' a couple of weeks later, on an afternoon in September. His smile was cheerful. The devotion in his eyes seemed undimmed. He'd brought neighborhood gossip, with which to amuse Flavia. He'd brought a fresh *Maryland Gazette,* which she seized with a happy cry and perused immediately.

A man of tact, Dennis Finny made no reference to his passionate declaration, and for this Flavia felt grateful. She wanted Dennis as a friend, not a suitor. He seemed to sense this, behaving accordingly.

When he arrived, Flavia was flushed with heat, working on the side veranda, sorting and sizing heaps of cucumbers. She'd been set to the task of pickle-making by Mrs. Byng, who was napping away the sultry afternoon in the house.

Alert to saving her a scolding from Mrs. Byng, Dennis Finny didn't interrupt her work, but pitched in and helped. As they worked, they talked cheerfully, conversation ranging far afield, taking in the weather, the Chesapeake sailings, Mr. Byng's Sabbath Day sermon, the market price of oysters, the Tate boys' school-house pranks and even the latest cheeky escapade of Betsy Simm and the notorious ne'er-do-well, Jimmy Barlow.

There was friendly ease in working side by side with Dennis Finny. Flavia couldn't help but notice that he was quick to preempt the heavy tasks, sparing her. Side by side, they scrubbed cucumbers, wrapped each in a washed grape leaf, packed the wrapped cucumbers into deep crocks and added dill, spices and salt. It was Dennis who carried each heavy crock around the house to the shed where the vinegar barrel stood. He filled each crock with vinegar, clamped the lid down tightly, much more tightly than she could've managed, and carried each crock to the cold cellar.

When the tedious task was done, they shared cold water from the dipper at the well. Then they sank down to the cool grass under a cottonwood tree. Flavia sighed tiredly, smoothing the damp clinging tendrils of hair from her brow. The day was hot. Hoping for a breeze to cool her head, she drew off her mobcap. As she did so, Dennis Finny's eyes went to her hair. A wistful look passed over his face. When he caught her studying him, he blushed violently and looked away.

So, Flavia thought. It's not over. He still hopes. How unhappy for him. She knew she must put him straight. He must waste no more time on her, but look in other directions for a helpmeet. There were many indentured girls who would cherish the security that a sober, industrious schoolmaster could offer.

She sat up and smoothed her muslin apron,

thinking what to say. The heat of the day was stifling. Even the slight breeze off the garden carried heat, and in the garden heat-loving grass-hoppers leaped high in some chaotic dance. Faintly, she could hear the dry, burring sound of their wings.

"Mr. Finny, your hours of leisure are precious and few. Those hours might be spent in a better fashion than toiling here at the Byngs'."

His intelligent gray eyes lifted to hers. A puff of garden-hot air stirred his damp muslin shirt.

"I call it not toil. I call it my heart's pleasure."

"Then your heart is ill invested."

He smiled patiently, as though she were a child.

"A heart is never ill invested when it seeks to love."

Flavia drew a frustrated breath, then expelled it. To extinguish the hope in those direct eyes, she would have to be blunt.

"Mr. Finny there is *no* future for you here at the Byngs'. *None*."

A moment passed.

"Then I ask no future, Mistress Brown. I will content myself with the present."

At his simple but eloquent declaration of where he intended to stand in the matter, she could only stare at him, bewildered.

"Are all Quakers so stubborn, so determined?"

At the utter seriousness of her question, the grave eyes began to twinkle with humor.

"You call us 'Quakers;' we call ourselves Friends."

"'Friends'?"

With a slight smile, Dennis leaned back on one elbow, rippling the grass between them with his free hand.

"Let me tell thee about myself, Jane," he began slowly. "I did not grow up as a Friend. I was born the ninth son of a country squire in Essex. Ninth, I had no hope of inheriting. My father determined I should go into the Anglican clergy. He sent me to Oxford to study. But I wanted no part of the church. I decided to seek my fortune in the New England. I shipped as an indentured schoolmaster."

Flavia nodded, leaning back in the cool grass. The smell of wild onion rose faintly from the grass, and a white cabbage moth fluttered up.

"The voyage was a hell for bondslaves, as well you know, Jane. By the second month, decent folk were behaving like a pack of wolves. Only one man took up the cause of justice. He defended the weak and the old. He pled the widows' case. He stood up to the Newgate convicts in their thievery. For this, he received harsh treatment from captain and crew, beatings from others."

Dennis raised his eyes to hers. Grave, steady eyes.

"I thought him a fool, Jane."

There was silence, silence so deep that Flavia could almost hear the beat of Dennis's heart. Moved, she reached out and touched his shoulder for a moment.

"The voyage was too much for him. When he died, I learned he'd been a Friend. His Bible came into my hands. Only one verse was underlined. Micah, chapter six, verse eight:

*"He hath showed thee, O man, what is good;
and what doth the Lord require of thee, but to
do justly, and to love mercy, and to walk humbly
with thy God?"*

Dennis's eyes held hers.

"I became a Friend that day. I received Jesus."

Flavia drew a deep, shaky breath. The admiration she felt for Finny's quest was swallowed up by her own sense of defeat.

"If you fight for justice, you fight windmills," she whispered bitterly. "Justice doesn't exist."

He looked at her evenly.

"Then we must make it exist."

The sudden, imperious click of heels on the wooden veranda warned that Mrs. Byng's nap had ended. Dennis Finny lunged to his feet and offered Flavia a hand. She got up, too, but slowly. Every muscle ached. She was just gaining her feet when Mrs. Byng swooped off the veranda and into the yard. From the expression on the woman's face, Flavia could see that Mrs. Byng was torn between the urge to scold for laziness and the stronger urge to grill Dennis Finny for gossip of the wealthy Tates. Indecision hovered in her sharp eyes, and Flavia took advantage of it, leaping in.

"Mr. Finny is just leaving, ma'am. He's brought you a gazette, and then he tarried to help with the pickles."

Mrs. Byng's peevish look faded. The woman always counted herself ahead when she got something for nothing. A free gazette *and* free labor amounted to a coup. Mrs. Byng granted Dennis a smile.

"Ah, Mr. Finny."

"Mistress Byng." He bowed slightly. But in the Quaker manner, he didn't remove his hat in deference to a superior. Mrs. Byng's smile chilled. Flavia knew Mrs. Byng found Quaker habits irritating. But the woman recovered herself and began to probe.

"How is dear Mrs. Tate? No doubt the dear lady is quite exhausted, always entertaining guests, as she is, always called upon, poor dear, to give dancing assemblies for her daughters. But then, if one has daughters as plain as Maryann and Deborah Tate, one must do *something* to attract suitors, mustn't one?"

She waited for an acquiescing nod or murmur of agreement from Dennis Finny, but he refused to accommodate her, and Flavia's respect for the dignified young bond servant soared.

Mrs. Byng trilled on. "But then, the Tates are Roman Catholics, and papists do love dancing assemblies and all manner of revelry. It is the pagan in them, Mr. Finny. The Reverend Mr. Byng says so."

She nodded excitedly. "Papists are only a stone's throw from their pagan roots, and there is not a one of them that would not rise up and murder us True Believers in our beds at night, if the wicked pope so directed. Oh, indeed, Mr. Finny!"

She stopped to catch her breath, and Flavia stole a glance at Dennis Finny. His intelligent eyes glinted with irritation.

"Thy opinion of dancing assemblies could not have come at a more opportune time, ma'am.

Mistress Tate is currently preparing invitations for her October assembly. Thee and the Reverend Mr. Byng were to have been invited. With thy permission, I shall endeavor to explain to Mrs. Tate that thee would not welcome such an invitation."

Flavia choked back a laugh. She knew Mrs. Byng would give her eyeteeth to be invited to one of the lavish, three-day dancing assemblies at the Tate plantation.

Mrs. Byng gulped, stumbled verbally for a bit, then sputtered her way to firmer ground.

"Thank you, Mr. Finny, but the Reverend Mr. Byng and I should consider it our sacred *duty* to attend the dancing assembly. If we refuse to mingle with papists, then how shall we convert them?"

She launched into more prying questions about the Tates, and Dennis Finny politely tried to take his leave without discrediting Mrs. Byng, the Tates, the pope, the Anglican or Catholic churches. It was a large order, and he managed it adroitly, to Flavia's admiration.

At last he managed to break away, and Mrs. Byng frowned after him in vague disappointment. She'd got no juicy tidbits. To Flavia's irritation, the woman made one more try.

"Oh, Mr. Finny," she called, arresting his escape. "Shall you hunt grouse in the fall? After corn harvest?"

Dennis turned patiently and rested his hand upon the low stone wall that fronted the yard.

"Yes, ma'am. That I shall."

"Well, then, good luck in the shoot, Mr.

Finny. Grouse are fine-tasting birds. Oh, indeed, Mr. Finny, the Reverend Mr. Byng always says there is nothing better to be brought to table than a fine fat grouse, roasted to perfection."

Dennis Finny paused. Flavia was amused to note that his pause was not long enough to be interpreted as impolite, but just long enough to be unsettling for greedy Mrs. Byng.

"May I prevail upon thee, ma'am, to accept a brace of grouse if my shoot goes well?"

Mrs. Byng's feigned wide-eyed surprise disgusted Flavia.

"Dear me! What an idea! No, I could not accept such a gift. No, indeed. Oh—oh, well. I daresay you will persuade me into it, Mr. Finny." She laughed lightly. "You are a very persuasive young man, and I am *quite* at the disadvantage."

"Not at all, ma'am," Dennis said solemnly. "It is *I* who am at the disadvantage."

Flavia ducked her head to hide the smile of amusement that leaped to her lips. When she looked up again, Dennis Finny had gone out the gate, had jumped the ditch full of honeysuckle and was loping toward the Tate plantation at a sure, steady pace.

She watched him go.

"I like you, Dennis Finny," she thought. "I respect you. And that is precisely why I shall never marry you. You deserve better than a wife who would lie in your arms each night grieving for another man."

Chapter 12

"Lud, Jane. I could speak the lines plainer than *that*. I could play Lady Macbeth better than *she*, and with a basket over my head."

Flavia burst into a giggle, then suppressed it.

"Shssh, Betsy. Everyone will hear."

"Let 'em. I say, that as an actress, Mrs. Hamilton-St. James makes a very fine cow."

Flavia giggled again. Betsy Simm's evaluation of the leading lady of the Hamilton-St. James Players was irreverent, but accurate. Anyone who'd frequented London's Drury Lane must agree. And Flavia had loved theater and gone often. So had Elizabeth Simm, before her father, the earl, banished her to the colonies under indenture, as punishment for promiscuous behavior.

Flavia and Elizabeth were sitting in the half-pence section, which meant they were sitting upon heaps of hay in the Tate warehouse, along with the other bond servants and poor. The warehouse had been lent as a makeshift theater for the traveling troupe. Chestertown's theater had been damaged by fire.

Flavia scratched her ankle. The hay itched. Stiff spears of it poked through her stockings. The hay was new-mown. Its strong pungent smell conjured up sneezes, and when anyone shifted haunch or leg, the actors' lines were lost in the loud rustling of hay.

The loft ran along the south end of the warehouse, the stage at the north. Between were rows of rough trestle benches, the pit. The ordinary citizens of Chestertown sat there. A few bewigged heads bobbed in the pit and a matching number of modest corded silk gowns. But most of the jackets that stirred in the pit were plain serge, and the gowns were Virginia-cloth with collars of homemade lace and white starched caps completing the gown.

Hastily constructed boxes flanked the stage. Here sat the gentry and anyone else able to pay dear. The Tates occupied the largest box, nearest the stage. Expensively bewigged and garbed in English silks, the family was dressed well but not showily. To the rear of the box, behind Maryann and Deborah Tate, sat Dennis Finny. Flavia was surprised. She'd thought all Quakers objected to theater. Dennis was flanked by two young Tate boys. A large book lay open across their knees, and Flavia guessed they were following the text of the Shakespeare play.

The question of "pit" or "box" seats had been

a touchy issue in the Byng household. From the first posting of the Hamilton-St. James playbill on the boards at the White Swan and at the Rose and Crown, Mr. Byng had declared himself for the pit. He could not, he vowed, part with an additional six shillings to sit three nights in a box. The pit would do them.

The pit would *not* do for them, Mrs. Byng had countered, setting off an explosive charge. Should all of Chestertown think the Byngs cheap and common, she'd argued, as Flavia and Neddy tried to stay out of range of the flaring tempers.

The argument went on two days. Mrs. Byng won, as Flavia had expected. Immediately Mrs. Byng packed her powdered wig into a rush-weave box and sent Neddy to town with it, to have it dressed at the wigmaker's. Unfortunately, Neddy wandered home from his mission by way of the creek. When he presented the box to Mrs. Byng, muddy water trickled from the rushing.

There'd been the devil to pay: a switching for Neddy and a hard slap in the face for Flavia when she'd tried to soothe the situation. Mrs. Byng's temper didn't cool until Flavia diverted her by offering to embroider red roses upon her calamanco dancing pumps, in preparation for the Tates' dancing assembly.

Mrs. Byng now sat proudly in her box. But the stiff set of her shoulders told Flavia she wasn't happy. And small wonder. Two things must grate, Flavia thought with amusement. First, Dennis Finny—a Quaker and a bondslave—

sat in the Tate box. Second, the town rogue
Jimmy Barlow and his gang of ne'er-do-wells
occupied the box behind hers.

With the handsome arrogance of a scamp who
cares not a whit what the town thinks of him,
Jimmy Barlow lounged low in his chair, feet
propped against the box boards, a sly grin on his
face. Bored with the play, he'd turned his chair
to face the loft and was making a public show of
flirting with Betsy Simm.

Catching his suggestive gestures, Betsy giggled admiringly.

"Jimmy Barlow is drunk!" she whispered.

"Drunk and out of his mind," returned Flavia
with a smile. "Why does he irritate the gentry
by hiring box seats?"

Mischief sparkled in Betsy's dark eyes.

"Because I dared him to."

"Betsy!"

"Oh, you're thinking he has no money, Jane.
But this week he has. Five men from Annapolis
rode all the way to Chestertown to challenge
Jimmy in Indian wrestling. The wager was ten
pounds. Jimmy won." She sighed admiringly. "I
guess Jimmy Barlow must be the champion
Indian wrestler of all America. Maybe of all the
world."

Below, the object of Betsy's admiration loudly
kissed the palm of his hand and blew the kiss
loftward.

Betsy giggled. "Oh, he *is* three sheets to the
wind!"

At the commotion in Jimmy Barlow's box,
Mrs. Byng turned and gave him a scathing look.

Mr. Byng did not. Cowardly, he pretended not to notice. Mrs. Byng pointedly shifted her chair, so that Jimmy Barlow should have the full of her corsetted, disapproving back.

With a wiggle of his finger, Jimmy Barlow alerted the loft and pointed toward Mrs. Byng. Elaborately he leaned toward the stiff, disapproving back and made his finger hover just inches from Mrs. Byng's wig. He pretended to follow the leaping itinerary of a louse in the wig. He snatched at the nonexistent louse, dashed it to the floor and ground it beneath the heel of his boot.

Betsy Simm giggled. The loft tittered, and from the stage the actors glared loftward. Even young Mary Wooster laughed happily for a moment, her fair, freckled face losing its downcast expression. And for this alone, Flavia silently blessed the outrageous Jimmy Barlow. Mary Wooster had never been the same since her public whipping in May. And the child's waist was thickened with still another pregnancy. Flavia's heart went out to her. She wished she could do something. But, what? She would do well if she simply managed to keep herself safe. But still . . .

"Mary," she whispered, "come sit with us."

Quickly, the girl complied, scrambling through the hay.

Encouraged by titters from loft and pit, Jimmy Barlow descended to additional buffoonery. His shining moment came at the expense of Mrs. Hamilton-St. James. The actress had just reached Lady Macbeth's most famous scene.

Wringing and rubbing her blood-guilty hands, she moaned with great emotion.

"*Out* damned spot," she groaned loudly. "*Out*, I say!*"

Jimmy Barlow stood up, swaying drunkenly.

"Ay, out with it. Out with the whole damned play! Give us comedy, m'girl. Give us "*A Hob in the Well*."

Immediately one of Jimmy's drunk cronies woke from his stupor and said, "Lesh go t' the Rose 'n' Crown."

As Flavia watched, wide-eyed, Jimmy Barlow evidently found the suggestion an excellent one. Or else the canny rogue realized he was about to be thrown out. For he bowed elaborately to the fiercely glaring Mrs. Hamilton-St. James, then strode out, laughing. His cronies trailed drunkenly behind.

Sighs of relief echoed from pit to highest box as the play resumed. The only sigh that was not one of relief was Betsy's. She sighed with deep admiration.

She whispered, "Too bad, Jane, that Jimmy Barlow isn't rich and well born. I shall have to wed dull old Mr. Gresham. And a poor second choice he is."

Flavia's glance flew to the box where the rich planter sat with his grown children. Mr. Gresham's expression was severe, and the look that followed Jimmy Barlow out the door was a black one.

"Your master?" whispered Flavia, dumbfounded. "But he has a wife."

Elizabeth shrugged.

"Mrs. Gresham has been an invalid for years. She grows worse and worse, poor thing. She hasn't left her bed in two months, and now she's spitting blood. It won't be long."

Mary Wooster set the hay hissing as she moved closer.

"Your master won't marry you, Betsy," she whispered bitterly. "If a master wants you, he takes you."

Elizabeth tossed her glossy black mane.

"*Not* if he intends to keep all the equippage he was born with. Jimmy Barlow has made it known from one end of Kent County to the other, that if Mr. Gresham forces me, Jimmy will—"

A natural actress, Betsy paused for effect.

"—will cut off his—his 'necessities,'" she finished.

Mary Wooster tittered, then grew wistful.

"I wish Jimmy Barlow liked *me.*"

And me, Flavia thought, then shook her head at her own ridiculousness.

As though one person, the three of them leaned forward and gazed out over the pit toward the Gresham box. The play was proceeding, but they ignored it. They studied Mr. Gresham. It was Elizabeth Simm who finally summed up their separate thoughts in one tart statement.

"He has," she said, "big ears."

Then she shrugged gaily. "Ah, well. So long as that's not the *only* thing big on him, I shan't be disappointed."

With a giggle, she seized her shawl and began scrambling through the rustling aromatic hay, heading for the ladder.

"Don't go!" Flavia whispered, suddenly realizing she'd not felt so lighthearted in months. Not since the days at Tewksbury when she'd sat on the nursery floor, playing with Robert and giggling at his antics.

Mary Wooster's face fell, too. "Betsy, you'll miss the comedy. You'll miss *Flora; or a Hob in the Well*. Where are you going?"

"Where?" Betsy flicked back her glossy hair. She whispered, "I shall decide 'where' when I reach the bottom of the ladder. Perhaps I shall flirt with the manager of the Hamilton-St. James Players and run away to become an actress. Perhaps I shall stay in Chestertown, marry Mr. Gresham and become a fine, rich lady. Then again," she whispered with a mischievous giggle, "perhaps I shall run to the Rose and Crown and let Jimmy Barlow give me a rum toddy and a kiss."

On a chilly night in late September, Flavia sat near the kitchen fire, embroidering Mrs. Byng's calamanco dancing pump as Mr. Byng read aloud to his wife. She dreaded the approach of winter. Winter would mean being shut in with the Byngs. Evenings would be too cold, too blustery for solitary walks or for sitting out upon the veranda. She would be forced to the hearth.

Mr. Byng droned on in a monotone, reading from a new *Maryland Gazette*, which he'd bought at the royal customs house on the waterfront in Chestertown. His voice made Flavia nod with sleepiness. She forced her fingers on, drawing scarlet threads through the coarse, impenetrable fabric.

In the interest of economy, Mrs. Byng allowed only one fire in the evening, and that was in the kitchen. In this Mrs. Byng reaped a dividend. The kitchen fireplace backed up to the Byng bedchamber. An iron box protruded from the kitchen fireplace into the bedchamber, forming a crude sort of warming stove that took the iciness from the sleeping arrangements.

Stingy, Mrs. Byng burned few candles in winter. Instead, she used a cheap rush lamp. The lamp sat upon the kitchen table, flaring and sending up nasty feathers of black smoke whenever Mr. Byng breathed too hard as he sat reading by its light.

Mr. Byng droned on. Even Mrs. Byng began to nod as she sat rocking in her new chair. The chair was an extravagance for the Byngs, and Flavia had noticed that Mrs. Byng's stingy little economies did not apply to her own comforts. Her latest purchase was proof of it. It was an expensive, all-wood Philadelphia chair, set upon rockers by a clever chairmaker in Annapolis. Never had there been such an unusual and wonderfully comfortable chair, and Mrs. Byng felt like a queen in owning the first of its kind in Chestertown. Everyone flocked to see it, and Mrs. Byng's proudest hour arrived when Mrs. Tate herself rode over in a stylish landau to examine the chair.

"Now the London society news, wife..." Mr. Byng droned on.

Flavia leaned forward. Often there was news of titled persons she'd known. Mr. Byng droned on, reading of sumptuous balls, of titled births, marriages, deaths...

."Her Grace, the duchess of Tewksbury—"

Flavia jerked. The sharp point of her needle jabbed into her finger. A drop of rich, red blood rose. She jerked the finger to her mouth and sat trembling. . . .

"—died of the smallpox on the twenty-first day of September, in the year of our Lord, 1753. . . . The earl of Dunwood set sail for Virginia on—"

Her ears roared. The slipper slid down her gown and fell to the floor with a light clunk. She couldn't get her breath. Fighting dizziness, she tried to find her feet, tried to leave. But her feet were numb stumps.

At last she managed to pull herself up. Panting, she stumbled to the door and went out. A cold wind cut through her thin muslin work dress, but she scarcely noticed. She lurched out into the dark yard, groped her way to the low stone fence and fell against it.

Dead... dear heaven, everyone thought her dead. . . . She'd assumed this, prepared herself for this; but now that the moment was here, she realized she'd made no preparation for it at all. Shock. Numbing, terrifying shock... her ears rang with her own death knell.

For the next few days, she went about her

chores in a fog. Dazed and heartsick, she tried
to come to terms with it. *Flavia Rochambeau is
gone . . . gone . . . only Jane Brown lives . . .
Jane . . . Jane . . . and what will become of this
Jane? Who is she? What does her future hold?*

Autumn deepened. The nights grew crisp and
leaves began to fall. Flavia's breath punctuated
the chill night air and hovered there—a trail of
icy steam in the lantern light—as she hurried to
the barn to settle Neddy for sleep. The boy
wouldn't be allowed to sleep in the kitchen until
December, and she worried about frostbite.

Pushing open the creaking barn door, she let
herself in, hung her lantern on a hook and
turned, smiling as Neddy's shout greeted her. A
single window spilled moonlight into the dark
barn, and Neddy had been playing with his top
in the patch of moonlight.

"Jane! Play—play."

She went to Neddy and patted his smiling
face. Peach fuzz sprouted on his cheeks. Soon
he would be a man physically, and life must
grow even crueler for him.

"No more playing, Neddy. Bedtime. But first
we must tidy up the barn. Come, get up. Help
Jane pick up things."

"No. Play!"

"Come, Neddy. Help Jane tidy up. If Mr.
Byng finds shovels and terrapin lances all over
the floor, Mr. Byng will scold."

The boy's face darkened with fear. He scrambled up and looked about him, bewildered by

the array of tools to pick up, unable to formulate a plan to begin. Tears of frustration rose in his eyes.

By accident, Flavia had discovered the boy could learn and remember if she set tasks to music. Music seemed to soothe and settle him. She began to sing softly:

"First Neddy picks up the lances, the lances, the lances..."

Neddy's face brightened. He joined in the singing and dove to the task. Soon the barn was tidy, and Neddy climbed into the hayrack, snuggling into his nest of hay and tattered blankets.

"Jane," he demanded, "find doll."

Flavia searched for the doll for several minutes. Finally she found it in the sheep pen, half under a ewe. She had to kick at the ewe's thick flank to get it to move. The smelly beast bleated, then lunged to its feet, turning and butting at Flavia.

The doll was a cornhusk one that Dennis Finny had made. Flavia had completed it, painting wild berry stain on its face for eyes and lips. She'd made a tiny jacket for the doll. Neddy spent hours putting the jacket on and off.

She put the doll into Neddy's demanding hands. He cuddled it under the covers and squeezed his eyes shut. He began to sing.

"Now Neddy go...sleep, sleep, sleep. Now..."

Shivering, she was glad to extinguish the lantern light and step back into the warmth of the kitchen, even if it meant another tedious evening with the Byngs. Shedding her cloak and hanging it on a hook, she gathered up her workbasket and sank to a bench by the fire. She threaded her needle with scarlet wool twist and picked up Mrs. Byng's calamanco dancing pump.

On the other side of the kitchen, Mr. Byng sat by the sputtering light of the rush lamp, reading his Sabbath sermon to his wife. She rocked in her Philadelphia chair, rubbing her face with a piece of cut lemon as she listened. The lemon was her nightly beauty preparation, to bleach and whiten her complexion for the Tates' ball. As she rocked and rubbed, she punctured her husband's dull droning with shrill outbursts.

"How true, Mr. Byng. You have hit the nail upon the head, sir. Lust is the cause of all sin and sin the cause of all lust.

"I shouldn't wonder that when your sermon reaches the ear of the bishop of London—

"La, sir, you shall be wanted at Kensington Palace.

"I shouldn't take it amiss, sir, to be called to London—"

Kensington Court? London? It was ludicrous, and Flavia couldn't help but snicker. Her scornful snicker was only the slightest sound, but the Reverend Byng caught it and looked at her immediately. It was as though he'd been tuned to her every movement, her slightest utterance.

"You've an opinion of my sermon, Jane?"

A chill passed over her. It was frightening to be watched so closely. And the curious flame that burned up in Mr. Byng's eyes...

"No, sir," she whispered, quickly dipping her head to her needlework. Instantly she regretted lowering her head. The firelight would play in her red hair, warming it to copper. Often she'd been aware of Mr. Byng staring at her hair, the lids of his eyes hooded to mere slits.

"Jane has no opinion," Mrs. Byng sputtered, rocking faster. "Jane is a bondslave. Bondslaves have no opinion at all." She turned to Flavia. "Go to bed, Jane."

Flavia rose to obey, but Mr. Byng lifted his hand.

"Jane shan't retire until after prayers, my dear. No one is excluded from evening prayers. Excepting Neddy, of course. But Neddy is a fool, and I can't abide praying over a fool."

Flavia tensed, as Mrs. Byng swallowed her annoyance and smiled sweetly at her husband.

"Nor can I, Mr. Byng. You've no idea, husband, how vexed I am at the thought of Neddy sleeping in the house this winter."

She threw Flavia a vengeful look.

"Perhaps, husband, Neddy could stay the winter in the barn?"

Flavia trembled for Neddy. Her hands stiffened and the calamanco pump thumped to the floor. Darting a scared look at Mrs. Byng, she snatched up the shoe, brushed it off and whirled to Mr. Byng.

"Please, sir? Neddy will freeze sleeping in the barn. It's too cold for the child."

When Mr. Byng seemed to consider Flavia's soft words, Mrs. Byng's annoyance warmed to anger.

"Neddy is *not* a child. He's a half-wit, an

animal. All animals have the knack of staying warm."

Flavia lost her senses.

"He's *not* an animal. He's a little boy. Trapped in a man's body."

Instantly, she knew she'd been foolish to argue. Color rose in Mrs. Byng's face. Clutching the shoe, Flavia backed away, fearing the woman would fly up out of her chair and smack her.

But Mrs. Byng attacked from a new and bewildering direction.

Smiling sweetly at her husband, she simpered, "I vow, sir. Should the wife of Maryland's best preacher endure a scolding from a mere bond-slave?"

Mr. Byng puffed up in pride.

"Indeed not, wife!" Flavia found herself the target of two sets of angry eyes.

"You will repent, Jane," Mr. Byng ordered. "Come here, chit. Kneel. We shall begin evening prayers at once."

Heart ticking fearfully, Flavia obeyed. Mrs. Byng came and knelt, too. A prim, pleased smile played over the tight lips. Mr. Byng knelt between them, placing one hand upon his wife's bowed head and one upon Flavia. His touch made her cringe. His touch frightened her far more than did the odd looks he sent her way when he believed no one was watching him.

Pompously and in a pulpit voice, Mr. Byng began to pray. Flavia tried not to listen, tried not to stiffen in growing anger when his prayer dealt with her.

"Lastly, Gracious Creator, there kneels before Thee the most contemptible of Thy creatures, Jane Brown. Thou hast put Jane into my care. Thou hast marked her with flaming hair that we might be warned of the lust that burns in her wicked heart. Cleanse and purify this miserable creature . . ."

The long-awaited invitation to the Tate dancing assembly arrived, and from that moment on, talk in the Byng household and talk throughout Chestertown centered on the ball. It was to be the grandest Kent County had ever seen. Mr. Tate was sparing no expense. Guests would come from Annapolis, Baltimore, Philadelphia and even Williamsburg. Gossips reported Mrs. Tate had ordered expensive guest "favors." Each gentleman guest would receive a silver snuffbox to commemorate the ball; each lady, a tiny silver nutmeg grater.

To Flavia's disgust, Mrs. Byng waxed ecstatic anticipating her nutmeg grater. She chattered that no woman of quality traveled about without one, and that at quality tables it was fashionable to take one's silver grater and nutmeg from one's bag and genteelly season one's food and drink. Indeed, she demanded of Flavia, hadn't Mrs. Tate so seasoned her rum toddy the day she'd called at the Byngs to see the Philadelphia chair?

Rumor said Maryann Tate was the reason for the lavish ball. Gossips predicted Maryann's betrothal would be announced. The same gossips insisted the silver favors would be engraved

with the entwined initials of the happy couple.
Privately, Dennis Finny confirmed both rumors
to Flavia. Flavia took a small, bitter pleasure in
withholding that news from Mrs. Byng.

A few days before the dancing assembly was
to open, Mrs. Byng went into a nervous tizzy.
No one could please her. Flavia couldn't iron
the flocked silk ball gown to Mrs. Byng's exact-
ing standards. Being a novice at pressing, she
had to do the gown over and over. Then, when
tears of hot exhaustion blurred her eyes and
she'd made a tiny scorch mark on the hem of
the underskirt, Mrs. Byng flew into a rage and
slapped her.

Mrs. Byng was also vexed that she had no
maid to take to the ball.

"Everyone shall arrive with a Negro, Mr.
Byng," she observed gloomily as she sat in the
dining room over an uneaten breakfast. "All of
the ladies will bring a slave to fetch and carry
for them. All except myself."

Mr. Byng helped himself to another square of
steaming corn bread as Flavia served the platter.

"Not so, my dear. Only ladies of quality will
bring their Negroes."

Mrs. Byng's sharp little cry pierced Flavia's
eardrums.

"Indeed, sir! Am I not quality? Are you not
quality?"

Mr. Byng scowled.

"Of course we are quality. There is no one in
the country to say we are not. But Negroes are
costly."

Mrs. Byng sighed. Propping her elbows on

either side of her uneaten breakfast, she rested her chin in her hands.

"I quite sympathize, Mr. Byng. The church is stingy." She sighed again. "Still, it will be *so* odious for you at the ball, Mr. Byng. It will be *so* humiliating for you to know that *your* wife must brush off her own shoes and powder her own wig between dancing sets."

Flavia glanced at Mr. Byng. He reddened, a sign he was becoming angry.

"You *shall* have a maid at the ball."

Mrs. Byng's small eyes glittered with triumph. She pounced upon the corn bread as Flavia held the platter to her.

"You shall use Jane," Mr. Byng announced.

Mrs. Byng dropped the corn bread as though it were poisoned.

"Jane!" she spat. "Jane is not a Negro, Mr. Byng. Jane is nigh worthless."

Flavia flushed, anger choking her. She would never get used to this humiliation, *never*. To be discussed as though she were a trussed chicken, hanging from a tree on Market Day.

Rashly she said, "I will not serve at the ball."

Two sets of astonished eyes turned to her. She quaked. Mrs. Byng was quickest to recover.

"You see, Mr. Byng?" she crowed. "You see how cheeky and insolent bondslaves are? No Negro would dare speak so."

Lest she drop it, Flavia set the shaking platter on the table. Mr. Byng's face was purple. He rose slowly, his eyes baleful.

"To my study, chit. At once. An hour of

kneeling in prayer will mend your disobedient ways."

Fear raced through her. She swallowed hard.

"Please, sir, I—sir, Mrs. Byng would have me finish her dancing slippers."

But he pointed to his study, and there was nothing she could do but obey. She moved toward it, gooseflesh racing up and down her arms. Behind her, Mrs. Byng's vicious snipe hissed.

"'Tisn't prayer Jane needs, but a whipping."

Mr. Byng's steps followed her into the study. The door banged shut, and Flavia knelt quickly, her stomach churning in revulsion. Mr. Byng's knees cracked in chorus as he knelt beside her. His breath was rancid, carrying the odor of a tooth gone bad. Flavia shrank from it, trying to prepare herself for the inevitable touch. His hand—hot and fleshy—slowly groped to her shoulder.

Listening intently, Flavia thrilled to the violin music that flowed out from the ballroom, spilling down to the brick terrace. Laughter drifted down, too, and the empty terrace was fragrant with the smell of lemon trees that stood in clay pots, gracing the brickwork.

Flavia hugged her shawl to her shoulders and stepped out of the way as a file of Negroes padded softly out of the night and began to trundle the potted lemon trees from terrace to greenhouse where the delicate trees would be safe from the night air. She supposed the pots would be trundled out again in the morning for the pleasure of the guests. The Tates had overlooked no detail.

The Negroes sang softly as they worked. They hummed to the rich violin strains, glancing over their shoulders at the brightly lighted ballroom windows where, in time to the music, silks and varicolored brocades whirled by.

When the Negroes were done, Flavia slipped up on to the terrace and hid herself behind a huge, brick-encircled oak tree where she might have a clear view. The ball was a splendid one. Brilliant light fell upon the terrace in patches. The music drew her ever closer, setting her heart alilt. Cares drained away. How she missed such pleasures!

She knew she should be knitting in the maids' cubbyhole, alert to Mrs. Byng's needs. But the night was too fine, the gaiety of the ball too seductive.

A sticky leaf drifted down from a high branch of the oak, catching to her skirt. She flicked it off. She must take good care of the gown, even if the gown was only cheap lutestring silk and heavily mended. It was a used gown Mrs. Byng had received from her sister. Too small for Mrs. Byng, the gown was destined to be unraveled this winter and its silk thread sent to the weaver to be rewoven into heavier cloth for chair pads. The gown fit passably well. Mrs. Byng's lips had pursed with annoyance, seeing its drab olive color come to life when set against Flavia's hair. Mrs. Byng had directed her back to the muslin, then again reconsidered. If the Byng maid wore muslin to the Tates, might not the Byngs be considered cheap?

The elegant violin music ceased in the Tate ballroom. Musicians in dark green livery filed down from the platform in the music alcove. Three black fiddlers ascended the platform. They raised their instruments and at once a merry country jig began. Laughter exploded and everyone clapped. With great hilarity, the strange, hopping step began.

The happy music was infectious. Flavia tapped her toe to the rhythm. On impulse, she lifted her skirts and tried to imitate the curious American step. She stumbled over her own feet, falling against the oak tree, laughing.

"Lord, but you're a clumsy wench!" a low voice teased.

Her laughter froze in her throat. She whirled around. She could see no one.

The good-natured voice came out of the darkness again.

"You must be a Londoner. Londoners never can catch on to our jigs. The jig is Negro, you know. To learn it proper, you must go down to the slave cabins at Corn Festival."

Seizing her shawl from where it had dropped, she made to go. But her way was blocked. Striding up into the light was a tall, very handsome young man with very black hair. He had Irish eyes. Eyes designed for laughter.

"Here, wench. Let me teach you."

He held out a hand for her to take, but the hand was encumbered with a man's powdered wig. He stared at the wig as though he'd forgotten he held it. His rich easy laughter made light of his gaffe.

"Lord, I'm an oaf," he said, tossing the wig aside and sending a scowl chasing it. "Damned thing's too hot. Boils my brain."

He laughed again and studied her. Ducking her head, Flavia moved to slip past him, but he'd have none of it.

He caught her wrist, and unwillingly she was pulled into the bright elongated rectangles of light that fell from the ballroom windows to the brick terrace.

"You want to learn the jig. And so you shall."

Fear fluttered in her throat. Not fear of the young man. Fear of Mrs. Byng.

"Please, sir. I should not be here. I'm only a bond servant."

"I can see that," he said good-naturedly. "No guest would wear such a ragged gown."

Her breath caught. The female in her made her hands fly to the largest of the mended spots, hiding them.

"It's a crime," he went on with insolent good humor. "Whoever made you wear that gown should be marched to the whipping post. No creature so ravishing should be made to wear such awful clothes."

She made to slip away again. Again he caught her wrist.

"You want to learn to jig, bondslave. And so you shall. Now, raise your right hand. Slap it to mine."

It was useless to argue. She'd best humor the

young man and get it over with. Within the ballroom, fiddlers had swung into an even jauntier jig. Shouts of gaiety echoed out to the terrace. She slapped her hand to his.

"Now," instructed the young man, "follow my feet. It is step-hop, step-hop, step-hop. Move backward on every hop."

He'd become so amusingly sober about playing the part of dancing master that Flavia giggled. Complying, she raised her skirts with her left hand and began to hop. She giggled at the silliness of the step. There was no dance like this in England. And certainly nothing so wildly improper had ever been danced at Tewksbury Hall. But the step and the music invaded one's blood. Soon she was laughing gayly and hopping about as enthusiastically as her dancing master.

"And with whom do I have the pleasure of dancing?" he teased as he jigged her backward across the terrace.

"Flav—"

She stopped dead.

The young man was forced to stop in mid-hop, too. That, or run her down. She tore her hand from his and clapped it to her booming heart. Fear surged through her. In the light-heartedness of the moment, she'd forgotten . . . forgotten . . .

"Jane Brown, sir," she gasped, gulping deep draughts of chill night air. "I am indentured to the Reverend Josiah Byng of Chestertown."

He bowed playfully.

"Your servant, Bondslave Brown. I am Raven McNeil."

She died. Died a thousand deaths. The terrace spun giddily. She was disembodied, numb. Had no legs, no arms, no tongue. She could formulate no reply, make no movement.

He grinned wryly.

"I see you do not care for the name Raven. Well, Bondslave Brown, you must blame the name on my mother. While my late mother was the grandest of women, she was also a bit of a jokester. It seems that as I was being birthed, the midwife caught sight of this." He gestured toward his thick black mane. "'Coo!' she cried out, 'it no be a babe, Mrs. McNeil, but a devil-black raven!'"

He waited for her to laugh. When she didn't, *couldn't,* he said lightly, "Perhaps it is 'McNeil' that Bondslave Brown objects to."

She groped for her voice. Long moments elapsed before she found it. Shakily, she whispered, "I don't object to either name. I have heard of the name McNeil."

He grinned cheerfully.

"Of course you have. Everyone in Maryland has heard of my brother. Captain Garth McNeil."

Her knees went to jelly. Reaching out to the oak tree, she steadied herself.

"He's not here?" she whispered.

"Who?"

He gave her a puzzled look. "Oh. My brother? Why? Do you think he would make a better job of teaching you to jig?"

She hung suspended in terror as he went on teasing her. Then, as an afterthought, he threw out the information she prayed for. "Garth isn't here. He's in Amsterdam. Or London. Or," he said with a laugh, "China, for all I know."

She went limp with relief. Staring up at Raven McNeil, she searched his face. Of course, they were brothers. The family resemblance was unmistakable. If the two were set side by side and put to a comparison, Raven McNeil would come off the handsomer brother. His features were more even than Garth's, his olive skin unroughened by sea wind. But Garth's was the dearer face. The face she longed to see.

She wanted to run. Run from this misery. Yet, if she did, she would be cutting this slight thread. This thread that carried her close to Garth. Staring up at Raven's handsome, puzzled face, she was overwhelmed with a larger thought. Raven was Robert's uncle!

Wrestling her wild emotions into subservience, she finally managed to ask, "And you, Raven McNeil. Are you a ship's master, too?"

He laughed as though she'd made an extremely funny joke.

"Lord, no. When I was ten, Garth took me to Barbados. I puked all the way there and all the way back. When I was twelve we tried it again. Same puking story. When we berthed in Norfolk, Garth took me aside." He cocked his head boyishly. "'Raven, old man,' Garth says, 'some of us are born to the sea, some to the land. You belong to the land. Stay planted, lad.'"

He laughed at the memory, adding, "I manage the land part of our business, procuring shipping contracts. We've three ships now and enough business to take all the pleasure out of life." He grinned. "I'd rather spend my time teaching bondslaves to jig."

The music in the ballroom flared up, and Raven's glance shot to the windows. He frowned and for a moment Flavia panicked, thinking he meant to go. There was so much more she wanted to know, wanted to ask.

"Do you live with your brother?" she blurted.

Again he laughed as though she were joking.

"God, no!" His eyes grew serious for a moment. "You've incredible blue eyes, Jane Brown," he murmured, then flitted to her question. "Live with Garth? Not likely. I'd be a damned intruder. Garth usually has a woman. Not a doxy, mind you. A lady of quality. His current lady is the Baroness Annette Vachon."

Her heart fell. She'd known, of course. But to hear it confirmed was a different matter. Sadness tugged her shoulders downward.

"Oh," she whispered.

Raven McNeil laughed cheerfully.

"See here, Jane Brown. I've taken a fancy to you and your incredible eyes. Will you become my mistress?"

Her head jerked up in shock.

"I shall buy out your indenture tomorrow. Tonight! This very hour!" he amended.

"No!" she cried out. "Oh, no. Never."

He grinned ruefully.

"I haven't the French disease. I've money. An even temperament. I'm always cheerful. Healthy as a horse. In fact," he said with a laugh, "feel free to examine me as you might a horse you contemplate purchasing." Hooking his finger into his mouth, he exposed even, white teeth. He accompanied this bit of foolery with a loud whinny.

Flavia's panic subsided to laughter.

"I shall buy your indenture, Bondslave Brown. I shall set you up in your own small house in Williamsburg. You shall breakfast on sweetmeats every morning and dine on them too, if you wish. You shall have three Negroes to flog. And you shall go to the theater every evening in your own landau. At the theater you shall be given your own bucket of spoilt fruit, and you shall feel free to pitch it at any actor who dares displease you."

She giggled. The young man was irrepressibly likable. She was so glad! Glad that her baby had a share in McNeil blood.

"Thank you, Raven McNeil," she said firmly. "But *no*, thank you."

He gave a theatrical sigh.

"Ah, well. Think it over, Jane Brown. I shan't accept this as your final answer. I shall call upon you at the home of your very Reverend Josiah Bang."

"Byng," she corrected, biting her lip to keep from laughing. "And you shall *not* call."

"Bing? Bang? What's the difference? He's likely a fool. Dressing a ravishing creature in tatty lutestring."

The jigging music had drawn to a close in the ballroom. There was the flourish of drums. Mr. Tate ascended the music platform to make his welcoming speech. It was now common knowledge that he would announce his daughter's engagement. Flavia could see slaves slipping among the guests, distributing special silver toasting goblets.

She turned to Raven. "You'll miss toasting the happy young couple," she said, hurrying across the brick terrace to retrieve his wig from where he'd tossed it.

"Hadn't you better go in?"

"Hadn't I better!" Raven McNeil agreed, reaching for the disheveled wig. "Especially since I am one-half of the happy young couple."

She was speechless. He knocked the wig against his knee in a futile attempt to tidy it. But he only managed to shower his blue silk breeches with powder. He clapped the luckless wig on his head.

"Yes, Bondslave Brown, I shall wed Maryann Tate. And make her a proper husband, too. She shan't complain of a cold bed." He grinned. "But I shall have *you* as mistress."

Still astounded, she floundered for something to say, something to dampen him.

"Raven McNeil, you are a sorry representative of your own sex."

He laughed.

"Straighten my wig, Jane. Then brush me clean of this infernal dusting powder."

She did so. When she finished, he playfully caught her round the waist. He tried to kiss her, but she gave him a stern motherly push, and his arms fell away. He looked so genuinely crestfallen that she changed her mind, stood on tiptoe and gave him a peck on the cheek.

He laughed his disappointment.

"Lord, wench. You kiss as badly as you jig."

He wheeled round, bounding off the terrace in the direction of a sweet, girlish voice that was calling, "Raven? Raven? Are you out here?" Just before he disappeared round a mulberry bush, he turned and hissed a complaint.

"That was a *sisterly* kiss, Bondslave Brown."

Her smile followed his fading footfalls.

"That it was, Raven McNeil," she murmured fondly. "That it was."

Chapter 13

Two weeks after the dancing assembly, a wood box arrived at the Byngs'. Posted from Williamsburg, the long box had journeyed by fishing boat, peddler's cart and finally in the indifferent arms of the boy who carried it from the Rose and Crown. It was addressed to Jane Brown, in the care of the Reverend Josiah Bang.

"'Bang,' indeed!" exploded Mrs. Byng as she snatched the box from Flavia's arms. "Who could be so ignorant?"

Anxiety rose in cold ripples. "Please, ma'am. The parcel is mine."

"Nonsense. Bondslaves do not receive boxes from Williamsburg." Mrs. Byng clunked the box down on the kitchen table, seized a meat knife and sawed the bands. She flung off the top of the box. It banged to the floor, and Flavia shut her eyes, trembling in fervent prayer.

Please don't let Raven—please—"

Mrs. Byng made a startled sound.

"My stars!"

Flavia's eyes flew open. Her stomach lurched as Mrs. Byng dove into the muslin wrappings and drew out the dainty bodice of a gown. It was rose-colored silk with tiny, exquisite rosettes worked into the neckline. Mrs. Byng gasped as she drew out matching silk underskirts, one after the other, the fabric rustling expensively.

Flavia swallowed in misery.

Raven, how could you!

The gift was an extravagant one and thoughtlessly cruel. Only an impulsive young man could fail to consider the consequences that such a gift must bring to a bondslave.

Mrs. Byng gave her a knowing look. The corners of her mouth turned down in contempt.

"With whom did you earn this gown, Jane?"

Flavia reddened, her misery swelling to anger. She was furious with Raven, but more so with Mrs. Byng. She was too agitated to risk answering. If she opened her mouth she would find herself at the whipping post or enduring the humiliation of public stocks. She stared at the floor, sullen with anger.

"Speak!" Mrs. Byng demanded. "Reveal your benefactor!" When she said not a word, Mrs. Byng smiled archly. "Very well, Jane. I shall place the matter in Mr. Byng's hands."

Flavia's heart jumped fearfully. Oh, not that! He would pray with her. Touch her. His touch hovering, threatening to become fondling. Her eyes flew to Mrs. Byng.

"Please, ma'am, I don't know who sent it.

Perhaps some lady at the ball took a fancy to me and sent the gown."

Mrs. Byng's eyes narrowed.

"A lady would send her discarded gowns. Only a man sends new."

Flavia swallowed, desperately trying to think. What could she say? How? She raked her mind. Greed. That was all Mrs. Byng responded to.

Quickly she said, "The gown was missent. It must be worth thirty pounds! It should be posted back to Williamsburg so that the true owner may claim it."

Mrs. Byng's eyes widened, then narrowed as she shrewdly considered her profit.

"Send it back? Nonsense. We shall retain it until the owner claims it. Box the gown, Jane, and slide it under my bed."

As she folded the lovely silk, tucking in the fragrant rose petal sachets that had been tucked in each corner of the box, Mrs. Byng patted her shoulder in a false, comradely way.

"Jane, dear," she trilled, "we mustn't talk about it, must we? The world is full of dishonest folk who'd claim the gown."

"Yes, ma'am."

"And don't trouble Mr. Byng about the matter. I'll not have the Reverend Byng's fine mind troubled with trivia."

Shaking with relief, her knees as steady as jelly, she packed the box and lugged it into Mrs. Byng's bedchamber. Kneeling at the four-poster, she moved the chamber pot and shoved the box into dark depths.

* * *

Dear Mr. Raven McNeil,
   There has been delivered to me a most unwelcome parcel. Were funds available, the parcel would be posted back to Williamsburg without a moment's hesitation.
   Further, any future parcels, letters or visits, shall be greeted with the utmost abhorrence. Indeed, no recourse shall remain but to consult Mr. Tate.

J. Brown

The letter was a severe one, but she sensed that only severity would work. She was sorry to threaten Raven with his future father-in-law. She'd liked Raven. Liked him from the first silly moment. But she had to protect Robert. And dearest Garth. If the duke should connect her with the McNeils...

She penned the letter on an afternoon the Byngs rode out for parish calls. She'd stolen a shilling earlier to pay for the first few miles of posting; the receiver would have to pay the remainder. Remembering Mab Collins's instructions, she'd done her stealing in plain sight, as Mr. Byng sat at the kitchen table doing his monthly count of Mrs. Byng's money box. Flavia had brought him tea and a Cornish pastie. Whipping the napkin into the air to catch his eye, she'd palmed a shilling, her heart banging in terror. But it had worked. Just as it had when Mab made her practice it over and over aboard the *Schilaack*.

"I thought," mumbled Mr. Byng after awhile, "I counted thirty-three."

In her Philadelphia chair, Mrs. Byng sipped tea.

"Count again, sir," she advised. "A shilling has no legs. It cannot jump up and walk away."

Mr. Byng reddened in irritation. He disliked being advised by a woman, especially his own wife.

He counted again, saving face by making the count come out right. But a puzzled look remained in his eyes, and Flavia took care to kneel to her scrubbing. She scrubbed the floorboards with vigor.

She posted the letter in a town six miles beyond Chestertown, where no one would remark on it. She'd run until her lungs gave out and a burning sensation began in her side. Then she'd walked, walked as fast as she could. Outside the printer's shop she'd caught her foot in a loose cobblestone. Pain shot through her ankle. She slowed to a cautious walk.

Hot tears rose. Not so much tears of pain, but tears of frustration. The Byngs would arrive home before her. There'd be no fire in the fireplace, unless Neddy remembered to come in and feed it. There'd be no supper on the table. There'd be the devil to pay.

She limped on. A farm boy gave her a ride in his oxcart for two miles, and as she bumped along she tried to enjoy the beauty of the afternoon. The crisp perfume of sun-warmed autumn leaves wafted upon the air. The oxcart crunched pleasantly through drifts of gold. The countryside glowed like a fine pastoral painting.

Cleared cornfields twinkled with shiny orange pumpkins. Flocks of birds soared overhead, the corporate sound of their beating wings making her glance around for a beehive.

The oxcart jounced over the highest ridge, and she gazed westward into the sun, squinting to see the Chester River. Three ships were asail, their sails snowy in the sunlight. She pretended one was Garth's. She watched it until it sailed out of sight, and was surprised to find foolish tears wetting her cheeks.

She left the oxcart and took the shortcut past the gallows field into Chestertown. In the valley it was dusk. Reflected firelight danced in the window of each house as she hurried through the dusty streets. The smells of supper drifted from each chimney. A dog barked at her, lunging out but then changing its mind and returning to a kitchen door to whine for supper.

She broke into a run, hobbling, her heart racing. Ahead, more dogs barked. The dogs of Chestertown were cowards by day, but bold and snappish at night. The same was true of the town riffraff. She was safe as long as light lasted. But after that...glancing fearfully at the vanishing twilight, she hurried. She'd take the shortcut, leaving the dirt road, crossing the bottomland that flowed down to Chester River. Even so, it would be dark by the time she reached the Byngs'. There she could expect a tongue-lashing at best. At worst—

She put it out of her mind with a shudder and hurried on. It was still light when she reached Dennis Finny's bottomland, the acreage that would be his along with a certificate of freedom in January. The land was already cleared. A garden site lay plowed, ready for spring planting. Looped from stake to stake, a hemp rope outlined the combination house-schoolhouse. Similar hemp skeletons suggested a barn and small outbuildings.

"Halloo!"

She stopped and swung in the direction of the sound.

"Halloo, Jane!"

Dennis Finny ran toward her, skirting scrub pines and springing over tumbled logs in his apparent joy to see her.

"Mistress Brown," he said, amending his earlier enthusiasm into more mannerly speech when he reached her side and stood panting from his run. "Does it suit thee, Mistress Brown?" He threw his arm, indicating his future property. "Is there ought which thee would change?"

She caught her breath. So he still hoped. The glow in his eyes told her so.

"Mr. Finny, I am only passing. I must hurry. It's late."

"Tell me thee approves," he insisted with boyish enthusiasm.

She shook her head, gently but firmly. "Mr. Finny, my answer remains the same."

The light in his eyes died a little. A sad little smile of apology tugged at the corners of his mouth. "Forgive me," he murmured. "I've no wish to offend thee." He gazed into her eyes as though searching for the tiniest glimmer of hope. Finding none, he sighed. He lifted his face to the sky and surveyed the darkening night. "I shall see thee safe to the Byngs'," he said with quiet firmness.

Flavia declined, knowing he taught Greek to the eldest Tate boys each evening. She told him she needed no escort. He didn't dispute it. But as she set out across the dark fields, he stubbornly fell into step at her side.

Wisely, he didn't call attention to his actions by engaging her in unwanted conversation. He held his silence. They trod through the dry rustling grass, watching the stars wink into glittering light, listening to the waking hoot of the barn owl. When a roaming dog bayed, wolflike, she started in alarm and quickly took his arm. Her cheeks warmed in embarrassment.

"Forgive me. I was rude," she admitted softly. "The night is very dark. I'm grateful for escort."

Sensitive to her embarrassment, he made no reply. But it was not many more steps before he sensed her bad ankle. Without asking permission, he stopped and picked her up in his arms. She was flustered to find herself carried along.

"Mr. Finny, I can walk."

"No, Jane."

It was said with such firmness that she knew it would be not only foolish but humiliating to argue. He was determined. Politely, he didn't ask what was wrong. The gentle man was a gentleman. Female limbs could not be discussed.

She settled into his arms, surprised at the wiry strength of the slightly built young man. Resting her head against his shoulder, she was surprised, too, at how fresh and clean he smelled. Few bondsmen were tidy about their persons.

Most smelled as rank as the animals they drove to Chestertown on Market Day. Dennis made no conversation as he carried her through the whispering fields, but his heart drummed loudly.

He set her down at the far end of the Byngs' stone wall. Before she could turn to go in, he seized her hand and drew it to trembling lips. Flavia was startled as he kissed her palm, kissed it with anguished passion.

"Jane," he whispered with fervent longing. "Oh, Jane!"

She jerked her hand away, jerked it so definitely and abruptly that his face went white in the dim light of the rising half-moon. He stared at her in shock, as though his fondest dream had been jerked from his heart, along with her hand. Stunned, he turned on his heel and ran off toward the Tate plantation.

Flavia's heart sank. She valued Dennis as a friend. She wished she had not reacted as though his kiss had been a bee sting. But she couldn't control such things. After Garth's kisses, she could bear no others. "Oh, Garth," she yearned softly. "Garth."

Heart heavy with sadness and with the dread of facing the Byngs, she let herself in the gate. The hinges shrieked, then shrieked again as she closed the gate. The complaining gate was echoed by a faint sound. A kittenlike whimper. She spun around, staring into the dark unmoving bushes. An injured animal?

She had no time to consider it. Loud, angry-sounding boots stomped across the darkened veranda and down the wood steps. She whirled around as Mr. Byng lunged out of the darkness, boiling with wrath.

"Who is he, Jane? Who do you sin with?"

She froze. Dumbfounded, she grasped to understand him. But she couldn't. She shrank back against the gate. Mr. Byng towered over her, shaking in rage. His eyes were wild. His white hair was in wild disarray as though he'd swiped at it in frustration.

"Who is he?" Mr. Byng demanded, shaking a fist in the direction Dennis had run. "Confess, Jane. I saw him slip away. You ran off to lie with him. Who is he? I promise you, he shall dance at the whipping post, my girl. As will you."

She gasped, suddenly understanding.

"Sir, please—I've not done anything—it was only D—"

She bit the name back. Bit her lip so hard she tasted the sudden rising of salty blood. She couldn't involve Dennis. Two months more and he'd be free, taking a respected position in the community as tutor to boys who'd go on to Harvard Seminary. Scandal would destroy him.

She backed away, backed into the gate so hard that wood pickets stabbed into her spine. Cornered, she looked up and defended herself. "Mr. Byng! I've not been with anyone. I went for a walk. I hurt my foot. My foot made me late—"

The flat of his hand cracked her cheek like a musket shot. The slap was so hard that at first she didn't even feel it. There was only numbness. Then the slowly building fire. Fire that drew tears.

"Liar."

Without giving her a moment to recover, he grabbed her arm, wrenching her along. Her feet flew out from under.

"You shall be punished, Jane. I know my duty when I see it."

Terrified, she tried to pull free. Her instincts pure and animallike. Run! Oh, God, run! She wrenched free and bolted, but he caught her by the hair as her mobcap flew to the ground. She screamed more in terror than in pain as he jerked her hair and threw her to her knees.

Half blinded by panic, she tried to get up and lunge toward the light that bobbed toward them from around the house. Her heart gave an enormous thud of hope, then died. It was Mrs. Byng, robed in a gray wool wrapper and carrying a flickering Betty lamp. Pursing her lips in approval, she urged her husband on.

"Whip her," Mrs. Byng advised. "She's wanted a whipping from the very first day. Indeed, sir, Jane has no respect for you. You must beat it into the chit."

Flavia bolted with a cry. "No! You have no right!"

But her ankle buckled and she pitched to the ground. She was roughly hauled to her feet and marched to the barn. Newly incensed by Mrs. Byng, Mr. Byng pushed her through the door, then slammed it shut as Mrs. Byng's Betty lamp bobbed ladylike toward the house. A lantern burned, hanging from an iron hook. Evidence Mr. Byng had been searching for her.

"Bare your back," he commanded, going for the whip he kept on a ledge in the barn.

Terror—terror greater than any she had known in her life—washed over her in waves, drowning her, paralyzing her. *This isn't happening! It isn't! I am Flavia Rochambeau. I'm asleep in my bedchamber at Tewksbury. This is a horrible nightmare—nothing more—*

But as he advanced upon her, she knew it was real. For the first time, she truly knew what Mary Wooster and the others felt as they were tied to the post. The racing panic. The thundering urge to run. But the paralyzing inability to do so. Fear choking the throat like a noose. Fear destroying all self-respect, so that one begged, cried, whimpered like a chained dog.

"Spare me," she begged. "I'll do anything—anything—"

"Bare your back," he commanded without mercy.

Her knees gave out. She melted to the floor, curling into a tight ball, curling against the inevitable first cut of the lash. She sobbed in hysteria as she heard the whip go up. She waited a lifetime for its descent. When the crack came, it came against the floor, as though deflected. There was a loud whoosh with it, and a thud as someone fell.

"Ooof—wha?"

Flavia jerked round. Mr. Byng crouched on the floor, rubbing the back of his head in stunned disbelief. Behind him, the stinking stable broom reared up in the air again.

"Neddy! Don't!" Flavia screamed.

The broom swung down with another loud whuff, this time missing its target cleanly and swacking the ground. It went up again as she drunkenly found her feet and rushed at the boy. She lunged at the broom handle, but Neddy was too wildly angered to be stopped. He wrenched the broom free of her and swung again. This time, a part of the handle hit a stout wood support post. The impact jarred the weapon from his hand. The broom flipped up and flew into the loft. Neddy stared at it stupidly, his mouth open. He burst into tears, suddenly a three-year-old again as Mr. Byng flung himself to his feet, brushing manure from his jacket and howling in anger.

"Fool! Attack me, will you? You shall be locked up in a lunatic house. Chained hand and foot like the animal you are. You'll do no more mischief, I warrant. Oh, no, Neddy."

Neddy fell to his knees, bawling in terror. He didn't understand the words, but he sensed the fearsomeness of the threat.

Heart pounding both in relief for herself and terror for Neddy, Flavia jumped between Neddy and Mr. Byng.

"Please, sir—Neddy didn't mean it—he won't do it again—I'll speak to him, sir—he won't—"

But Mr. Byng would not be placated. Pushing her aside with an order to get to her neglected work in the kitchen, he seized the bawling boy by the collar and cuffed him, slapping him hard and yanking on his ears.

Flavia flew out the door, gasping and crying, but knowing Mr. Byng would hit him the harder if she stayed. Wobbly-kneed, she staggered out into the chill night air and drew deep draughts of it. *Please, God ...please ...*

She prayed desperately, prayed Neddy's thrashing would end. When it finally did end, tears of relief coursed down her cheeks. Dizzily, she made her way through the mudyard to the house, wiped her wet cheeks, went in and quietly set about doing her chores. She glanced unhappily at Mrs. Byng. The woman smiled at her smugly, obviously pleased with her red swollen eyes, her beaten, downtrodden spirit.

Despite their professed devotion to the quiet, meditative life, Flavia knew the Byngs were never so exhilarated as after conflict. Mr. and Mrs. Byng went to bed directly after Neddy's whipping. After a discreet interval, Flavia could hear their loud whistling snores from where she sat at the kitchen table.

Drained, emotionally at the end of her tether, she lay her head in her arms. Over and over, the events of the evening marched roughshod through her heart. She winced, remembering Neddy's terrified cries.

Sleep would be impossible tonight. She was not like the Byngs, thriving on conflict, even deriving sexual arousal from it. Their distant snoring went on. Listlessly she dragged herself up and put another log on the fire. Sparks whooshed as she sank back on her haunches, staring into the flames. She scarcely cared when a spark jumped out of the fire, singeing a tiny hole in her skirt before winking out.

The tall case clock in the parlor bonged twelve times. October was over. This was November. Six years and three months still to go. Then she would be free. But free to what?

The question hung over her like a pall. Six years and three months. How could she endure it? She stared into the fire. Every snap and pop of the fire shouted, "Run!" But to where . . . to what . . . few bondslaves managed to escape. Most were captured. Her mind flew to Mab Collins. Mab had evidently made it. The subscription for her apprehension continued to appear in gazettes. How had Mab managed it? Where had she gone? Certainly she'd gone first to Hampton to steal Sarah Bess. Mab wouldn't leave without her daughter.

A faint scratching came at the window. Tiredly, she got up. It was Neddy's signal, the signal she'd taught him. Lifting the door bolt, she quietly let herself out. Neddy was there, jumping up and down in excitement.

"Uh—uh—Jane—"

She placed her fingers on his lips, shushing him. She led him toward the barn, out of the Byngs' hearing.

Neddy danced up and down.

"Uh—uh—Jane—lady—" He waved his hand excitedly toward the barn, and the fine down on the back of her neck prickled. Mab? Could it be Mab?

She ran to the barn. Neddy had left the door open, and the thin watery light of the November half-moon trickled into the barn, disappearing in gloom. She picked her way through the

darkness. She could hear sheep stirring restlessly
in their pen and the rasp of a horse's rump as it
lazily scratched itself against the wood stall.
Then came loud, violent panting, followed by a
mewling sound. It was the same kittenlike whimper she'd heard earlier in the yard.

"Mab? Is it you, Mab?"

The anguished panting came again. The whimper that followed intensified into a stifled whine
of pain.

"Jane?" the gasping voice whispered. "Jane?
Oh, Lord, Jane, help me!"

Blindly she plunged into the darkness, stumbling over a broom, losing her balance as her
foot kicked against rake or hoe. The cry came
from the darkest corner, an empty stall where
hay was stored. Flavia felt her way, her eyes
useless, adjusting to the gloom with maddening
slowness.

"Mab?" she whispered, as she felt her way
into the dark stall. Gradually a figure material-
ized. It was a girl. She was lying on her back in
the hay, and she seemed all belly. As Flavia
looked, the belly contracted violently. The girl's
whimper of pain climaxed in a sharp yelp.

"Mary!"

Flavia fell to her knees, watching helplessly
as Mary Wooster rode her violent contraction,
then sank back into the hay, still as death.

She seized the girl's cold hand and chafed it
roughly. "Mary!" She swung her head to Neddy,
who stood gawking. "Neddy, run to Dennis. To
Dennis, Neddy. Tell him to bring the plantation
midwife. *Midwife*, Neddy."

But the boy only continued to gawk, and Mary's eyes flew open in fear. "No," she gasped. "No one. Master—he shall—"

She lost her words as the panting began again. Pain closed in like a vice. Flavia bit her lip in panic, lunging to catch Mary as the girl's head and shoulders shot forward. Sweating with anxiety, she held Mary through the contraction. When it ended, Mary collapsed, dead weight in her arms. Flavia strained, trying to lay her down gently. Mary's eyes rolled, then sank into her skull.

Flavia bent over her, aghast. This wasn't natural labor. Mary's labored sweat stank like noxious poison. Her breath was vile. Frightened, Flavia moved to go for Mr. Byng. He must be wakened. He must ride for the doctor. But the rustling hay alerted the girl. Mary reared up, then choked in pain, clutching her belly.

"No one," she begged. "I've runned away— oh, Jane, it hurts—it hurts—"

She sank into the hay, crying. Helpless, thoroughly frightened, Flavia held her hand. She snapped at Neddy to bring the horse's water bucket. When he did, she tore off her apron, dipped it into the water and gently swabbed Mary's face. She held her through another contraction, murmuring words of comfort she could not believe herself. She sent Neddy to fetch his own bucket of drinking water, then held the dipper to Mary's lips. The girl drank thirstily.

"He give me tea," she whispered faintly. "My master did . . . tea boiled up from them twigs of

the pretty flowerin' trees. . . . He made me to
drink it. . . . I didn't want to, Jane . . . but he
said . . . said he'd whip me . . ."

Her words died away as she panted her way
into a new contraction. Flavia held her fiercely,
anger granting new strength. How dare he!
How dare he do this to a child! She'd heard of
it, of course. Plantation masters aborting their
helpless bondwomen, covering their own trails
of foul lust. Dear God, a fifteen-year-old girl!
Did no one care?

During the next hour of contractions, Flavia
worked feverishly. She forced Mary to drink
water. Water would flush the abortive. She made
the girl comfortable, wiping her face with a cool
wet cloth between contractions. She gave her
hands to Mary during each pain. Mary clutched
them, unknowingly driving in her nails at the
height of her agony.

At last the rhythm of the labor changed. Mary
reared up, her eyes alive with raw fear. She
shuddered.

"It's coming," she gasped. "Lord of my saint-
ed mother, it's com—oh—oh—help—it's com—"

Too terrified to think, Flavia reacted with
instinct. Gathering all the strength she had, she
pushed down on the girl's rock-hard belly. Mary
screamed. There was the gush of waters and the
infant slid out into the straw. Mary Wooster
fainted, and Flavia fought her own light-head-
edness.

She stared at the infant. It lay wet and
glistening. As unmoving as a child's doll. She
was frightened to touch it. Equally frightened

not to. She swallowed hard for courage. Shaking, she picked up the slippery doll and held it to her ear, listening for a heartbeat. None. Terrified, she swiped fluids from the doll-like face and blew air into the little lungs. She slapped its bottom. Slapped with hard sharp cracks that woke Neddy. He ambled into the stall, curious. Then he burst into tears, fearing she was hurting a doll.

She worked on the infant for a fruitless eternity, then knelt on her haunches, dazed, exhausted. Wiping away her own tears, she put the body aside. She turned to Mary, kneading the unconscious girl's belly, encouraging the after-issue.

Mary remained mercifully unconscious for a quarter of an hour. When she came to, she stiffened in fear, clutching her flattened stomach.

" 'Tis over?"

"Over."

Mary wept in relief.

"Dead?"

Flavia nodded tiredly.

Mary lay back in the hay, staring blankly at the dark rafters where horse harness and tools hung. The night was passing. Dawn was near. Eerie gray light crept into the barn, elongating shadows and changing the shapes of things.

"I'm glad!" Mary whispered passionately, the hay rustling viciously under her. "May God forgive me, but I'm glad."

Flavia squeezed her hand, understanding.

"Mary? The baby must receive a burial."

Mary Wooster's eyes grew luminous with fear.

"Jane, no! They'll say I birthed a bastard and killed it. They'll hang me!"

Flavia shuddered. Mary was right. An indentured woman who gave birth to a stillborn was at the mercy of the court. Depending upon the caprice of a jury of men, she could be exonerated or she could be sentenced to death.

Flavia rose wearily. Straw crunched underfoot as she went to the horse stall and took the horse blanket from its cubbyhole. When Mr. Byng discovered the blanket missing, he would blame gypsies. Wrapping the infant in the blanket, she collected a shovel and then the wide-eyed Neddy. They buried the bundle in an isolated copse, halfway to the creek.

The sky was beginning to lighten as she helped Mary up to the low loft above the sheep pen. It was smelly there. But the rank odor was an ally. Mr. and Mrs. Byng never willingly visited the sheep pen.

She was tired when she finally slipped back into the kitchen. As tired as she'd ever been in her life. Her ankle throbbed. Coals still glowed in the fireplace. She sprinkled kindling slivers upon the coals. The kindling caught. Fire hissed up. She added logs and swung the kettle trivet over the flames. She made tea, warmed a leftover potato stew and carried all out to Mary. In the barn she quickly forked clean hay over the birthing spot, then paused to cover the sleeping Neddy with a blanket. She flew back to the house in a limping run, shucked her soiled outermost petticoat, scrubbed it in a basin of water and stretched it over the hearth to dry.

She was just in time. She was just measuring cornmeal into a cracked blue bowl when Mrs. Byng emerged from her bedchamber.

"As to yesterday, Jane," Mrs. Byng began irritably, "I shall speak to the magistrate. He shall be persuaded to indemnify me for the lost hours. Oh, yes, indeed, girl!"

She waited for response. When Flavia gave her none, refusing to be baited, Mrs. Byng's eye twitched in vexation.

"As to your wicked sinfulness," she went on, her voice rising, "you had best remember the penalty for whelping a bastard. Oh, indeed, missy, you are a wanton one." She smiled in cold satisfaction, adding, "You shall dance at the public whipping post one of these days. Mark my words!"

She hid Mary Wooster for almost two weeks while word spread through Chestertown that a bondwoman had bolted. A notice of reward for capture went up on the church notice wall, on a tree at the market square and at the Rose and Crown. The notices had to be repenned often, as they tended to disappear. At Sabbath services Flavia learned why.

"Poor Mary!" Elizabeth Simm whispered during Mr. Byng's windy sermon. "She's but a child. I hope she runs and runs far. I told Jimmy Barlow, I did—'Jim, were the notices about poor Mary to disappear, I should feel obliged to throw my arms round you and kiss you'—"

Betsy's furtive whisper was cut off as a pole jabbed her between the shoulder blades. She swung her head round, spearing the warden with a haughty look. The warden backed off, reddening in confusion, and Flavia smiled inwardly. So he, too, had heard Betsy Simm would be the next wife of the very rich and powerful planter, Ira Gresham.

The cold sleeting rains of November began. Tentatively at first, then with wintry determination. Gray rain bludgeoned the countryside, dragging the last foliage from trees and swirling colorful heaps of autumn leaves into sodden, mud-colored mounds. The goldenrod was gone, the showy bright yellow blossoms washed down to the creek. House yards flowed with mud. Flavia couldn't leave the house to do chores without wearing wood pattens over her shoes. Even so, the awkward stiltlike pattens flicked cold wet mud up her stockings as she walked.

Inside the house, spits of rain shot down the chimneys, sizzling like hot fat in the fire. On a night after especially heavy downpours, she'd gone to bed to find her blankets wet. A drip had sprouted in the loft roof.

The barn roof was sound, but the wetness of the outside air pressed in. The air grew musty. Absorbing the moisture, the hay sent up a thick strong odor. One couldn't breathe the air without coughing, and Mary Wooster lived in terror, fearing Mr. Byng would come in and hear her cough. She was determined to run as soon as the rains abated.

Her heart aching for the girl, Flavia listened to Mary's childish plans for escape. The plans were inept, unworkable, the wishful fantasies of a young girl. She knew she had to obtain help for Mary. But from whom?

From Jimmy Barlow? Elizabeth Simm? Flavia sighed sadly. She might as well announce Mary's whereabouts from the pulpit as use those two. Dennis? No. She couldn't ask so much of him. Aiding a runaway bondslave was a crown offense. In January Dennis would begin life anew, a free man, a respected schoolmaster. She couldn't ask him to jeopardize his future.

Her mind flew to Raven and as quickly fled him. Raven would help if she asked. Somehow, she felt certain of it. But Garth's brother seemed given to grand, cavalier gestures. Raven would try to play the hero and make hash of it. Mary could only end up the worse off...

If only... if only...

No! No! No! Dear heaven! Never!

But her aching heart flew there again, and she was forced to consider it. Her pulse raced erratically, blood thundering in her ears. Garth ... if only she could send Mary to Garth.... His keen eyes would read and understand Mary's woebegone face in a glance. He would sense her awful plight and he would help. She knew it! Knew it as certainly as she knew she adored him. Garth's help would be mature. Decisive and discreet. Unlike Raven, he'd feel no need to play the hero. He'd hide Mary aboard the *Caroline*. He'd take her to safety, to another colony, or to England—anywhere she could start free.

It was a foolish fantasy, she admitted sorrowfully. It was dangerous. More foolish and dangerous

than any of Mary's childish plans. She pushed it
from her mind. But it kept coming back. She
was forced to consider it. Two nights later,
serving supper to Mr. and Mrs. Byng, she was
jerked into urgent action.

"I heard noises again, Mrs. Byng," Josiah
Byng began in his nasal voice, carefully buttering
all sides of his corn bread. "In the barn. I
wonder if gypsies—"

Flavia's breath caught.

"'Tis rats, Mr. Byng," Mrs. Byng interrupted,
delighted to be consulted. "Rats driven in by
the weather."

"I wonder..."

"Oh, indeed, sir. 'Tis rats, I do assure you.
What is wanted, Mr. Byng, is a Rat Kill."

Flavia's hand trembled as she ladled more
stew into Mr. Byng's dish. In her nervousness
she flicked a speck of gravy to the white linen
cloth. Mrs. Byng sent her a killing look, then
sweetened her countenance and smiled over the
spotted cloth at her husband.

"Perhaps the boys of the parish would enjoy a
Rat Kill, husband. We might give a prize. Oh,
nothing of value, of course."

"Of course," Mr. Byng agreed, brightening at
the prospect of ridding his barn of rats at no
expense. "I shall attend to it, my dear. When
the weather clears."

"It clears tomorrow," Mrs. Byng pressed. "Mr.
Franklin's Philadelphia *Almanack* predicts it."

Flavia felt ill.

"Then I shall attend to it at once," Mr. Byng

insisted. "Neddy can drive the animals to pasture. The boys shall bring their cudgels. I shall set smoke lamps in the barn. When the smoke rises, the rats will run." Pleased with himself, Mr. Byng leaned back, basked in his wife's admiration and signaled Flavia for another helping of stew.

"As to the prize for the champion rat killer, my dear. A leather pen wiper? Eh?"

"A *felt* pen wiper," Mrs. Byng countered, mentally counting her pennies.

When the Byngs retired, Flavia stole parchment, ink and quill pen from the study. Quickly she penned the note that had undergone a hundred mental revisions as she'd sat knitting winter stockings, waiting for the Byngs' first yawn.

> *Dear Captain Garth McNeil,*
>   *If ever you have known the joy of true love, honor the memory of that love by helping this girl.*
>
>   *One Who Beseeches You*

She held the letter to the fire to dry it. She folded it in thirds and addressed it to Captain Garth McNeil of Williamsburg and Hampton. Slipping it deep into her apron pocket, she scavenged food for Mary's supper and went out to the barn.

Mary Wooster left the following night. The rains had blown out to sea. Wind and a day of sunshine had made the mud roads solid enough to support a human, but not so solid as to allow horse or cart. Conditions were ideal. No rider would be out for a day or two.

She went with Mary to the fork in the road, just beyond the gallows field, south of Chestertown. She'd taken a stout sack, packed it with food and put in a book Mr. Byng wouldn't miss. Mary could sell the book. Or trade it for passage across the Chesapeake to Hampton.

They parted at the crossroads, embracing as the chill November winds slapped at their cloaks. Flavia hugged the girl for good luck.

"Remember, Mary, you carry my life in your hands," she warned. "I can't explain. But my life will be in danger if *anyone* discovers I sent you."

Mary Wooster's freckled face shone strong and determined in the watery moonlight.

"A man wrote the letter for me," she said firmly. "A traveler I met. I never saw him before. I don't know where he was a-travelin' to. I don't remember what he looked like."

On sudden impulse, Mary threw her arms around Flavia and hugged her tightly.

"Don't worry, Jane. Depend on me. I owe you my life. I shall die before I say aught that will hurt you."

Behind them, in the road toward Chestertown, a faint light began to twinkle. Taverngoers were wending their way home, carrying a lantern.

Flavia urged the food sack into Mary's arms. The girl seized it, shaking with frightened excitement.

"Farewell, Jane," Mary whispered passionately, turning and running, her cloak slapping in the wind. "We shan't meet again! God be with you!"

Flavia put a hand to her thudding throat.

"And God be with *you*, Mary," she called softly. "Farewell!"

Chapter 14

.

It was Militia Day in Williamsburg. Every able-bodied male between sixteen and sixty was expected to turn out. *That* includes shipmasters, McNeil wryly reminded himself, blinking against the sharp shaft of sunlight that was knifing its way over the sill of the east window in his bedchamber.

He burrowed deeper under the goosedown coverlet. The November morning was chilly and the featherbed warm and appealing. Not the least of its appeal was the woman sleeping next to him.

Lazily, he shifted up on one elbow, studying her. She looked particularly fetching this morning. Black hair, loosed of restraining pins and combs, fanned out upon the pillow in silken waves. He smiled, spotting a single silver hair

among the glossy tresses. He wondered how
she would react when she found it. The dark
luster of her hair was repeated in thick, sooty
lashes. The lashes flickered slightly, as though
the approach of morning carried her up to the
level of dreams. Her lips were parted, and one
hand—naked and oddly childish without its usual
array of jewels—curled round the edge of the
coverlet, clutching it.

She slept in her chemise, a gossamer-soft
garment of thin peach-colored silk. The warmth
of her body mingled with the exotic scent of her
perfume, sending a delicious invitation to his
waking senses. He had the sudden urge to kiss
her, but he didn't. Quietly he lay back on his
pillow, hands clasped behind his neck. Let her
sleep. They'd been out late.

They'd gone to the theater to see the Hamilton-
St. James troupe perform. The celebrated Mrs.
Hamilton-St. James had been an abomination as
Lady Macbeth, but in *Flora; or a Hob in the
Well*, she'd found her footing. The actress did
comedy tolerably well. However, he suspected
that her best role was "Mrs. Hamilton-St. James."
He doubted there'd ever been a General
Hamilton-St. James, to whom the widowed ac-
tress tearfully dedicated each performance.

Forgetting the actress as quickly as he'd thought
of her, he let his mind drift over the other
events of the last evening: late supper with a
crowd at the Governor's Palace, an hour or two
of dancing at a public dancing assembly, and
Annette's squeal of surprise at the ball when her
ticket won a Negro in the raffle.

Lazily, his eyes roamed the bedchamber. He'd been back from Europe a week, but he was not yet used to the room. All was changed. Much to the better, he admitted with a sleepy grin. In her bold, commanding way, Annette had decided to refurbish his Williamsburg house in his absence. She'd plunged into the project like a chicken plucker diving to her work. Blithely, she'd sent all bills to Raven. She'd begun with the bedchamber. But *that*, he thought, grinning, was only natural to the baroness.

Everything was freshly painted in white and robin's egg blue. All of his furniture—including the four-poster bed in which he and Raven had been born—had been sent out to be refinished. The cherry wood glowed. Annette had done the bed curtains and canopy in red velvet, throwing red at the windows as well. New chairs flanked the fireplace.

Downstairs, Annette had attacked foyer, drawing room and dining accommodations with equal zest. She'd not spared his wallet. She'd used velvet, silk and damask as though it were cheap as sackcloth. He'd come home to find himself the astonished owner of peacock blue silk draperies and a foyer floor of black and white checked marble.

Though the rest of the rooms lay drab—crying for similar refurbishing—he could pronounce his Williamsburg house worthy of a king's visit. Worthy even, he thought acidly, of a Wetherby visit.

The thought gave him an unpleasant jolt.

A sharp and very real pain in the neck.

Rubbing his neck, he glanced guiltily at Annette as she lay sleeping. He'd not told her yet. He'd told no one about Eunice. He'd been back a week, but somehow the moment never seemed appropriate to tell her. Cowardly, but there it was. She'd greeted him so happily. She'd pranced like a child, showing him all she'd done with his house. And, as always, the first touch of her hand on his had set off the old familiar vibrations. Within thirty minutes of seeing each other, they'd catapulted into bed. She'd been wantonly loving. An angel of passion compared with the diffident, prissy fiancée he'd left behind. She'd banished all memory of Eunice. Almost, she'd banished the memory of Flavia.

He turned his head as she gave a little gasp in her sleep, then trembled. Once. Twice. He shifted up on his elbow, watching her. A dream. Perhaps not a pleasant one.

"Annette," he said softly. "Annette?"

It took her a few moments to waken. She glanced about, confused. Then her eyes found his face and she smiled sleepily.

"Where? Oh—did I spend the night at your house?"

"You did."

"Did we—"

"Twice."

She laughed contentedly, her sleepiness mellowing her sultry giggle, taking it to lower and even more appealing levels. She stretched like a cat, then sighed. With one finger she idly traced the grizzle that was sprouting on his jaw.

"And did you like it, Captain McNeil?"

"No, Lady Annette."

She giggled at the absurdity of his answer, but responded to it with sleepy soberness.

"Then I shall have to try harder."

He grinned.

"By all means."

With a happy sigh she slipped her hands around his neck and drew him close to her warm breasts.

"Now?" she suggested.

He shook his head.

"Militia Day."

"Pooh. Miss it."

"Can't."

"*Can.*"

"No."

She gave him a little push of frustration. "Damnation, McNeil!" He laughed at her unbaronesslike outburst and rolled out of bed. Hitting the floor, he grabbed a robe and built a fire. When the kindling was crackling, he went to the cherry-wood wardrobe, flung open the doors and rummaged for underbreeches. He pulled them on. Deerskin breeches followed. He rummaged deep in the recesses of the wardrobe, emerging with nothing but a tart, "Annette, where the devil is my buckskin shirt?"

"How should I know?" she tossed across the room.

"The devil you don't. You've refurbished everything else. Likely you've sent it to the cabinetmaker. To have the fringe done in brass."

She giggled appreciatively.

"An excellent idea, McNeil. Marry me, and

like a good wife I shall set about obliterating
your wardrobe immediately."

His breath caught unpleasantly. He slammed
the wardrobe shut. There it was again. It would
have to be dealt with. Sooner or later the news
of Eunice would reach her ears. Should she
hear it from some malicious gossip? Or from
him?

Damnation! Steeling himself to tell her, he
drew a heavy breath. The day suddenly smelled
sour. Shirt forgotten, he went to the bed and sat
down heavily. The bed bounced and Annette
giggled.

"Naughty, naughty." She wagged a finger in
his face. "Militia Day, Captain McNeil."

He caught her annoying finger. "Annette," he
began carefully, "what would you say if I told
you I were bethrothed?"

Her gay laughter pealed.

"I would say nothing."

"'Nothing'?" He was seized by astonishment.
The astonishment burst into bubbles of relief.
So she wouldn't care! They could go on as usual.

"I would say nothing," she repeated, lunging
up and grabbing him by the ears. "I would
simply *shoot* you."

He pushed her away, more annoyed than
startled. Then, as he sensed the justice of her
position, he broke into laughter, wondering if
shooting by the baroness might not be prefera-
ble to a lifetime of climbing into bed with
Eunice.

"Bray like a jackass, will you?" she snapped.

He ducked her slap. She cursed and lunged

again. He caught her, flinging her deep into the goosedown, imprisoning her. He kissed away her shrieks, kissed her until her furious struggles turned to gasps of desire. When she lay quiet beneath him, he spoke.

"Annette. Annette, I must tell you—"

His attempt was sabotaged. The heavy carved door flew open, banging hard into the robin's egg blue paint. Loud boots clumped in. Harrington's booming voice greeted him, and the opportunity was lost. Garth swore under his breath.

"Mornin' Cap'n! 'Tis Militia Day! About them twelve-pounders, Cap'n. Be we firing the twelve-pounders today? If so, Jenkins and me'll be needing a voucher to draw powder from the magazine." He paused, casually doffing his cap at Annette. "Mornin' ma'am," he said politely, as though finding a woman in his captain's bed was nothing out of the ordinary.

Annette steamed. She grabbed the coverlet.

"Really, McNeil. You should train your servants. They shouldn't be allowed to come crashing in."

Garth said, "Of course they should be allowed. Many's the ship that has come to calamity because a tar had to observe the protocol of knocking on his captain's door." He grinned at Harrington. "Besides, Harrington is *not* a servant."

"'Deed not, ma'am. Ye might say, ma'am, I be the Cap'n nurseymaid."

Annette was not amused. She wrenched the coverlet to her chin.

"Get out, lout!"

"Yes, ma'am." Harrington edged for the door. Garth stopped him with a gesture. Ignoring Annette and lunging off the bed, Garth renewed his search for the buckskin shirt, banging drawers, riffling through suits of clothes in the wardrobe.

"We'll give the men practice firing the eight-pounders. You'll find the powder voucher on the desk in the library. And, Harrington—"

He paused, finding the soft buckskin shirt hidden on a peg in the rear of the wardrobe. He pulled it out and yanked it on.

"It wouldn't hurt to 'nurseymaid' Raven today. Keep an eye on him. Raven cost me fifty pounds last Muster Day. He got drunk at Raleigh's Tavern and bet half the town he could shoot the yellow tailfeather off Governor Dinwiddie's prize fighting cock." Garth grinned sourly. "Blew the damned bird to Kingdom Come."

Harrington chuckled, then threw a scared look at Annette.

"Ay, Raven's a true McNeil. Even if the lad *can't* walk a gangplank without puking."

A sputter of vexation came from the bed.

"McNeil! Get him out of here!"

Garth ignored her, driving his stockinged feet into brown leather boots. He swung toward Harrington.

"Is Trent up?"

"Up, fit as a fiddle and perky as a jaybird. Trent be in the kitchen, talkin' up a storm to anybody what'll listen. He be taking his breakfast mush with cook. Cook says she'll bring him round to watch the Muster."

McNeil's face softened.

"Tell cook not to take the boy too near the artillery. The boom of the cannon might scare him. And tell her to bring along a lunch. Trent can eat with me on the Palace Green."

Harrington touched his cap in the affirmative, grinned at Annette, launched himself off the sea chest and clumped out.

As the door banged shut, Annette made a small, exasperated sound. Petulantly she said, "Damn you, McNeil. I think you care more for that Amsterdam orphan than you do for me."

Her dark eyes flashing, she waited for his denial, but he refused to give it. Coolly, he ignored her reference to the boy. He went to the washstand, sloshed water from pitcher to bowl and doused his head. The less said about the boy, the better.

But a chill fingered its way up the back of his neck as he finished his slapdash grooming. If Annette noticed his partiality to the child, others would notice too. And question. Suppose the duke of Tewksbury got wind of it?

He knew he should put the child in the charge of a nursemaid and ignore him. But it went against the grain. This was his son. His *son*. Whenever he swung the laughing child up into his arms and gazed into those intense eyes, he saw Flavia. And he saw himself. The boy was all he had left—all that remained of their love.

With a vexed sigh, the baroness swung her legs out of bed, rose, went to the wardrobe and fished out a wrapper she kept there. Shrugging into peach silk and Flemish lace, she leaned against the door, blocking his way as he sought to go. Her eyes flashed angrily.

"You haven't an iota of sentiment in you, McNeil. Yet you take pity on an orphan and bring him into your home. You treat him like a *son*. Why? Why do you do this?"

He scented danger. Danger for Trent. His eyes narrowed. With rough disregard, he pushed her away from the door.

"Why?" she persisted. "Why should you collect orphans?"

He eyed her with coldness.

"A habit I have, Baroness. A habit of collecting other men's castoffs."

His implication was ruthlessly clear. Hurt rose in her eyes. A dot of color began to burn in each cheek. Her nostrils flared defensively. She seemed to hover between lashing out and weeping. Indecisive, she drew a long quivering breath.

"In your absence, Garth," she said, her voice unsteady, "I've received offers of marriage. Lord Dunwood of Baltimore. Peter Hayes, the plantation owner. Mr. Fisk, the Boston shipbuilder. But I hoped..."

"Hoped I would help you choose?"

It was deliberately wounding. And meant to be. Anything to divert her thoughts from the boy.

He was satisfied to see the hurt in her eyes change to wild anger. Her small fists clenched.

"You—you—damned fornicating sea rover. So I am good enough to be your mistress, but *not* good enough to be your wife!"

"Precisely."

With a shriek she hurled herself at him, her pummeling fists ineffective in the heat of her passion.

"Oh, go to your Militia Day," she cried as he captured her wrists. "Go and be damned. I *shall* wed Lord Dunwood. And I warn you, McNeil—I warn you, I shall be *exceedingly* happy."

She'd hurled her final utterance as though it were the direst of threats. He couldn't help but laugh.

"*Exceedingly?*"

She twisted free of his grip, backed away and bared her teeth like a she-wolf.

"Yes!" she hissed. "Exceedingly! And you needn't make fun of Lord Dunwood. He may be a bit stout, but he is younger than *you* and very, very virile."

"*Exceedingly* virile?" he taunted unkindly.

With a curse, she whirled from him, flew across the room and flung herself onto the bed. She pounded the quaking mattress in frustration.

He started to go out, then changed his mind. Annette was only his mistress, not his first mistress and surely not his last. But in her odd, promiscuous way, she'd been damned loyal. He owed it to her to behave decently.

Closing the door, he turned and walked back to the bed. He sat. She wouldn't look at him. Belowstairs, servants clumped about, doing chores, talking. Someone was whistling. The faint smell of frying ham wafted up from the distant kitchen, melding—humorously, he thought—with the exotic scent of Annette's perfume.

At last she rolled over. She looked at him. For a woman of forty-five, she had a young-seeming face. Just now her expression was such a childish mix of both pique and the eagerness to forgive that he laughed and kissed her.

She warmed to him at once. She drew him into her arms, her lips parting eagerly. The familiar urge, the animal instinct, stirred hot and delicious in his groin. He kissed her again, hungrily.

"You'll be later to Muster," she whispered happily.

"*Exceedingly* late," he agreed.

It was ten o'clock before he swung out of his house on York Street, struck north on Waller Street and headed for Nicholson Street. He was on foot. To take a horse on Militia Day would be foolhardy. Already, the dusty streets were choked and congested. Farm wives hauled their wares to market in handcarts. Street jugglers performed wherever a willing audience of two or three gathered. Children erupted everywhere, like an outbreak of measles.

He passed Campbell's Tavern, skirting a group of children who'd gathered in the manure-pocked street, organizing games. They laughed excitedly, huddling like quivering puppies in a tight group.

"Run, sheep, run!" their leader shouted from the center.

The group broke like a starburst. McNeil dodged flying arms and legs.

To compound the chaos, British regulars drilled on Militia Day, too. The redcoats did this—not in a spirit of cooperation—but in rivalry. The spit-and-polish redcoat and the casual Virginia-born Englishman harbored an instinctive and competitive dislike for one another. While the redcoat prized soldierly obedience and could be marched off a cliff without batting an eye or missing a step in cadence, the independent Virginian chafed at such folderol. Eager to show his individuality, the Virginian marched to his own drumbeat. Often, he made his drill performance deliberately sloppy as a statement of independence.

The American-born Englishman could be led, Garth admitted. But he could *not* be driven.

Each militia elected its own officers and gave only nominal heed to the redcoat officer assigned by the royal governor to the unit. Friction was the natural result; skirmishes were inevitable. Once the ale began to flow, not even the governor's stern warning of punishment could keep the Virginian and the redcoat from going at one another. McNeil counted himself lucky if at day's end the men under his command tallied in with only a few black eyes and a broken nose or two.

But the tone of *this* Militia Day should be different, more cooperative, he told himself. The problem with New France was escalating. The French were infringing upon Virginia's frontier. A year ago, the French had seized a half-built English fort on the forks of the Ohio River. As a waterman, McNeil knew the gravity of this encroachment. Control the forks of the Ohio, and you controlled access to the great Mississippi River. Control the Mississippi, and you controlled a whole continent!

Aware of this and alarmed, Governor Dinwiddie had sent a warning to the French commander who'd seized the English fort on the forks. He demanded withdrawal. The ultimatum was carried into the wilderness by a twenty-one-year old volunteer, a Mr. George Washington.

Alone except for one white companion and a few Indian scouts, both Washington and the ultimatum he carried were treated with contempt by the French. Washington was sent packing. Slogging through the freezing wilderness in hard winter, the young man survived treacherous ambush by his own Indians, as well as near drowning in an icy, rushing river. Tattered, disheveled, tail tucked between his legs, the governor's valiant young emissary made his ignominious escape. The news was relayed to London. Virginia tensed, waiting for Parliament to deal with the New France issue.

Despite the seriousness of the Muster, American enthusiasm for mixing business with pleasure refused to be dampened. It was only ten o'clock, and already Williamsburg was a pot on the boil. Livestock mooed, brayed, baahed and whinnied as it was driven toward Francis Street and Market Square. Avoiding the pungent droppings, McNeil skirted the animals and cut across

a field behind the Capitol. In the field, Negro
slaves tended wicker cages of fighting cocks.
Wearing leather gloves and aprons, the blacks
carefully groomed their masters' roosters for the
afternoon contests. Wagers would fly fast and
furiously. Gentry would use tobacco vouchers
for currency. Poorer folk would bet buckskins.

Nicholson Street was crowded. Men should-
ering muskets ambled toward their units. Scarlet-
coated officers were already abroad, riding in
landaus with their ladies and sneering benignly
at the provincials.

"Maple sugar sweetmeat, sir?" a young vendor shouted.

A second vendor shouted louder, drowning
out the first.

"Buy a new English steel scalping knife, sir?
Get ready for the French and their hairdressers,
good sir! Only ten buckskins, sir. Only ten
bucks, good sir!"

McNeil pushed past. A crowd milled at the
jail. Prisoners were being exercised, and onlookers taunted them, yelling opinions as to
what they might get after they faced the general
court that afternoon. McNeil slowed his pace
and studied the prisoners as he passed. Occasionally a promising seaman might be found
among the riffraff. Jenkins had come into his
employ that way, and he'd never regretted paying
the man's fine.

He scanned the group, instantly rejecting the
lot. The only person who stood out as someone
with spine was a woman. McNeil scowled. Thin
as a scarecrow, she was scarcely as attractive as

one. A runaway bondwoman, no doubt. And one who'd compounded her crime with theft.

She'd go to the whipping post for sure. McNeil scowled again. It went against the grain to see a woman's back bend to the lash. It set his teeth on edge. Not that this stringy-haired trollop was likely to wilt under the whip! Judas, no. She had a strong, pridey look to her. There was an insolent set to her mouth. He didn't doubt that if she chose to do so, she could open that mouth and flail her taunters to jelly with her tongue.

He pushed on. But the brave look of the chit lingered. It occurred to him that she might make a nursemaid for Trent. She'd not be soft like cook, letting Trent get away with mayhem, letting the child eat himself sick on sugared flan simply because he demanded it. But the woman had not struck him as harsh, either. The eyes flashed rebellion, not cruelty.

He'd consider it.

If time permitted, he'd break from militia drill and interview the jailer. If she was a runaway, her master would probably be glad to be rid of her at a cheap price.

Ragged drum rolls sounded. He broke into an easy trot down Nicholson Street, cut across the bowling green near Chowning's Tavern and hurried down Duke of Gloucester Street. The smell of baking bread filled the air around Chowning's. Yeasty, mouthwatering smells drifted out of the tavern toward Nassau Street, as though drawn along by the drumming. The heavier richer smell of oyster stew drifted along, too. On Militia Day the stew was cooked outside in

Chowning's enormous iron pots, to accommodate the ravenous men who would clamor for it.

He was just leaving the bootmaker's shop in his dust when frantic hallooing from within the shop broke his stride. It was Raven. One foot bestockinged and one foot in half-fitted leather, Raven crashed down the steps.

"Garth! Wait, Garth."

He did so, but with ill grace. How typical of Raven to start out for Muster and end up at a tailor or bootmaker!

"Damn it, Raven," he said when his brother caught up, "you belong at Muster."

Raven laughed.

"So do you."

Garth flared, then checked his temper. Raven had the knack of hitting a nail square on the head. This quality, combined with a deceptive air of flightiness, was responsible for much of the growth of McNeil & McNeil. Few shipping clients realized they were dealing with a shrewd businessman until long after Raven had them signed, sealed and delivered.

"Well? Are we to have the pleasure of your company at the eight-pounders, Raven? Or have you the tailor and the barber yet to visit?"

Raven laughed, impervious to sarcasm.

"I'll be there." He kicked the foot encased in leather. The leather flapped foolishly. "I can't go a-marrying in old boots, can I?" He frowned, his quick mind leaping to a new subject. "Garth, I must talk to you. About a woman—"

"Not now."

Garth swung round as the ragged rat-a-tat-

tats of unpracticed farm boy drummers came from Nassau Street. The patchy drumming contrasted with the smooth professional drum rolls of the redcoats who were assembling a quarter of a mile away, on the Palace Green. Down Nassau Street, he caught sight of Jenkins. Jenkins was supervising cannon placement. The cannon mules were behaving like mules—stubbornly. He started to go, but Raven caught his sleeve.

"Garth, you must listen. I need your help. I intend to take a mistress and—"

Downfield, Jenkins looked up and waved. Impatiently Garth waved back, signaling he'd come soon. He swung back to Raven.

"Goddamn it, Raven, you've only a month to wait to bed Maryann. If you can't wait, take yourself to the doxy house in Yorktown. Or slip round to Mrs. Daws."

Raven shrugged impatiently.

"No, no, God, no. You don't understand. I'm in *love*. She's a bondslave and—"

Garth snorted his opinion.

Raven reddened. "I *love* Jane," he argued angrily. "I *will* make her my mistress."

Garth shrugged.

"Suit yourself. But *without* my help."

He looked downfield. Jenkins waved urgently, and he set off at a trot, his boots kicking up dust.

"Damn it, Garth, I need your help," Raven called plaintively.

McNeil glanced over his shoulder as he ran. "It's not help you want, but a *keeper*," he yelled. "Nobody but a lunatic would ask for the misery of both bride and mistress."

He reached the field, and it wasn't until he was thoroughly immersed in the day, squatting and going over each cannon with his hand to find firing flaws before allowing eager sixteen-year-olds to learn to fire them, that the irony of his own words sank into his brain like acid.

"Nobody but a lunatic," he muttered, "would ask for the misery of both Eunice and Annette."

At two o'clock he lunched on Cornish pasties with Trent at the Palace Green. The child had been overjoyed to see him.

"Cap Mac!" he shouted. He broke from cook's firm grasp and threw himself into Garth's arms. Trent's kiss was sugary and sticky. Testimony that he'd not walked past a sweetmeat vendor without putting up a fuss.

They ate sitting on the grass at the edge of the redcoats' drill field. If he'd expected the child to be awed by the pageantry—the low thunder of marching boots, drum rattles, the flash of officers' swords in the bright sunlight—he'd been mistaken. Trent's attention went elsewhere. A fat puppy, drawn by the smell of their food, trotted up to Trent and played the beggar. Laughing delightedly, Trent fed the puppy his lunch. Every scrap. The pup gorged himself, then staggered away.

Garth made a mental note: *Get dog for Trent.*

When lunch was done, cook gathered the basket on one hip, the boy on the other.

Jiggling him, she urged, "Be saying good-bye to Captain McNeil. Captain McNeil is your benefactor, Trent. It's a fortunate lad you are, to be found by Mr. Harrington and given shelter by Captain McNeil."

Trent eyed him soberly, his expressive eyes showing he understood nothing of the cook's lecture except that he should offer a farewell.

"Good-bye," he murmured, shrinking shyly against cook.

McNeil fought the urge to take Trent in his arms and give him a whiskery tickle, as any natural father might do. Instead, he let his hands fall empty to his side.

"Good-bye, Trent," he said. "Cook? Thank you."

Without allowing himself the luxury of a backward look, he loped off to rejoin his unit.

In his absence, Raven had been left in command. After shepherding the men to Chowning's for oyster stew and beer, Raven had returned in high spirits. He'd taken it into his head to lengthen the firing field and increase the charge. Jenkins had tried to dissuade Raven. Harrington, too. The town's cows, usually pastured in common on the fields used today for militia, were hobbled a few hundred yards beyond, out of cannon and musket range. But Raven had pooh-poohed the danger, and by the time Garth reached the unit, the worst had already happened. A milk cow that had broken her hobble and wandered back toward familiar pasture, had been hit square on the head and knocked dead. It hadn't been just any cow. It was Governor Dinwiddie's cow.

"Bad luck," Raven offered cheerfully by way of explanation when Garth lit into him.

"'Luck'!"

Raven shrugged uncomfortably. "Don't worry. I'll mollycoddle the governor at the ball tonight. These things, er, well, they *happen*, Garth."

Garth sighed in disgust.

"Only to you, Raven."

By four o'clock the air on Nassau Street was a haze of musket smoke and cannon residue. McNeil's eyes burned. He was sweaty with grime. The work was over for the day, and marksmanship contests had begun. The contests were nearly always won by keen-eyed, sixteen-year-old farm boys. Next would come the well-earned revelry: taverning, carousing, wrestling matches, impromptu horse races, cock fight wagers. As the sun went down, the militia would gradually break up, dividing into social class. The gentry would gravitate toward home or inn and clean up for an evening of theater or public balls. The lower class would make for cheap taverns, drinking ale until money ran out.

As McNeil stood watching the young sharpshooters, a flash of amber silk caught the corner of his eye. He turned. Down Nassau Street he caught sight of Annette. She was approaching on the arm of a flashily dressed dandy. He watched her trip daintily along. As she drew closer, McNeil could see mischief dancing in her eyes, and he realized she'd waited until he

looked his goddamn dirtiest to introduce him to
her Lord Dunwood.

For surely this was Dunwood. The description fit. About twenty-five years old. Short and
fat. So flashily dressed that he looked like a
pregnant parrot. A yellow silk waistcoat swathed
his rotund chest, and green silk breeches dropped
to the knee where ribboned garters fastened to
yellow silk stockings. His jacket was blue brocade, and his hat sported an ostrich plume so
long that it looked like a parrot's tailfeather.

McNeil frowned in irritation.

In contrast, Annette was understated elegance.
Her chaste high-necked dress was a spill of
amber silk. Her hat and short cape matched the
dress. Dark curls bobbed against her silk shoulder as she tripped along.

"Captain McNeil, isn't it?" she called out
demurely, uncertainly.

McNeil scowled. Forced to fall in with her
game, he strolled to the couple.

"Yes. Garth McNeil at your service, Lady
Annette."

She smiled her dazzling smile and tightened
her hold on Dunwood's arm.

"Lord Dunwood, may I present Captain Garth
McNeil."

With a quick black look at Annette, Garth
offered his grimy hand. Lord Dunwood was
forced to take it. Garth pumped the hand,
pumping the grime in. Annette's dark eyes flashed
with irritation, then with humor. She coughed
delicately into her kid glove, perhaps hiding a
giggle.

The three of them exchanged amenities, and Garth confirmed what he'd already suspected. Dunwood was a bore. But a rich, amiable bore. If Annette wed him, she'd have no trouble. Dunwood seemed easily persuaded to any side of any issue, as if taking a stand on an issue required too damned much work. If they wed, Annette would rule Dunwood; and Dunwood would adore her for it. The thought annoyed Garth beyond belief.

Amenities drifted into the evening's entertainments, the governor's ball. Annoyed, Garth took a stab at shaking Annette's composure.

"Perhaps, Lady Annette, you will grant me the honor of a dance at tonight's ball?" Garth said.

She smiled archly.

"Perhaps. However, Lord Dunwood tells me he intends to claim every dance. I am quite his servant in the matter."

Lord Dunwood laughed proudly, muttering an abashed, "My dear!" Then, to Garth, "A pleasure to have met you, sir." Garth smiled grimly and again stuck out his hand. Dunwood was forced to take it.

"A pleasure, sir," Garth agreed, stabbing Annette with a look. "An *exceedingly* great pleasure."

It was five o'clock before he remembered the girl at the jail. His inclination was to forget it and head for home with Harrington. He was dirty and tired. He wanted the hot bath that waited in his bedchamber at the close of Militia

Day. But as he swung down Francis Street, the memory of the chit's fierce, proud eyes kept intruding.

"Harrington," he directed irritably, jerking his thumb toward Blair Street. They turned and strode north toward the jail and the noisy throng that had gathered for public punishments. He told Harrington his intention.

The court had convened after the noon dinner hour. Because each crime and its allotted punishment was explicitly laid down by law, long deliberation was seldom necessary. The general court sat just twice a year, and a proper court could deal with a dozen or more lawbreakers in an afternoon. Already, ten prisoners had been marched back from court and stood in the jail yard, some awaiting punishment, some already undergoing it. A man hung at the whipping post, enduring his stripes none too bravely. An adolescent girl cried as she crouched in wrist and neck stocks. Two urchins with wild turkey feathers darted past the girl, tickling her nose.

McNeil surveyed the prisoners. "There she is," he muttered tiredly to Harrington. "That one," he said, nodding.

"Ahhh," Harrington whispered after a long moment. "She be a fine-looking woman, Cap'n."

Garth shrugged irritably. "You're looking in the wrong place. The one standing under the maple. The one in the filthy gown. Hair like a worn-out mop."

Harrington nodded.

"Ay, sir. I see 'er. Ay, she be a *fine*-looking girl."

McNeil shifted, glancing at Harrington. The man's ruddy, beaky face softened foolishly as he gazed at the bondwoman. McNeil chuckled. Well, there's no accounting for one's taste in women, he supposed.

The town drunk was released from the post, and the woman was next. Her charges were read aloud. She'd run away from Mrs. Spencer's employ and been gone eight months. She'd stolen her mistress's earbobs, which had been recovered. But she'd ruined the clothes she stole. Her fine was sixty pounds of tobacco or twenty lashes to the bare back. Also, a year added to the indenture. At the end of the reading, the crowd clamored for the whip.

"Shall you speak up now, Cap'n?" Harrington urged.

"Wait. Let's see if that pridey spirit turns to mush when she's led to the post."

The crowd shouted in excitement as the jailer walked toward the bondwoman. He grabbed for her hand, but she snatched it away. Pushing him aside with an earthy curse, she marched to the post. Head held high as the sail of a proud ship, she angrily unlaced her own bodice. Closing her eyes, she let the bodice fall to the dust and angrily thrust her wrists to the post to be tied. The crowd jeered, the drunks shouting bawdy comments about her small, thin breasts.

"Now, Cap'n?" Harrington asked anxiously.

Garth pushed through the crowd.

"Wait!" Garth yelled to the court's representative. "I'll pay the woman's fine. I'll buy her indenture."

The crowd groaned its disappointment, and at the post, the girl whirled round, blinking in astonishment. She snatched up her bodice, yanking it to thin breasts. Her eyes narrowed warily.

A shrill voice came from the crowd, followed by its owner, Mrs. Eliza Spencer. In moments the bargain was struck and disappointed spectators wandered off, seeking the cock fights. It was agreed McNeil would pay the original price of the indenture and would indemnify Mrs. Spencer for lost clothes by sending over two bolts of flocked tabby silk, fresh from England and imprinted in the latest fashion. Mrs. Spencer tripped out of the jail yard well pleased.

"Good fortune to you, Captain McNeil," she trilled. "For you shall have need of it. She's Newgate trash. A thief, a liar and a runaway. I'm glad to have no more truck with her."

At the post, the girl still crouched warily, so astonished that she didn't think to put on her bodice rather than hide behind it. But when Garth strode to the post, she lifted herself tall. Distrust and wariness flashed from narrowed eyes. Garth scowled.

By God, she was a cheeky one for a woman who smelled like a pigpen and had jail lice crawling in the hair. He guessed she would require the same rough indoctrination he used on pridey new seamen.

"Name?" he demanded.

"M—M—" She had to lick her lips before she could speak. Good, he thought. So she wasn't as

fearless as she'd pretended. Her mouth *had*
gone dry in fear of the whipping post.

"Mab Collins, sir," she whispered.

"Louder!"

Her eyes flashed with quick anger before she
threw her glance to the ground.

"Mab Collins, sir."

"'Mab'?" He turned to Harrington and laughed
derisively. "A stupid name. A name suitable for
a cow. Or," he said, pausing deliberately, "a
sow."

At his side, Harrington shuffled uncomfortably.
He'd seen the scenerio played before. But never on a woman.

Mab Collins's head jerked up. Again the anger flashed. This time it was tempered with
hate.

"If you say so, sir."

"I *do* say so," he said unpleasantly. "Mab is a
sow's name. But it suits you."

She looked at the ground, drawing quick
angry breaths.

"Put on your bodice!" he ordered, and she
jumped to obey. He nodded toward Harrington.
"This is Mr. Harrington. You will follow him to
my home. He will assign your duties. Obey him
to the letter, and he'll beat you no harder than
he beats the Negroes."

She flinched, throwing Harrington a scared
look that she tried to conceal. Garth turned on
his heel and strode out of the yard. To his
surprise, a loud shrill shout chased after him.

"I'll not be your doxy!"

He swung around.

"Sir," she added, as though to ameliorate what she'd shouted.

He stared at her in astonishment. Judas, the chit had conceit! Did she think him so hard up for a female that—it was laughable. But he was too tired and exasperated to laugh. He strode back to where she stood shaking and stared her down. Even in her terror, she managed a shaky whisper.

"I'll be *no one's* doxy, sir."

He studied her with growing irritation. He wanted his bath, not a confrontation with this bag of bones.

"You're to be a nursemaid," he snapped. Her eyes widened. "Nursemaid to an orphan who lives in my house. That is, if you're not too stupid a sow to tend a child!"

Her shoulders stiffened. Her eyes dropped angrily to the ground.

"I had two o' me own."

"You will be nursemaid to a little boy. Treat him harshly, and I will beat you. Treat him too soft, and I will beat you twice as hard. Understood?"

She jumped.

"Yes, sir," she whispered, but he wasn't fooled by her seeming docility. He turned to Harrington, who was having trouble hiding a grin.

"Take her home. Before you let her into the house, burn those pigsty clothes and see that she bathes. I'll not have cooties in my house."

* * *

He turned to go just as Mab Collins's eyes flew up in horror.

"A all-over bath? Judas, Mary, Matthew! I'll not do it. 'Twill be my death. You can't make me, sir. I'm a Englishwoman. I know my rights."

It was time to change tactics. Garth shrugged, nodding to Harrington.

"I've changed my mind. I don't want the sow. The bargain is off. Call the jailer. Tie her to the post."

"Ow, sir!" she screamed. "I'll take the bath! I will!"

"Too late," he threw out callously, turning on his heel and tramping down Nicholson Street.

Mab Collins flew after him. She trailed in his dust, begging, pleading. He paid scant attention, walking so fast that she had to run.

"Sir! I beg! Please! I'll be a right good nursemaid! Why, sir, I can teach the child. I can read. And cipher."

"Ha!"

"And I know my manners, sir. Please! I was taught lady-ways by a duchess."

"Ha."

"Well, she claimed to be a duchess at first, sir. Aboard ship, sir. She did, sir. The girl what taught me."

He stopped in his tracks and swung around. The chit was a bigger liar than he'd bargained for. Perhaps it *would* be better to sell her off. Perhaps she'd be bad for Trent.

Sensing that her life was in his hands and being decided for good or ill, Mab Collins bowed her head, nervously clasping and unclasping her hands. She began to weep. Not ladylike tears, but great gasping sobs as though the tears had been dammed up for years.

He was moved, but clearly it wasn't in his best interests to show it. When Harrington caught up to them, Garth said coldly, "Take her home. And tell her what we *do* to bondslaves who steal, run away, or tell lies."

Harrington nodded uncertainly, but made a passable pretense of certainty with his hearty, "Ay, ay, Cap'n."

But when McNeil strode off, Harrington bolted after him for a few steps and whispered in his ear.

"Cap'n? What is it we do, sir? To bondslaves?"

Garth grinned wearily.

"How in Hades do *I* know? Make up something."

Whatever Harrington told the homely girl must've been more outrageous than her own lie about keeping company with a duchess. For when he rounded the corner at York Street and glanced back over his shoulder, Mab Collins was following Harrington, meek as a lamb.

McNeil grinned. He wasn't such a fool as to believe what he saw. The chit was not as easily cowed as she pretended.

If he thought he'd left his vexations behind him on Francis Street, he was wrong. Inside the house, Raven waited. Lounging deep in a new Queen Anne chair, with polished boots crossed upon a new ruby velvet footstool, Raven clasped a goblet of Madeira in one hand, two buns of minced chicken in the other. He was cheerfully gorging himself on what had been intended for McNeil's own supper.

Raven burst into chatter. Ignoring him, McNeil strode to the sideboard in the dining room, wolfed the remaining bun, washed it down with Madeira and went upstairs for the warm bath that waited near the crackling fire in his bedchamber.

To his annoyance, Raven followed.

"Danm it, Raven, if you mean to share my tub too, you will have gone too far."

Raven laughed.

"I've already been in it. And thank you."

The scum floating along the waterline of the brass tub confirmed it. McNeil stared sourly at it, then sighed, shucked boots and buckskins, and got in. The warm water carried away his temper along with the grime. He groped for the bar of lavender soap that Raven had left melting on the bottom. He scrubbed hair and body, only half listening to Raven's persistent chatter. He shaved in the tub, with Raven holding the mirror.

"So you see, Garth, it's quite simple," Raven went on enthusiastically. "You've only to sail up to Chestertown, seek out the Reverend Josiah Byng and buy Jane Brown's indenture for me."

The water whooshed as he stood and got out, toweling himself dry.

"No."

"Damnation, Garth! Have you no family feelings? I'm dying of love and you'll do nothing to help me! I only ask you to buy her indenture so

that the Tates will not find out. I can't have
Maryann knowing."

Garth snorted, went to the wardrobe and
began to dress for the ball.

"If you take a mistress, let me assure you,
Raven, that a wife always finds out."

Raven followed him to the wardrobe.

"No, she won't. You recall my telling you
about the little house I bought for Jane? On
Capitol Landing Road?" He shrugged boyishly.
"Well, I bought it in *your* name, Garth."

McNeil jerked around.

"Goddamn it!"

Mildly vexed with Raven before, he was
thoroughly vexed now.

"Brother, you have finally gone too far! What
of *my* good reputation? Do you think I have no
use for it?"

Raven wilted. But not in total. He grinned
weakly.

"Well," he tried, "you're not married."

"The hell I'm not! I'm betrothed. That's just
as binding."

Raven's eyes grew large, then narrowed, flashing with humor. "Not the Vachon? Not Annette?"

McNeil fumed. He'd snapped out the news
without thinking. Damnation and hellfire! Now
he'd have to entrust Raven with the secret.

"Not Annette," he snapped unwillingly. "Miss
Eunice Wetherby. Cousin to the earl of Wetherby.
I became betrothed to her on my last sailing. In
Amsterdam."

Raven plunked down in a chair, whistling his
surprise.

"Annette doesn't know," Garth admitted quietly. "No one knows yet. I trust I can count on *you* to keep your damn mouth shut."

Raven stared at him, still as stunned as a gaffed fish pulled out of water. Again, Raven whistled in disbelief.

"We'll count on each other," Raven said, warming to the conspiracy. "I'll keep your betrothed a secret from your mistress. You keep my mistress a secret from my betrothed."

Garth wrenched a ruffled shirt of cream silk from the wardrobe, jerked it on and buttoned it with quick angry twists.

"Gallows humor," he said sourly.

"But if you could help me—" Raven started again.

"No."

But no did not mean to Raven what it meant to others. He brushed it away like a gnat. "There is one additional small problem that you must help me with. Jane is not completely persuaded to become my mistress."

Garth snorted.

"Not *completely*?"

Raven laughed self-consciously.

"Actually, Garth, she has said no."

Garth stabbed his legs into brown brocade breeches, then drew on cream silk stockings and black shoes. He threw his brother a cynical look.

"Occasionally, Raven, 'no' means no."

Raven brushed the argument aside. He sighed with longing. "If only you could see her, Garth, you would understand. She's as beautiful as an

angel. Her hair—God, her hair! It glows like
the richest copper. And her eyes are incredible.
They're not quite blue, but they're not quite
green, either."

Raven went on extolling the beauty of his
intended mistress until Garth lost patience and
sent him packing. His mood spoiled by Raven,
he kicked the door shut behind his brother,
found a cigar in the new enameled Persian box
on the low cherry-wood table, dipped a sliver of
kindling into the crackling fire, lit his cigar and
sank into one of Annette's new purchases. He
propped his feet on the stool and smoked the
cigar without tasting. Outside, twilight was
descending, stealing light from the room and
leaving behind only melancholy shadows.

Raven's chatter had set his teeth on edge. No.
It had done more. It had unsettled him. He,
too, had once known a girl like the girl Raven
described. A girl with red hair and incredible
eyes. A girl whose sweetness sent the heart
soaring.

He drew viciously on the cigar, and as viciously
spat out the biting smoke.

"Goddamn you, Raven," he muttered.

Outside, the sun had set. Militia Day was
finishing. A few drunken shouts still echoed
from Francis Street. Dogs still barked, but
hoarsely, as though they'd barked themselves
out. The oil lamps that fronted his brick house
were being lit. Soft laughter drifted up as the
scullery girl carried oil to the lamplighter and
stood conversing with him.

He'd not sat and thought deliberately about Flavia in a long time. He'd tried to forget. When memories pressed in, he'd made it a habit to throw himself into some sort of activity. Anything to bury the ache. But today, egged into it by Raven's chatter, he allowed himself to think about her. He remembered so much. She'd worn the scent of heather. Fresh and light as spring rain. He remembered the rabbit-quick beat of her heart as he held her close. The gentle innocence of her voice as she'd declared her love for him. Her startled gasp when his touch upon her soft body had brought her a pleasure she hadn't expected.

The old misery settled upon him like a pea-soup fog enveloping the *Caroline* at sea. His sails went slack. He sat motionless in the flickering firelight, his ship becalmed.

Lost. She was lost to him forever.

Before Flavia, he'd thought loss was simply a feeling. It wasn't. Loss was a physical weight. Under its oppression he sank low in the chair, smoking. The air in the room smelled of cigar and of melancholy.

Abruptly he lunged out of the chair, slung the cigar into the fire, grabbed waistcoat and jacket and flung the door open with a bang.

Stomping down the stairs, he bellowed for his staff, bellowing Flavia out of his mind.

"Cook! Damnation, where's my supper?" he thundered, though he knew good and well supper waited on the sideboard. "Patsy! Come brush my jacket this instant or you'll get the

cat-o'-nine! Toad, bring the landau at once! Drive
it to the front stoop. Trent! Where are you, you
little scamp? Come kiss me good-bye!"

His household exploded. The furor of scam-
pering, excited servants, and Trent trying to kiss
him while stoutly imprisoning a meowing cat in
his small arms, sent melancholy flying. He stood
at the sideboard in reasonably good humor,
devouring chicken buns while his jacket and the
shoes on his feet were brushed. He downed a
goblet of Madeira and was about to sprint for
the landau when cook bustled in.

"Cap'n McNeil, sir? At the kitchen door, sir.
A servant girl begs to speak with you."

"Send her away," he directed, leaving.

"She says she carries a letter of introduction."

Garth shrugged his annoyance.

"Leave the letter in the library. I haven't
time."

"She won't leave go of it, sir," cook argued,
following him to the door.

"Then the hell with her," he said pleasantly,
flinging the door open. "Good night, cook."

"Good night, sir."

"Sir? Captain McNeil?" said cook. "The girl is
back."

McNeil looked up from his writing table in
the library and scowled. He was in a foul mood.
His head pounded like ten devils. He'd drunk
too much at the ball, smoked too many cigars,
stayed up too late. His luck had soured at the
gaming tables. He'd drawn an idiot partner for
whist. Between them they'd left fifty pounds at

the table. Further, it was rumored McNeil &
McNeil would lose Governor Dinwiddie as a
shipping client. The governor had not been
amused by Raven's artillery expertise on the
muster field. He'd not been won over by Raven's earnest explanation that Raven had thought
the cow was a bull's-eye target, painted on
sacking and tied to a hay bale in the distant
field.

"A bull's-eye!" he mumbled to himself, ignoring cook, who still stood before him. "Raven's a
bona fide lunatic!"

The night had gone from bad to worse. Concerned to play the role of prim, proper widow
during Lord Dunwood's visit to Williamsburg,
Annette had shaken her head at Garth's unspoken invitation to spend the night. Bidding him a
cool, polite farewell, as though they were the
merest of acquaintances, she'd tripped off on
Lord Dunwood's arm, going chastely to her own
mansion near the Governor's Palace on North
England Street.

In front of his desk, cook sighed heavily.

"Shall I bring her in, sir? The servant girl?
The girl with the letter?"

McNeil scowled. What the devil was cook
blathering about? He racked his brain.

He remembered. Something about a petition.
Scowling blackly, he vowed to dispatch of the
nuisance as swiftly as possible. Waiting, he stared
around the room. The library seemed suddenly
rough and utilitarian compared with what Annette
had done in other rooms.

The girl crept in like a mouse. Expecting a

girl, McNeil was startled to see a child. She couldn't be more than thirteen. Her face was white with fear. Against the pallor, childish freckles stood out like a spatter of red clay on a whitewashed wall.

"Give me the letter."

She did so, shaking so badly that she dropped it twice before she got it to him. He broke the seal, opened the letter without interest and began to read.

> Dear Captain Garth McNeil,
> If ever you have known the joy of true love, honor the memory of that love by helping this girl.
>
> One Who Beseeches You

He jerked his head up. He lashed the girl with a black look. What fool nonsense? Something copied from an almanac or a bad theatrical play? He read the note again, stirring uneasily. Who would dare!

"You!" he accused. "You wrote this."

The child blanched.

"I can't write, sir," she whispered. "Nor read."

"Then, who!"

She swallowed, shaking visibly in fear.

"A man, sir. He said—"

"What man? Where?"

A tic jumped in her cheek.

"A stranger, sir. 'Twas on the road. Between Baltimore and Williamsburg, sir. He said—"

"He was gentry," McNeil accused hotly. "The note is written without a single misspelling."

Her eyes slid away. She swayed as if she might 'fall.

"I don't know, sir—"

"Why did he send you to me?"

"He—he—said Captain McNeil would help me."

McNeil lunged to his feet and strode to the window. Out on York Street, two boys rolled and chased a wood hoop as they made their way to parish school. A dog chased the hoop, too, yapping and growling at it as though it were alive.

He turned and eyed the girl with cold suspicion.

"Who are you?"

"Mary Wooster, sir."

"And your trouble?"

The white face blanched even whiter. She threw him a terrified look, then bowed her head and stared at the floor.

"I've runned away, sir. From my indenture."

"That is a crown offense," he said flatly. "I can't help you."

Her shoulders curled forward in pathetic hopelessness. McNeil stared at the letter. He reread it. Then read it again. He was mystified. Who, among his acquaintances, would dare make such a demand of him? And refer to love! Annette? Raven? Ridiculous. He swung back at the child.

"Why did you run away?"

She shook her head.

"Did your master beat you?" he prompted.

Red color swam up to her face, drowning the freckles. She shook her head in the negative, still staring at the floor. McNeil's anger began to abate as he glimpsed her plight. It was the old story. Common to plantation life. King of all he surveyed, the plantation owner made himself the chief rooster.

"How old are you?" he asked more gently.

"Fifteen, sir," she whispered.

"How long has your master been forcing you?"

She cringed in shame.

"I birthed a month ago," she whispered, her voice scarcely audible. "When I was fourteen, sir—I birthed then, too."

He choked.

"You went to the post for bastardy?"

Too shamed to answer, the child let her cloak fall to the floor and tugged at the neck of her soiled dress, revealing a small patch of upper back.

McNeil sucked wind. The snakelike scars of the whip stood out in livid purple. She'd be thirty before those scars disappeared, he estimated.

He strode to the window, threw it open and sucked in the clean, chill air of approaching winter. When he turned again, the child had retrieved her cloak and stood swathed in it, awaiting his judgment as though awaiting the gallows.

He went past her to the door and flung it open.

"Toad!" he bellowed. "Toad, the landau at

once! You're to drive me to Hampton. And God help you if you don't make tracks. You're to have me there before the *Hampton Belle* sails today to Barbados."

Chapter 15

ELIZABETH SIMM scandalized all of Chestertown by ordering her wedding dress from the dressmaker eight days before the long-ailing Mrs. Gresham died. It was a shockingly expensive gown. Elizabeth paid for it in full upon ordering, paid with a tobacco draft written in Mr. Gresham's own land.

The gossip had traveled on quick hot tongues.

"Ira Gresham grows senile!"

"That dark-haired chippy bewitched him!"

"Scandalous! Mrs. Gresham not yet in her grave!"

"Taking a *bondslave* to wife."

"Poor Mrs. Gresham. Her bed'll have no chance to cool 'ere Betsy Simm climbs into it!"

When news had reached the Rose and Crown, where Jimmy Barlow and his cronies were gambling at dice, Jimmy Barlow had taken to the cup. He drank himself nearly senseless. Seizing a cudgel, he'd leaped drunkenly upon his horse and galloped down Water Street, smashing out every oil lamp that burned before Chester River mansions. He'd been caught and thrown into jail. The scandal had intensified when, at noon of the next day, Betsy Simm had marched boldly to the jail and had paid Jimmy Barlow's fine with *another* tobacco draft written by Mr. Gresham.

Gossips had had a field day, and Flavia was glad. Mary Wooster's disappearance was forgotten. Even the schoolboys, who spent spare hours beating the bushes for Mary in hopes of claiming the reward, forgot her. With each day that passed, Flavia breathed easier. She had faith that if Mary had managed to reach Garth, Mary would have found a safe haven.

Meanwhile, Betsy's scandal had gone on.

"The brazen chippy," Mrs. Byng had summed up to a visiting friend, as Flavia served tea. "What Mr. Gresham sees in that girl, I cannot fathom. He quite spoils my plan. I meant to bring my sister from Philadelphia. Prudence would've made him a good Christian helpmeet. True, she's lost a tooth or two. But she don't limp much anymore. Not since she took my advice to eat honey for joint pain."

The visiting friend had set cup into saucer with a startled click and a bewildered, "But Mrs. Gresham is still alive."

"Well, she won't be," Mrs. Byng had snapped crossly, as Flavia passed the raisin cakes. "And Mrs. Gresham can blame it upon rhubarb. I advised her in the matter many years ago. 'Have your cook boil it two hours,' I said. But, no. She *would* have it boilt only thirty minutes."

Mrs. Byng's lip curled in contempt.

"Well, there she lies, bedridden five years and lately spitting blood. And there's the Simm chit, planning to walk the aisle of the church, bold as brass."

"Disgusting," the friend had murmured, biting into a raisin cake.

"Outrageous," mumbled Mrs. Byng, chewing her cake.

Mrs. Gresham had grown worse. Throughout Kent County, black gowns and black suits were pulled from wardrobes and given stiff brushings. Mr. Gresham had sent to Annapolis for two hundred pairs of kid gloves, the appropriate gift for a rich planter to give funeral guests. He'd ordered a mourning ring, and it was reported that in a touching moment Mrs. Gresham herself had selected the lock of hair to be cut off and put into her widower's ring as a badge of their eternal union.

This done, her affairs tidily in order, the poor woman had bade an affectionate farewell to husband, children and grandchildren. Easing into a deep unnatural sleep, she had lingered one more day, then passed.

Mrs. Byng was keen to attend the sumptuous two-day funeral feast, and flew into a temper when word came she was needed in Philadelphia. Her sister had fallen and was lying in bed with a bad leg. Grumbling, Mrs. Byng clattered off in the church warden's inferior one-horse chaise to catch the public coach that ran between Baltimore and Philadelphia.

Flavia nearly jumped for joy to see her go. But she was uneasy, too. Except for Neddy, she'd be alone with the Reverend Byng.

But Mr. Byng spent funeral week at the Greshams', fawning over the stricken family. With both Byngs gone, Flavia reveled in the luxury of freedom. It was a freedom she'd never known. Always she'd been under someone's domination: her parents, the duke, the indenture. Always she'd had responsibilities. As eldest of six daughters, she'd sensed early in life that she was expected to sacrifice herself for her younger sisters. She'd done so, obediently marrying at fifteen.

But freedom.

Freedom!

It was as heady as wine. Lighthearted, laughing breathlessly, she ran through the wintry, sparrow-picked fields for the sheer joy of running. She sang at her chores. She spoiled Neddy with raisin cakes. She bundled up warmly and tramped to the low bluffs of the Chester River. She counted eleven ships under sail and told herself the finest and fastest was Garth's. She pretended he stood at the wheel, his strong shoulders straining as he guided the ship, making her leap and race like the wind.

Nights, she sat by the fire reading and musing. She thought about Garth. She dwelt fully and indulgently upon Robert, imagining his growth. He was no longer a baby. He was past two. Sturdy, handsome, adorable? Surely! And did he talk now? Did he know the names of animals? Was there someone he sweetly called Mama? The thought wrenched her, left her sick with unbearable yearning.

By the time Mr. Byng returned home from the Greshams', Flavia had Neddy entrenched in the kitchen for the winter. His pallet and blankets visibly occupied a corner. Mr. Byng scowled when he saw. He was forced to say nothing, for the weather had turned bitter. Only a barbarian would make a human being sleep out in it.

She felt an immense, trembly relief. Neddy's presence was her shield.

The November sky over St. Paul's Church was a rare bright blue. The sun shone, and from the northwest came a crisp, chill wind. The Chesapeake Bay air smelled fresh and clean, like new beginnings. Flavia hoped it was a good omen for bride and groom.

Closing her cloak against the wind, she took Dennis Finny's arm and turned to watch the bridal carriage. It was an open carriage, and the bride stood tall in it, fairly dancing with excitement.

"Get ready!" the bride shouted gaily to a group of about twenty horsemen whose mounts were shying nervously.

"One!

"Two!

"Three—ride for the bottle!"

The ground vibrated under Flavia's feet as horse hooves thundered away from the church. Whooping and yelling like Indians, the score of

horsemen tore off for the Gresham plantation.
The wedding was over. The traditional wedding
game of Ride-for-the-Bottle had begun. The
winner would be the first rider to reach the
white-pillared veranda of the Gresham mansion.
Scooping up the waiting bottle of rum, the
winner would gallop back to the approaching
wedding procession and claim his prize: a kiss
from the bride.

"I pray Jimmy Barlow does not win," Dennis
Finny murmured.

Flavia met his concerned eyes and smiled.

"So do I."

But a glance at the wedding carriage con-
vinced her the bride prayed quite the opposite.
Elizabeth Simm Gresham danced on tiptoe,
tossing her shining black mane in excitement as
she watched the riders go. She was lovely in a
gown of ivory satin with a red velvet cardinal
cloak tossed carelessly back from her shoulders.
At her side sat Mr. Gresham. He tugged at her
cloak, silently bidding her sit. Elizabeth absently
brushed at the annoying hand and continued to
stand. She didn't sit until Jimmy Barlow's horse
galloped out of sight. Then she dropped into the
cushions with a pleased sigh that reached even
the rear of the entourage where Flavia and
Dennis stood.

Flavia glanced at Dennis. He shook his head.

Mr. Gresham signaled and the procession
moved forward. It was as awkward an assortment of wedding guests as Flavia had ever seen:
bond servants on foot, tavernkeepers on their
mules, well-dressed gentry in landaus, in chariots,

on handsomely saddled horses or carried in Negro-borne sedan chairs. The retinue surged forward, tight-lipped and ill at ease.

Flavia had to smile ruefully at Betsy Simm's stubborn loyalty. Betsy would not marry, she'd told Mr. Gresham, unless she could marry in St. Paul's and invite her friends to the celebration. Mr. Gresham had given in, and Flavia suspected the gentry would never forgive Betsy for this untidy mix of guests. They'd have forgiven her for marrying into their ranks if she'd done so quietly and with decorum. She was, after all, the daughter of an earl and titled by birthright.

For some twenty minutes they sauntered along in the chill November sunshine, chaises rattling ahead, an occasional wheel squeaking. Finally Flavia heard the distant sound of pounding hooves. Riders broke over the crest in the road. Flavia's hand tightened on Dennis's arm.

"Is it Jimmy?"

"I don't know."

Shouting to the carriage driver to stop, Betsy jumped up, squealing in excitement, her hands clapped to her mouth. The winning rider came charging like thunder, bottle hoisted high in one hand, the bottle's gay ribbons streaming in the wind like the gold and scarlet banner of a knight.

"Jimmy!" Betsy squealed.

Thundering up to the retinue, he jerked his horse to a halt, leaped down and pushed his way through the crowd to the wedding carriage.

He grinned, his white teeth flashing.

"My prize, Mrs. Gresham?"

Betsy giggled. She stooped to give him a chaste kiss on the mouth. But he'd tossed the beribboned bottle to a friend, and with a quick unexpected movement, he grabbed Betsy round the waist and swung her up and out of the carriage. Betsy shrieked in shock, and the crowd gasped its astonishment.

Mr. Gresham jumped up.

"Here, now! Stop, I say! Stop!" the elderly bridegroom stormed as his young wife's petticoats went flying and a silk-stockinged leg flashed.

From atop his horse, Mr. Byng joined in.

"Mongrel! Cur! Stop, we say. What God hath joined—"

Jimmy Barlow paid no attention. He set Betsy on her feet. He drew her into his arms. He kissed her soundly and with obvious enjoyment as a shocked buzzing rippled through the crowd. It was a long kiss, and when they parted, the moistness of their young lips attested to the intimacy of it. Flavia swallowed hard, her eyes misting. The kiss had been sweet and fervent, carrying her back to what she'd shared with Garth. She remembered his strong warm arms sheltering her. She remembered his thrilling kisses, his tongue seeking hers.

Without meaning to, Flavia clutched Dennis's arm. He looked down at her. But whatever he saw in her misty eyes must have given him pain, for he looked quickly away.

In the carriage, Mr. Gresham stood stiffly, his face purple under his white powdered wig.

"Elizabeth! Get into the carriage at once."

Apoplectic, Ira Gresham tore at the carriage

door latch, finally flinging the door back with a loud bang that shied the horses and rocked the carriage. "Get in!" he repeated.

As Flavia watched, the soft joyous happiness faded from Betsy's face. She jerked herself from Jimmy's arms, put a hard bright smile on her lips and jumped up into the carriage.

The incident provided more grist for the gossip mill, and the mill eagerly began to grind. Trailing along in the dusty rear of the party, Flavia unhappily caught bits of it.

"Indecent! Everyone knows what she's been to Jimmy Barlow!"

"How could Ira Gresham wed such a tramp?"

"They say his grown children are livid. Imagine burying a mother one week and greeting a stepmother the next!"

"Mind you, there's always a reason for haste. But I think *I* can count to 'nine' as well as anyone else in Kent County."

"Is it true that now we must call her *Lady Elizabeth?*"

Angrily, Flavia shut her ears to the sniping. Her loyalty lay with Betsy. And even with Jimmy Barlow. Crude ruffian that he was, he'd done his bit to cover Mary Wooster's tracks.

Within the carved and paneled splendor of Gresham Manor, the bride's receiving party proved to be as awkward and stiff as Flavia had feared. Guests gathered in two camps, a large no-man's-land of polished ballroom floor between. Hostility bristled from each camp.

In deference to the scarcely departed Mrs. Gresham, there was no music, no dancing. But buffet tables sent out tantalizing aromas of plum pudding, buttered smoked oysters and all manner of delicacies. Wine, ale and rum toddy bowls abounded.

While most of the lower class huddled like sheep, scared to sample food or drink lest they spill, the upper class began to celebrate with haughty confidence. Begrudgingly, they paid their respects to the bride, and Betsy's clear gay voice rose above the rest.

"It is *Lady* Elizabeth," she said with crisp maliciousness, correcting a guest who'd addressed her as "Mrs. Gresham."

Flavia and Dennis exchanged looks of amusement. Across the ballroom Betsy clung demurely to the velvet-jacketed arm of her haughty bridegroom. But with each sip of wine, her glance flew more boldly across the room to Jimmy Barlow, who stood amused and drinking at the toddy bowl.

Betsy's hand pulled from the velvet sleeve. Her heels clicked over the empty expanse of no-man's-land. Rich satin swooshed against Flavia's green lutestring silk gown as Betsy linked arms with her.

"Stroll with me, Jane," she commanded, disguising her intent. Flavia demurred, but she was drawn along. By a circuitous route Betsy made her way toward the laughter at the toddy bowl. Jimmy Barlow's laughter died as Betsy suddenly stood before him, a ravishing dark-eyed gypsy, her lovely bosom rising and falling as she looked up at him.

He stared at her and she at him. Flavia could

almost feel the regret that flowed between them. They were unsuited and yet they loved. Her heart melted with sympathy. To know love and then to lose it—wasn't that life's greatest sorrow?

As though he could stand no more, Jimmy Barlow rudely turned his back on Betsy and flirted with the tavernkeeper's daughter. Betsy's lips trembled, but immediately she gave her dark head a toss. With a forced gay laugh, Betsy tugged at Flavia's arm, drawing her across the polished ballroom floor toward the gentry.

"No, Betsy—please!"

But it was useless, and she was suddenly very glad she'd cut material from the deep hem of the green lutestring gown, fashioning silk rosettes to cover the patches Raven had so made fun of the night of the Tate ball. She knew she needn't be ashamed of her appearance. With Mrs. Byng still gone, she'd managed a tub bath, washing her hair and brushing it dry before Mrs. Byng's mirror. Her hair was shiny and clean, its color a deep wine red that spilled to her shoulders and framed her bosom. Her cheeks and lips felt rosy from the long walk in nippy air. Glances from the gentry confirmed what she knew. She looked pretty. Only Mr. Byng's glance was not an admiring one. He scowled, throwing a look that commanded her to stay on the other side of the room with the bondslaves. But she couldn't. Betsy grasped her arm firmly, drawing her along.

She endured Betsy's introductions, feeling comfortable only when she met the Tates. The large Tate family was as unpretentious as Dennis

had described them. She was delighted to meet
Maryann Tate. The eighteen-year-old wasn't a
beauty, but she had a sweet eager manner.
She'd make Raven a good wife. And, she thought
with sadness, Maryann would make Garth a
sweet, kind sister-in-law.

The eldest Tate son, a young man just returned
from studies at Oxford, invited Flavia to stroll
the ballroom. She couldn't refuse. As she drifted
off on William Tate's arm, Mr. Byng glared at her.

Following in the wake of other couples, they
politely reviewed the ballroom portraits, admired
the marble mantelpieces and considered the
distant view of the Chester River from each of
the tall front windows. Conversation went naturally to Maryann's wedding, and Flavia plucked
up her courage, inquiring tremulously if Captain Garth McNeil would attend. He would,
William Tate assured her. Flavia's knees grew
wobbly.

"You are highborn," he said suddenly. "Like
Mrs. Gresham."

Flavia jerked, startled.

"No! No, sir. I—I—once served as maid. In a
duke's house."

"Where?" he asked, smiling in mild curiosity.

She'd not expected him to press. Her mind
whirled. Glasses tinkled against wine-bottles,
voices rose in the ballroom as wine and rum
toddy did their work. Her hesitation had brought
a quizzical look to his face. "Tewksbury Hall,"
she blurted, her mind a sudden blank.

He smiled, nodding.

"I've been there."

She felt faint. He drew her along to the next window and considered the sheep-cropped lawn that rolled gently down to the Chester River. He was done with the subject of Tewksbury, jumping in about the tobacco harvest. She hardly listened. Trembling with eagerness, she knew she should leave the subject of Tewksbury closed. But she *had* to know. Had to find out.

"Then you met His Grace?" she asked, her voice shaking.

"What?" He swung an odd look at her, as though they occupied separate worlds. "What? Oh, the duke of Tewksbury? Yes. And Her Grace."

" 'Her Grace'?"

Shock exploded in her brain like wood splinters flying from the ax.

He smiled pleasantly. "I believe the duke's last wife died of some ghastly disease. Smallpox, if you will. His Grace married his late wife's sister. Valentina."

"Oh!"

It was an utter shock. She stared at the floor, trying to take it in. Valentina! She felt a surge of terror for her sister. *Oh, Valentina, be careful!* But relief galloped in on terror's heels. If the duke had married Valentina, then her family was still safe. Her little sisters were assured a good future. Mother and Papa were secure. She drew a steadying breath. Valentina had been a doting, loving aunt to Robert. She would mother him.

"See here, are you ill, Miss Brown? If you're ill—"

Flavia jerked her head up.

"Oh. Oh, no."

He smiled in relief, drew her along and plunged into a discourse on tobacco. They'd almost circled the room. Circle completed, courtesy would demand they part, and William Tate would invite another young woman to stroll. She dragged her feet. Her opportunity to ask more, to ask about the baby, was fast vanishing. She gulped air to steady herself.

"The duke's son," she uttered softly, unable to say more without losing control.

"What? Oh, yes. A pity, wasn't it?" He veered from the subject. "I should consider it an honor if you will allow me to call upon you at the Byngs."

He waited for her answer. She stared up at him, frozen dumb. A pity? Robert? Raw fear coursed through her. Her hands turned to ice. She was terrified to know. *More* terrified *not* to know.

Her lips were wood. "The marquis?"

William Tate blinked his bewilderment.

"Oh, that. Yes. A tragedy. The child was sent to live in Germany. He drowned in the Rhine River in August." He smiled sympathetically. "May I call on Tuesday next, Miss Brown?"

She stared at him. Not comprehending, then fighting comprehension. She shook her head.

"No. No!"

He smiled uncertainly.

"Perhaps Wednesday?"

Beside herself with shock and horror, she whirled from him. She stumbled to the center of the room, drifted there without feet, with legs gone numb. The silver chandelier above her head began to spin slowly. She reached out, seeking something to hold on to. The room spun. Turquoise brocade, saffron silk, parrot green velvet, ivory fans, lace, and bondslave muslin spun round her like the streamers of a child's Fair Day stick. Colors whirled dizzily, madly, fast, faster, closing in. The floor lurched up, crashing against her hip and an instant later, her head.

She fell into merciful darkness.

"Your drunkenness is a disgrace! A blot on my good name," Mr. Byng raved. "All of Chestertown will speak of it. 'She drank herself into a swoon,' they will say. They will laugh behind my back, saying the Reverend Byng employs a wanton, drunken chit!"

Flavia sat collapsed at the kitchen table. She sobbed in grief, her arms abandoned upon the table, her cheek resting upon the rough wood. Dead. Her bright-eyed darling was *dead*. All that sweetness—

"What have you to say for yourself, Jane?" Mr. Byng demanded, his boots stridently hitting the floor planks as he paced.

She made no response. She couldn't. She couldn't stop sobbing, even though the deep muscles of her stomach hurt from the endless, wrenching sobs. Dead. Dead since August. She had rejoiced on his second birthday in September, and all the while he had been dead. *Dead*.

"Speak," Mr. Byng ordered, bending over her and shaking her. She pulled away. The odor of his bad tooth flowed to her, melding with the salty taste of her tears, making her gag.

She didn't know how she got back to the Byngs'. Vaguely, she recalled Dennis Finny's drawn, worried face. Vaguely, she recalled William Tate and Dennis lifting her up to Mr. Byng, upon Mr. Byng's horse. The funereal clop of hooves. The strong equine smell. Dazed, she'd heard none of Mr. Byng's irate lecture. She was sobbing when he'd pushed her into the house. Her sobs had upset Neddy. He'd begun to bawl, babbling, "Jane—uh, uh—Jane hurt—"

"Fool!" Mr. Byng had thundered. "Tend my horse. Get to the barn and stay there." Neddy had scurried to obey.

The fire crackled, radiating waves of warmth, but she felt no warmth. She was cold as a stone. Still ranting, Mr. Byng thrust a cup of steaming tea at her. Its fragrance made her gag. She rolled her head away, too grief-laden to lift her head.

"Go to bed," he said in disgust.

She tried to find her feet, but could not. Irritably, he pulled her up, stripped off her cloak and pushed her toward the loft. She stumbled numbly to the ladder.

"You're too drunk to climb it," he said. With an angry push, he shoved her toward Neddy's pallet. She fell upon it, curling up into a ball of grief. The pallet smelled of barn. The worn sheet covering it was as cold as ice water. Water. Oh, God! She saw him. In her aching numbness she felt his bewildered shock as the cold Rhine closed over his head. She saw the bright happy eyes go wild with fear. Tiny hands clawed. She felt the torture of the first lungful of water, the tormented gasp for air. His baby-fine hair swirling in the dark waters as he fought.

God. Oh, God.

She gagged at the vision, sobbing and curling into a tighter ball. The vision tormented her, freezing her to ice and then burning her with hellish, feverish heat. She twisted and turned, unable to sleep. She bit her lip to keep the vision at bay and scarcely noticed when Mr. Byng retired, casting a long last hot look at her.

She burned with thirst as a sleepless hour crept by. Dragging herself up, she stumbled to the water bucket. She drew the shaking dipper to her mouth with two hands. Her throat was too choked to swallow. Water trickled to her crushed, ruined gown.

She shivered. She was suddenly cold again, cold as stone. Dizzy, she found her cloak and pulled it on. A door creaked open on hinges that cried for oiling. Dully, she turned toward Mr. Byng's bedchamber.

He stood there, still fully dressed, glowering. His face crimson in the firelight.

"So. I caught you, you red-haired bitch. Not too drunk to sneak out, eh? Who waits out there, eh?"

Too grieved to understand, she could only stare at him. He thrust an accusing finger at her, wagging it at the cloak she wore.

"Brazen chit! I watched you play your charms

upon young Tate. So you planned to shame me by feigning drunk, did you? And then sneak out to meet him?"

She shook her head, understanding not a word. Robert... Robert. Like a predator, her master lowered his head and stalked toward her. Softly. His boots noiseless.

Fear knifed through the numbing fog.

"Mr. Byng," she whispered, backing away. "Please, sir—"

Alert now, she saw what she'd been oblivious to as she rode home in his angry arms. His face was flushed, highly colored and puffed with passion. As she stared, his hooded eyes closed, snakelike.

"You shan't wait for the whipping post," he whispered in a thick, shaking voice. "You shall be whipped this instant. Go to my bedchamber. Prepare yourself."

She gasped, fear exploding like musket shots. She tensed. The words were a lie. She knew it. Knew he did not intend to whip her. Knew exactly what he intended. Whirling in panic, she flew for the door. But he caught her, grabbing her wrist, twisting it, wrenching it until she fell against him. She struck out wildly and a chair clattered over.

"Submit, Jane."

He pawed her, trying to kiss her. Her feet went out from under. She struggled to get her balance, stiff with fright, trying not to breathe in the foul odor of his bad tooth.

"No!" she cried out. "Let me go!"

But he was beyond reason. He tried to kiss her again. She tore out of his arms with a scream. He slapped her silent, a great crashing crack on the cheek. The blow sent her reeling. She feel to her knees, cradling her burning face in her palms.

Aroused by the violence, he seized both her wrists. He dragged her to the bedchamber. She broke free with one hand and clawed at the doorframe, trying to hold on. She felt her nails split to the quick as he wrenched her through the door.

She sobbed in pain and terror.

"Please—I beg—don't—"

She managed to lunge away, reeling into the bedpost. She grabbed it, strangling it, clinging to it as though to life itself.

Again he wrenched her loose. With the last breath she had, she screamed. But he'd seized her hair, he'd forced her to the quaking bed, crushing all air from her lungs. She gasped for air but drew in the stench of his mouth, the acrid stale smell of his serge coat. The smells brought her terror to a screaming head.

"No! You cannot!"

In a frenzy she clawed at him. He bellowed in pain as her nails raked his face. For a moment, he let go. She lunged off the bed. She tried to run, but her own skirts trapped her. They were caught under him. With a sob of desperation, she tried to jerk the skirts free. But he caught her, caught the slippery silk. She jerked again, jerked desperately until the silk wrenched free of his fist. She lunged from the bedchamber, her feet clumsy wooden things that would not, could not move.

"Jane!" he roared, chasing her.

In her terrified flight, she tripped over the extended rocker of the Philadelphia chair. She crashed to the floor, knowing she'd come to the end. She had no strength left. She curled into a ball and sobbed her despair. She did not look up as his boots slowly clipped across the floor and stopped, not inches from her skirt. She could hear his determined panting.

"You *will* submit."

Weeping, she did not hear the kitchen door open until it banged to the wall. She looked up through tears. Neddy swam in the doorway. She blinked, trying to see him clearly. He held something in his hands. She blinked again. What he held made no sense at all.

"Fool! What do you think you're—"

Flavia reared up in terror, finally understanding what Neddy held.

"Neddy—oh, no!"

Neddy charged like a buck. In a single motion he thrust the lance in, lofted the flailing terrapin on his lance and flung it hard to the floor. Like the hunts at the creek, the terrapin lay belly up.

Flavia froze as blood spurted. Its rich redness glistened in the firelight. She stared, as the spurt ended and a dark red pool slowly spread across the floorboards, seeping down the cracks. The sickly sweet smell of death crept into the air.

Unbelieving, she stumbled to her feet.

Neddy dropped the bloody lance with a cry of fright. The lance rolled, bumping along until it hit the table leg and stopped. Neddy burst into tears, swiping at the blood on his clothes, his hands.

"Dirty," he sobbed in distress. "Dirty—uh, uh—Miz Byng—whip Neddy—uh, uh—dirty—"

She was dazed. Too dazed to move to the boy.

A cold draft blew through the open kitchen door and with it came the distant sound of approaching voices. Boots crunched through the mudyard, then stomped across the stoop.

She felt dizzy, floating. She turned, staring out at the sounds, staring from glazed eyes. Vaguely, she heard someone say, "Odd. The door is open." As she stared, two men seemed to swim into the doorway.

"Jane?" Dennis Finny began, "Mr. Tate and I walked over to see if you're feeling—No! Oh, my God!"

"Lord Almighty," whispered William Tate. "What's happened here?"

Chapter 16

MAB COLLINS ran away.

Garth had anticipated it. He'd alerted the servants, warned Harrington and Jenkins. As a result, Mab got no farther than Dray's Ordinary on the Hampton Road, five miles beyond Williamsburg. Jenkins tracked her. He threw the kicking, hollering chit across his saddle and trotted home with her.

Now she'd have to be dealt with, Garth fumed. He slammed a business ledger shut. Lunging from his chair, he crossed the small study in two strides, fumbled into a tin box for a cigar and, finding none, irritably slung the box away.

Damnation. Was there no end to female trouble? What next! It was enough to try a saint: Raven chewing at him every blessed moment about the Chestertown bondwoman. Eunice sending urgent letters from London, demanding his presence. "Demanding!" he thought blackly. "Ha!" Annette turning suddenly virtuous—dressing up in lace collars like a sixteen-year-old virgin and tripping about town with that parrot, while she knew damned well he ,wanted her stripped to her shift and lying in his bed upstairs. Then the business about the freckle-faced girl—what was her name?

He snapped his fingers, irritably jogging his memory.

Mary. That was it. Mary Wooster. He'd sent her to Widow Richards, a motherly innkeeper in Barbados. "Fine!" he sneered at himself. "Done! And a star for your crown in heaven, McNeil." But the worry about the letter remained. Who had sent it?

And now he'd the Collins chit to deal with.

He snorted in self-disgust. In the old days, he'd walked out on domestic problems, leaving them to solve themselves. And he'd certainly not spent five minutes mollycoddling any of his mistresses. He'd lived the sailor's rule: when a woman ceases to be an amusement, sail on, brother, sail on. Even now he chafed to jump on a horse and ride to the peace and quiet of his small house in Hampton. Or better yet, escape to the *Caroline* and the inviolate sanctuary of his captain's cabin.

But he couldn't. And he was at a loss to say why. Was Trent the cause? Partly. Home had never before been so appealing. He was getting used to sticky, enthusiastic kisses. Getting accustomed to sinking into a chair only to find he'd squashed a remnant of sweet bun or a toy soldier. He'd miss those homely things at sea or in Hampton, he admitted. But there was more to this curious deterioration of old chauvinist ways, and he lay the blame on Flavia. He'd loved her with shattering intensity. She had melted into his heart, become part of him. Because of Flavia, he looked at the world with new eyes. She'd softened him, taken away the old "cutting edge." He felt like a fish out of water.

A tap at the door broke into his musing. The tap was followed by the door pushing cautiously inward.

"Now, Cap'n? Will y'see Mab Collins now?"

Garth scowled. Harrington's red beaky face was twisted with concern. The look he popped at Garth begged for amnesty. The old tar had taken a shine to the chit. Behaved like a mother hen.

"Bring her in," he snapped, squelching Harrington's hope. As he waited, he caught furtive whispers outside the door as Harrington coached.

"Remember, lass, beg his forgiveness—"

"I'll not!" a saucy hiss snapped back.

"Come, lass, make it easy on y'self. The Cap'n's not a mean man, but if ye rile him—"

McNeil caught the girl's derisive snort.

The door swung in. Harrington tugged at Mab Collins's soiled sleeve, mother-henning her into the study. She shrugged off his hand and threw an angry, blazing look toward Garth. Damnation! She looked about as meek and repentant as the Queen of Sheba. He'd have to get rough.

He returned her stare. Returned it with cold ruthlessness. She quailed slightly. She dropped her eyes to the floor.

McNeil sauntered to his chair, casually dropped into it, propped his feet atop the writing table and indolently leaned back. He stared at her, saying nothing.

The silence was as loud as thunder. He could see it made her nervous. A tie flared in her cheek. Once, then again. Good. So, silence was more effective torture for Mab than scolding...

At last, she could take no more. She flung her head up. Her gray eyes shot fire.

"Whip me, then! See if I cry one peep! A whipping don't matter. I'll run again. First chance I gets."

"Now then, lass," Harrington put in.

McNeil scowled him into silence. He smiled coldly. Jerking in fright, she cast her eyes to the floor. McNeil considered the matter. She must be punished, must be brought into a cooperative spirit. But he doubted beating would work. She was a London drab. No doubt cuffings had been daily fare as she grew up. One more would only be water off a duck's back. No, he had to go deeper. He sat mulling it over.

"Are you afraid of the *dark*, Mab Collins?" he asked coldly.

Her head jerked up. Some unnamable emotion skittered through her eyes. "I ain't afraid of nothing." But the tremor in her voice contradicted.

"Do you like to *eat*?" he continued malevolently.

Her wary eyes widened. She covered her fear with brassiness.

"Don't everybody?"

"Good," he said pleasantly. He turned to Harrington. "Lock her in the attic. It's dark as sin there. She is to have water but *no* food. Leave her there until she decides to be a proper bondslave."

She gasped. Harrington puffed and reddened.

"Y'can't do that," she cried. " 'Tis against English law! I know my rights, I do!"

McNeil yawned. Dismissing the matter with a bored wave of his hand, he turned to Harrington. "Tell cook I want lunch. Those delicious Cornish pasties will do. A cold glass of buttermilk, a wedge of cheese and," he added malevolently, "a thick slice of plum cake with lemon sauce."

Mab Collins stared at him in shock. As he'd rattled off his menu, her tongue had darted to the corners of her mouth. No doubt she was famished, having run off before breakfast.

Tugging at her sleeve apologetically, Harrington led the shocked girl off. McNeil was pleased that it took her to halfway up the stairs to retrieve a portion of that pridey spirit.

"Git your hands off'n me," he heard her say shakily. "I can walk by meself, I can."

Harrington's low apology drifted into the study.

"Come now, lass. No one means you ill—"

"Stuff it in yer hat."

*   *   *

To McNeil's surprise and grudging admiration, Mab Collins stuck it out three days before capitulating. He wasn't fooled by the contrite manner in which she resumed her duties. The chit still had a peck of pride in her. But he was satisfied to see she was scared silly of him. He was also satisfied to note that she and Trent took to each other. Happy laughter pealed in the nursery, and yet, Trent was somehow being made to toe the line. He no longer wailed his demands, and he'd come to some new understanding about sweetmeats and the long-suffering kitchen cat: they were *not* his to snatch at will.

Garth closed negotiations on a new ship in December and shook her down in the Chesapeake, testing her responses to various winds and weather. He would assign a shipmaster in January. But he was finicky about his ships. He liked to match ship to master as carefully as any marriage broker matched bride to groom. A well-matched pair meant smooth sailing; an ill-matched pair . . . sourly, he thought of Eunice.

Taking tea in Annette's drawing room on a rainy afternoon, he'd offered to transport the ever-present Lord Dunwood back to Baltimore on one of the shakedown sailings. Annette had shot him a black look; but the young man accepted with alacrity, and McNeil choked back a chuckle. Already he'd overstayed, Dunwood admitted sheepishly. His elderly mother was expecting him back. He must oversee preparations for a Christmas ball.

When Dunwood scurried out to alert his valet

at The King's Arms, Annette whirled round in the splendor of her damask and rosewood drawing room. She planted her fists on her hips, and McNeil found himself the recipient of a look that was pure fury.

"No doubt you think you are being clever, McNeil?"

His grin built slowly.

"I missed your bed."

Her chin shot up.

"And you shall continue to miss it. I'm finished with you. Lord Dunwood proposes marriage. He respects me. You?" She tossed her head. "All you ever propose is bed."

Ignoring her pique, he moved toward her, crossing the Oriental carpet. At his movement, she whirled round and took refuge behind a settee, her skirts rustling.

"No," she snapped. "McNeil, no. Do not presume—"

He went round the settee after her.

Flaring, she seized her skirts and marched round the settee, out of reach. She whirled and faced him.

"Behave yourself. You act like a child."

But he knew it was in his best interest *not* to behave. "Behave" and he'd end up out in the icy rain. Misbehave and he'd gain a rainy afternoon spent in a warm featherbed. He moved toward her.

She backed away, shaking a furious finger at him.

"I am *not* your plaything, McNeil. I'm a human being. I have feelings. I have—"

He caught her jeweled finger and drew it to his mouth, gently kissing the tapered nail, then each knuckle. He took her hand and buried his lips in the softness of her palm.

She whispered, "Don't, McNeil. Please. Let me go."

He drew her into his arms and kissed the rosy flush on her throat, kissed her white shoulders. She struggled to pull away, but it was a token struggle, and he ignored it. He thrilled to the feel of her soft breasts against his hard chest.

"McNeil, I won't let you—"

Her whisper faded as he kissed her mouth. He knew her body, knew it well. He felt the familiar shiver of her rising desire. Slowly, her jeweled hands crept up his chest, curling round his neck. It had been a long time . . . most of November . . . into December. He kissed her hungrily.

The fire crackled in the grate. The mellow smell of burning hickory wood scented the air. Rain pattered on the roof, and occasional icy dots of sleet hit the window.

She shivered in his arms. As he raised his head and looked at her, Annette's eyes slowly opened.

"It's warmer upstairs," she whispered, then caught herself and began to plead. "Oh, no, Garth, I—Lord Dunwood."

He kissed her.

"*Much* warmer, Annette."

McNeil & McNeil's new ship was small, but sleek and fast. It was a provisions ship, built for quick sailings to the Caribbean. The times were changing and so must shipping, Raven had pointed out. Garth agreed. The tobacco economy was fading. Trade in grain was on the upsurge. A new strain of grain had been developed in Maryland. The grain was mildew-resistant—a phenomenon! For the first time, grain could make it to the Caribbean without rotting along the way. Planters were quick to visualize profits. The West Indies colonies were crying for grain and willing to pay dearly for it. Tobacco land in Maryland and Virginia was being plowed under. Grain sprang up everywhere, and McNeil & McNeil meant to take a bite of those profits.

Garth sailed the new provisions ship up to Chestertown for Raven's wedding. Annette accompanied him. Having taken her stand during Dunwood's visit to Williamsburg, she'd recovered her amiable good humor and was back in his bed where, in his opinion, she damned well belonged.

When they dropped anchor off Water Street in Chestertown, he and Annette found the rural eastern shore buzzing with news of a bizarre murder. It was all anyone wished to talk about. Annette found the murder dull. She found a different, somewhat related story much more amusing.

It seemed that at the wedding party of the rich planter, Ira Gresham, a woman fainted and caused quite a stir as guests sought to aid her. During the to-do, some callow ruffian abducted the bride. He boldly galloped off on his horse, clutching the shrieking bride. Chaos had erupted.

The wedding celebration had disintegrated. Riders thundered off in all directions, searching for the bride and her abductor. The bridegroom was reported to have been purple with fury.

But the bride and her cavalier could not be found. Some hours later, the bride managed to drift home on her own, looking none too chagrined for her ordeal. The tartest-mouthed gossips snickered that the shocking state of the bride's gown made it all too evident that the bride had begun her honeymoon *without* her bridegroom.

Her lilting laughter ringing, Annette tucked the risqué anecdote into her memory, swearing to Garth that she couldn't wait to regale all of Williamsburg with it.

Raven's wedding proved to be a lavish affair. The Tates spent a fortune on wines, delicacies and costly favors. Everyone who was anyone in Maryland society attended. The Tate mansion bulged with guests, sometimes six or eight to a bedroom.

Garth found his brother little reformed. Not an hour from the altar, Raven pulled him from the congratulatory throng and into the privacy of an empty gaming room. When the oak door thudded shut upon the merriment, Raven began belaboring the same old subject.

"About Jane, Garth. You must ride over at once and—"

"No."

Raven flung his hand impatiently.

"You don't understand, Garth. The Chestertown murder? It was Jane's master! She was there!"

Garth sighed his annoyance. Beyond the closed doors, violin music was beginning. A gay tune lilted, lifting above the hubbub of happy excited voices.

"Then you're well quit of the bondwoman, Raven. Be sensible. You're a married man, now. You don't need scandal mucking up your—"

"When I want your advice, Garth, I'll *ask* for it! At the moment, all I am damn well asking is your *help*."

Garth set his wineglass on the billiards table with an angry clunk. The witless pup. Did he think life was so simple? Bark loudly at what you want, and it shall be dished up to you posthaste?

"Grow up, Raven! You've taken a wife, you've vowed fidelity. Break Maryann's heart—break the heart of a loving girl, and you prove yourself still a fool schoolboy."

With an abrupt movement, Raven jerked around and banged his wineglass onto the billiards table. Wine sloshed. He ignored the damage, his color rising.

"Lecture me on matrimony and the treatment of women, will you! God, Garth, you've got crust." He drew a ragged breath. "I suppose when *you* wed that cold fish you caught in Amsterdam, *you* will behave the model husband. I suppose *you* will collect your slippers from under the Vachon bed and take them home?"

Garth flushed.

"We're discussing you, not me. And leave Annette out of this."

"We'll discuss *you*, and we'll leave Annette *in* this," Raven contradicted, his voice heating. "Don't preach morality at me, brother. From you it rings hollow."

Garth's pulse thudded angrily in his throat.

"Lower your voice. The guests—"

Raven ignored the warning, flinging up his arm in melodramatic fashion.

"You want to discuss ethics, Garth?" he challenged. "Very well! Let's discuss the ethics of breaking hearts. Vachon loves you, and yet you feel free to treat her like dirt. You haven't even the decency to tell her of your coming marriage." Raven snorted. "Knowing you, Garth, you'll duck out on a shipping and leave Vachon to read the news in the *Gazette*."

Garth burned with anger. Not the least of his anger was that he'd been toying with doing exactly that.

"Enough, Raven! I warn you!"

Raven laughed harshly.

"'Enough'? Not enough by half. You're a taker, Garth, not a giver. And your morality stinks!"

Garth's fist shot upward, almost cracking Raven's surprised face before he seized control of it and drew the fist back to his side. He was shaken. He'd not hit Raven since Raven was ten and had carelessly set fire to a neighbor's hen house.

He turned on his heel, a blinding surge of blood rushing headward. He made for the door with a furious, "As to this bondslave, I order you to forget her! You've made your bed, Raven. Now lie in it!"

"I won't!" Raven shouted back, wrenching off the wig that had gone askew, and whipping the wig to the table, where it sent the wineglasses crashing. "I love her, damn you! I love her!"

Just as Garth grabbed for the door latch, the door slid hesitantly open. Maryann peeped into the room, giggling a shy, sweet giggle.

"Whom do you love?" Maryann said, throwing a quick, shy smile at Garth, then gazing at her bridegroom with unabashed adoration.

Garth held his breath. In the long, strained moment that followed, Raven pulled himself together by degrees. Then, smiling his rakish smile, Raven strolled to Maryann, took her glowing face in both his hands and kissed her mouth.

"I love *you*," he swore. "Only *you*."

Maryann blushed with joy, looking almost pretty in her gown of ivory satin, with a wreath of orange blossoms woven into her plain-colored hair. She threw Garth an ecstatic look, and as he left the room he caught her soft, "Oh, Raven, you are my *world*. My whole *world*."

"And you," Raven lied charmingly, "are mine."

Garth gritted his teeth in anger. He'd be damned if he'd help Raven break that sweet girl's heart! Raven could beg until the cows came home. He would *not* help him procure that bondwoman. In fact, he thought with vengeful satisfaction, perhaps he could put an end to the matter.

A covey of fan-fluttering, chattering ladies floated toward him. He shook off the scene with Raven, put a smile on his face, greeted the

ladies and set himself to playing the role of
brother-to-the-bridegroom. But his mind dwelt
on the problem. Supposing he bought this Jane
Brown, supposing he sent her to New York or to
Barbados, where Raven would be unable to
trace her. . . . He needn't bother to see the girl
himself, he thought, as he bowed over a dowa-
ger's proffered hand, then amiably greeted her
husband. He could put the matter in the hands
of his agent.

He caught a flash of gold brocade across the
crowded ballroom. Annette. Extricating himself
from a woman who was gushing about Raven's
made-in-heaven marriage, McNeil accepted a
glass of wine from a servant and waited for
Annette to work her way across the room. She
looked dazzling. The neckline of her gown exposed a good deal of bosom, drawing looks of
frank admiration from men and collecting stares
of envy from less well-endowed women. He
smiled in amusement, watching people react to
her. But the smile felt stiff. Raven's accusations
stung: *You haven't even the decency to tell
her. . . . You're a taker . . .*

In annoyance, he downed his wine and rid
himself of the goblet. He watched Annette as
she wove her way toward him. Once, she became trapped by three garrulous old gentlemen.
With the easy grace born of her station, she
endured their hand-kissing and their compliments, granting each a dazzling smile as she
swished out of their circle. She wore the bright
formal smile until her eyes caught his. The
smile softened. A girlish glow lit her middle-

aged face. Where had he seen that look before?
Maryann . . . going into Raven's arms. Damn.

"Dance with me, Garth?" The perfume she'd
dabbed behind ear and in bosom floated up to
him.

He deliberately put her in her place, leering
into her cleavage, like a tar at a chippy. He
wanted her to realize that she was only a mistress. It would be easier that way, in the long
run.

"Dance? I would rather—"

Hurt flashed in her eyes for an instant. Then
she banished it and stabbed him in the rib with
her folded fan.

"Jackanapes! Why do I bother with you,
McNeil!"

Angry with Raven and fearing a freeze in the
Chester River, he decided not to stay for the
entire week of wedding festivities. He made his
apologies to the Tates and took a stiff farewell of
Raven.

"My mouth shot off like a twelve-pounder,"
Raven said, fishing for an apology.

Garth shrugged, unwilling to forgive but wanting, at least, to reach neutral ground.

"Spilled milk."

Brightening, Raven released a sigh of relief.
Even as a child, Raven never had been able to
bear being on the outs with him.

"That, er, delicate—matter I spoke of, Garth.
Er, ah, Jane? You'll help?" Raven tendered the
request gingerly, stiffly.

Garth's temper began to rise. But something

in Raven's face—a young hopefulness, a vulner-
ability—quashed his temper. Had twenty-two
always been so young? So passionately vibrant,
so easy a target for anyone who chose to sling
hurts?

He'd forgot. God, twenty-two seemed a cen-
tury ago.

He sighed softly, tension and irritation draining
away. Reaching out, he tousled Raven's dark
hair as he used to do when Raven was a hero-
worshiping puppy of ten. In those days, Raven
had dogged Garth's tracks, and Garth had hardly been able to turn around without trodding on
the boy. Garth felt a surge of tenderness as an
easy grin sprang to Raven's face.

"I've a confession, Raven. I called you a fool
schoolboy. But you are a venerable old sage
compared to what I was at twenty-two."

Raven's brow lifted quizzically.

"When I was your age, I was 'head over heels'
for Mrs. Daws."

Raven's face opened with incredulity. His shoulders hunched, as laughter built. His laughter
came in erratic spouts, like a whale.

"No, Garth!"

"Absolutely. Mrs. Daws had been my first
'lady,' and I was confusing a good bounce in bed
with this mysterious thing called 'love.' I went
so far as to take it upon myself to defend the
lady's honor."

More whale spouting. Raven wiped tears of
laughter.

"Some task! Mrs. Daws has a gentleman cal-
ler almost every night. She must've been might-

ily annoyed with you, beating up her callers and decimating her income."

Garth laughed.

"She was."

"Then what happened?"

"The good lady developed a yen for a bolt of brocade from the Orient. Nothing would do except that I should sail and get it for her. By the time I returned eight months later, I'd come to my senses. I was cured of Mrs. Daws."

Raven laughed and clapped a hand to Garth's shoulder.

"Ah, our Mrs. Daws. Still a divine bounce in bed."

Garth smiled wryly.

"As you discovered at sixteen."

Raven's mouth went slack.

"You knew?"

"How could I not? For days before you got up courage to knock on her door, you were jittery as a cat. And the house reeked of the French scent you were slapping on yourself."

Raven's face grew thoughtful.

"So that's why Mrs. Daws didn't send me packing, as she did to youngsters who knocked on her door. You intervened, Garth."

"Not really. I sent her a tobacco voucher for twenty pounds. I enclosed it in a note: *If Mr. Raven McNeil should come to call, please treat him as you'd want your own son treated when he comes of age.*"

Raven laughed sheepishly. "I don't know whether to thank you or punch you in the nose."

"Let's make it a handshake."

Raven thrust out his hand.

"A handshake, then."

They shook hands, then embraced awkwardly in farewell.

"About Jane Brown," Raven began as they strolled to the door.

"I'll consider the matter."

"You promise?"

"Yes. I suppose a mistress is not altogether out of the question."

He did not add, however, that Jane Brown as mistress was indeed out of the question. Jane Brown was known in Chestertown, known by the Tates. If word slipped out—and word *would* slip out—the Tates would be scandalized, and McNeil & McNeil would lose a lot of Maryland shipping. No, he must dispose of Jane Brown and find Raven a mistress in some distant port, such as Norfolk. He patted Raven's shoulder and left.

On the last day of December, Garth and Annette arrived back in Williamsburg. The year 1754 was a hair's breadth from becoming 1755, and Garth worried what the new year would bring to the colonies.

If the fat wasn't already in the fire on the frontier, it would be by summer. The humiliating clash of untrained militiamen and French regulars had signaled that certainty at Fort Necessity. Garth doubted that the members of the Privy Council, sitting on their fat, brocaded asses in London, would succeed in preventing all-out war with the French. And King George turned a deaf ear to colonists' cries for British troops. The king preferred to listen to his minister, the duke of Newcastle, who advised: "Let Americans fight Americans."

But on this eve of 1755, Williamsburg pretended trouble was not imminent. The capital bubbled with holiday merriment: balls, galas, horse races, theatricals. All business halted as Williamsburg played, playing well into the new year. With shipping temporarily forestalled, Garth plunged into the gaiety.

On the fourth of January he crossed the bounds of gaiety; he got irresponsibly drunk. The fourth was a date he habitually found hard to tolerate. It was the anniversary of his first encounter with his beloved Flavia.

He arose on the fifth, paying dearly for his sins. His head hurt like the devil. Slouching at his writing table in the study, a fire snapping on the hearth and a pot of strong coffee at his elbow, he made a stab at sobriety by attacking business matters. He tried to map out new shipping routes for McNeil & McNeil, in the event of war. War would mean privateers, and he didn't intend to lose a ship to any buccaneering Frenchman.

When the maps and charts proved to be jumble to his aching head, he slung them aside and turned to another matter. Raven's nonsense. He wrote out a draft on his bank for fifty pounds, a second draft for one hundred pounds and a third for two hundred. Irritably, he scrawled a legal paper, releasing one "Jane Brown" from indenture to Captain Garth McNeil of Williamsburg. Then he sent for his agent.

The pounding in his head lent precise brutality to his instructions: as soon as the weather eased, the agent was to make tracks for Chestertown. There he was to locate the Byng household and purchase Jane Brown's indenture. If the agent could get her for the generous fee of one hundred pounds, good. If not, offer two hundred. Only a lunatic could refuse.

Then the agent was to take the girl directly to Philadelphia, buy her passage to England, and see her securely aboard the ship. He was to give the chit three things: her freedom papers, fifty pounds in sterling, and a severe warning. The chit would be skinned alive if she ever again set foot in the colonies.

It was arbitrary, and Raven would thunder when he got wind of it. But so be it. Garth could weather the storm, and Raven would recover. The lad's past love affairs had had all the longevity of a sudden summer squall.

This disposed of, he attended to the January shipping schedule. Finally, reluctantly, he turned to a touchy personal matter. Annette. In his silent drunken brooding over Flavia, he'd spurned what Annette tried to offer. She'd left in a huff, deeply offended.

He rose cautiously, babying the devils that danced in his skull. As careful as a ninety-year-old, he maneuvered the stairs, entered his bedchamber, washed himself from head to toe, splashed on a scent Annette had given him and then got dressed.

He sent round for the landau and was about

to plunge out into the January wind when a thought surfaced: only an idiot strides defenseless into the den of a wounded lioness. He shut the door against the stinging wind and stood in the foyer, considering. As his mother's handsome old case clock chimed the hour, he moved thoughtfully toward the kitchen.

The kitchen was cozy, a moist spicy smell filling the air as cook stirred the pumpkin mush that simmered in an iron pot over the fire. At the far end of the trencher table, Trent and Mab had their heads together. They were picking seeds from pumpkin pulp, dropping the seeds into a roasting pan.

"One, two, five," Trent counted.

"One, two, *three*," Mab corrected.

At the sound of Garth's step, Trent's head popped up, then his whole body. Garth went to the boy, scooped him up and stood him upon the table.

"Trent, old man, I'm going to hide behind your coattails. How'd you like to pay a visit to Lady Annette?"

The Flavia-eyes worked earnestly. A grin began to build.

"Yady Annette! Presents! Toy ship—" Trent clapped his hands in glee, and McNeil found himself wiping a dollop of airborne pumpkin pulp from his jaw.

"Trent's *not* going out in this weather," Mab snapped from the end of the table.

Garth turned and sent her a baleful look. The pounding in his brandy-soaked skull left him in no mood to be crossed. The look was effective. About to say more, Mab shut her mouth and jumped up to get Trent's things.

"Beg pardon, sir, Captain McNeil, sir," Annette's elderly footman stammered, pausing often to clear his throat. "My lady, she—Lady Annette has left word that Captain McNeil is not—ah—not to be admitted?" The footman's voice lifted in question, as though to sugarcoat his message.

McNeil stepped in, closing the door and setting Trent down in the foyer. Outside, the wind howled.

"Announce Master Trent."

The footman blinked in fresh alarm.

"Please, sir? My lady, she's in foul mood."

"So," warned McNeil, "am *I*."

The footman jumped at that. Turning, he shuffled across the foyer and pumped up the wide stairway in woebegone slow motion. At the top of the stairs he applied a reluctant knuckle to the boudoir door, sidling in when so bidden.

When the door opened again, it opened with a bang that rattled the mansion from top to bottom. Annette stalked out to the landing, wearing a dressing gown of burgundy velvet. She jammed her fists onto her hips.

"Are you out of your mind! Taking a child out in sleet and ice!"

Then she stooped, her arms going out toward Trent, her voice softening.

"Come here, darling. Quickly. There's a fire in my boudoir. We'll have you warm in a trice."

Trent toddled up the stairs. McNeil followed,

feeling foolish. Annette swept the boy into her room, but when McNeil tried to follow, she slammed the door in his face. The bang stirred up his hangover anew. He stood there, considering what to do, when the door jerked open. Ignoring him as though he had no more substance than a ghost, Annette shouted through him at the footman descending the stairs.

"Hot chocolate, Paddington! A pot of it for Master Trent."

The door slammed again. McNeil steadied his thudding head. A green humor stirred sickly in him. Well, if she wanted her revenge, she was getting it. At the expense of his head.

He stood staring into the carved paneling of the door, feeling victim of a disease to which he'd hitherto been immune: unsureness. He supposed an apology was due, but the thought rankled. One didn't apologize to one's own mistress.

Behind the door, Trent's chatter rose, punctuated by the occasional ring of Annette's laughter. Taking a deep breath, he grabbed the door latch and let himself into the familiar room with its turquoise bed hangings and floor splashes of bright Persian rugs. He shut the door behind him, gesturing at the fire that crackled a warm invitation from the fireplace.

"I'm cold, too," he tried, grinning.

It was cold mackeral. She ignored him, stripping off Trent's bundlings.

He tried again.

"You're angry, Annette."

Her head swung toward him.

"Brilliant, McNeil!"

He floundered for something to say, something to turn the trick. Not an outright apology, of course, though something close. But she gave him no chance.

"I'm finished with you, McNeil. So you can well march yourself out of here. I've written Lord Dunwood. I intend to wed him at the soonest."

A false threat. But her willfulness was as irritating as the headache that had set up housekeeping in his skull. Almost, his good intentions flew out the window. Almost, he snapped: *May you and your parrot be very happy!* Only a kind Providence held his tongue. And an interruption from Trent.

Trent tugged at Annette's hand.

"Toy ship?" The blatant little beggar turned an appealing smile on Annette. She tore angry eyes from McNeil and looked down at Trent, softening.

"Darling, I haven't—" Her eyes swept the room. "Come, Trent, we'll make a pretend ship."

She stalked to the small round cherry-wood table where Garth kept his things. Seizing his teak and ivory pipe box, she banged the contents out on the table. Garth winced at the unmistakable sound of his favorite pipes cracking. She seized an enameled tin box of tobacco, wrenched off the lid, strode with it to the fire and shook the tobacco into the flames. She strode back to the table.

"Now, for sails on our pretend ship..."

He winced audibly as she pounced on his

treasure, a seventy-five-year-old ship's log. She flung the book open and ripped out two pages. When the "ships" were a-sail, she carried them to the bed and rumpled the turquoise spread.

"See the blue ocean, Trent. See the big waves."

With a squeal of glee, the little traitor forgot him and scrambled up into the bed to play ships with Annette. When the hot chocolate came, the two made a party of it, with the tray an island in the blue sea. Garth wasn't invited.

A large chunk of time passed. Giggles. Happy chatter. Ships sailing to London. Cargoes of silver teaspoons. The sailors threw him not the slightest glance.

At last, Trent remembered. Clutching the pipe box ship, Trent slid down from the bed, ran to Garth and pressed the ship into his hand.

"Play!"

Annette did not look up at the sound of his footfalls. The bed jiggled violently as he lounged across one end. Annette coolly retreated to the far end. Trent crawled to the center, kneeling and barking commands.

"Sail here!" Trent pointed to Annette.

McNeil slowly maneuvered the ship toward Annette. When it was about a foot from her and she still hadn't thawed, he quipped, "Can't do it, old man. That sea is full of icebergs."

He watched for the telltale twitch of her lips that would signal a return to good humor. It didn't come. He tried other ploys, all of which he considered extremely clever. No response.

With a sigh, he hove to and limped back to home port. So it was a full apology or nothing, was it? He flushed. He'd never apologized to a woman before. Well, cook and his mother and a few assorted aunts didn't count. He drew a last breath, waded into deep water and crossed the Rubicon.

"Perhaps the ship needs a new cargo," he told Trent, who knelt on the bed, bouncing up and down in excitement. "This," he said, taking a teaspoon and placing it in the pipe box, "is Captain McNeil's confession: He behaved like an ass." He picked up another spoon, putting it in the box. "*This* says he is sorry." He fumbled for another spoon. "This says—" He swallowed, the words sticking. "—says—forgive me?"

Annette didn't move, didn't raise her eyes to his. So he sailed the box across the turquoise sea and up the burgundy velvet dressing gown until it rested in her lap. She still didn't move. Garth held his breath. *You treat Vachon like dirt. You haven't even the decency to tell her—*

Holding his breath, he vowed he would play fair with Annette from now on. He would make a clean breast of things, tell her of Eunice...

At last, her hand twitched. She touched the spoons. Silver clinked as she picked up the spoons and slowly brought them to her heart. To Garth's amazement, she burst into tears.

Bewildered, he said, "Don't cry, Annette, don't."

Frightened, Trent scrambled to Annette. He patted her cheek and shook his head. "Don't cry, Yady Annette."

Annette mopped her tears, ruffled Trent's

dark hair and kissed the boy. Finally, she dragged her eyes to Garth.

In a watery whisper she said, "I'm not crying because I'm *unhappy*, you stupid oaf. I'm crying because you've made me wonderfully happy."

Still weeping, she came into his arms. From that point on, the day did not seem to be quite the right one to tell her about Eunice.

Outside his house, the snow fell wet and thick, fell erratically without pace or pattern. Through his drawing room window he watched the snow's futile attempt to cover the brightly burning oil lamp. But each lump of snow lasted only a moment on the brass, melting and sliding. The lamp burned on like a beacon. As the world turned white, the lamp glowed ever brighter, reflecting the whiteness. Outdoor sounds ceased, muffled by blanketing snow. He sipped wine and watched.

Inside, the fire crackled a pleasant invitation: *Be lazy. Do nothing*. And from the nursery drifted the distant sound of an amusing altercation: Mab putting Trent to bed, Trent escaping from the bed and running to the window, Mab trying again. It went on for several minutes. Then he heard the firm slap of hand to fanny. Token wailing. Then silence. He grinned. Mab Collins was working out well. Mab was fond of Trent, and she and McNeil were no longer the enemies they'd been.

Silk rustled behind him. Annette's warm arm entwined his as she gazed out at the falling

snow. She too held a wineglass. The amber
liquid in her goblet caught the firelight, blazing
golden.

He smiled down at her. Since his and Trent's
visit to her house, the words "Lord Dunwood"
had vanished from Annette's vocabulary. And
he, having recovered from what he assessed to
have been a near-fatal attack of conscience, had
put off announcing news of his betrothal. Such
news could only upset the applecart; he preferred to keep the cart upright for as long as
possible.

With the snow increasing, they settled down
over a chessboard in front of the fire. They were
ten minutes into the game—Annette moving in
rash intuitive spurts and he cutting off her
retreat with simple, classical moves—when he
caught the muffled clop of hooves. Horse harness jingled. Coach wheels grated to a stop.

"Who the devil? On a night like this?"

He got up and strode from the drawing room,
closing the door behind him to prevent a draft.
He beat Toad to the front door and wrenched it
open.

"Yes?"

For a moment, the figure before him seemed
unrecognizable. The figure was heavily cloaked,
and the snow was falling like a blanket. But
when recognition dawned, it was a severe jolt.
He stiffened, blinking in disbelief.

"Don't stand there as though you've seen
some dreadful apparition, Garth," Eunice
Wetherby said. "Do let us in." She glanced
over her shoulder to where a very fat figure and

a slim one clung to the arms of the coachman as they made their way up the walk. "Auntie is freezing, and my companion has a cough. The ocean crossing was dreadful. *Dreadful* coach journey from Hampton."

Cold, snow-flecked cloaks brushed him as the covy of clucking, complaining women entered, stamping snow from their shoes.

"Terrible climate."

"Inferior to England."

"—will be the death of me."

Speechless with shock, Garth groped for words.

"Eunice, I didn't know you were coming," he said stupidly.

Dropping her cloak into Toad's arms, she turned to answer. But Lady Wetherby jumped in.

"Of course you didn't know, dear boy. There was no time to send a letter before sailing. Besides, our dear Eunice was not certain you could *read*, for you do not seem able to *write*, dear boy."

"Auntie!" Eunice's plain, birdlike face colored to scarlet.

The foyer vibrated with resentment. True, he'd not written, and he'd paid scant attention to the silly, gushy letters Eunice wrote him. Like a skiff with a loose rudder pin, he tacked about for a reply, but Lady Wetherby sailed upwind of him, cutting him off.

"Come, come, dear boy! We forgive you, don't we, Eunice? All's well that ends well. Now that you two lovebirds are reunited," she paused, beaming at Garth and then at the flushed

Eunice, "we shall set the date and we shall live happily ever after!" Lady Wetherby extended her hand.

Date? We? As he kissed Lady Wetherby's hand and then the hand of Eunice's companion, his hackles rose. Truss and roast him, would they? He was on the verge of rudeness, when the harrowing night at Bladensburg came rushing back. *Trent.* Eunice was the key to Trent's safety. So were the fat aunt and even the mousy companion. If the duke's suspicions should ever be stirred...

Swallowing a lump of anger, he took Eunice's hand.

"Eunice," he said, trying and failing to pump enthusiasm into his voice.

"Dearest Garth."

She offered her cheek. He kissed it perfunctorily. Her cheek was cold, and the scent that rose from her was heather. Heather had been Flavia's scent. He jerked away at the first whiff of it and turned from her.

Lady Wetherby and Mouse stood appraising his foyer, their eyes totaling up the cost of the black and white marble checkered floor, the silver chandelier that Annette had ordered.

Annette!

"*That* must be the drawing room," Lady Wetherby said, nodding to the door he'd earlier shut. "Come, ladies. We'll thaw before the fire." With proprietary aplomb, she marched to her target.

Garth sprang forward.

"Wait!"

Before he could stop her, she'd opened the door and gone in. Eunice and Mouse obediently fluttered after. Halfway to the fire, they froze like three rabbits felled by a single shot.

Across the room, Annette's plum-colored silk glowed in the firelight. Although her garb was silk, she wasn't attired in a gown but a dressing gown tied over white dimity petticoats. It was the sort of attire a man's wife might wear on an evening no company was expected.

Silence thundered. There was only the snap and hiss of the fire. While Eunice's face went pale, Lady Wetherby and Mouse flushed red. Annette drew herself up, chin held high, a spot of bright color burning on each cheekbone. Her glare stabbed first at him, then at the invaders, settling with uncanny female intuition upon Eunice. Eunice returned the glare. Then, four sets of accusing eyes swung to him.

He wished he were in China. Or at sea, riding out a simple, sail-splitting typhoon. But neither option presented itself. There was no solution but to bite steel and get it over with. He drew a deep breath.

"Lady Wetherby, may I present the Baroness Annette Vachon."

The two women nodded stiffly. He stumbled through the introduction of Mouse. He'd forgotten her name. With an air of injury, she supplied it. That left Eunice and Annette. He took a last breath.

"Lady Annette, may I present Miss Eunice Wetherby. Miss Wetherby is my—my—"

Eunice and Annette were scarcely breathing,

hanging on his every word. "My—" he began again lamely.

To his fury, Lady Wetherby crisply finished for him.

"Betrothed. My niece is Captain McNeil's future wife."

Annette jerked, then stood still as death. For some moments she seemed not to breathe. When breath again came, it was in childlike spasms. Overwhelmed with the sudden urge to comfort her, he started forward, but she shot past him, flying from the room. He dove after her.

"Captain McNeil!"

"Garth," Eunice whined.

Ignoring them, he strode after Annette as her heels clicked down the long corridor toward the kitchen.

"Toad!" she called out. "The landau at once! Mab? Get my cloak and boots. Collect my things."

"Annette, wait! I tried to tell you—"

But she'd reached the kitchen. Turning, she stopped him in his tracks with a look of pure fury. She slammed the door shut. The bolt shot home, locking him out.

He exhaled with a curse, but had no time to pursue the matter. Servants bustled everywhere. Luggage bumped in the foyer as the hired coachmen lugged it in. Cook chattered at his elbow, asking directions for room assignments and refreshments.

It was an hour before the servants finished settling them in, an hour before he resumed his interview with Eunice. Preparing himself with a swallow of brandy in his study, he straightened his shoulders and headed for the drawing room. Eunice and her aunt were waiting, perched on a settee with a low tea tray before them. Eunice's eyes were red.

"I would like to speak with Eunice alone, Lady Wetherby."

The woman's several chins jiggled in indignation.

"Perhaps *you* feel free to do things improperly, but *we* do not. Eunice shall require a chaperone until she is properly married."

His temper flared. With effort, he checked it.

"Who *is* that low woman?" Lady Wetherby began.

"Yes," Eunice echoed, taking courage from hiding behind her aunt's skirts. "Who *is* she, Garth?"

He considered a lie, then thought better of it. He'd only be digging himself into a pit. Besides, with peckish, hennish women like the Wetherbys, it was always safer to be blunt. Bluntness deprived them of future territory at which to peck and scratch.

"Annette has been my mistress for the past few years. You will do well to absorb that fact and then forget it."

Eunice gasped.

Lady Wetherby's jowls puffed. "A gentleman would not admit such a thing! And to his betrothed!"

He was on the verge of snapping out about Lord Wetherby's "gentlemanliness"—his penchant for writing Garth for loans, but he bit the words back. The loans were lost money. An investment in keeping Trent safe.

He turned to Eunice. "Why did you come, Eunice? I told you I would fetch you myself. We would wed in London."

Eunice opened her mouth to respond, but Lady Wetherby jumped in.

"You *didn't* come, dear boy. You didn't even write. You didn't acknowledge Eunice's letters. It was humiliating for her. Her friends, her cousins, everyone asking about the wedding— oh, it was not to be borne!"

Nodding at each point Lady Wetherby made, Eunice dropped her face to her hands and wept bitter tears of injured pride.

He felt the stirring of pity. He sighed tiredly, wondering how many marriages had as their foundation, pity. *More than the world dreams* . . . he went to Eunice and patted her shoulder.

"How can I make it up to you?"

Her head came up, bird-eyes shining with hope.

"I—I—"

"You can set the date, dear boy. And purchase the marriage license."

He drew an annoyed breath.

"I will give it thought. After my next sailing."

" 'Thought'! Dear boy, you will set the date *now*. And as for that despicable woman—"

He swung on his heel, striding to the door, and Lady Wetherby gasped uncertainly, changing her tack.

"Dear boy, where are you going?"

"Garth?" Eunice chirped in alarm. "Where are you going?"

He turned and gave the women a scathing look.

"Enjoy the hospitality of my house, ladies. Eunice, tomorrow I shall instruct my bank to honor any bills you might incur in my absence."

"'Absence,' Garth! But where?"

He smiled tightly.

"I may not be a gentleman, but I *am* a workingman. A shipload of barrel staves awaits delivery. Where am I going? For tonight, you may find me in my study. Tomorrow? You'll find me in the Caribbean."

He shut the door with a satisfactory bang.

With characteristic ill timing, Harrington barged into the study where he'd been brooding for an hour or more, staring out at the gently accumulating snow. He'd not been thinking of Eunice, but of Annette. Wondering what move to make. Annette would come round sooner or later, of course. He preferred sooner.

"I know why she does it," Harrington boomed jubilantly, ignoring McNeil's black mood. McNeil sent him an even blacker look. Harrington refused to be discouraged.

"Cap'n, I know why she does it."

McNeil groaned. Harrington had a bee in his bonnet. The signs were unmistakable. He lunged up to make a strategic retreat to the drawing room, but then dropped back into his chair with a sigh. Harrington would only follow him.

"What the devil are you nattering about?"

Harrington rubbed his beaky nose, unknowingly polishing its ruddy color to a bright red glow.

"*Her,* Cap'n. *Mab Collins.*" Harrington uttered the name as though it were sacred. "I know why *she* runs away. 'Tis *her* child. A little girl not more'n six. Had to be sold, Cap'n, when her Pa died on the *Schilaack. She* runs off because she wants to steal the tyke. She be bound to a farmer near Hampton."

McNeil closed his eyes in irritation, trying to sort out the disjointed story. Harrington was a first-class sailor; but on land and in conversation, he was a ship without rudder.

"So?" he said when he'd sorted it out.

"So ho, Cap'n!" Harrington hitched up his pants, his face splitting into a grin. "I mean to buy Sarah Bess and fetch 'er here. That is—" His booming confidence waned a bit. "That is, sir, if ye'll have 'er?" He paused, rushing on. "Why, Cap'n, a little girl don't eat more'n a bird. She could bunk with Trent. Why, Trent and her—they'd sail plumb smooth together, they would."

Garth frowned, considering it. Mab hadn't totally proved herself yet. He was inclined to wait. His thoughts jumped to Eunice. Eunice would question the presence of one orphan in his house. *Two* might be easier to swallow. The girl might deflect attention from Trent. An old diversion: When taking aim with one cannon, fire all the rest to confuse the enemy.

Harrington waited, scarcely breathing. Garth nodded his permission.

"Thank ye, Cap'n!" Harrington boomed.

"Does Mab know?"

Harrington shook his head.

" 'Tis my surprise," he said proudly.

"Well, be quick about it. The *Caroline* sails tomorrow."

"I'll go at once."

The snow ceased during the night, leaving a fresh-smelling blanket of white. Garth rubbed steam from the kitchen window and looked out. Williamsburg's dogs were cavorting as wildly as the boys who pelted them with snowballs. A rangy mutt leaped into the air, snapping at a snowball and catching a mouthful of cold-shock. The dog shook his head and slunk away.

Avoiding the ladies, he was breakfasting early and in the kitchen. Cook fussed noisily at fireplace and oven. The steamy fragrance of simmering corn mush and chicken-en-fricassee wafted everywhere. He ate standing at the window, one booted foot propped on a bench. Toad, Mab Collins and the scullery girl sat at table, chattering about the storm. Trent dipped into his breakfast between mad flights to the window. Trent was in a dither to go out and play. Mab would not allow it until his mush bowl stood empty.

Garth glanced curiously at the back door as a muffled knocking began. Wiping hands on her apron, cook rushed to open the door. Harrington stomped in, big and blustery, an enormous bundle of rolled-up wolfskins in his arms. He stamped snow from his boots, looked round at the placid assembly and gave a loud bark.

"Here now, Mab Collins! Up lass, and help me with this bundle."

Mab glanced up with bristling disinterest.

"Stuff it in yer cap," she advised.

Garth chuckled. Harrington was the lone remaining recipient of Mab's insults. At first Garth had assumed Mab had taken a hot and instant dislike to Harrington. But the ensuing weeks proved the opinion premature. If anything, he suspected Mab liked Harrington too much and covered this weakness with insolence.

Harrington persisted with good humor.

"Come now, Mab. Me arms be ready t'fall off."

"Stuff it in yer—"

The bundle wiggled. From within came a muffled cry.

"Mama?"

Garth's glance shot to Mab. Her face went slack, all expression sliding away. Her spoon clattered to her trencher. She stared at the wiggling bundle.

"Oh ho, now," Harrington boomed, setting the bundle down and unpeeling it, layer by layer. Fair hair was the first thing to appear, then blinking blue eyes, a small nose, thin lips.

"Mama?" she chirped uncertainly. "Mama?"

Mab's bench hit the floor with a crash as she lunged up, diving for her daughter. She fell to her knees, grabbing the child and nearly crushing her to death.

"Sarah Bess—"

She pressed a hundred violent kisses upon the girl until Sarah Bess shrieked happily. McNeil's eyes met Harrington's in approval.

Not to be outdone, Trent scrambled from his bench, scooped up a toy soldier and ran to the girl, holding it out in a gesture of invitation. Sarah Bess giggled. Wiggling out of her mother's arms, she dropped to the floor to play.

Mab panted. Swatting the moisture from her cheeks, she tore her eyes from Sarah Bess and swung toward Harrington.

"Don't you go thinkin' you'll bed me because of this!" she shouted belligerently.

McNeil's breath caught sharply. Of all the damned cheeky bitches!

But Harrington did not appear to be perturbed.

"I'll not be supposin' that, lass," he returned mildly.

Her eyes flashed.

"And don't think I'm pea-assed green grateful! Because I ain't!"

"Course you ain't," Harrington agreed good-naturedly.

Trent whooped something about more toy soldiers. He snatched Sarah Bess's hand. The two ran gleefully toward his room. Mab stalked after the children, pausing in the doorway to throw one more spear.

"Don't be thinkin' it means anything to me. It don't! I would've got Sarah Bess m'self, by and by. I can take care of m'self, I can!"

"Of course, lass."

His gentle agreement seemed to disconcert her. She jerked around, making to go. Then she turned one last time. Her lips trembled. McNeil could see the hard shell was cracking. She fought it. Fought to regain her angry fire. But it was a losing battle. She threw one final desperate look round the staring assembly, then flew across the room and into Harrington's burly arms. He caught her as though she were as light as a feather and as welcome as sunshine in January.

"Oliver—" she cried out, using Harrington's Christian name. "Oliver—oh, Oliver!"

What Harrington's response was, McNeil never knew. Tapping Toad and the scullery girl upon their gawking heads, he ejected the staff from the kitchen with a curt "Out."

He shut the door firmly behind him.

Chapter 17

"THEE SHOULD NOT COME."

In the hushed stillness of gently falling snow, Dennis's voice seemed large and cavernous. Flavia couldn't answer. Instead, she took his arm for support as they walked on.

The falling snow lent an unreal quality to a day that was already horribly unreal. The snow dropped steadily. Without wind, each snowflake fell with vertical precision, as though following the master carpenter's plumb line. Familiar landmarks were disappearing into dubious shapes. A white world was closing in.

She wanted to flee. Or scream until the world came real again.

"Thee has been ill. Thee should *not* come," Dennis persisted.

"I must."

She heard him draw a long breath of the cold, snow-sweetened air. Snow squeaked under their boots in somber rhythm.

"Ay," he agreed softly.

The familiar walk to Chestertown seemed alien and endless. It was like moving in a dream. With every step she took, her heart cried out to turn and run. She forced herself on. When she faltered, Dennis's arm came around her, strong and comforting. He brushed the accumulating snow from the shoulders of her cloak, then patted her cheek.

"Courage, Jane."

But when they finally reached the small miserable jailhouse, courage fled. She stood in the snowy, empty street, too ill to go in. She clutched the oilskin packet of raisin cakes to her breast.

"Shall I take thee back?"

She longed to respond to the compassion in his voice by crying, "Yes! Oh, please—yes." But she couldn't. She must be strong. Stronger than she'd ever been in her life.

Shaking her head, she stepped out of the snow and up onto the creaking, uneven boards of the stoop. Dennis banged once on the rough-hewn door, then pushed it in. As they entered the jailer's rude quarters, heat and the greasy smell of bear stew rushed toward them. The jailer and his disagreeable family were at their noon meal. Following lower-class custom, the jailer and his wife sat at the table while their four raggedly dressed children stood. The children had no plates. They waited in obedient silence until it pleased one of their parents to hand them a dripping hunk of meat or a bread sop. The family glanced toward the door without interest.

"Open the cell," Dennis commanded without a greeting.

The irascible jailer showed no inclination to rise. Instead, he chomped steadily on a meaty bone, loudly sucking off the flesh.

"It ain't time," he mumbled, grease dribbling down his chin.

Worry shot through Flavia.

"Oh, Dennis—"

"Open it *now*," Dennis ordered.

The jailer threw them a sullen look. Then, seeming to judge that it wasn't in his best interest to offend the respected schoolmaster, he got up, viciously snatched his key ring from a peg on the wall and lumbered to the cells in the adjoining room.

Flavia's knees jellied. She followed Dennis and the jailer, her stomach turning. The cells were cramped, windowless boxes accommodated with straw. Unheated, they were not fit to house animals. The gagging odor of unemptied chamber pots hung in the air. Sickened, she backed away, backed out to the jailer's one-room quarters. She waited, throat tight with anxiety. She set the packet of raisin cakes aside. Five sets of greedy eyes flew to the packet.

At last, Neddy came forth. Straw clung to his hair, to his dirty, disheveled clothes. He blinked at the unaccustomed light, his eyes slow to focus.

"Neddy? I've brought raisin cakes this time."

Her voice was queer, unnatural. But he knew it at once. His eyes lit with happiness.

"Jane? Uh, uh, Jane?"

Jo Ann Wendt

She went to him on stiff legs, taking him into her cold arms. He wiggled like a delighted puppy, and a wave of terror coursed through her.

"Jane—uh, uh—doll—find doll—"

Her eyes misted. She nodded at Dennis.

"He's lost his doll. Will you?"

A quick search of the cell turned up no doll. Dennis returned, his usually placid features contorted in anger.

"Who has it?" he snapped at the dining family. "Who's taken Neddy's doll?"

The jailer's wife lifted her stringy, unwashed head. "The lunatic don't need no play-doll," she drawled belligerently. "Now, me *own* girls—"

Flavia's eyes roved the messy crowded room. She spotted the cornhusk doll atop soiled bedding in the family bedstead. Untangling herself from Neddy's affectionate embrace, she flew to get it. The two girls broke into petulant whines at her action, but Dennis glared at the jailer.

"Silence yer yaps," the jailer growled at his daughters, "or I'll slap 'em silent. Ye'll soon have the doll. He'll not need it an hour from now."

Flavia fought the hysteria that rose. She pressed the doll into Neddy's eager arms. Her eyes flew to Dennis for comfort as Neddy dropped happily to the floor, crooning to his doll.

Dennis touched her shoulder.

"Thee has done everything possible. Thee gave testimony at the trial. Indeed, thee put thyself in jeopardy, Jane. Thy testimony did not set well with the parish. It cannot set well with

Mrs. Byng—the things thee revealed about Mr. Byng." His forehead wrinkled in deep concern. "Jane, if Mrs. Byng and her sister are mistreating thee, I swear I shall—"

"No." She shook her head tremulously. "At first, yes. But no more. Betsy Simm came to call on Mrs. Byng." She paused, attempting a wry smile but failing. "*Lady* Elizabeth, I mean. It seems Mr. Gresham is in the habit of granting a widow's pension to wives of clergymen. Betsy threatened to make Mr. Gresham stop Mrs. Byng's pension if Mrs. Byng is in any way cruel to me."

"Good for Betsy."

"Yes," Flavia whispered, looking down at the floor. She could not add that in those first days she'd been oblivious to Mrs. Byng's cruelty. *Robert. Robert.* She'd been numb with grief. Mrs. Byng could've whipped her bloody, and she'd hardly have noticed.

Playing on the floor, Neddy laughed in sheer happiness. Her chin trembled at the sound, and Dennis patted her cheek for courage.

"*Why*, Dennis?" she whispered passionately. "*Why* must this happen? He's of accountable age, but his mind is that of a small boy!"

Dennis drew a sharp angry breath.

"The jury were landed men, slave owners. The thought of a slave killing his master, Jane?" Dennis shook his head. "'Tis terrifying to the slave owner. It wakens a fear that the rich try to suppress. No. Clemency was not in their hearts. Not even Mr. Tate would help. Though Mr. Tate's new son-in-law was sympathetic."

"He was?"

"Ay. Mr. McNeil spent three days going round to the jurors with me. But . . ."

Tears swam in her eyes, tears both of gratitude and despair, tears she must control. If Neddy saw . . .

Dropping to the floor beside Neddy, she took the oilskin packet from the stool and carefully unwrapped the raisin cakes. They were squashed, but the rich aroma of molasses curled upward, seizing Neddy's attention. With a gleeful shout he fell upon the cakes.

"'Tis a waste," the jailer's slack-jawed wife drawled from the table. "Givin' bonny good cakes t' the fool. In a hour, he'll be—"

"Be silent, woman!" Dennis exploded. "Or by God, I'll throttle you!"

At the unexpected outburst from the mild-mannered Quaker, the jailer and his family ducked to their food and remained cowed.

Flavia watched Neddy enjoy his cakes. She tried to straighten his hair a bit, raking her fingers through it. But to touch him brought tears. As Neddy finished and licked the last buttery crumb from his fingers, Flavia heard the stomp of boots on the porch stoop. Her stomach lurched, curling round the cold pit that was her heart.

The deputation!

Her eyes shot to Dennis. He whitened, got up and went out to speak to the men. It seemed an eternity before he returned, and yet the time was not long enough.

The deputation would forgo the shackles, he

told her. He and she would be allowed to escort Neddy. She felt dizzy, weak with relief and revulsion. Choking back a sob, she scanned the room for Neddy's old patched coat. She spotted it on the jailer's son, a surly-looking lad of about thirteen. She jumped up, went to the boy and wrenched the coat off. No one made a peep or even met her blazing, angry eyes as she stared round the table.

Neddy chortled in happiness as she and Dennis stiffly bundled him in coat, scarf and Dennis's warm gloves.

"Home?" he asked.

Dennis's eyes went to Flavia.

"Ay, lad," he said softly. "Thee be going home."

Flavia gave in to one wrenching sob, then fled out into the freshly falling snow. Neddy followed, then stopped suddenly in astonishment. He stood gaping at the feathery whiteness. His eyes lit with wonder.

"Jane! Uh, uh, Jane—pretty!"

Flavia choked on her despair.

"Snow," she managed to say. "It's snow, Neddy."

"Pretty," he whispered in awe, then dropped to his knees and swirled his hands in it. He brought some of it to his mouth, tasted and then laughed in delight.

One of the black-cloaked deputation stepped forward to jerk Neddy to his feet. But Dennis stepped in front of the man.

"A moment to play," Dennis said firmly.

The man fell back, shrugging. "This gives us no pleasure, Finny. But the court has ruled. Justice must be served."

"This is not justice," Dennis said bitterly. "It's murder."

Flavia shuddered. She felt ill with cold. It was not the icy chill of the weather, but heart-chill, soul-chill. Weakly she reached for Dennis's arm. He supported her and coaxed Neddy along. Flavia forced herself on. The snow was falling thicker and faster. Neddy reveled in it. Never had she seen him so joyful. It was as though the purity of the snow's beauty communicated with the purity of his soul. He couldn't speak of his joy or even comprehend the concept of joy; but joy frolicked in him and radiated from his eyes.

"Jane—pretty!" he called every few minutes as he gamboled along.

She felt ill. Ill to death. She fought the urge to vomit. Dennis sensed her weakness. His arm shot around her in increased support. She leaned heavily upon him and stumbled on.

Huddled in shawls and cloaks, stray onlookers joined the procession, eerily appearing like gray apparitions rising from the falling snow. Children ran along, kicking snow with loud whoops of delight. Her heart twisted as Neddy tried to imitate the kicking children.

"Who is to hang, Mother?" a child's cheery voice rang out in the hushed snowy air.

"Hesh! Mind your manners, Susannah."

Flavia shuddered. The shudder would not stop.

"Oh, Dennis," she whispered, collapsing against him. "I'm going to be sick to my stomach. I can't—Dennis—"

She pulled away, lurching through the thick

snow and stumbling into an alley off the street. The procession moved on without her as she retched violently. Falling to her knees in utter weakness, she could not stop retching. She retched beyond the point of bringing anything up. She knelt panting in the snow, her hands and her legs ice.

The procession had been swallowed up in snow. Even their voices had vanished. She gagged one last time, then dragged herself to her feet. She was in the alley that ran beside the fiddle maker's house. Unconnected violin notes rang out as the craftsman worked. Fleeing the sounds, she stumbled out into the street and forced herself on. The footprints of those who'd gone ahead were already rounding, filling with snow. She hurried.

The snow was falling like a blanket now. Blindly, she stumbled on, following whatever prints she saw. When the huge oak in Market Square loomed up, she knew she'd lost her bearings. Turning, she ran through the thick impeding snow, panting as she rushed. At last she sensed the gallows field, sensed its presence rather than saw it. She ran faster.

God, no. No, no, no.

It came to her suddenly that the snow was a blessing. Neddy couldn't know where he was going. Even the gallows must be heaped with snow and unrecognizable.

She ran on, slipping, falling, dragging herself up again. At last, faint gray shadows took shape in the snow ahead. Spectators? She gagged, clutching her stomach and running on.

Suddenly, a clear happy voice rang out.

"Jane? Pretty! Pret—"

Rope whirred. There was the sickening snap of human bone breaking, then murmurs flowing from the crowd, flowing toward her like an enormous ocean wave. She swayed as it hit her.

"Neddy?" she cried out. Then, when no answer came, "*Neddy!*"

She was hovering there, frozen in disbelief, when Dennis found her. He said nothing. He picked her up in his arms and carried her away in stony silence.

When the first wave of shock passed, she struggled to get out of his arms.

"No, Dennis—I must take him down—I must bury him—oh, help me—we must—"

He avoided her eyes, and then she remembered. She let her head fall to his chest. She wept bitterly.

The jury had decreed. Neddy's body must hang three months. A visible warning to bondslave and Negro.

"Let me shelter thee, Jane. Let me buy thy indenture. Let me take care of thee. Let me . . . husband thee," he urged gently.

She'd been sitting by the fire in his rough, unfinished schoolhouse for hours. Although he'd wrapped her in every blanket he owned, she was still shaking. He fed her hot rum tea with his own hands, since hers shook too badly to manage the cup.

"It's true I don't have the money just now—" He gestured round at his house, and, dully,

Flavia's eyes followed. Furnishings were sparse:
a bedstead, a trencher table and benches. She
was sitting in his one chair. The opposite end of
the schoolhouse fared better. Expensive books
stood in wall shelves. Carpentry tools lay neatly
upon the school desk that was under construction. Four finished desks gleamed with the pa-
tina of oil rubbed lovingly into the fine wood.

Dennis went on. "I shall borrow the money,
Jane. From Mr. Tate. Or," he said, hesitating,
"from Mr. McNeil."

Flavia was too heartsore to respond. She let
him talk. Taking her silence as possible assent,
he said, "Yes, I'll consult Mr. McNeil. As soon
as possible. Before he travels to Williamsburg,
to his brother's wedding."

The words sliced through her fog.

"'Wedding'?" She shook her head. "Not Captain McNeil?"

Dennis nodded in the affirmative.

"Mr. Raven McNeil tells me his brother will
wed soon."

Flavia's fingers dug into the arms of the chair.
No! It was too much. She could stand no more.
She'd tried to endure the duke's cruel punishment—oh, she'd tried. Then Robert and the
agonizing doubt that overlay his death, the night-
mares in which the duke found out and cold-
bloodedly murdered her son. Neddy... Robert
... Garth... Valentina filling her shoes as duchess of Tewksbury... Uncle Simon and Father,
Mother, going on... living...

She was as dead to them all as if she had truly
died. But if Flavia was dead, Jane Brown still

lived. What should "Jane" do? What would
become of her? She'd be a prideful fool to turn
away from the comfort, the kindness of this man
and the safe refuge he offered.

She looked at Dennis. He was squatting by
her chair, his face tender with concern. She met
his worried eyes.

"I—I'll marry you, Dennis."

The sadness of Neddy didn't leave his face,
but quiet joy suffused it. Too choked to speak,
he fumbled into the blankets for her hand, drew
it out and pressed a soft kiss into her palm.

"When may I claim thee, Jane?"

Awash with sorrow and resignation, she couldn't
think.

"After, after—Neddy is buried," she said at
last.

Dennis kissed her hand, then gently tucked it
back into the blankets.

"In April, then?" he said.

She nodded, the last fragment of her old
life—of "Flavia"—seeming to fall away, leaving
her just Jane.

"In April."

Chapter 18

GARTH RETURNED FROM THE CARIBBE-
AN to find the forsythia in bloom, the air
smelling of spring planting and his life going
to hell in a handbasket.

The first annoyance was his steward. The man
was aboard the *Caroline* almost before the
Caroline settled into her berth in Yorktown
harbor. It was a bad omen, Garth thought sourly.
Good news will wait. Bad will not.

Garth was right. The steward reported he'd
failed to buy Jane Brown's indenture. Another
had beat him to it. A Quaker schoolmaster, a
Mr. Finny. Jane Brown still lived in Chestertown.

And Raven still pines for her, Garth thought
in irritation. He gave his agent a black look.

"Use your head, man. Buy her from Finny
and get her out of the colonies at once."

The man shrugged apologetically.

"I tried, sir. Mr. Finny would not sell."

Garth raised his eyebrows. "Not for one hundred pounds?"

"Not even for two hundred, sir."

Garth laughed cynically. "Then she's Finny's whore."

"It did not appear so, sir. Mr. Finny is highly respected in Chestertown. Three seminary students board with him, sir."

Garth frowned in puzzlement, then listened to the rest of the bad news. Raven had got wind of his brother's actions. He was so furious he was spitting tacks. Raven had ordered his own steward to go to Finny and offer *three* hundred pounds.

Garth sighed. A pretty mess. What if Maryann heard?

His second annoyance while trying to settle the *Caroline* was Mab. He was dealing with the royal customs officer on deck when he spotted a horse hightailing down the Williamsburg-Yorktown road. The rider was chucking about in the saddle as if he or she possessed no riding skills at all. He went on with his business, glancing up now and then in curiosity. To his annoyance, he began to recognize the gait of his favorite mount. He looked sharply. Mab's long thin figure hove into view atop the horse.

"Damnation! She can't ride. She'll ruin him," he fumed, grabbing quill pen, jamming it into the inkwell and scrawling his signature upon the customs papers. He went to the rail where Harrington leaned, grinning at the approaching rider.

"Tell your woman she is *not* to use my mounts."

Harrington's grin broadened. With the back of his hand he rubbed his beaky nose, polishing it to a ruddy glow.

"Ay, Cap'n. I'll tell 'er."

"And tell her a horse is steered by reins. *Not* by shouting curses into its ear."

Harrington laughed happily.

"I'll tell 'er."

With customs papers disposed of, the noisy unloading of cargo began, Jenkins supervising. Mab clattered on to the wharf, dismounted clumsily, gave the horse a slap that was pure vexation and abandoned McNeil's mount to a small boy who stood watching. Without ceremony she pushed her way up the gangplank, cursing a path for herself through the string of porters trundling cargo from ship to waiting wagons. She threw herself into Harrington's grinning embrace, but immediately twisted free of him to hiss fire at McNeil.

"*She* sent him away, *she* did. That hoity-toity pale-faced bitch of your'n. And Sarah Bess, too!"

It was several minutes before they could calm her, several more before her story made sense. But when it did, Garth's temper went on the boil. *Eunice, damn her.* It seemed the children's presence had been an annoyance to Eunice and Lady Wetherby. Trent and Sarah Bess were too loud, too boisterous. Since they were merely orphan and servant's child, Eunice had dispatched them to a farm on the outskirts of Williamsburg, putting them to board with a farmer and his wife.

Anger throbbed in his throat. Eunice. By God, he'd like to throttle her. How dare she meddle with his *son*? He needed several deep breaths of the fresh spring air before he could control himself.

"Do you know where Trent is?" he demanded of Mab.

Whisking back the long hair that was flying in the wind, she snorted her contempt for his question.

"Course I do. I sneak off to visit him and Sarah Bess, mebbe thrice a week."

He turned to Harrington.

"Hire a chaise. Take Mab. Get the children and bring them home."

Leaving Jenkins in charge of the unloading and deliveries to warehouses, he threw a coin to the boy holding his horse, swung himself up into the saddle and quickly left the port of York behind. He was glad for the few miles that stretched between Yorktown and Williamsburg. The distance helped him cool down. By the time he trotted up to his own front door, he was cool with determination. Eunice ruling the roost? *His* roost? Ha!

He threw the front door open and stamped into the foyer. A cursory glance revealed that his mother's fine old case clock had been moved. In its place stood a ridiculously fragile table with finger-thin legs. On the table, a vase of flowers. Not real flowers, but ones made of silk with button centers. He eyed them with displeasure. Fancywork done by Eunice, the fat aunt and Mouse, no doubt. He slammed the door, noting with childish satisfaction that one silly flower tumbled to the floor.

The slam of the door brought the immediate swish of silk. "Garth, dear, you're home!" Eunice rustled down the stairs, shadowed by her excited, twittering companions. "We've been expecting you at every moment, ever since word reached us that the *Caroline* had arrived."

She stopped short when she saw the fallen flower. With a little cry she swooped down upon it, rescued it and tucked it back into its nest. Then she offered him her cheek. Politeness decreed he make the effort to kiss it. Seething, he did so, then greeted the others with as much civility as he could muster.

"I want to talk with you at once, Eunice." He motioned toward the open drawing room door.

She preceded him in, twittering happily. "Oh, yes, Garth, we've so much to plan. Auntie and I have such lovely ideas for the wedding."

When Auntie and Mouse made to follow them in, he was forced to make it clear that he intended to talk to Eunice alone.

The aunt blinked her dismay. "But—but a chaperone, dear boy?"

He forced himself to be civil. "Lady Wetherby, this is *my* house. I've not needed a chaperone in it since I was six years old and fell madly in love with cook."

She blinked again. Then she gushed, "As you say, dear boy. Naturally you wish to see Eunice alone. So romantic and, of course, the wedding plans and—"

He shut the door on her gushing. A glance at the drawing room revealed Eunice and Auntie had made their stamp here, too. Annette's striking peacock blue silk draperies had vanished. Pale, insipid green hung in their place. He pursed his lips in growing annoyance, went to the sideboard and poured himself a steadying glass of port.

"About the wedding date, Garth," Eunice bubbled. "Auntie suggests—"

He interrupted her.

"Where are the draperies?"

She caught her breath at the harshness in his voice, and he watched her eyes dart from drapery to drapery.

"I took the liberty of—that is, Auntie and I thought—" She drew a quick breath and began again, this time with confidence, as though she'd been coached. "Since I shall be mistress here very shortly, dearest, I took the liberty of replacing them. The draperies were—how shall I put it? Garish, perhaps. In poor taste."

"*I* liked them."

It took the wind out of her sails, but not completely. With a surprising show of spirit, she said, "You liked them because *she* picked them out. Oh, yes, Garth, the servants left me in no mystery about *that*."

She reddened at her own daring. Irritably, he took a swallow of port. It proved to be as sour as his feelings for Eunice. He set the wine aside.

It was time to take a stand. That or be forever

ruled by a triumvirate of Auntie, Eunice and Mouse.

"Eunice, hear me and hear me well. You may change the window hangings hourly, for all I care, and shuffle the furniture like cards. But there is one thing you will *not* do. You will *not* interfere with the children who live in this house."

Her small eyes widened in genuine surprise. She drew a trembling breath.

"But—but—they were only servant children. I was only trying to make our home more perfect, Garth. Someday *we'll* have children. We shan't want them associating with that saucy little girl or with Trent."

His annoyance rose.

"What's wrong with Trent?"

She took a deep breath and plowed in.

"His low-class origin is all too apparent, Garth. He has no manners. His speech is no better than Toad's." She shuddered delicately. "I shouldn't wonder that he harbors some dreadful disease."

McNeil seethed. Biting back a hot retort, he grabbed the glass of sour port and downed it without tasting. His breath came in harsh draws. He mustn't defend Trent. If Eunice thought him lowborn, so much the better. Still, it rubbed him raw. Her snipes at Annette had been bad enough. But to criticize his and Flavia's son? He longed to throttle her. He wrestled with his temper, not speaking until it was under control.

"The children will stay, Eunice."

Her eyes fell away. Her mouth trembled, then settled into peevish sulky lines. Lifting her skirts, she rustled to the door. She paused, hand on latch.

"As you say, Garth. But as for that *woman,* she'll trouble us no more."

He looked up, questioning.

"She's wed the earl of Dunwood. In Baltimore."

McNeil was stunned. So Annette had gone and done it! Willfully burning her bridges. He drew a quick breath. Damn her headstrong ways!

Eunice went on. "All Williamsburg gossiped of it, Garth. A woman marrying a man who is young enough to be her *son.* You may be certain the earl's mother, Lady Dunwood, put up a fight. Lady Dunwood still opposes the match and privately threatens to have the marriage annulled—if immorality can be proved on the part of the baroness, by testimony other than servant gossip."

Garth's eyes narrowed.

"What sort of testimony?" Hating the thought of Annette's marriage, he hated this even more. Annette boxed in, under threat . . .

Eunice colored. With a stiff reluctance she said, "Proof the baroness has given birth to an illegitimate child."

Garth snorted in relief.

"Annette Vachon has never had a child."

Relief seemed to surge through the stiff figure facing him, too. "Oh! Oh, I'm so glad," she cried out in a happy rush, picking up her skirts and rustling across the room to peck his cheek. "I was afraid that—" She blushed, retreating toward the door. Seemingly overwhelmed by her own thoughts, she turned, opened the door and bolted.

Garth stared after her, puzzled. It was several moments before daylight broke through. Had Eunice thought that Trent was . . . that he and Annette had . . ? Idiot woman!

He shrugged it off. He started for his room, but halfway up the stairs he heard an Indian raid commence in the distant kitchen. Whoops, cries of welcome and the excited shrieks of children split the air like tomahawks. With a happy grin he descended the stairs, strolled down the long corridor and into the chaos.

Trent was already chasing the kitchen cat. Sarah Bess knelt on the floor, setting up toy soldiers and scolding whenever Trent and the cat leaped through the army, scattering soldiers.

"Cap Mac!" Trent shouted, diving for his arms. McNeil caught him, threw him toward the ceiling, caught him again and hugged him, kissed him. Trent shrieked his delight. The imp chattered in a dozen unrelated directions and then demanded to be let down. McNeil obeyed.

"Does the man like *me*, too, Mama?"

Garth turned. Fair-haired Sarah Bess stood staring at him shyly, one finger lost in her rosy mouth. He laughed, went to her and swooped her up. She was a slight thing, long-limbed and skinny like Mab. No sooner was she up in his arms than she wriggled to be set down.

She scooted across the kitchen to Mab, hiding in Mab's apron. "Mama, I'm hungry!" Trent ran to Mab, too. "Mama, I'm hungry!" he demanded.

Mama? Garth was surprised, then pleased.

The little monkey was evidently devoted to
Sarah Bess, aping everything she said and did.
Well and good, he thought cynically. Mab could
be "Mama" to Trent. It would keep Eunice and
Auntie in a state of royal confusion.

A week after he returned, Garth ran into Annette.
She was coming out of the milliner's shop on
the Duke of Gloucester Street just as he popped
out of The King's Arms tavern. She was on the
arm of her parrot. Marriage seemed to have
brought the parrot into full feather.

He's become a goddamned bird-of-paradise,
McNeil thought as the gaudily dressed earl of
Dunwood strolled toward him, automatically
extending a hand in greeting.

"Charming to see you again, Captain McNeil,"
Dunwood offered, with only a lightning-quick
glance to check Garth's hand for cannon grime
before pumping it. McNeil smiled sourly. Had
he known, he'd have stopped off at the arsenal.

"Charming," he agreed.

Annette wouldn't look at him. Her lips were
pursed tightly. When politeness required that
she return his own terse greeting, she did so
without wasting a syllable. And rather than look
into his eyes, she fastened her gaze on his chin.
Irritated, he stooped slightly, trying to intercept
her line of vision. She jerked her head away.

"May I offer my congratulations, Lord Dunwood."

The parrot's hat feather bounced.

"Indeed you may!" he said, his chest puffing
in pride. "And thank you, sir. My *wife* and I are

here for the spring horse racing." He sent Annette a fond, doting look, and Annette smiled charmingly back. "My *wife* and I brought two horses down from Baltimore. I daresay our Maryland filly will give Virginia fillies a run for the money, haw, haw."

McNeil made the expected reply. Dunwood rambled on, wearing out the expression "My *wife* and I." The phrase grated on Garth's ears. When Dunwood paused for breath, Garth swung angry eyes to Annette.

"I trust you are exceedingly happy, Lady Dunwood?"

The parrot preened, proudly awaiting her answer.

Annette's dark eyes flashed with fury.

"Yes!"

Immediately, she took Dunwood's arm.

"Dear, I've a silly little headache," she said. "Could we return to North England Street?"

Dunwood nearly swooned with concern, and McNeil bit back a malicious offer to run for leeches and bleed her on the spot. Dunwood ushered Annette into the waiting chaise as though she were made of porcelain. The chaise creaked as Dunwood got in. Wheels squealed a single complaint, then began to roll. Annette rode off without a backward glance.

McNeil strode home in a vile mood, blaming the hollow niggling feeling in his gut on the oyster pie he'd downed; that tavernkeeper had always been one to pass off yesterday's oysters as today's.

His mood suffered no improvement when he

reached home and found himself met at the
door by cook, who had an irritating request.

Cook's daughter and son-in-law were ill with
the ague. Cook's grandsons needed tending.
Could cook bring the little boys here to live for
a few weeks?

"Why not!" Garth snarled. "The more the
merrier! There's nothing I relish more, after a
night's drinking, than little screaming devils
running up and down the house!"

Cook looked at him calmly, absolutely unruf-
fled. Service to two generations of McNeils had
left her immune to McNeil tempers.

"It's settled, then, sir," she said. "The little
ones can sleep in my bed. Thank you, sir."

Garth glared at her.

"Perhaps, cook, after you've settled them in,
you'd like to take a staff and lantern, and go
hawking the streets of Williamsburg shouting,
'Come one, come all! A free living's to be had at
Captain McNeil's!'"

Calmly, she pursed her lips. The look he got
from her was the same look he'd got often when
he was a schoolboy.

"Master Garth," she said firmly, "your attitude wants mending."

Garth avoided being pinned down to the wedding date with all the nimbleness of a seasoned
sailor scrambling in and out of a ship's rigging.
His excuses were beginning to sound feeble
even to himself. He dodged prods from Auntie
and Mouse. And his own brother was no help in

his nimble dance to postpone matrimony. There was blood in Raven's eye; Raven was out for revenge. Raven had been outraged at Garth's effort to rid Maryland of a certain bondwoman. Raven was extracting his revenge in small pieces, as though to prolong the pleasure.

Settled in his Williamsburg house with Maryann, Raven came often to tea or dinner. He took special delight in setting off the ladies with his vicious: "Well, well, well. And have we set the wedding date?"

Raven would sit there, wickedly savoring Garth's discomfort as female voices fluttered to the subject like a flock of birds to a piece of suet.

"Thank you very much, Raven," Garth would mutter, "and go to hell."

Raven's handsome grin—not quite friendly—would flash.

"You're welcome, Garth. And age before beauty."

Wisdom decreed he should marry Eunice. The pack of women—Auntie, Eunice, Mouse—lent an air of respectability to his house, which in turn protected Trent.

He worried about Trent. He longed to adopt him. But if he adopted Trent now, in his bachelor status, he would draw unwanted attention. The evil-minded would whisper that Captain McNeil had spent too long at sea; he'd developed a taste for "boys." Even decent folk would find such an adoption odd and would look at Trent with new eyes, speculating on his origin. If such trivial news should reach the duke of Tewksbury? He shrugged away a shudder. The duke was a shrewd, calculating man.

No, the adoption must wait until he had a wife. As for the wife, he supposed he could make no better choice than Eunice. Some of her ways were irritating; but on the whole, she seemed eager to please him. She covered that night at Bladensburg—if ever that night should need covering. Her family tree was sprinkled with titles. In later years, the tie to Lord Wetherby would prove a boon to Trent. If Trent chose to do so, he could enter the highest social circles in England. Flavia would have liked that for her son, would she not?

Well, he would have to decide. Eunice was becoming increasingly resentful of his offhand manner. If he intended to marry her, it was time he played the suitor. What was he waiting for, he wondered cynically. Love?

No, he'd not love again. Not like Flavia.

Two days later, the scales tipped, once and for all, to Eunice.

Early on the day of the Silver Cup Races and the governor's ball, his first mate, Jenkins, rode in from Hampton. Catching a first glimpse of the man, Garth's initial reaction was irritation. Jenkins meant work. Garth had intended the festive day for play. But quickly he shrugged off his irritation. Jenkins was his best man, quick-minded and intelligent. Trustworthy. Both he and Jenkins knew that the next ship purchased by McNeil & McNeil would find Jenkins as its master.

Garth led the way to his study. When he'd shut the door and dropped into his chair behind the writing desk, he said, "Sit down, Tom."

Jenkins didn't sit. He riffled one hand through his dark hair, then spread his hands on the writing table and leaned forward.

"I thought you should know," he said quietly. "The duke of Tewksbury has landed in Hampton."

For a long time, McNeil listened to his own heart thud. At last he drew a deep breath.

"The duke's business?"

Jenkins nodded.

"I took money from the *Caroline*'s cash box and went taverning to find out." A wry half-smile twisted his lips. "A man finds himself a lot of new friends when he goes taverning with a fat purse."

Garth nodded, leaning forward.

"First I cozy'd up to His Grace's wardrobe man and then to a young footman. Oiled 'em well at your expense, Captain. 'Twas the footman's first taste of good French brandy. The young braggart sang like a nightingale."

Jenkins straightened up, loosely hooking his fingers on his belt.

"When the duke's steward come into the tavern, I made his acquaintance careful-like. He's a pridey man. But not so pridey as to look down his nose at a free bottle. So we punished the bottle for a bit. A tight-mouthed fellow, the steward. Still, he let a thing or two slip."

"Such as?"

Garth pushed his chair back with a loud scrape, got up and went to the window. Trent and Sarah Bess were playing outside, shrieking and chasing a butterfly. Anxiety prickled through him.

"Puzzling out what each man said, I'd guess His Grace is here on a large matter and a small. The small is a bondslave he wants punished. She—"

Garth flicked his hand.

"That's of no account. The large matter?"

Jenkins smiled grimly.

"You know the *Bountiful Lady* and the *Virtue?*"

Garth nodded, his eyes narrowing. "Both ships from Norfolk. Both with rather unbelievable navigation records. Long crossings to London, long enough to first put into the Irish sea and pay a visit to the Isle of Man."

"Ay, Captain. The smuggler's island."

"When the ships finally make London, the waterline on the hull sticks out like a sore thumb. Even a blind man can see that a few ton of cargo have vanished between Norfolk and London."

Jenkins added, "Yet the ships' paperwork is in order, cargo tallying with the Norfolk royal customs officer's certificate."

McNeil drew a sharp breath, wondering where Jenkins was heading, but trusting the man to deliver.

"A dangerous game, smuggling," Garth said. "Especially with England tottering on the brink of financial collapse because of lost revenues, Parliament screaming for smugglers' necks and the royal customs force doubling daily."

Jenkin's eyes met his.

"Not dangerous if the ship's captain has a friend on the Board of Trade."

Garth's eyebrows shot up.

"Tewksbury sits on the board. Are you saying—"

Jenkins shook his head.

"I'm only sayin', sir, that the duke received two interesting callers as soon as he arrived. The captain of the *Bountiful Lady* and the master of the *Virtue*."

Garth whistled. It was a whistle of both surprise and relief. So it wasn't Bladensburg that brought the duke. Thank God! Garth had heard rumors that the smuggling network extended into high places. But *this* high?

He turned to Jenkins and shook the man's hand in dismissal.

"Thank you, Tom. Well done."

For a long time, he sat in his study, thinking. He was annoyed that his inner tension didn't dissipate, but instead, increased. Tension dug its teeth into the deep muscles of his neck. He rolled his head, irritably rubbing his shoulders, seeking relief. He got up, went to the window and watched Trent play.

Tewksbury would pay a formal visit to Williamsburg, of course. His position on the Board of Trade would make a call on the governor *de rigueur*.

Entrenched in Williamsburg's highest social circle, Lady Wetherby, Eunice and Mouse would flutter to parties given in the duke's honor. The subject of Bladensburg would come up. Garth broke into a cold sweat.

Get your ducks in order, McNeil. Trent's life depends upon it. Set the damned wedding date!

"You look very pretty, Eunice."

It was the best Garth could do. A poor start, perhaps. But a start. *It'll never go down in the annals of great courting speeches, McNeil!*

He was in the drawing room, taking wine and a cigar as he waited for the ladies to assemble for the governor's royal ball. A spring breeze wafted in through the open window, stirring Eunice's dull green draperies. Outside, the landau waited, fresh washed and gleaming in lamplight. He could hear the horses shaking their traces as Toad clucked to them.

At his compliment, Eunice lit up with pleasure.

"Why, Garth! Thank you. That's the sweetest thing you've said to me since I arrived."

"Then I've been remiss."

She blushed happily, dropping her shining gaze to her gown.

"You really like it?"

"Yes."

The gown suited her, he admitted. Its rosy color cancelled the sallowness of her complexion. She was slightly chicken-breasted—breastbone protruding a bit—and the gown's fussy neckline hid this feature in laces, ribbons, rosettes. A traditionalist, she wore a formal white wig. She looked like . . . like a wife, he thought bleakly.

Encouraged by his attention, Eunice burst into a flurry of the silly chatter he'd come to expect of her.

"Garth, you *do* look handsome in dark blue brocade. I can't wait to stroll on your arm at the ball. I shall be the envy of every woman. Oh, I do so admire dark blue on a man, but I wonder, Garth, if you might not be just the tiniest more handsome in your *light* blue brocade."

He swallowed his rising temper, trying not to envision a marriage that had as its stability "handsomeness" and "brocade jackets." *Get on with it, man. Do it.*

"We must set the wedding date," he said briskly.

Eunice's mouth fell open. She blinked in astonishment.

"Garth! Dearest! I had begun to fear—"

For answer, he went to her and lightly kissed her tight cool lips. The fragrance of heather rose from her. Flavia's scent. *Flavia...Flavia*. Abruptly he pulled back.

"June," he snapped with harsh decisiveness. "When I return from my next sailing."

"June," she echoed in awe, whirling to face Auntie and Mouse as their ball gowns rustled into the room.

"It's to be *June*," she cried out in giddy triumph.

Elated chatter erupted. Coos and kisses swirled round Eunice. Garth returned to his wineglass and drained it. He slung the suddenly tasteless cigar into the fireplace. He'd set his course. The rudder was locked. No turning back. Still, the scent of heather lingered in his nostrils. *Flavia...Flavia*.

* * *

Torches blazed along the boulevard leading to
the governor's mansion. Torchlight played upon
the sleek rippling rumps of carriage horses,
burnishing each hide to a rich dark luster. The
boulevard was noisy, crowded with conveyances.
The going was tortoise slow.

Had Garth been alone, he'd have walked the
distance and found it a fair night to do so.
Spring had arrived in Williamsburg. Fruit trees
bloomed with masses of pink and white blossoms. The sweet fragrance of the evening air
teased the senses and almost coaxed away the
tension that had gripped him all day, following
Jenkins's visit.

"Oh, look. The cupola is lighted," Eunice
cried out, pointing her fan down the palace
green toward the governor's estate.

Mouse and Auntie "oohed," and Garth stirred
himself, trying to be attentive. At the terminus
of the boulevard, beyond the black iron grill-
work gate with its crowned royal lion, the governor's three-story brick mansion glowed in torchlight and lantern light. On the flattened, top-
most section of the slanted roof there marched a
square of fencing. Within the fencing, a two-
story cupola glowed in lantern light, shining out
over Williamsburg like a beacon.

"The cupola is lighted for special occasions,"
he said. "For royal birthday balls and, tonight,
for the Silver Cup Race Ball."

Lady Weatherby gushed, "It's a beautiful estate, simply beautiful. I'm sure I do not comprehend why you Virginians look down your

noses at it, why you sneer and mock at it, calling it the governor's 'palace.'"

"Because we Virginians *pay* for it," Garth said more tartly than necessary, "in unreasonable taxes." The landau swayed as a wheel caught a rut.

Eunice wrinkled her nose and tapped him on the sleeve with her fan. "Politics! Garth, I do hope the talk at the ball will not center on the Virginia frontier again. Such a bore. I shan't allow such talk at our wedding party."

His temper flared at her stupidity. Or was it the Tewksbury thing that made him edgy, impatient? He made an effort to be civil.

"Eunice, were you a settler on the forks of the Ohio tonight, you would pray that the ball centers on exactly that."

The women scrambled back to wedding talk, and the landau bumped indolently along. He was glad when Toad finally made his way up in the queue, and they could alight at the gate. Scarlet-coated British regulars handed the ladies down. Offering one arm to Eunice and one to Auntie, Garth led the ladies past the flanking buildings, up into the courtyard to the main house. Mouse trailed behind. He supposed he made quite a sight—a goddamned rooster with his clutch of hens. Raven's grin, when Raven saw him in the noisy, crowded antechamber, corroborated Garth's impression.

"Well, well, well," Raven began predictably as he sauntered up with Maryann on his arm. "And have we set the—"

"June," Garth snapped.

"'June!'" Eunice trilled, echoed by Auntie and Mouse's cries of, "June! June!"

"June!" Maryann cried out in delight, and another flurry of wedding chatter burst forth as Maryann embraced her future sister-in-law and generously hugged the twittering Auntie and Mouse, too. All of the ladies began talking at once, like a flock of chickens.

"June!" Raven mimicked, grinning like a cat who is satisfied that the rat is trapped. "Well, well, well."

"One more 'well,'" Garth muttered, "and you'll find yourself eating it."

Raven continued to grin, but a flash of anger lit his eyes.

"As *you* will eat *your* words, Garth, if ever again you speak up and interfere in my personal affairs."

Garth drew a sharp breath. The bond-woman again.

"It was for your own good."

"You were misnamed. Your name should be Judas."

The women bubbled on, talking trousseau and wedding trip, proposing parties in honor of the event. Garth's head ached. The worry about Tewksbury. Now this.

"Raven, let's be done with warfare."

"'Done'! Not by half. I want my pound of flesh, I want—" Raven's jaw tightened as their eyes met. "What's wrong?" he demanded, his voice changing. "Trouble?"

Garth nodded. Raven darted a look at the happily engrossed women. Their laughter rippled.

"Business?" Raven asked with concern, his boyish facade falling away as the shrewd, canny businessman in him emerged.

"No. Personal."

Raven lifted his hands slightly.

"If I can help, Garth . . ."

"Some squalls have to be weathered alone."

New arrivals poured into the antechamber, the ladies ridding themselves of light evening wraps. Candles burned brightly, catching the irridescence of silk. The air smelling of hot melting tallow and musky perfume . . . laughter.

Garth wished the ball were over, wished he could turn the clock ahead; or, he mused, turn the clock back. Back to a time when his life had been a simple and controllable matter. When the thought of marriage had made him laugh, when the sea was everything, when women were bedded and discarded, when his brother had been a malleable youth.

Abruptly, Garth turned to Raven.

"The habit of 'fathering' you is damned hard to break. You were eight when Father died, twelve when Mother fell sick."

A wry half-smile twisted Raven's lips. Over Garth's shoulder, Garth heard Maryann's shy, excited, "We will fete you and Garth at an elegant dinner, Eunice, and then—"

"Apology accepted," Raven said.

Garth flared. "I'm not apologizing, damn it."

"Yes, you are. About Jane Brown, and I accept."

"Raven—"

But like a small flock of elegantly feathered birds, the ladies turned and fluttered toward

them. Garth found his right arm claimed by
Eunice, his left by Lady Wetherby. The group
flowed from the antechamber into the ballroom,
joining the glittering throng of guests. It seemed
to Garth that every fancy plume and silver
buckle in Virginia had been dragged forth and
worn tonight. Even somber, no-nonsense mer-
chants wore suits of pink brocade. The trad-
itionalists wore stiff white wigs; America-born
Englishmen, like Garth and Raven, tended to
wear their own hair.

The dancing was about to begin. The music
changed from dignified chamber pieces to dance
tunes. Garth's eye swept over the crowd, a
pinprick of tension tingling in his neck. No sign
of Tewksbury. He released the breath he'd not
been aware of holding. *Overreaction, McNeil.*
Stop it.

Across the room, Annette and Lord Dunwood
were smiling their way through the crowd.
Annette looked striking in ice blue satin. She
wore her own hair, piled dark and glossy
atop her head, and Garth could only suppose
she was making some sort of fashion statement
in the sea of stiff white wigs. A new necklace of
ice blue diamonds glittered on her bosom.

He felt Eunice stiffen on his arm as she
caught sight of Annette. While Eunice might
have been able to snub Annette when Annette
was a baroness and a widow, Eunice couldn't do
so now. Annette was the wife of an earl. The
wife of an earl stood a hundred times higher
than the cousin of one.

Dunwood's glance fell upon Garth. With characteristic lack of understanding, Dunwood charged toward him, a smile on his face. Garth saw Annette blanch, but on the arm of her husband there was nothing she could do to stop the encounter.

Lord Dunwood pounced upon them with the zest of an eager puppy. Introductions went round, hands were shaken and kissed. Except for Maryann and Dunwood, who knew nothing of Garth and Annette, and except for Raven, who found a perverse humor in this sort of thing, conversation was arctic. Eunice, Lady Wetherby, Mouse and Annette froze into silence. Conversation moved forward with glacial speed.

To Garth's irritation, Raven took it upon himself to spice things up.

"Lady Annette," Raven began, "have you heard the news? Miss Wetherby and my brother have set the date of their marriage. It's to be June."

"How nice," Annette replied crisply.

Garth threw Raven a murderous look, but Raven missed it. Dunwood whinnied his congratulations, then launched into an extemporaneous homily on the blessings of holy wedlock. He talked on and on, finally finishing by declaring he must dance with the bride-to-be. Overwhelmed by the earl and obviously not knowing how to refuse, Eunice took the earl's arm and went off to dance.

Maryann burst into admiration for Lord Dunwood, and Annette acknowledged the compliments with tight little thank-yous and "you are so kind." To Garth's relief, Maryann seemed to sense she'd waded into deep waters. She retreated by shyly stammering her admiration of the governor's residence.

"Isn't it grand? They—they say the estate is three hundred fifty acres; ten acres of it in formal gardens." She threw an uncertain, hopeful look at Raven. "Oh, Raven, could we see the gardens *now*? Before the evening grows too cool?"

Garth saw his opportunity to be alone with Annette and jumped at it.

"Do indulge Maryann, Raven. Perhaps Lady Wetherby and Miss Turner would enjoy strolling the gardens with you."

"Oh, yes, do come along, ladies," Maryann offered from her shy, generous heart.

Garth earned a black look from Raven, but Auntie and Mouse accepted with alacrity, visibly relieved to escape Lady Dunwood's company. Raven was obliged to exit with a show of good grace, leading the ladies off.

Garth found himself alone with Annette. But only for a moment. Flicking her fan shut with an angry click, she gave him her satin-clad back. She stalked off into the crowd. He was forced to go after her. When he'd bumped into and excused himself to a half-dozen guests, he finally caught her elbow.

"Annette, we must talk."

She twitched her elbow free of him. Without a word or a glance, she swept onward. McNeil leaped after her, feeling a fool.

"Annette."

Nothing.

Garth stopped in his tracks. Her silent rejection cut deep, deeper than could her sharpest word. He flushed, pride counseling retreat; heart vetoing. He went after her.

Sensing his pursuit through the milling crowd, she fled the length of the ballroom and went into the supper room where glasses of wine and cups of apple cider awaited the first wave of refreshment seekers. The room was empty except for livery-clad Negroes fussing at the tables. At the far end of the room the garden doors stood open, framing the distant fruit trees in blossom.

Annette's heels clicked across the supper room. She swished up to the wine table and took a glass. Garth followed, taking the glass that had sat next to hers. Vexed, she crossed the room to the table opposite. He followed.

"Damn it, Annette, you might spare me a word. After all we've been to each other, I—"

She whirled around, her eyes blazing.

"And just what have I been to you, McNeil? Tell me! I would be amused to know."

He set his wineglass down. The Negroes retreated to another table and began fussing at the glassware there. He swallowed hard, stuck for an answer.

"Annette—I—"

His hesitation made her eyes grow bright with angry tears.

"Please don't cry," he whispered.

Setting down her wineglass, she uttered a harsh laugh.

"'Cry'? Don't flatter yourself, McNeil. I shall never shed another tear over *you*, never!"

He drew a deep breath. This was harder than he'd imagined. He hated seeing the tears in her eyes, hated her pretending the tears weren't there.

"Stroll the garden maze with me. The maze is private. We can talk."

"No! Why should I! Why should I risk anything for you!"

She caught hold of the fan hanging from her wrist and whipped it open, holding it in front of her like a shield. He stared at the fan. It was an ivory one, delicately carved. Yet the way she held the fan, it might have been a barrier of steel. He reached for the fan, fumbling to slowly fold it.

"Don't do this to us, Annette."

Her dark eyes blazed with flame

"Me? It's you. *You.* What have I ever done to you but love you, McNeil!"

At her confession, she whirled around, giving him her back and dropping her head. He could hear her tears, her anger.

"Damn you," she hissed. "Now you've done it. You've made me lose my composure." She swiped at her eyes.

Footfalls sounded in the supper room as a party of four drifted in toward the wine table. Garth glanced around, then took Annette's elbow.

"The maze, Annette."

She hesitated. The supper room began to fill with chatter and laughter.

"Damn you," she hissed. "The maze, then."

Avoiding the paths that led to the ornamental boxwood garden, to the falling gardens and to the canal, Garth led Annette north toward the maze. He knew the maze well. Every boy growing up in Williamsburg knew it. Trespassing in the governor's garden and leading the gardener on a merry chase through the maze was a dare every boy took. Selecting the first four right-hand alternatives and the remaining alternatives to the left, he quickly led Annette to the heart of the maze, to the shadowy retreat with its marble bench.

When they were surrounded by the privacy of hedge and the crisp, faintly tangy smell of yew, Annette turned on him like a wounded lioness.

"Why did you betroth yourself to that—that *nothing* girl? *Why*, McNeil?"

There was no answer he could give. He stood there, mute as a sheep and feeling as stupid as one.

"It was necessary."

Annette whirled round at his limp words. She paced the small enclosure, her slippers crunching the crushed shell path, her pale blue satin gown shimmering when moonlight struck it.

"'Necessary'! Bah. Don't lie to me, McNeil. At least give me *that* much respect."

He tried again.

"My betrothal to Eunice is a matter of life and death. More I cannot tell you. If you won't believe that, then believe what you will."

She stopped suddenly in her pacing, stopped like a butterfly alighting and resting its blue satin wings for a moment. A startled look captured her face. She shrugged it away.

"Bah! Don't lie to me. I know you met her in Amsterdam. I know you followed her up the Rhine. I know you followed her to Bladensburg." She began to pace again, then stopped, looked up at the sky as though searching for some sense there. She gave her head an impatient shake.

"Bladensburg, of all places! And after all your trouble with the duke of Tewksbury."She whirled round and eyed him. "McNeil, does your ancestral tree contain much insanity?"

His mouth twisted in a wry smile.

"I've often wondered."

She ignored his lame attempt at humor, at bringing peace between them. She charged on.

"You might have married *me*. Me! We'd have been wildly happy, McNeil, and you know it!"

Unbidden, a small halfhearted laugh escaped him.

"And which of us would have ruled in the marriage? You've a ruling nature, Annette; so have I. Our marriage would've been a cat-and-dog fight, a battleground."

Her lips quivered. Her dark eyes grew shiny in the moonlight.

"You might have at least given us the chance to fail," she whispered. "It would've been a *magnificent* failure. But you never gave us a chance. And for that—I shall never forgive you." Her mouth trembled. "Oh, Garth, how *could* you?"

He stepped toward her, stepped forward to take her in his arms, when voices rang out in the maze. Shoes crunched lightly on the paths.

"Garth? Are you out here, Garth? Garth!"

Recognizing his brother's voice, McNeil swore. He drew a quick breath and heard Maryann's sweet voice sing out.

"Perhaps Garth is in the ballroom, Raven."

Crunching footsteps drew closer.

"No, Maryann. I'm sure I saw him duck into the maze."

"Alone?"

"With Lady Dunwood." Raven renewed his efforts.

"Garth! Halloo!"

Annette tensed. Garth wanted to murder Raven.

"With Lady Dunwood'?" Maryann said. "Oh, my."

"Bosh, Maryann. Entirely proper, I do assure you. Lady Dunwood is—er—a longtime family friend."

"Oh."

While Garth seethed, there was a moment of silence. Footsteps crunched the path, drawing closer. Damn Raven! He and Annette had come just a heartbeat short of making up.

"Raven?" Maryann's voice was just on the other side of the yew hedge now. "How is it you seem to know the maze so well? You told me you had never brought any other girl out here."

Silence.

Then, "Keen instinct, Maryann. Unerring navigational ability. All we McNeils have it. Did you know we McNeils are descended from the Vikings?"

"Oh, my! Raven, you are *so* wonderful."

Garth gave up. Raven would search until he

found him. With an angry sigh, Garth took
Annette's wrist and led her through the maze,
colliding at last with Raven and Maryann.

Raven gave him a wicked, knowing grin.

"A message has come for you, Garth," he said
cheerfully. "You're wanted at home."

Garth tensed, his thoughts flying to Trent.
Was Trent ill?

"What's the matter? Is the house afire?"

Raven smirked at the sarcasm.

"You've a visitor, Garth, and a fancy one, at
that. The duke of Tewksbury."

Raven wiggled his eyebrows as though im-
pressed, then turned on his heel, leading Maryann
back to the dancing.

"'Tewksbury'?" Annette whispered.

Garth stood like stone, scarcely breathing as
Maryann's and Raven's footsteps faded, then
disappeared. So it was come . . . this thing that
he'd dreaded, this thing that haunted his dreams
when he slept. . . . His mind shot out in a
hundred directions. He could take Trent and
flee the country. A stupid solution, solving nothing. He could brazen it out, sticking with his
story. Trent is only an orphan. To stick by his
story would put the onus of proof upon the
duke . . .

"The duke of Tewksbury?" Annette said again.
"Surely he's not journeyed all the way to Virginia to accuse you of stealing more jade pieces?"

"No."

Annette half laughed, bewildered.

"Then what can he want?"

Garth drew a long, shaky breath.

"Trent," he said softly, "I'm afraid he wants Trent."

Leaving Annette standing there, gaping in astonishment, he rushed from the maze, sprinted through the garden and into the supper room. He pushed his way through the crowd, skirted the dancing formation in the main ballroom and made for the antechamber.

"Garth, dear? Where are you going?"

Eunice seized his arm, stopping him in mid stride. He'd not seen her, so fierce was his concentration. His impulse was to shrug her off, but he reconsidered. He'd do himself no good, rushing off half-cocked. He would only play into the duke's hands. But suppose he arrived home in a leisurely fashion, on the arm of his bride-to-be. That was hardly the action of a guilty man.... He smiled grimly, determined to outwit the duke.

"Come along, Eunice. We've a visitor at home. The duke of Tewksbury."

She gazed up at him, openmouthed.

"His Grace?"

Garth nodded. "You know His Grace?" All the better if she did, he thought grimly.

Eunice smiled. "Yes, of course. The duke was acquainted with my father. I've been to Tewksbury Hall several times. I took tea with his last duchess, the one who died of smallpox." Eunice's smile retreated into a vain pout. "Some persons thought her pretty. I did not. All that red hair, those too-large eyes. Not ladylike, I'm sure."

He snapped his jaw shut and propelled her along, excusing his way through the silks and brocades.

"But my chaperone, Garth?"

He took a deep, long breath, trying to stifle the anger that forked through his fear. Criticize Flavia, would she? By God! He had to swallow several times before he was able to reply with a modicum of civility.

"A premarital landau ride is hardly the cardinal sin, Eunice."

A large black-lacquered coach with six horses waited outside his house on York Street, dwarfing his own modest landau and making even the house appear small. A half-dozen attendants and drivers lurked about the coach: big, brutish men with cudgels stuck in their belts. McNeil's pulse raced. He wished Harrington and Jenkins were not in Hampton.

He let himself in without ceremony, drew one last steadying breath of air, then preceded Eunice into the drawing room. Cloaked in black, the duke stood at the fireplace. A small spring fire had been kindled as a gesture of respect, and refreshments had been brought, but it was obvious His Grace had not touched them. The man was as McNeil remembered: arrogant, pompous and deadly dangerous.

The duke turned as he entered, and McNeil met the icy scornful eyes with casual coolness, his own eyes narrowing. He was alarmed at the fury the man stirred in him. He'd wanted to remain cool, intelligence and reflexes on the alert. But he found himself heating. This titled popinjay had had access to Flavia—touching her, bedding her whenever he'd chosen.

It galled him.

Eunice swished into the room with a pleased chirp.

"Sir, what an honor to see you again," she trilled, tripping across the room and offering her hand. "May I offer you my belated but most sincere condolences, sir. Such a tragedy at Bladensburg."

The duke seemed momentarily startled at her presence, then recovered himself. With inbred politeness that requires no thought, he bowed over her hand and kissed it.

"Thank you, Miss Wetherby. However, such condolences are no longer necessary. I have reason to believe my son lives." Turning from her startled glance, the duke turned scornful eyes on McNeil. Coldly and with matching contempt, McNeil returned the look. *Your move, Your Grace. I'll not tip my hand with needlessly spoken words.*

The duke's glare was icy, frost seeming to rise from his eyes.

"I will speak with you in private, Captain McNeil."

It was not a request. It was a command. In the foyer, Garth's mother's case clock struck the hour. Waiting until it was done, until the echo had faded, he replied, "You will speak with me here and now, or not at all."

Eunice gasped in horror. "Garth, it's His Grace! You cannot say such things."

The duke drew himself up, his face darkening. He glanced meaningfully out the window at his coach. McNeil understood and tensed. Trent ...sleeping innocently upstairs. The bullies could seize him at will. Beads of sweat broke out on his forehead. Mentally, he went to his study. There were weapons there...

"*I want my son.*"

Eunice fluttered in bewilderment. "Sir?" she asked, staring at the duke and then at McNeil. Both the duke and Garth ignored her.

"I have had you under surveillance, McNeil. Ever since the night of my son's natal ball when you so freely helped yourself to my—" He paused, spitting out the last word with contempt. "*Treasure.*"

Eunice gasped.

Garth's throat tightened in anger. He struggled to remain calm as his temper went on the boil. Some inner sense warned him the duke was not speaking of jade but of Flavia. His mind shot back to Tewksbury Gardens. Vaguely, he remembered Flavia's alarm when a clay pot had plopped to the greenhouse floor as they stood talking. Or was the duke bluffing, hoping to entrap him?

Boiling, he held himself in check, saying nothing.

The duke went on.

"I obtained a writ for your arrest that very night, and then I instructed my steward to—"

"Plant your damned jade pieces on the *Caroline.*"

The duke smiled frigidly.

"Yes," he admitted proudly, airily. "It amused me to use you for another purpose. A double stroke, if you will. I obtained my purpose, and I obtained your humiliation. You dared touch my duchess that night. No one touches what is mine."

McNeil clenched his jaw, checking his fury. To hear Flavia spoken of as if she were of no more value than a damned jade piece! He shook with the urge to strangle.

"I don't understand," Eunice whispered. "Garth?"

The duke ignored her.

"I would have seen you rotting in Newgate, McNeil. However, you slipped through my net. Then, Captain, you sought revenge for the jade planting, did you not? You went to Germany. To Bladensburg. You stole my son, and you made it appear that my son drowned."

Eunice uttered a sharp cry.

"Two months ago," the duke went on, "I received certain information. Two days after my son 'drowned,' an orphan was brought aboard the *Caroline*. He was the same age as my son. He was brought to Virginia, and he lives here— in *this* house."

Eunice gasped. "Trent? Sir, it cannot be so. Trent is as common as a stable hand."

The duke swung her a cold look.

Eunice sputtered on in bewilderment. "Sir, you must be ill. Ill with grief. Your son drowned. I remember the night, I recall it well because of the bright hunter's moon. Garth was with *me* —in Köln."

"All night?" His Grace asked pointedly.

Eunice rocked at the insult, reddening. Garth held his breath.

"Indeed *not*, sir," she replied angrily.

Garth broke into a sweat.

Angered, Eunice went on. "I could not sleep that night. Nor could my aunt, Lady Wetherby. The moon, sir. So Auntie and I strolled the gardens. Garth's room was in the ell of the wing. His candle was burning."

The duke laughed coldly. "A candle proves nothing. You're being used, Miss Wetherby."

Eunice blinked uncertainly. "Sir, Auntie and I *saw* Garth through the window. He sat at his table, reading."

Garth had been holding his breath. Slowly, cautiously, he let his breath escape. So the charade with Jenkins *had* been necessary. To think he'd almost not bothered.

The duke seemed to waver at Eunice's testimony. It was time to jump in. Garth strode into the center of the room, giving a casual wave of his hand.

"Enough," he said, affecting a slightly bored, irritated demeanor. "If His Grace wants an orphan bastard to call 'son,' then His Grace shall have one. The boy Harrington brought from Amsterdam is a damned nuisance, anyway."

Wheeling round, he went out of the drawing room and into the foyer. He shouted up the stairs.

"Mab! Up at once!"

In a few moments, Mab appeared at the top of the stairs, rubbing sleepy eyes with her knuckles. She was in a wrinkled flannel nightdress and her hair was braided for sleep.

"Bring Trent down at once," he ordered loudly. "The duke of Tewksbury wishes to make him his heir!" Mab blinked in astonishment. He turned back to the drawing room, then had a better thought. He barked at Mab again. "Wait! Go up to cook's bedchamber. Her grandsons are sleeping there. Wake them. Bring all three boys into the drawing room at the same time."

Mab blinked her amazement, and he strode back to the drawing room, closing the door with a firm click.

"You *will* be able to recognize your 'son,' Tewksbury?" Garth sneered. "You *will* be able to pick him out of a group of three?"

The duke faltered slightly, then covered himself with an arrogant "Naturally." But uncertainty tinged the word and the duke's thin, hawkish face flushed with anger.

Score one, McNeil thought. *So the old goat doesn't know what Trent—Robert—looks like.*

The minutes ticked by. Hostile silence settled upon the room. Bewildered by everything, Eunice sank weakly upon the settee and nervously wrung her hands.

"I wish I had stayed in London," she whined. "I should never have—oh, the disgrace—whatever will people say?"

As though unconcerned with events, McNeil strolled to the sideboard and poured a glass of port. He gestured toward Eunice, offering a wine, but she merely looked at him and shuddered as though he were an ominous stranger. Contemptuously, he held a glass toward the duke. His Grace merely stiffened in icy silence.

With a careless laugh, Garth quaffed the wine himself.

At last, commotion began upstairs. Doors banged. Children's sleepy voices rang out. Garth tensed, the sweat beginning. A few moments more and Mab—her nightdress covered with a serge wrapper—shepherded the children in.

"Over here, by the candles," Garth snapped coldly. "The duke of Tewksbury will want to see well when he picks out his 'son.'" Deliberately, he made the word "son" ring with irony.

Dumbfounded, Mab obeyed, and the duke strode forward, flinging back his cloak. He studied each sleepy child. They were of a piece: dark-eyed, sandy to dark hair. The duke flushed, a blue vein thumping dangerously in his temple. He swung toward Garth.

"Enough of your games. Which is my son?"

Garth laughed scornfully.

"Take your pick. Any one of them will be well pleased to inherit the Tewksbury title and all of its wealth."

He'd hit a nerve. The duke's complexion darkened.

"I'll see you dead for this!" he hissed, lunging toward the window to signal his men. Just then, a landau clattered into the street. Garth froze in his would-be dash to the study for weapons. The front door banged open. Heels clicked on marble, then on wood as Annette burst into the drawing room. Her color was high, her bosom rose and fell with panting.

Breathless, she dropped a little curtsy to the duke, then turned to the sleepy children. Garth was stunned. Goddamn it, what was she doing—

"Trent," she cried out. "Trent, dear, come to me."

Garth found his voice. "Annette, damn it," he swore, starting for her. But it was too late. Trent was fond of Annette. With a sleepy smile he stumbled into her waiting embrace and was crushed to the blue satin gown.

The duke smiled his triumph.

"Thank you, Lady Annette—or Lady Dunwood, I should say. You have just identified my son. If you will kindly release him—" The duke started toward Trent, and Garth tensed to spring. He'd not wanted violence. But if it came to that, so be it.

"*Your* son?" Annette said loudly, hugging Trent. "How dare you, sir! Trent is *my* son. My son born out of wedlock to Garth McNeil. A secret I had to guard, sir, from my late husband, the baron."

The astounding announcement froze the assembly. The duke tottered a bit in shock, and McNeil stared at Annette, dumbfounded. He drew a hoarse breath.

"Mab, take the children away," he ordered quickly. Wide-eyed, Mab jumped to do his bidding. On the settee, Eunice burst into tears. She lunged to her feet, sending a dagger of hate at Annette and a sword at Garth.

"How *can* you disgrace me like this? I shall be the laughingstock of all London! To think that you and this low woman . . . Oh, I hate you!

When Auntie hears—when my cousin, the earl—
I *shan't* stay another moment in this house."
Eunice ran out.

The front door banged shut, and in a few
moments McNeil recognized the creak of his
own landau as it moved off.

The duke glared at Annette.

"Do you know what you are admitting to,
Lady Dunwood?"

Annette blanched, and only then did Garth
begin to sense what she'd done to herself.

"Yes," she said boldly. "If you refer to my
husband's mother—and I think you do, sir—you
are quite right. She now has grounds to annul
my marriage."

The duke eyed her with contempt.

"I grant you one last opportunity to deny the
boy is yours. Else you become the joke of
society." He laughed coldly. "Had you borne a
bastard to the Prince of Wales or to someone
highborn, London would forgive you. But to
bear a bastard to a sailor!" He snorted, as the
lords and ladies of London would snort when
they heard.

Annette's eyes fluttered to the floor, and Garth
held his breath. Social position was everything
to Annette. She reveled in it, enjoying status
and power. As wife of the earl of Dunwood, she
would enter even higher circles on her return to
London. His heart hammered.

"I—I—" She stopped and drew a quivering
breath. Softly she began again. "I will not deny
my own son. Whatever the cost."

As her tears began to spill, Garth growled at the duke, "Get out of this house. Get out of Virginia. Get out of the colonies."

The duke drew himself up arrogantly.

"In due time. Do not presume to order *me* about. I've unfinished business in the colonies. I mean to finish it."

There was threat in his words, but threat of what? Garth had no idea.

"Get out," he repeated. "If you do not, the Board of Trade will receive very interesting information. The board will learn that in September of 1753, a jade piece was planted aboard the *Caroline* so that all harbor attention would be focused on *her* and not on two incoming ships, *Virtue* and *Bountiful Lady*."

He paused as the duke flinched.

"The board will also learn that when the duke of Tewksbury landed in Virginia, his first callers were the captains of *Virtue* and *Bountiful Lady*."

The duke's eyes widened in alarm for a moment, then narrowed to dangerous slits.

"Be careful, McNeil."

Garth met the cold, shrewd eyes without blinking.

"May I offer Your Grace the same good advice?"

They stared at each other, adversaries who hate and who are a hairbreadth from attack, but adversaries who sense the wisdom of a standoff.

Latching the fastenings of his cloak in a slow, deliberate manner, the duke strutted to the door like a peacock. He turned with an unpleasant laugh.

"As to the boy, I suspected he was *not* my son at first sight. There is a common, mongrel air to the bastard."

The duke strutted out. Within seconds, harness tracings jingled and snapped. The uneven clopping of six horses echoed into the drawing room, and the carriage creaked off.

Sweating with released tension, McNeil went to Annette. She came limply into his arms. They didn't speak. The house lay hushed and silent. A breeze blew in the open window, bringing the faint hint of plum blossom and riffling the lace that trimmed her gown.

He was overwhelmed. Stunned by her generosity and loyalty. Did she love him so much, then, this foolish little woman? She'd sacrificed everything. His arms went around her tightly, protectively. Her gallantry left him speechless, left him ashamed.

At last he murmured into her hair, "You know that Trent is my son, don't you?"

"And Flavia's."

"How? How did you figure it out?"

Unwillingly, she met his eyes.

"The bits and pieces began to come together tonight, after you left me at the ball..." Softly she told him. The clues had been there. Two years' worth of clues. Finishing, she whispered, "The dock girl? The one you searched for in London? Was she Flavia?"

He nodded. "I didn't know she was Flavia. Not until the night of the natal ball."

A long unhappy sigh came from her. She

clung to him. Gradually, she tried to brighten.
The old brassy sparkle flickered.

"Well, McNeil, shall I spend the night?" She
gave an unhappy, self-deprecating shrug. "All is
lost, anyway."

He kissed her forehead, then put her at arm's
length, keenly aware as he did so that he
already missed the warmth of her willing
body.

"No, love. No, Annette. Go back to the ball
before Dunwood misses you. All is *not* lost. I
doubt the duke will hurry to spread the news.
He is more clever than that. He will keep the
news to himself, hoping to use it against you
and Dunwood at a later time. When it better
serves his purpose. With luck, that time may
never come."

Her eyes grew large with hope.

"But Eunice?"

Garth smiled sadly. "The story is Eunice's
humiliation, too. She'll not say 'boo.'"

Annette laughed hopefully. With a quick
breath, she turned and rustled to the door, only
pausing to whisper, "Did you mean it, McNeil?
When you called me 'love'?"

He was taken aback. He'd not remembered
saying it. He strolled to the sideboard, fumbled
for the brandy decanter, but his hand slid away.
He turned and looked at her.

"At this moment there is only one woman I
still love more than you," he admitted. "And *she*
is dead."

Annette's dark eyes jumped in joy.

"Oh, Garth," she breathed, "Oh, Garth, good night."

"Good night, Lady Dunwood," he said. And for once he said it without sarcasm.

As the rumble of her landau faded into the spring night, he returned to the brandy decanter and poured out a healthy portion. But when he tried to bring the glass to his mouth, the glass shook. He set it down with a clunk, disgusted. So this sort of evening got to him, did it? He'd not known he had "nerves." They'd never reared up at sea, not in storms, not in pirate attacks.

Abandoning the drink, he went out for a walk. As he walked, he sorted everything through. It was finished, he realized in relief. Trent was his. He and Trent would begin life anew. He wished Flavia could know.

He strolled on in the quiet night, fruit trees showering him with pink and white blossoms at each gust of spring wind. He thought of Annette. God, she'd been loyal. It made him feel like a dog, treating her like a convenient eager tart all these years. He was ashamed; he was thirty-three and not yet grown up. God!

He thought of Eunice. Vaguely, he wondered where she'd gone to, then admitted to himself he did not care. He supposed he would forfeit the two thousand pounds dowry money he'd loaned to Lord Wetherby. He shrugged. Small price to be rid of Eunice, and the two thousand pounds would go far in smoothing her ruffled feathers.

He returned home and drank the brandy with a steady hand. Its cleansing fire burned a trail down his throat. He poured a bit more, then sank into a wingback chair, surveying the room. His first step, he thought with childish pleasure, would be those damned sickly green window hangings. He wanted the bright blue silk ones back. Annette's. Not Eunice's.

He was still slouched low in his chair, bemused and mulling over the extraordinary evening, when a tap sounded at the open door. It was Mab. Her flannel nightdress peeped out of a dark wrapper. Her hair, even in its braided state, managed to look stringy.

"Yes?"

She hung in the doorway.

"I heared that name somewheres. That Tewksbury name. But I can't remember where."

McNeil sighed tiredly.

"Forget it, Mab. Forget everything you saw and heard tonight."

She persisted.

"It bedevils my sleep, Cap'n. Tewksbury. It sticks in m'brain. Like a sliver in a thumb."

"Then pull it out," he said irritably. "You will do well to forget the name. In fact, I insist."

At the rancor in his voice, her head reared up in the old pridey way. She opened her mouth to say something snippy, but McNeil rose from his chair. He was in no mood for servant trouble, on top of everything else.

"Yes, sir," she whispered and went flying.

Two nights later, he was roused from deep

and dreamless sleep. It was Mab again. Her intense face hovered over his bed.

"I remember, sir," Mab whispered excitedly.

"What the devil?" He growled like a bear roused from hibernation, then came suddenly awake. "Trent? Is he sick?"

Mab shook her head, grinning.

"Then get out of here," he barked. "Whatever it is, it can wait till morning." He rolled over, punching his pillow and settling into it. The day had been damned trying: a frigid interview with Lady Wetherby, who was staying at the Governor's Palace with Eunice and Mouse. A tongue-lashing from the governor, who'd been told only enough by Lady Wetherby to lead the governor to believe Garth had taken liberties with Eunice. The dissolution of the betrothal. Annette leaving for Baltimore with Dunwood...

To his deepening annoyance, Mab shook his shoulder.

He rolled over.

"So help me, Mab, you're asking for the whip!"

She ignored him grinning.

"That Tewksbury name, sir. I remember!" she crowed victoriously. "I know where I heard it!"

Chapter 19

"For thee, Jane."

Flavia's smile trembled as she accepted the small, utterly perfect bouquet of flowers. They were lilies of the valley. Still moist with morning dew, the tiny white bells shivered upon stems of dark green, exuding a heady fragrance. She brought the bouquet to her face, inhaling sadly. Her wedding bouquet.

Tears welled up. She blinked them away.

"Thank you, Dennis. They're lovely."

He stood studying her with an earnestness that threatened to become anxiety. She tried to give him an assuring smile, but only half managed it. Still, the smile seemed to cheer him. His eyes lit with love.

He looked fine; ready for the altar, Flavia admitted. He was wearing his best: a brown suit of wool serge, new white stockings, a new ruffled linen shirt that was Betsy's wedding gift to him, and his only pair of shoes, which he'd carefully repaired and polished almost to a state of newness. It touched her that he'd combed his hair carefully over the balding spot on the crown of his head.

"Thee hast not reconsidered, Jane?"

His voice was tight with dread, and his Adam's apple shot up and down.

"No," she said quickly, not daring to pause and think.

"I want only thy happiness, Jane."

She tried to meet his eyes.

"I shall try to be a good wife to you, Dennis."

"Jane," he whispered passionately. "Beloved Jane."

To hide the tears of despair that rushed to her eyes, she lifted her mouth to be kissed. He flushed. It was their first intimacy. Touching her cheek with carpentry-roughened hands, he timidly brought his mouth to hers. His lips were dry and hot, trembling with passions he was too gentlemanly to unloose before the wedding vows. "Jane," he whispered. "Dearest love." He allowed himself a moment's kiss, then drew back in propriety. The marriage ceremony must come first.

"I'll fetch the chaise," he said, moving out the door to get the chaise and horse that William Tate was lending them for the day.

Alone, Flavia turned slowly and sadly surveyed her surroundings. When next she stepped into this little schoolhouse, she would be Dennis's wife. Her eyes moved to the cozy area Dennis had made for her in one corner of the kitchen. His only real bedstead was there. When he'd bought her indenture from Mrs. Byng—paying three times what it was worth—he'd also gone to the wharf in Chestertown and bought old, wind-worn sails. He'd sewed rings to the sails, then slipped the rings on poles and fastened the poles to wall and rafter. She'd been able to draw the curtains closed whenever she wished, gaining a somewhat private bed area.

Dennis and the three boarding students who were preparing for the seminary slept on cots in the unfinished attic.

He'd also bought a cracked mirror for her, mending it as best he could and encasing it in a maple stand. She moved to the mirror and checked her appearance. Except for the regret in her eyes, she looked like a bride. Betsy had seen to that, buying Flavia a wedding gown of silk taffeta. The color was royal blue, and the rich hue stirred fiery highlights in her loose, brushed hair. To Mr. Gresham's irritation, Betsy had given her a royal blue wool serge cloak as well. Dennis's delicate bouquet completed her ensemble.

She sat down to wait in the new wingback chair that was William Tate's nuptial gift to Dennis. Her eyes roamed sadly over the sparsely furnished kitchen to the schoolroom area. Working nightly, Dennis had completed ten student desks and a larger one for himself. His prized books now stood in wall shelves that had been worked with all the pride of a master carpenter. Dennis did everything with care, not content to do a slap-dash job. She knew he would treat their marriage with the same loving care, and she knew she ought to be happy because of it. But she wasn't.

Garth . . . oh, Garth . . . Robert . . . sweet lost son. . . . She'd carried Garth's child with joy. . . . How joyfully would she carry Dennis's children?

Tears rose. She dashed them away. She was determined to thrust grief from her mind for this one day. For Dennis's sake. Dennis was a good man. He deserved to bring a willing, happy bride to his bed this night. Not a reluctant, weeping one.

She sprang to her feet, pacing, determined to concentrate on Dennis's many kindnesses. He'd shared everything with her: his material goods, his every thought, his hopes for the future. Only twice had he shut her out, and that was when he was visited by men who appeared to be business agents. On those two occasions Dennis crisply sent her into Chestertown on errands she knew to be unnecessary. He never revealed the nature of the men's business, but she'd sensed it had something to do with her indenture. She'd noticed thereafter that Dennis cooled when anyone mentioned the name McNeil. Had Raven tried to buy her indenture?

The rhythmic creaking of a chaise jolted her. Taking a deep breath and clutching her bouquet, she forced a smile to her lips and went out to Dennis. The boarding students were running alongside the chaise. They'd tied sprigs of wild flowers to the whip stand. When she'd taken her place on the seat beside Dennis and the boys were shouting their good wishes, Dennis turned to her. His gray eyes searched hers.

"Ready, Jane?"

She swallowed. She knew he asked more than if she were ready to ride to Quaker's Neck Landing to be married in the small Quaker meetinghouse. In his humbleness of spirit he was offering her one last chance to refuse him. She placed her cold hand upon his warm one.

"I'm ready, Dennis. Truly. I'm honored to become your wife."

His smile began slowly, but when it had begun it was like the sun rising. To her surprise, he gulped two great breaths of relief. Clucking to the horse, he gently shook the reins and the chaise jerked forward. The seminary boys whooped and cheered them off.

Dennis drove on in joyful silence, his happiness too large for words. They bumped along Quaker's Neck Road, well inland from the Chester River. The sky was the thin blue sky of spring. White cloud puffs raced overhead, and the air smelled of freshly plowed earth. Dennis was elated. She could see it in his eyes. As for herself... she dropped her gaze to her wedding bouquet. *No. I won't think of Garth...*

At the paupers' graveyard, south of Chestertown, Dennis called, "Whoa." It was a stop they'd planned. Flavia's heart sank at the sight of the desolate, abandoned burying place. Neddy belonged in a churchyard. But as a murderer, he'd been refused church burial. On the day his crow-pecked body was allowed to be taken down from the gallows, Dennis had gone to town to see Neddy decently buried.

Dennis got down and tied the reins to a

scruffy pine tree, then helped Flavia alight.
Together they climbed the hill to the mound of
raw, sun-baked earth. Dennis removed his hat,
and Flavia stooped to pluck the weeds that had
already sprung up. On impulse she untied the
bridal bouquet she carried. Gently she spread
half the flowers upon Neddy's grave. The soil
was warm and the delicate perfumed bells wilted
almost instantly. Eyes misting, she let Dennis
lead her back to the chaise.

"Quaker's Neck Landing is not far," he offered
softly.

She tried to match his encouraging smile,
then lowered her eyes to her flowers when she
could not.

*You're wrong, Dennis. Quaker's Neck Land-
ing is a lifetime away.*

"Faster! Get your speed up, man," Garth ordered, nervously raking his fingers through his
hair. "She's moving like a tortoise."

Harrington snorted. "Any faster and ye'll tear
holes in the mainsail."

"Then we'll buy new," Garth said, knowing
he was spouting irrational nonsense. The
Marabelle was already leaping through the
Chesapeake as fast as she could go. She was a
provisions ship, sleek and quick, shallow-bottomed
and able to navigate up rivers to farmers' wharves
where grain and salt pork were loaded for the
West Indies.

He paced the deck frantically, well aware that
Harrington, Jenkins and the crew thought him
mad. But he couldn't contain himself. *Flavia,*

alive! God, he was afraid to believe it. Alive. All this time. Alive and subjected to servant work and to God knows what other abuse. Frightened for her life, no doubt. In terror of what the duke might do next. It made him crazy with anxiety for her.

And to think she was Raven's "Jane Brown"! Why hadn't he listened to Raven's chattering about the sweet, red-haired bondslave with the incredible eyes? And why hadn't he tumbled to the *big* clue? "Jane Brown" had refused to become Raven's mistress. No sensible bondwoman would do that. The life of a mistress was easy; servanthood—burdensome and even degrading under the wrong master.

Alive!

He was torn between wild exhilarating joy and the urge to commit murder. So great was his rage when he thought of the duke that he nearly blacked out. He wanted to kill the cur, do murder with his bare hands.

His first urge, when he'd made head and tail out of Mab's yammering, had been to hunt the duke, hound him down, tear him limb from limb for what he'd done to Flavia. But the overwhelming urge was to fly to Flavia.

The *Marabelle* had never before suffered such a rough and abrupt departure. A crewman who'd dawdled on the wharf had been left behind, waving from the pilings, shouting his pleas. Early morning had brought fog, slowing the *Marabelle* and pitching Garth into a fury of frustration. The day passed in insufferable slowness. Night was worse. He was on deck hours before dawn, driving the crew on. When his pilot missed the mouth of the Chester River and sailed past it, he'd nearly thrown the man overboard.

But now the wharves, warehouses and red-bricked mansions of Chestertown's waterfront were coming into view at last. He paced the deck, gritting his teeth at the maddening slowness with which the buildings grew to normal size. When the *Marabelle* finally pulled into a slip at the wharf near the royal customs house, he didn't wait for the gangplank to crash down. He leaped from ship to wharf while the *Marabelle* was still bumping into the pilings, settling into her berth.

He hired a mount at the livery stable, tersely inquiring for the schoolmaster. He'd forgotten the man's name, had paid no attention to it when his steward had reported it in York harbor. The stableman was dense. Garth had to mention the Reverend Byng, a name Mab had put in his ear.

"Oh, he be dead, sir. Driv straight through the heart with a terrapin lance, sir. 'Twere an awful to-do." Happily, the man launched into the tale, but Garth cut him off sharply.

"I want to find the bondwoman who worked at the Byngs'. Jane Brown."

"Oh *her*," he said, leering and wiping his soiled hands on his leather apron. "There's some as says she told the truth at the trial. There's some as says she dint. I'm of a mind—"

"Damnation, man! Direct me to Jane Brown."

The man licked his lips. "Don't know as I

'member rightly." His tone hinted, and Garth complied, digging irritably into his leather jerkin pocket for a coin. He tossed it and got the information he wanted at once.

His heart thudded with fearful expectation as he jumped from the horse at the Finny place. Slinging reins around a fence post, he strode through the neat yard to a schoolhouse that still looked raw from construction. Cackling chickens scattered from his path. His boots clumped loudly on the small veranda, but not so loudly as his heart. The door stood open to the spring day. He pounded on it, then waited, each passing second a lifetime. Flavia . . . how would she look? . , . was she well?

Boots thumped the length of the schoolhouse. A lad of about fifteen hove into view. "Yes, sir?" he inquired respectfully.

For a moment Garth's mouth went dry. He couldn't speak. He took a deep breath.

"I'm here to see Jane Brown."

The boy smiled widely. "They've already gone, sir. They must be in Quaker's Neck Landing by now. Doubtless the ceremony is over."

A prickle of apprehension crawled up his neck.

"'Ceremony'?"

The boy smiled again, delighted to disseminate news.

"'Tis their wedding day, sir. Mr. Finny takes Mistress Brown to wife."

It was like being socked in the gut. Sucking wind, he put his hand to the doorjamb, steadying himself.

"Tell me how to get to Quaker's Neck Landing."

The boy told him, finishing with, "You're the second to ask for Mistress Brown today. A stranger came earlier. An odd sort of wedding guest, if you ask me! Ugly big brute. His companion, too."

Garth froze. An image flashed. The duke's black coach waiting in front of his house. The attendants, tall brutish thugs. What had the duke said? Unfinished business?"

"Have you any weapons?"

"'Weapons,' sir?"

He began to sweat.

"Pistols," he snapped. "Musket, sword, anything."

The boy's eyes rounded in bewilderment.

"There's Mr. Finny's hunting musket. And a cudgel for killing rats. But I say, sir. I cannot—"

"Get them. They'll be returned. If not," he paused and dug into his jerkin pocket, pushing coins at the boy, "this will buy a half-dozen muskets."

McNeil rode off, galloping toward Quaker's Neck Road, riding like the wind. His heart raced ahead. Flavia! God, no. Not that. The duke could not! But he was fooling himself, he knew. The duke was a madman. Heartless enough to sell her into slavery, he would have no qualms about killing her. Flavia, sweet Flavia . . . lying still and cold in death.

Viciously, he kicked the horse in the ribs, spurring him on. He crouched low in the saddle, urging the horse on.

"Finny, protect her," he muttered, as wind

and horse mane streamed in his face. "Take care of her, keep her safe."

Her bouquet was beginning to wilt. The dewy morning moisture was long gone from the flowers. The delicate tips of the bells were beginning to turn brown. She'd been waiting two hours in the austere, empty meetinghouse where, when prayer meeting began, she and Dennis would quietly stand up and declare themselves married.

Before God and these witnesses, I make thee my wife, Jane.

Before God and these witnesses, I make thee my husband, Dennis.

But the prayer meeting was delayed. One of the Friends had lost a horse that morning. A leather gate latch had worn through in the night, and when the man arose, his horse was gone. He and all of the other men and boys had gone to search.

"It won't be long, Jane," Dennis said, slowly pacing the room and pausing to gaze out each window as he passed it. Outside in the yard women were setting up a long table to hold a wedding feast. Flavia knew the feast was to honor Dennis, not her. When the customary Quaker committee of women had called upon her to determine the suitability of the proposed marriage, Flavia had felt their unvoiced disapproval. She could only suppose that Dennis had received more than unvoiced disapproval when the committee of men paid its premarital visit. Yet he was undeterred.

"It won't be long," Dennis said again, fingering the pocket that held the marriage license.

She forced a smile.

"We've a lifetime," he said softly, his eyes seeming to drink her in. She tried to look enthusiastic, but her lips trembled.

"Yes!" she said, too brightly.

A shadow darkened his countenance. Abruptly, he left the window, came to the chair where she was sitting and dropped to one knee. He set her bouquet aside and took her hand in both of his, cradling it with the utmost gentleness, as though he held a fledgling bird that had fallen from a nest.

"I know thy heart dwells elsewhere, Jane. I read it in thy eyes the first day I met thee. But let me *try*. Let me *try* to make thee happy."

With a groan of passion, he lay his head in her lap. Awkwardly, she stroked his thinning hair. There was no other response she could make. Could she pledge love? No, not after Garth, she thought, her heart aching. She was fond of Dennis, grateful to him. But in no way did her feelings for him even begin to approach what she'd felt for Garth. In Garth's arms she'd found the meaning of her womanhood. She'd been shaken by it and forever changed.

Sadly, she stroked Dennis's head.

"I will be your wife, Dennis. I promise. Your wife in every way."

The eyes he raised to hers shone with a light that was pure and selfless. "Jane...sweet, beautiful wife of my heart..."

The moment was broken by the sound of horses' hooves.

"They've returned," Dennis said joyfully, jumping up and drawing her to her feet. Flavia clutched at her bouquet, her knuckles whitening. Dennis slipped his arm possessively round her waist, led her to the open door, then frowned as the two horsemen proved not to be the Friends.

Puzzled, they watched the men dismount. They were not the sort of men who usually came to Quaker's Neck Landing. They were huge and brutish-looking. The larger man was missing half his right ear and the smaller had an evil grin that displayed teeth as cracked and broken as the blade of a saw. The men were armed with musket and club. A knife glinted at the larger man's waist.

Flavia felt a cold chill. "Dennis?"

"Get behind me."

He pushed her roughly and she stood trembling at his back, her hands on his serge coat. Fear quickened. She'd heard of such things happening. Ruffians swooping down upon a community, robbing, raiding. But surely not here in peaceful Quaker's Neck, where there was nothing to steal and where homes seemed to commune in tranquillity.

Afoot, the men loomed even larger. Ignoring the huddle of humble houses and vegetable plots, they swaggered straight toward the meetinghouse. Flavia's hands stiffened on Dennis's shoulders. Though the approaching men towered above Dennis, he staunchly blocked the door.

"What do you want?"

"Your purse, matey," said the ragged-ear.

Dennis dug in his coat, then flung the purse to the dirt at the men's feet. The thin clack of copper made the men roar in evil laughter. Ragged-ear scornfully scooped it up.

"Ain't got much, has you, matey?"

"You've got what you want. Begone!"

Flavia shook like a leaf as the saw-toothed one continued to swagger toward them. Her eyes darted round the room, trying to conjure up another door. But there was none. She and Dennis were trapped.

"I've nothing else of value," Dennis snapped. "Be gone!"

The saw-toothed one laughed. "You has one thing more we'll be taking. The girl. Jane Brown."

Flavia choked, her heart stopping. Dennis spread his arms to the doorjamb and planted his feet.

"There is *no* Jane Brown here. Begone."

But the saw-toothed one kept coming. Flavia swung round in terror. There was nowhere to hide. The meetinghouse was bare except for a dozen straight-backed chairs. She fled into the room, seeking pitiful shelter behind one chair.

She stared in growing terror as the saw-toothed one batted Dennis out of the way with his musket stock and stomped in. Dennis crashed to the floor, and seemingly for the sport of it, the ragged-eared one kicked Dennis hard in the chest. Flavia screamed as she heard his rib crack. Dazed, Dennis crawled to his hands and knees, groaning.

"Jane, run," he ordered. "Run—"

She tried to obey, but her legs were sticks. The men roared anew at her feeble efforts to stumble away from them. They seemed to take pleasure in stalking her, slowly cutting off her escape, slowly backing her into a corner. When she fell over a chair, the saw-toothed one leaped upon her and dragged her up by the hair. She fought him, flailing at him with the wedding bouquet she still clutched.

He laughed at her, his garlic breath hitting her full in the face.   rung you a message from His Grace, my pretty."

She froze in new terror. The duke? Oh, my God!

"No—no—please let me go—don't—"

The ragged-eared one said, Give 'er a ear-to-ear smile, matey."

With a laugh of pure relish the man drew out his knife, and the will to survive jolted through her. She twisted violently, throwing herself about like an animal caught in a trap.

Dennis was dragging himself across the room.

"Run, Jane," he gasped, coming toward her. A musket barrel whipped out, smashing Dennis to the floor.

The knife came up again, and this time Flavia couldn't move. The man had her pinned. He jerked her head back by her hair. She screamed, screamed until no more sound would come.

"Wait," directed the ragged-eared one. "His

Grace said to kill 'er. But he didn't say nothing 'bout taking our sport with 'er first. Come on. Bring 'er. Let's have a toss, first. After that—" He grinned.

They dragged her from the meetinghouse. She fought and screamed, her screams futile echoes. The roughness of their hands, the crude stable smells of the men hit her with terrifying reality. They dragged her toward their horses.

"Help me," she screamed at a woman and her daughter, who fled from the feasting table. They ran to a nearby house, banging the door shut in panic. An elderly woman with stiff gray hair poking out from under a starched cap marched out of her house, wielding a musket. Dropping to one knee by her stone well, she took aim at the ruffian who ran toward the horses. The musket cracked, but the shot went wild, and the ragged-ear turned in fury. Running to the woman, he seized the musket, smashed it against the well and kicked the old woman to the ground.

"No!" Flavia shrieked, sobbing in despair. Could no one help?

A hoarse cry from behind made her captor pause for a moment. Flavia tried to wrench free, turning. Dennis was pitching toward her, bleeding from the head. He limped, but still he came doggedly.

Flavia shrieked again as the saw-toothed one leaped back at Dennis, slashing with a knife. The sleeve of Dennis's coat split open. Flavia screamed at the sudden flash of white linen and the terrifying spurt of blood.

"Dennis!"

She tried to twist loose. The brute who'd slashed his knife at Dennis laughed loudly as Dennis continued to stagger toward her.

"Jane," he gasped, "run—run—"

The brute kicked Dennis's legs out from under him. Dennis crashed in the mudyard, his blood flowing. For good measure, the brute kicked him in the arm that was bleeding.

"No! No!" she shrieked, twisting and wrenching herself. She fought wildly, fought now for her life as both men dragged her toward the waiting horses. She kicked and slashed out with her teeth, her wild struggles making the horses balk and skitter sideways. Angered at her struggles, the ragged-eared one smashed his hand across her face, slapping her into submission. Her face exploded with fire. Her ears rang from the blow, rang so loudly that she wasn't sure she heard the thunder of horse hooves until one of the brutes cried out in alarm.

Their hands fell away suddenly, and she ran in terror. A shot rang out, and then she heard the thud of a cudgel striking flesh.

"Run! Me arm, matey!" squealed one of the brutes. "He's broke me arm!"

Flavia ran, ran wildly, ran until shame stopped her. Dennis! Dear God, Dennis bleeding to death! She turned and ran back. The horseman had dismounted. His cudgel swung in fury, and as Flavia ran frantically toward Dennis, running and stumbling over uneven ground, the ruffians fell, mowed down like hay slashed by a scythe. One of the brutes tried to crawl away, and two

Quaker women came running with barn pitch-forks. The women thrust the glittering tines toward the man's throat, and the brute cowered as the women held him at bay. Flavia flew toward Dennis, her eyes on the tall dark-haired horseman and his swinging club. When the brutes huddled in a heap, bawling and clutching their wounds, the horseman dropped his club and turned...

Garth turned, his heart hammering in dread of what he might see. Had she been hurt? God, he would kill them! When he'd ridden in and had seen that flash of red hair, that small figure being dragged through the mudyard, he'd gone crazy. Now, breath gone, panting, half blinded with anxiety, he looked for her. His eyes flashed over the scene. To his right, at a stone well, an elderly woman was struggling to get up from the ground. A girl rushed out of a house to aid her. Ahead, the yard of the small meetinghouse lay in chaos. A trencher table lay overturned. Cakes and a cider jug lay smashed, the smell of apple cider strong in the air. A man was on the ground, dragging himself to his knees, clamping a hand to a head that spurted blood. Flavia?

Fear half blinded him. He forced his eyes to focus. He sent his eyes searching. Beyond the meetinghouse, blue silk flashed in the sunlight. His heart gave a gigantic leap as he saw the red hair. Framed against an April blue sky and white cloud puffs racing in from the Chesapeake, she came flying. She flew toward the mudyard, flew toward the man who knelt bleeding on the ground.

Garth lunged forward.

"Flavia!"

At his shout, her head jerked. She pitched forward in her frantic run, stopping, her arms flying out and freezing in midair, as if she were a delicate statue, a work of art.

His steps froze too. Not twenty feet from her, his feet seemed to root into the ground. He couldn't move. He stared at her, stared in shock, stared in dumb joy.

"Garth?" she whispered. "Garth?"

She hovered there, trembling, her trembles growing into violent shaking. Her face went white. She swayed. As she swayed, he leaped forward. Uttering a sharp little cry, she came tottering into his arms.

He caught her, caught the sweetness he'd spent years yearning for and crushed it to his chest. God... God! The scent of heather. The rabbit-quick beat of her heart. Her small body— so small a man could lose her in his arms.

Hoarsely, he whispered, "They've not hurt you? You're all right?"

Ice cold with shock, she seemed not to hear.

"Garth, is it you? Is it really you?" she asked over and over. "Is it you?"

Like a blind person, her shaking fingers trembled to his face. She touched his mouth, his jaw, his eyes. Her fingers trembled to his hair, his temple. "Is it you? Is it you?" The freezing coldness of her hands jolted his very soul. He held her, his heart breaking at what she'd endured since that first encounter on the London quay.

"I'm here, Flavia. You're safe with me. The duke can do you no more harm...no more harm."

She continued to tremble, staring up at him, her eyes wide with shock and terror. He drank in every feature of her face, drank it in as a man dying of thirst drinks water when finally he finds it. It came to him with a jolt that she was not the girl he'd loved; she was much more. The sweetness was still there, but it was a different sweetness—one that had survived the searing crucible of suffering. There was strength in the sweet face. The girl was gone. A woman had been born.

She raised her face to him in new terror.

"Garth! Oh, my love, you must leave me at once! If the duke finds out, he will try to kill you. Oh, Garth, I should die if you were harmed. I couldn't bear it. I've already lost more than I can bear. I've lost our—"

She caught herself and stood gasping in his arms.

Garth's heart wrenched from its mooring.

"Our son, Flavia?"

Her white face turned to chalk. Her eyes filled her face.

"You know Robert was yours?"

He tried to smile, but the agony in her face broke his heart.

"I know," he whispered, "I know, beloved, I know."

Bursting into tears, she buried her face in his chest.

"Our son is dead, Garth. He drowned in

Germany. I don't know if—if—it was an accident—
or if—if the duke—" She ground her head into
his chest. She sobbed, "Garth, our son is dead.
He's dead, dead."

It took every ounce of willpower to bite back
what he longed to tell her. He knew he mustn't
tell her now. Her small, shaking body was already icy with shock. He feared what might
happen. He cradled her close to his warm,
pounding heart, kissing her fragrant hair, whispering endearments as she clung to him.

The mudyard burst into a flurry of activity.
Quaker women in plain Virginia-cloth dresses
and white starched caps came running, some
with pitchforks to guard the attackers, some
with ointments, linen for bandaging, bottles of
medicinal brandy. Men on horseback straggled
into the yard, gaping at the chaos they saw. A
flurry of excited voices rang out.

"Attacked Mistress Brown, they did!"

"Widow Jordan fired her musket and they—"

"Rode in out of nowhere!"

"Fought 'em barehanded, Mr. Finny did."

"Mr. Finny—'twas the bravest thing I ever
did see."

"Mr. Finny's bad wounded."

As Garth held Flavia, she jerked her head up.

"Dennis! I must go to him."

She twisted out of his arms, but he caught
her.

"You're not fit, Flavia. You'll be no help;
you'll be a hindrance. Let me handle this."

She shook her head vehemently, but he called
two women and put her in their charge, asking

them to take her into a house and give her brandy.

He strode to Finny. A life at sea had left Garth no stranger to treating wounds. Accidents were a sailor's lot. Three women had brought a blanket and were encouraging the bleeding man to lie on it.

"Help him sit up," Garth directed, kneeling to the work ahead of him. "Prop him up. His head will bleed less."

"Finny?" he said, when the women had propped him.

Strong, intelligent eyes lifted to his.

"Jane? Is she all right? You've saved her?"

Garth felt he was looking into a mirror as he looked into Finny's eyes. The anguish in those eyes was the same Garth had felt twice in his life—first when he'd thought he'd lost Flavia to the smallpox; second, when Mab had told him about "Jane Brown" and Garth had suddenly known what the duke intended to do to Flavia. So this Finny loved her, too...loved her more than his own life. Garth swallowed, a humble respect for the man welling up.

"She's safe," he said softly. "But I didn't save her. You did. If you hadn't fought, delaying the scum in their evil work, they'd have ridden off with her. By the time I got here..."

His mouth tightened in revulsion as he visualized what he would have found in the countryside when the scum had finished with Flavia.

Garth set to work on Finny, directing the women in their efforts to help. He tended the head wound first. Though blood flowed copiously,

the wound was no worse than that which the
sailor got when a studding sail boom broke loose
and went swinging. Directing the women to
find a flat stone, he wrapped the stone in linen
and tied it hard against the wound. The arm was
next. A superficial slash, but a painful one. He
wrapped it after dousing it with stinging brandy.
He fashioned a sling. Finny's painful breathing
indicated bruised ribs, if not a cracked one.
Working with the women, he opened Finny's
shirt and bound the pale chest with tight lengths
of linen.

"Who are you?" Finny said, gritting his teeth
in pain as Garth worked.

Garth hesitated.

"McNeil. Captain Garth McNeil."

The grave intelligent eyes flashed with sudden anger, the anger gradually dissolving into a
look of bitter pain.

"Enough," Finny said, taking the last end of
the linen strip and tucking it into his rib bind-
ings. With a groan of rib pain, Finny hove
himself to his feet, buttoned his shirt with his
free hand and limped toward a one-horse chaise
that stood waiting beyond the mudyard.

Flavia shook her head at the second offer of
brandy. She felt calmer now, and at the same
time she felt her nerves would explode in shock
and in joy. Garth! Garth! Her heart singing, she
snatched at the bodice a young woman held out
to her. The women had stripped off her gown
and put it to the fluting irons and to the pumice
stone to gently rub dirt streaks from the shining

blue silk. Her skirt was brought and she dove into it, binding it just as the door opened and Garth came in. With a cry of joy, she ran into his arms.

He caught her, and she reveled in being crushed in his arms, crushed so close to his pounding heart that every breath she drew smelled of him. Giddy with joy, she held him tight, weeping, laughing, weeping.

"Flavia," he whispered in a choked voice, his rough warm fingers fumbling toward her tears, as though to stop the flow. "My little love . . . my life . . ."

At last, arms still entwined, they made their way out into the sunshine. Flavia blinked against the sudden brightness, then caught her breath as she recognized the quiet figure standing near William Tate's chaise. Dennis! Waiting for her. In her dazed joy she'd forgotten. Forgot this was her wedding day. Forgot the beating Dennis had taken for her sake. She stiffened in Garth's arms, and his hands reluctantly released her.

"Go, sweetheart. Speak to him."

On wobbly legs, she slowly made her way across the littered yard. Dennis was being tended by a tall, slender girl with shining chestnut-colored hair. The girl fussed gently with his bandaging, her anxious smiles darting up at his pain-whitened face. Flavia winced. The girl was doing for Dennis what she herself should be doing.

At her approach, the girl turned, rested her hand on Dennis's shoulder for a long moment, then ducked her head and slipped away. Flavia's

eyes flew to Dennis. She bit her lip at the
bloody head bandage, at the arm cradled uselessly
in a sling. A white line of pain edged his lips,
and she sensed the pain was not entirely physical.

She strove to find words. Kind words. But
when she could finally bring herself to look into
his eyes, she saw she need say nothing.

He smiled bitterly.

"Is it *he*, Jane? Is he the one who has
kept thy heart prisoner all these past years?"

She longed to soften it. She couldn't bear his
eyes.

"Yes," she whispered.

The spark of hope flickered out as she watched.
He exhaled painfully, holding his bound ribs.
Turning to the chaise, he fumbled to find his hat
and put it on. Then he gazed at her intensely, as
though absorbing her into himself, memorizing
every feature. His eyes moved to the ground.
Her wedding bouquet lay scattered there, torn
and crushed in the attack. The delicate white
bells lay smashed in the dirt. Painfully, Dennis
eased down on one knee and fumbled for one
green stem with its mutilated, still-fragrant blossom. He stood, tucked the flower into the breast
of his coat and painfully eased up into the
chaise. He clucked gently to the horse and the
chaise squeaked forward. She watched him go,
watched the chaise grow smaller as it went to
meet the low, scudding spring clouds. Watched
from the warm shelter of Garth's arms.

"Flavia?"

"Jane," she reminded him with a little laugh.

"Jane, then." He leaned back in the rocking landau, content and feeling a peace he'd never before known. He'd hired a landau and driver at the port of York. Williamsburg was fast approaching. It was time to tell her.

"Happy, sweetheart?"

She twisted in the seat to look him full in the face, her large eager eyes melting into his. "Oh, yes, Garth." But her eyes were tinged with a sadness she didn't speak of.

He'd ached to make love to her that first night on the *Marabelle*, as they'd slept in the port of Chestertown. The breezes had hummed through the rigging and water had lapped gently at the hull, faintly rocking the ship. A perfect night for love. But he'd held himself back. Flavia's nerves were raw, fearful things. Hysteria lurked beneath the surface. One moment she would be laughing joyfully with him; the next, her body would chill to ice, and she would shake in some nameless terror. He'd realized she needed simply to lie in his arms like a trusting child.

They'd slept little. They'd talked endlessly. When he'd asked for an account of her past years, she'd told him everything, though he suspected she'd dwelt little on her sufferings in order to spare him pain. In turn, he told everything she'd wanted to know about his years since that first meeting on the quay. He'd felt the need to be honest. He confessed to Annette and to Eunice. The only thing he held back was the subject of Trent. She wasn't ready for that shock.

They'd not made love until the next day, when the *Marabelle* had sailed out of Chestertown and was out upon the choppy waters of the Chesapeake. He'd come down to his cabin to find her standing at his washstand, completing her toilette. She was wrapped in toweling, her fiery hair brushed long and loose, a washcloth still dripping from her hand.

She'd caught her breath as he entered, her eyes lifting to his. His heart had given a violent twist. Dear God, she was lovely! More lovely than he'd remembered. The childlike eyes had deepened with a new wisdom, a lingering sadness. The curve of her small breast was no longer girlish but womanly, promising the fullness of a woman's passion. His loins had ached to have her.

"Flavia?" he'd whispered in a cracked, husky voice.

She'd dropped the washcloth. It fell to the floor with a wet plop. Her eyes filled with fearful anticipation.

"Make love to me, Garth?" she'd whispered. "Now?"

Choking on his emotions, he could only hold out his arms. She'd flown into them, and he'd stripped away her towel, lifting her off her feet until her lips trembled against his.

"I want to please you," she'd whispered. "Please you so much that you forget every woman you've ever had."

He'd kissed her, a slow, searching kiss that brought him the sweet taste of her tongue, the long-remembered moist intimacies.

"You've already done it, Flavia. I can remember no one. No one but you."

The landau jounced along. He drew a deep breath as the first houses of Williamsburg hove into view.

"Flavia, I have good news for you."

"Jane," she corrected him with a smile.

He tensed. "The news will come as a shock."

She gave him a startled, wondering look. He took a determined breath and tightened his grip around her small waist.

"Our son is *not* dead. He's alive."

The expectant smile froze on her face. Her eyes did not blink. It was as though she'd frozen to marble. Even her heart seemed to stop.

He shook her gently. "Sweetheart, Robert is alive. He lives with me in Williamsburg. Mab Collins is his nursemaid."

It was well he'd been holding her tightly because she pitched forward. Her breath returned in harsh, choking gasps.

"Don't, Garth—my God! Don't—don't—"

"It's true," he went on, holding her close. Quickly he sketched in what he'd done. Her heart thumped wildly. Her teeth chattered uncontrollably.

"*Again*. Tell me *again*."

He did so. This time, slowly and in detail. He recounted all of it, from the first moment it had dawned on him. He didn't spare himself. He told her of the necessary betrothal to Eunice. He told her of Annette's sacrifice. When he finished, she burst into tears. He took her into his arms and began the story again.

Flavia felt she was stretched tight as the skin of a drum by the time Garth opened the door of his house and ushered her in. A clock was chiming the hour and her heart jumped at every stroke. She'd coached herself as the landau clattered through Williamsburg. She would resist the urge to grab Robert—oh! *Trent!* She wouldn't snatch at him or scare him with ferocious hugs. She wouldn't frighten him by weeping.

"Mab? Trent?" Garth bellowed, his voice echoing down a corridor.

A woman blustered down the corridor. She looked to be a cook, and she told Garth that Mab was on an errand. Trent was in the garden, playing with Sarah Bess.

"Send him in," Garth ordered.

Flavia's pulse leaped like a rabbit. Garth carefully led her into a drawing room that was bold and cheerful with bright red chairs and peacock-colored silk draperies. Her knees wobbled.

"Are you all right, sweetheart?"

She nodded stiffly, then negated the gesture by staggering to a chair and sinking into it just as her knees turned to jelly.

Garth kissed her trembling lips, strode to the door and bellowed toward the kitchen.

"Trent! Where are you, you scalawag? Come greet me. I'm home!"

Flavia shook in anticipation. At last, a child's excited whoop sounded and small feet beat a patter down a wooden corridor. Clutching the arms of her chair, she leaned forward, staring at

the door. In a moment, an explosion of dark
hair, dark eyes, sturdy chubby arms and legs
charged in. The child dove into Garth's waiting
arms.

"Cap Mac!"

"Oh!" she cried, bursting into tears she'd
sworn she wouldn't shed. Hastily she swiped at
the tears as Garth tossed their son to the ceiling, then caught him expertly and settled him
in the crook of his arm.

More tears came, and through the wetness
she could see her child staring at her, decided
disgust on his small face.

"She's a crybaby," he accused, pointing a
finger at the disgrace she was trying to mop up
with a handkerchief. She giggled wetly. Talking
so well? And not yet three? Tears of pride
washed down.

Garth chuckled softly and brought Robert
near.

"Yes, Trent, she's a terrible crybaby. Still, you
will love her. I assure you."

Flavia gasped for breath. "Oh, Garth, he's
wonderful. He's so beautiful. I never dreamed—
oh, Garth."

Garth jostled her son proudly. "I've brought
you a gift, Trent. A real mama. Are you happy?"

Trent considered it, then decisively shook his
head no.

"I want a puppy," he proposed instead.

Flavia giggled tearfully. She held out her arms.

"You shall have your puppy, Trent. I'll see to
it. But now you must give me a hug or you'll
break my heart."

He studied her, considering the proposals. Garth chuckled, jostling him and giving him a pop on the fanny.

"Scamp. Go to your mama," he ordered.

With a wicked, gleeful laugh and a nonstop demand for a puppy, he dove into Flavia's arms. At the healthy, wiggling weight of him she felt her heart would stop in pure joy. Oh his clean little-boy smells! His firm sticky cheek, still smelling of tea cakes! She began to weep again and her son demanded, "Down!" in no uncertain terms. She let him go and he went thundering out, flying back to his play.

She was speechless with happiness, light as a feather as Garth drew her up from the chair and took her into the warm strong circle of his arms. Chuckling, he lifted her straight up until her lips were on a level with his. He kissed her with tender playfulness. Once, twice. Then he lowered her to her feet and kissed her with searching passion. She shivered as his mouth searched hers, searched for the response she gladly gave. After a bit, he drew back and smiled down at her playfully.

"We've done passably well producing a son, Jane Brown," he teased. "Should you like to collaborate on a daughter?"

She didn't answer. She stared up at him, her small bosom rising and falling, her chin trembling. Then she flung her arms round him and pressed her face to the rough serge of his jacket. He heard her tears begin.

It was all the answer he needed.

Epilogue

GARTH AWOKE AT FIRST LIGHT, keenly aware of the date, keenly aware of which ship would sail to London on this date and which titled lady would be aboard.

He stirred uneasily. He couldn't deny that the port of York pulled at him today. Guiltily, he shifted upon his elbow and gazed at Flavia sleeping peacefully beside him. He felt the familiar fierce surge of love for her—for this "Jane Brown" he'd taken to wife a year ago in Bruton Parish Church. She was his. She was safe. Safe.... Not a week after arriving in the colonies, the duke of Tewksbury had been recalled to London to answer charges of conspiracy to smuggle. A wealthy and powerful man, His Grace had easily eluded the net of human justice. But he'd not eluded a higher justice. His Grace had suddenly fallen ill and succumbed to a mere child's disease—measles.

The duke's death had freed Flavia to reach out for her beloved family. Garth had expected her to demand an immediate sailing to London. But, no. Tenderly solicitous of her sister Valentina, and unwilling to do anything that might hurt Valentina's position as the widowed duchess of Tewksbury, Flavia wrote first to her Uncle Simon, telling him all. The old man, overjoyed, had thought the matter through, then carried the news first to Valentina and then to Flavia's family, wisely counseling all into secrecy. A deluge of loving letters poured across the Atlantic. Seeing Flavia's ecstatic joy, Garth had determined to take her and the children on a visit to London as soon as the war with France ended, as soon as sea routes were completely safe again.

Watching the rise and fall of Flavia's bosom as she slept on, Garth drew a guilty breath. The port of York pulled at him like a magnet. Still, he watched Flavia sleep. He hated to leave her, even for a day. Especially now. Her time was approaching, and as it did, he felt the cold chill of fear. Childbirth had its dangers, did it not? What if he lost her?

No, damn it! He'd not think such things.

To assure himself, he reached out and touched her cheek. Her skin was soft as a child's. She looked lovely, her mass of red hair curling upon the white pillow. Only a tinge of blue beneath her eyes hinted at the strain of pregnancy. And, of course, the large mound that sat where her small waist had been.

At his touch, she moved. Sleepily, she opened her eyes, panicked a moment to find him, then found him and smiled.

"Garth, are you going out?" she whispered.

"Business," he lied.

Her eyes slid away for a moment, then lovingly returned to his face.

"You'll be back by evening? Raven and Maryann dine with us tonight."

He bent and kissed her cheek. It was warm, rosy with sleep. She smelled of heather—fresh, sweet, young.

"If Raven's coming, I certainly shall be back. I refuse to leave you in the company of that lunatic. Whenever he gets a moment alone with you, he demands you become his mistress."

Her soft sleepy giggle flowed musically to his ears.

"Raven is only teasing."

"Half teasing," he corrected.

She laughed again, then sighed and patted her bulk.

"A fine mistress I'd make in *this* condition."

"I'm satisfied," he said softly.

Her eyes filled with love.

"Truly?"

"Truly."

With an order to go back to sleep, he kissed her, tucked her in, then got up and dressed.

Flavia curled into the featherbed, her face to the wall. Her heart pounded with anxiety. She, too, was aware of what date this was and what ship sailed and which particular titled passenger would be aboard. Unbidden tears collected in

the corners of her eyes. She brushed them away
as unworthy. *I will not be jealous of Annette. I
will not think ill of her. Didn't Annette save
Trent from the duke?* Still, tears came.

Love me, Garth.
Don't love her.
Don't go to her.

The last-minute disorder that precedes embar-
kation was in evidence upon the wharf. Ship
officers barked at sluggard porters, fearing to
miss the tide. Curses and shouts split the air
as porters collided with one another on the
gangplank. Well-wishers mucked up the works,
getting in the way as they bade passengers
farewell.

He scanned the wharf for Annette and found
her standing in a circle of friends. Dressed in a
travel costume of sapphire blue velvet, she was
reigning over the departure like a queen. Her
dazzling smile went everywhere. Only occasionally did her glance skip out, anxiously searching
the wharf.

He grinned. He strolled toward her, and she
caught sight of him at once. Her shoulders
jerked. She bade a hasty good-bye to her friends,
then whirled to Lord Dunwood.

"Be a love? Check to see if my trunks are
safely in our cabin?"

Flushing with pleasure, the parrot bounded
off, the feather of his hat jauntily stabbing skyward. Annette turned and clipped toward him,
one curl of her shining black hair bouncing
upon her velvet shoulder.

"So you've come," she said as she reached him.

"Yes."

"So it's good-bye, then, McNeil."

He nodded. He'd seen her seldom during the past year and had touched her only a few times, taking her as dance partner at public balls.

She laughed with forced brightness.

"Shall I see you in London?" she asked.

The question was casual, but her voice caught, betraying her. He understood. He shook his head gently.

"Not in the way you mean."

Her eyes fell to her jeweled hands.

"Oh."

She was silent a moment. Then she drew herself up and forced a bright smile. Giving a brittle little laugh, she extended her hand in farewell.

"We have been an amusement to one another, McNeil, have we not!"

Her hand was still extended, trembling slightly. Ignoring it, he put his hands on her blue velvet shoulders and pulled her to him.

"McNeil, don't."

But even as she protested, she lifted her mouth to his. His mouth came down hungrily, and he felt the old rush of desire, the lust she would always awaken in him. He kissed her with satisfying completeness, his tongue roaming the moist familiar territory. He tasted the farewell sherry she'd sipped with her friends, tasted the almond biscuit she'd nibbled in hasty breakfast.

He tore his mouth away. "Damn it, we've been more to each other than amusement! And *well* you know it."

With an eager cry she threw her arms around him and kissed as though to remember the kiss for all eternity. Out of the corner of his eye, he saw Lord Dunwood's bobbing feather on the deck of the ship. He pushed her away. She hovered there, panting. Her eyes were bright with unshed tears. Her voice shook.

"McNeil, had you merely kissed my hand in farewell, I never should've forgiven you— *never.*"

He swallowed. Softly, he admitted, "And I never should have forgiven myself, Annette."

She gazed at him a moment longer, then whirled round and fled, sapphire blue velvet darting through a throng of dirty, shabby porters. He watched her go. Was she running out of his life? A hollow, empty feeling settled upon him, gnawing its way into his being. The hollowness—the wasteland—did not begin to dissipate until a startling thought knifed through him.

If it were Flavia running to that ship, I would not stand here. I would move heaven and earth to stop her.

It was dusk when he arrived home. The oil lamp out front was already flaring and Raven's chaise waited with its driver.

His step in the foyer brought Flavia on the run. He was about to scold her for it, when he saw her face. She looked scared and vulnerable, incredibly lovely despite the ungainly mound that pooched out under a gown of delicate pink.

She ran into his arms. "Garth! You're back! I was so worried."

He held her carefully, tensing in fear.

"Your time? Is it happening?"

She stared at him in bewilderment for a moment, then dashed the tears from her eyes and laughed.

"No, silly. Not that. I was afraid—Garth, I know I'm being ridiculous, but I was so worried you would—"

She stopped. He had to prod her.

"Would what?"

Her eyes searched his face. "—sail for London," she whispered.

He was taken aback. God! So she'd known! And she'd not stopped him this morning by pleading her pregnancy or any of a hundred things a wife might plead. Instead, she'd endured a day of utter hell. Tenderness welled up, and respect. He swallowed hard, feeling a love for her that was even greater than anything he'd felt for her before. He drew her close, his breath husky.

"Why would I sail to London, when everything I want is right here, Flavia—right here in my arms?"

Flavia felt a surge of purest joy. Throwing her hands around Garth's neck, she kissed him with shameless abandon. She felt she was soaring, and in her giddy flight, pictures flashed past: Garth toasting her at the fire in a shoddy tavern bedchamber; Garth's lobster red son, shattering the quiet of Tewksbury Hall with his loud birth cry; Garth's marriage vow, ringing strong and clear in Bruton Parish Church.

She kissed him wildly, hardly aware of footfalls behind her.

"Indecent," Raven scolded. "Behave yourselves."

"Go away," she and Garth murmured in unison, kissing.

Raven sighed his complaint.

"Well, I suppose I must make my own fun. Maryann!" he shouted. "Come here, my good girl."

In her haze of happiness, Flavia barely heard the rustle of Maryann's skirts or Maryann's startled "Oh, my!"

"Maryann," said Raven. "Pucker up, my good girl. You are about to be kissed. And *not* decently."

Get the whole story of
THE RAKEHELL DYNASTY

BOOK ONE: THE BOOK OF JONATHAN RAKEHELL
by Michael William Scott   *(D30-308, $3.50)*

BOOK TWO: CHINA BRIDE
by Michael William Scott   *(D30-309, $3.50)*

BOOK THREE: ORIENT AFFAIR
by Michael William Scott   *(D30-771, $3.95)*

The bold, sweeping, passionate story of a great New England shipping family caught up in the winds of change —and of the one man who would dare to sail his dream ship to the frightening, beautiful land of China. He was Jonathan Rakehell, and his destiny would change the course of history.

THE RAKEHELL DYNASTY—
THE GRAND SAGA OF THE GREAT CLIPPER SHIPS AND OF THE MEN WHO BUILT THEM TO CONQUER THE SEAS AND CHALLENGE THE WORLD!

Jonathan Rakehell—who staked his reputation and his place in the family on the clipper's amazing speed.

Lai-Tse Lu—the beautiful, independent daughter of a Chinese merchant. She could not know that Jonathan's proud clipper ship carried a cargo of love and pain, joy and tragedy for her.

Louise Graves—Jonathan's wife-to-be, who waits at home in New London keeping a secret of her own.

Bradford Walker—Jonathan's scheming brother-in-law who scoffs at the clipper and plots to replace Jonathan as heir to the Rakehell shipping line.

ROMANCE...ADVENTURE...DANGER

__DAUGHTERS OF THE SOUTHWIND
by Aola Vandergriff

(D30-561, $3.50)

The three McCleod sisters were beautiful, virtuous and bound to a dream —the dream of finding a new life in the untamed promise of the West. Their adventures in search of that dream provide the dimensions for this action-packed romantic bestseller.

__DAUGHTERS OF THE WILD COUNTRY
by Aola Vandergriff

(D30-562, $3.50)

High in the North Country, three beautiful women begin new lives in a world where nature is raw, men are rough...and love, when it comes, shines like a gold nugget. Tamsen, Arab and Em McCleod now find themselves in Russian Alaska, where power, money and human life are the playthings of a displaced, decadent aristocracy in this lusty novel ripe with love, passion, spirit and adventure.

__DAUGHTERS OF THE FAR ISLANDS
by Aola Vandergriff

(D30-563, $3.50)

Hawaii seems like Paradise to Tamsen and Arab—but it is not. Beneath the beauty, like the hot lava bubbling in the volcano's crater, trouble seethes in Paradise. The daughters are destined to be caught in the turmoil between Americans who want annexation of the islands and native Hawaiians who want to keep their country. And in their own family, danger looms...and threatens to erupt and engulf them all.

__DAUGHTERS OF THE OPAL SKIES
by Aola Vandergriff

(D30-564, $3.50)

Tamsen Tallant, most beautiful of the McCleod sisters, is alone in the Australian outback. Alone with a ranch to run, two rebellious teenage nieces to care for, and Opal Station's new head stockman to reckon with —a man whose very look holds a challenge. But Tamsen is prepared for danger—for she has seen the face of the Devil and he looks like a man.

Don't Miss These Other Fantastic Books By HELEN VAN SLYKE!

__ALWAYS IS NOT FOREVER   *(A31-009, $3.50)*
(In Canada A31-022, $4.50)

Lovely young Susan Langdon thought she knew what she was doing when she married world-famous concert pianist Richard Antonini. She knew about his many women conquests, about his celebrated close-knit family, his jet-paced world of dazzling glamor and glittering sophistication, and about his dedication to his career. Here is an unforgettably moving novel of a woman who took on more than she ever counted on when she surrendered to love.

__THE BEST PEOPLE   .   *(A31-010, $3.50)*
(In Canada A31-027, $4.50)

The best people are determined to keep their Park Avenue cooperative exclusive as ambitious young advertising executive Jim Cromwell finds when he tries to help his millionaire client get an apartment. In this struggle against prejudice, the arrogant facade of the beautiful people is ripped away to expose the corruption at its core.

__THE BEST PLACE TO BE   *(A31-011, $3.50)*
(In Canada A31-021, $4.50)

A NOVEL FOR EVERY WOMAN WHO HAS EVER LOVED. Sheila Callahan was still beautiful, still desirable, still loving and needing love—when suddenly, shockingly, she found herself alone. Her handsome husband had died, her grown children were living their separate and troubled lives, her married friends made her feel apart from them, and the men she met demanded the kind of woman she never wanted to be. Somehow Sheila had to start anew.

__THE HEART LISTENS   *(A31-012, $3.50)*
(In Canada A31-025, $4.50)

Scenes from a woman's life—the rich, sweeping saga of a gallant and glamorous woman, whose joys, sorrows and crises you will soon be sharing—the magnificent tale ranging from Boston of the roaring twenties through the deco-glamour of thirties' Manhattan to the glittering California of the seventies—spanning decades of personal triumph and tragedy, crisis and ecstasy.

__THE MIXED BLESSING   *(A31-013, $3.50)*
(In Canada A31-023, $4.50)

The sequel to THE HEART LISTENS, this is the story of beautiful young Toni Jenkins, the remarkable granddaughter of Elizabeth Quigley, the heroine of the first book, torn between her passion for the one man she desperately loved and loyalty to her family. Here is a novel that asks the most agonizing question that any woman will ever be called upon to answer.

BEST OF
BESTSELLERS FROM
WARNER BOOKS

—THE CARDINAL SINS
by Andrew M. Greeley　　　　　(A90-913, $3.95)
From the humblest parish to the inner councils of the Vatican, Father Greeley reveals the hierarchy of the Catholic Church as it really is, and its priests as the men they really are.. This book follows the lives of two Irish boys who grow up on the West Side of Chicago and enter the priesthood. We share their triumphs as well as their tragedies and temptations.

—THE OFFICERS' WIVES
by Thomas Fleming　　　　　(A90-920, $3.95)
This is a book you will never forget. It is about the U.S. Army, the huge unwieldy organism on which much of the nation's survival depends. It is about Americans trying to live personal lives, to cling to touchstones of faith and hope in the grip of the blind, blunderous history of the last 25 years. It is about marriage, the illusions and hopes that people bring to it, the struggle to maintain and renew commitment.

—TO THOSE WHO DARE
by Lydia Lancaster　　　　　(90-579, $2.95)
They were society's darlings. They were born to marry for wealth and position, rear respectful children and take tea with the elite. But they chose love instead of prestige, principles instead of pride. In a growing town on Erie Canal, they dared to follow their dreams.

Perspectives On Women From WARNER BOOKS

__**GLASS PEOPLE**
by Gail Godwin   *(A30-568, $3.50)*
Godwin's protagonist, Francesca, is a cameo figure of perfect beauty, but she is her husband's possession without a life or depth of her own. Francesca travels East, to home, to find answers to her own life in her own way.

__**VIOLET CLAY**
by Gail Godwin   *(A30-567, $3.95)*
Violet Clay is at a turning point in her life. She is facing the need to find validity in her work as a painter and in herself. To do this she journeys mentally and physically to a new environment, breaking the constraints of her past to strive for the ideals she has felt imprisoned within herself.

__**THE PERFECTIONISTS**
by Gail Godwin   *(A30-570, $3.50)*
The relentless sun of Majorca beats down upon a strange group of vacationers: a brilliant English psychotherapist, his young American wife, his small, silent illegitimate son and a woman patient. They look at one another and themselves and see the unsavory shadows that darken their minds and hearts.

More From
Valerie Sherwood...

__RASH RECKLESS LOVE
by Valerie Sherwood   (D90-915, $3.50)

Valerie Sherwood's latest, the thrilling sequel to the million-copy bestseller BOLD BREATHLESS LOVE, Georgianna, the only daughter of Imogene, whom no man could gaze upon without yearning, was Fate's plaything...scorned when people thought her only a bondswoman's niece, courted as if she was a princess when Fortune made her a potential heiress.

__BOLD BREATHLESS LOVE
by Valerie Sherwood   (D30-702, $3.95)

The surging saga of Imogene, a goddess of grace with riotous golden curls—and Verholst Van Rappard, her elegant idolator. They marry and he carries her off to America—not knowing that Imogene pines for a copper-haired Englishman who made her his on a distant isle and promised to return to her on the wings of love.

To order, use the coupon below. If you prefer to use your own stationery, please include complete title as well as book number and price. Allow 4 weeks for delivery.